THE MARCH HARE

THE MARCH HARE

by

TERENCE DE VERE WHITE

LONDON
VICTOR GOLLANCZ LIMITED
1970

MADE AND PRINTED IN GREAT BRITAIN BY
THE GARDEN CITY PRESS LIMITED
LETCHWORTH, HERTFORDSHIRE

"Have some wine", the March Hare said in an encouraging tone. Alice looked all round the table, but there was nothing on it but tea. "I don't see any wine", she remarked. "There isn't any," said the March Hare.

For Deborah

I

S HE SAT IN the corner, never altering the sullen expression
which made her small fair face look old. The dress of mourning,
bought quickly and cheaply yesterday, would have lent her pathos
were it not for the defiance that was apparent in her eyes and in
every reluctant movement of the undeveloped body under the
misery of black cotton. The family, gathered as close as feeding
hens, cast occasional apprehensive glances in her direction. It was
not anyone's fault, except possibly his own—and at this moment,
who in charity could even think of it—that Arthur had fallen off an
outside-car. And everyone agreed that while it was hard on Milly to
lose her father just at that age, it would make a much more painful
change for Dolly (who had just 'come out') and Carrie, a widow at
forty—what a drear prospect for her!

Nobody knew—and just now, before the funeral, nobody even
liked to think about the money question. Arthur Preston had a large
practice, but he threw money about—they lived like kings—and as
there was no private fortune there (Dublin always knew these
details) it was most unlikely that he would, at his age, have put
anything substantial by. It was assumed that as well as the anguish
of his loss, the Prestons would have to come down in the world.

Dolly, who was pleasant-looking but plain, had swollen eyes from
crying herself to sleep. By frequently blowing her nose she had
made it red. But she was untiringly busy, fetching cups of tea,
taking the weight of the occasion off her mother, who walked round
in a daze. Uncle Joe, in a corner, missing nothing, helped himself to
whiskey from the decanter in the dining-room. He, too, shared
Milly's detachment; but the expression, never far from laughter, on
his face, was out of keeping with her relentless gloom.

He felt a kinship with this girl of seventeen that was conspicuously lacking towards the rest of her relations. They were hud-
dled together. He and she, on the other side of the fence, were
looking in. She shared, he was certain, his ironical amusement at
their flatulent piety, vying with one another in unctuousness to the
deity, who, from any detached point of view, had given this family

9

a knock-out blow. Emily, a cousin in drab circumstances, had already hinted—when closeted with a few—that it was a judgment on Arthur's extravagant manner of life. Her hearers nodded, glad to hear God's attitude so neatly explained, and not disposed to argue. If that was the case, then the sins of the father were being visited upon the children with a vengeance.

Joe had liked Arthur, enjoyed his society, which was sometimes brilliant and always flippant, and borrowed from him regularly; and at his death owed him not less than a thousand pounds. He would be a real loss to Joe, who compared his own reticence with the caterwauling of these women whom in life Arthur avoided; and looking at Milly, sullen and sad, told himself that she was excluding him from the arc of her disapproval. In this he was wrong: she realised that he had lost a source of perpetual succour and would be unaware of any obligation to his dependants. She also noticed the whiskey: how typical of Uncle Joe to take a jorum of his sister's supplies at such a moment! Neither did she share his amused contempt for some of her strait-laced cousins who had already offered to help if help were needed and who had passed over the regrettable circumstances of Arthur's death with considerate delicacy. Her expression—attributed by nice Dolly to shock—was indicative of rebellion. She had loved her father and thought that she understood him much better than Dolly or her mother, whose idolatry was fatuous and, she knew, bored him. She perfectly understood that his death would leave them destitute; and in the year 1900 to be gentlefolk without means was like living on the moon without an oxygen supply. Their mother would lose comfort, dignity and pleasure; Dolly, with that large nose and receding chin, unsupported by any influence, was unlikely to marry now; as for herself, she disliked the convent she was at in England and wouldn't mind if she had to leave it; but the prospect of respectable penury was galling. The alternative was too vague for even her adventurous mind to contemplate. However you chose to look at it, there was nothing but misery in the present situation, and she for one felt under no obligation even to pretend to propitiate the power that had willed it so. And if all was accident, the proceedings were farcical.

In pairs the whispering ladies crept upstairs to view the corpse: a band of plaster covered the fractured skull; they came back edified by the spectacle, kissed 'poor Carrie', sipped the tea Dolly offered them, and made their way out with sympathetic nods and sad little smiles. The last were aimed at Milly whose demeanour had frightened all but the hardiest. She gave no acknowledgement. She was on her own now, outside the range of comfort.

Joe watched the play, and thought that a current was passing between him and his niece. He saw them as both in the same plight. It was true inasmuch as they appreciated Arthur for his real qualities—a Dionysian figure if ever there were one—and these others lacked the intelligence to see behind the mask, the cheerful manner, the easy good-nature, the stateliness he put on with his working clothes. Joe saw another Arthur, slightly flushed, on his second bottle, daring in talk, easily contemptuous; or at a dinner, taking notice of the bosom, which fashion decreed should be on view, across the table. Often morose at home, the presence of company aroused the wit in him. He was Sheridanesque. Dublin lawyers prided themselves on their humour; but it consisted of anecdotes. Arthur was an original: his contribution was already in the common stock. Old benchers drew on it to maintain a reputation for conversational brilliance. All this Joe understood, and Arthur had been grateful for his intelligence. It cost him, on average, two hundred pounds a year.

Lying on the road, his face smooth and white as marble: his thick brown hair soaked in the blood that ran over the edge of the pavement—the kerb had cracked his skull—the scene would haunt Milly for ever; but she had made it up, put together from what she heard (whispered) and read in the newspapers. The memoirs of childhood are a tangle of experience and hearsay for anyone with a pictorial memory. Her father's death was the dividing line in Milly's life. Her last and most vivid recollection of childhood was imaginary. But not the scene that displaced it when she jerked her mind towards her obscure cousins from the country, Christopher and Cathleen and Dick and Willie and Tom. Nothing left there for imagination to supply; nor by Margaret and Fanny and Emily and Violet, nor by Uncle Joe, who had slipped away for a fraction of time and returned with his tumbler replenished. These she would also remember with the clarity of a Goya etching.

When the relations, neighbours, and well-wishers cleared away, Joe abandoned his position of detachment and sat beside his sister. In her agony of grief it was certainly right that he should be at her side—her only brother, the head of his house.

"Your bed is made up," she said, as he put his conspicuously elegant hand on her shoulder. "Tell O'Brien to tell cook that Mr Dunne will be staying for dinner," she said to Dolly. The house in Merrion Square was well-staffed. Tomorrow would be time enough to think of retrenchment.

"I'm very tired. I think I'll sit down," the widow said. "Milly, dear, will you ring the bell for Mary to put some coal on the fire."

I N A L A N D S C A P E that visits to the gallery in the city had taught her was like a picture by Cuyp, Milly walked with a companion at the front of the line: Sœur Dominique, with a martyr's expression, stalked along in front; a cheerful little Sister brought up the rear, clucking like a mother hen at stragglers. Sœur Dominique turned round occasionally, fixed the whole line with a look of stern reproof, mentioned someone by name, causing a flutter; and then turned again, Prussian fashion, and marched on.

The girls whispered and giggled, except for the very good ones who took Sister's complaints to heart—the school's credit was involved when they were out walking. Milly's companion whispered to her, but received monosyllabic replies or none at all. This did nothing to discourage her; the girls, except for the few who were jealous, worshipped Milly.

She was tall and, though slender, strong. Her bright fair hair had reddish half-tones. If she looked serious, and sometimes severe in repose, this, by contrast, gave radiance to her smile. When she was amused it showed round her eyes, which were blue and slanting, and her mobile lips. Her voice was too clear to be sweet; but could, on rare occasions, be tender. Her unfriendly manner was part of her legend. She had a fine contempt for the nuns, but it did not take the form of childish behaviour in the street. She was quite capable of leading the girls and would have imposed her own discipline.

To win a smile Gertrude, the fat girl walking beside her, pretending to settle her dress, extracted a sweet, wrapped in brown paper, that she was carrying in the elastic of her bloomers, and pressed it into Milly's hands. It was a considerable sacrifice; the child doted on sweets, and the gesture amounted to a gift of her heart. Milly, aware of everything, averse to the sweet, its wrapping and its recent lodging, handed it back.

Gertrude, rejected, blushed; but she admired Milly more than ever, and on reflection was glad to recover the sweet. The girls were marched as far as the wood, which could be seen across the flat fields from the convent windows. They were allowed to stop and rest and admire the wild flowers that grew there, but they were forbidden to pick them. After quarter of an hour, still very hot, they walked back again.

Indoors, in the passage richly scented with bees-wax, Gertrude caught Milly by the arm, looked round furtively, and then pushed a few drooping primroses into her hand.

"I picked them for you," she whispered.

Milly frowned. "You'll get me into trouble."

"I picked them specially for you."

"But you shouldn't. You were told not to. You'd have been punished if ma Sœur had seen you; and they are not worth it."

The last sentence made Gertrude's eyes brim with tears. She had seen herself as the martyr who puts his hand in the flame. And this was all her reward.

"Milly, what have you got there?"

Sœur Dominique, the nun in charge of the afternoon's expedition, had heard voices and came back to see who was lingering in the passage. She disapproved of loiterers, and was ever on the alert to ensure that girls were not getting into holes and corners together. Less than five girls in a group spelled danger in Sœur Dominique's eyes. As she had lived all her fifty years in convents, her opinion was backed by experience.

"Give them to me. You were told not to pick flowers. It is disgraceful that one of the senior girls should give wicked example. I will report you to ma Mère."

"I did not pick any flowers, ma Sœur."

"How can you say that? I see them in your hand."

"I did not pick them, ma Sœur."

"Then, they grew there. Is that what I am to tell ma Mère?"

"I am not claiming any miracle, ma Soeur. I am merely denying that I picked them."

"You know you are lying."

"I do not tell lies, ma Sœur."

"I have seen the flowers in your hand."

"I do not tell lies, ma Soeur."

"How did the flowers get into your hand, then?"

Silence.

"You will tell ma Mère."

"I shall tell ma Mère what I told you, ma Sœur."

"Oh, Milly, my child. Why are you so proud and stubborn?"

"If I picked the flowers I'd have said so, ma Sœur."

"I will believe you if you tell me how they got into your hands."

"You are tempting me to lie, ma Sœur."

"You must not say such a thing. How can it have entered your mind? Can you imagine a Sister telling lies? Why are you so stubborn, Milly? I ask you: can you imagine such a thing? Your silence says you can. Milly, this is a dreadful sin."

Gertrude, who had prayed to be made invisible, gave a groan. To her fear of the nun, which was paralysing, Milly had added apprehension of divine wrath. The blasphemy passed without supernatural intervention, but the groan attracted the nun's attention.

"Go to your class-room, Gertrude."

The Dutch girl slunk away; devotion and shame gave her the appearance of a beaten hound; Milly seemed to have forgotten her existence. She looked very pale and like a goddess, Gertrude thought, blubbering as she went away, ashamed of her cowardice, her betrayal. In the hall a steel engraving of St Peter listening to the cock crowing caught her eye for the first time although she must have passed it a thousand times. Its aptness struck her as a reproach from Heaven. But she lacked the courage to confess; and what was worse, she saw in the encounter with the nun that Milly didn't expect anything better from her. Milly saw the nun as her antagonist and had forgotten Gertrude's part in the drama. It was awful to love a goddess. All Gertrude could do now was to put the bookmarker of Florentine leather her aunt had given her, under Milly's pillow.

"Pride is the most deadly sin. You are full of pride. It was the reason that Satan was cast out of Heaven. It will bring you to sin."

The nun had changed her tactics. The truth had possibly dawned on her as she watched Gertrude's undignified departure. For all her austerity, Sœur Dominique had more insight into the girls than some of her gentler companions. She had had to fight terrible battles in her own soul; and this hard, proud girl who challenged her authority was someone she could understand and fear for.

She knew the details of her history, that poverty was the explanation of her presence in a Dutch convent, and the reason she had not gone home for two years; the journey cost too much. And yet she was as proud as Lucifer and made no secret of her contempt for her surroundings. The Irish, Sœur Dominique understood, had suffered for the faith and were an oppressed people; but Milly had an imperious manner. When the girls criticised the English on account of the Boers—they had recently capitulated—Milly took their remarks as a personal affront. They expected her to be pleased. But she seemed to be on the English side.

She still held the flowers, clutching them defensively.

"Give those to me."

The girl contrived to do so in a way that was not rude but conveyed disdain for the operation, and made the sad little bunch look ridiculous in the nun's hand. She felt them as a stain which she wanted to wash away; but the passage was as empty as it was clean and there was no receptacle into which to throw them. For the first time in their encounter Milly felt an ascendency; she smiled inwardly at the nun's dilemma. Had she been handed a new baby to hold, her embarrassment would not have been more obvious. She crushed the flowers into a ball. There was something cruel in the action; a revenge on the innocent; outraged impotence.

"You may go," she said. "And remember what I said."

Her face was very white.

That was the last but not the first of Milly's controversies. The nuns were relieved that she was leaving at the end of this term. She was uncommonly clever and talented and law-abiding; but she gave the impression that she obeyed the laws because it suited her own convenience. Minor infringements, for which there were ordained punishments, would have been easier to cope with than her persistent argumentativeness. She had no respect for authority, accepted nothing as gospel, and caused the greatest scandal in living memory by keeping to her room when the Bishop paid a visit. The girls had new dresses for the occasion, for which their parents paid; but Milly refused point-blank to put her mother to the expense of a new dress. Even when the Reverend Mother interviewed her at length, she persisted.

"I don't want to see the Bishop," she said.

For the nuns his visit was the highlight of the year; and at first they were sorry for Milly because they explained her conduct to themselves as evidence of her awful poverty. Sœur Dominique and the Reverend Mother, the most intelligent members of the Community, did not think it wise to confide the truth—that Milly was glad of the excuse, not to avoid the ceremony so much as to show her superiority.

But the Reverend Mother gave her rosary beads as a farewell present, and Sœur Dominique a beautifully bound copy of Thomas à Kempis. She would have been surprised to learn that Milly, reading it in the train, brushed away a tear.

Milly was as glad to leave the convent as if she had finished a term in prison. But she was not blind to the advantages of her two years in Holland. As a convict may acquire some knowledge of a trade in prison work-shops, she knew that she came away with a few solid advantages—German and French, as well as Dutch, drawing, needlework, music (she played the piano really well) and a meticulous hand-writing—these were all assets. She needed them. She needed any accomplishment she could acquire because her future depended on what she could do for herself. She had no illusions about the prospects at home. Merrion Square and an insurance policy were the only provision Arthur Preston had left his family. When she appreciated the situation, Carrie bought a small house in Rathgar, a retreat, in social terms, as emphatic as Napoleon's decision to leave Moscow.

Here she contrived to live with Dolly on an income of three pounds a week. Much of Dolly's time was taken up by Lady Kelly, the widow of a fashionable doctor, who had rented the Prestons' house on lease. The rent was ridiculously low, being based on Lady Kelly's suitability as a tenant, not Mrs Preston's needs or prevailing rates. Lady Kelly had long been an acquaintance of the Prestons; her husband had doctored the family in his time. And it was she who had come forward when the Prestons' poverty was common knowledge to suggest the arrangement. She had contrived to present it as a favour; and it had been received in that spirit. The solicitor who looked after the transaction was as jealous as the two ladies that nothing savouring of commercialism should enter their lives. Carrie Preston had been shielded from the harsh realities of life since her childhood, and she wanted to be saved from the world's stain even now. She was quite intelligent; but she had been encouraged to believe that it was ill-bred and unattractive in a woman to have any knowledge of business. Lady Kelly endorsed this belief. To spare her friend the unpleasantness of calculations, she had gone to considerable trouble; her lawyer and Mrs Preston's lawyer concluded the transaction in a leisurely and well-bred manner. They, too, were behaving well. A sale would have been more advantageous to their interest; but they showed a more than professional concern for the widows, whom they called upon, sparing them visits to law-offices and business details.

Lady Kelly went further. She 'took up' Dolly. Having no daughter of her own, and her niece, a sister's child, being wedded to hunting in Limerick, Dolly was eminently suitable as a protegée. Her not being pretty was an advantage. It kept her steady; and she was more available than a belle would have been in a city where Army officers were the aim of every unattached female.

To attach her even more closely to herself Lady Kelly called Dolly her secretary, and thereby solved the problem of a girl who was hard-up and could not lose caste by taking the only sort of employment for which she was qualified. A lady without money was in a predicament. Dolly had been presented at the Castle and enjoyed a Dublin season, including a ball in Merrion Square. Arthur Preston, secretly lamenting her lack of looks, did everything a man in his position could to launch her. If she had married, he would have made her an allowance.

Dolly's season had been exciting and anxious; but it had led to no proposals. The very plain son of one of the attorneys upon whom her father depended for briefs had been assiduous in calling; but Dolly, nice to everyone, had given him no exceptional encouragement, and he had never disclosed matrimonial intentions. If he had, she would have considered them. She had a romantic heart but a sober estimate of her attractions.

Lady Kelly's proposal—she regarded it in her secret thoughts as a supplement to the rent—involved no salary. Dolly called every day, sat with her, drove out with her, and passed round the tea-things. If her employer received a disagreeable letter or a bill, Dolly undertook the correspondence in the third person.

There were occasional presents, visits to the theatre, and a promise of a ball. The last never materialised; but Lady Kelly cadged a few invitations for her and they were presented as a discharge of the promise, coupled with an offer to give a ball for Milly. Dolly was quite satisfied with that. She was not in the least jealous of her younger, prettier sister, and much concerned for her future.

Carrie's letters to Milly were not very revealing. She had very little to say that was cheerful and she was too good to complain. Nearly every letter contained a reference to what Lady Kelly was doing for Dolly.

Dolly's letters gave Milly a clearer picture. She wrote well and with humour, and made no bones about the fact that a little money from Lady Kelly would be far more useful than the side benefits of the association; but she was afraid to imperil what she saw as the last link left with the world in which they must struggle to retain a foot-hold.

Buttercup Square in Rathgar was a place to escape from. To mix with the residents meant social oblivion. Dolly was amused by the incessant attention of the family next door to breaking down the barrier. Mrs Preston would not have been more exclusive and apprehensive of her neighbours had she moved her family from Merrion Square to a cage in the zoo.

Milly had done a lot of thinking and before she left the convent decided to make herself understood by Dolly, at least. She purposely avoided upsetting her mother, to whom her letters were quiet and affectionate.

Convent of the Sacred Heart,
Guelderland

July 1st, 1902.

Dear Dolly,
Please thank Mama for my ticket and the money, and tell her they arrived safely. Don't either of you trouble to meet the boat. I can take a cab from North Wall, and I would much prefer to do this than to think of either of you waiting on those draughty docks. I have enough money to pay the driver.

Am I supposed to write to Lady Kelly and thank her for hinting at the possibility of a ball? Don't be cross with me, Dolly; but I must make it clear before I come home that I want to have as little to do with her as possible. Ever since Papa died she has loomed large in our lives and patronised us; but we hardly knew her in the old days and Papa used to laugh at her.

I know you think I am hard and ungrateful; but I have had time to think, and from a distance I may see things in better perspective than you can. I am convinced that Mama should be getting a much higher rent for Merrion Square. I know you will say that Lady Kelly does 'so much' for you; but I would prefer if she salved her conscience in some other way. From your account she benefits more from the association than you do; but you are too good a goose to see this. I won't interfere with you, and I hope you won't try to exert the privileges of an elder sister. I see our case as desperate but not hopeless; and I intend to employ desperate remedies.

If I have enough talent I should like to be an artist. I am much better at drawing and painting than any of the girls here.

Don't tell Mama, but I might even go on the stage; I'm by far the best at theatricals in the school, and I have a good voice. My recitations of 'To be or not to be' and 'The quality of mercy' are star turns; the last time the Bishop came—I condescended to meet his Lordship on this occasion—I recited both for his benefit. As he doesn't understand a word of English he must have found the entertainment a great bore. He patted me on the head afterwards, a tribute that I could have done without. I noticed when I kissed his ring that he had black hair on his fingers. I found this highly objectionable.

I wonder if I could get a temporary job teaching drawing or languages in the mornings. It would give me some money and something to do. Mama plans for me to sit at home and look ladylike; but who is to see me in that misleading guise? I should become dangerous if I had no employment. Here, at least, one is never idle. I can sew and embroider. I must practise cooking; then I shall be equipped to face the world.

There is really nothing to be afraid of. When I came here, not able to speak the language, I was quite miserable; but one day talking with girls in my form (as soon as I could make myself understood) I realised that in every group there would always be a majority less bright than oneself. This revelation had an extraordinary effect on me. Since I had it I have never had a moment's fear. The other girls live in terror of the nuns; when they are caught out in a fault they lie—all except the two English girls. It is a bond I found we had in common, that, and not cheating at games. But they are dull and take their superiority for granted.

My only friend is Dutch; I prefer her to the Germans. She is quite as sentimental, but not sly.

Uncle Joe sent me a pound. Can you believe it? The greatest miracle since Moses struck the rock. He won it on the Derby. I never had so much money in my life. I should really give it to

Mama to repay a little of what she has spent on him. He is very satirical about everyone, including Lady Kelly, whom he calls the Marchioness of Merrion Square. He says that she is robbing Mama; and *he* ought to know. I feel a frightening affinity with him. You remember what Papa used to call him: 'My unregenerate brother-in-law'. Of course we weren't meant to hear. But I have been hearing things I shouldn't hear ever since I was born. How can we be sisters, Dolly?

Is it that all the good—and there's so much good in Mama—is concentrated in you and all the wickedness in me? Not that I have done anything very wicked yet—unless it is wicked not to want to kiss a Bishop's ring—but I feel so antagonistic to your Lady Kelly and so unshocked by Becky Sharp and so bored by Amelia that I fear I am heading for the pit. Love to Mama.

Yours affectionately,

Milly.

III

DOLLY ACCOMPANIED LADY KELLY to the Spring Show: a dressmaker had been kept very busy for some weeks beforehand; her ladyship's dress was calculated to distract attention from the exhibits, Dolly's was simple, becoming her years, good enough not to disgrace her exalted companion, not good enough to attract attention to herself. Lady Kelly gave Dolly her dress and paid the dressmaker's bill. Thirty shillings in all it cost her; and she received a touching letter from Mrs Preston for yet another act of kindness.

Dolly had the knack of being happy, and she enjoyed looking at the crowds, the horses and the cattle. If she shot occasional glances of concealed admiration at passing figures, looking splendid on horseback or gallant in uniforms, it was not with discontent. She made no claims on her own behalf.

Only the socially desperate gave much time to Lady Kelly: Dolly's company not only saved her from being solitary a great deal, it attracted acquaintances who would otherwise have passed the 'old dragon' with a rapid hail and farewell. If young men did not lay siege, Dolly was liked by everyone. Lady Kelly should have paid rent for her if their arrangement was put on an equitable basis.

Their perambulation of the ground was interrupted by frequent halts and exchanges of civilities and comments on the crowd, the weather, the band. All, in Lady Kelly's opinion, showed a falling off since the days of her prime. Not since Dr Kelly received the accolade from her then Majesty's representative, the Earl of Zetland, had anything ever been quite the same. That was the meridian. Since then there had been a decline.

"There's Uncle Joe," Dolly said.

The mention of a man always produced a sensible reaction in Lady Kelly. She raised her head like a horse when a neigh sounds in the vicinity. It was only when she remembered that Uncle Joe was not a connection to be proud of that her eagerness subsided. But he had decided to talk to his niece, and he was not to be put off. He was in full fig, and as he had a male companion also dressed to kill, Lady Kelly condescended to recognise him.

Uncle Joe cut quite a dashing figure; but his lifelong addiction to betting on horses had left its mark. He had the look of one who was ready to take off at any moment without warning; his eyes never kept still; when conversing he gave the impression that he was listening to another conversation behind his back. But he was elegant and slim and not without a raffish charm. He seemed to be always laughing at you, even when he put on an expression of immense gravity, talking to Lady Kelly.

His friend was unknown to Dolly. He was very large and dark, and out of place at a Dublin agricultural show. His eyes were dark, oriental, and unfathomable. To set off their exotic impressiveness he was dressed in rather loud checks. Uncle Joe was obviously proud of his company and introduced him with a flourish as his 'friend, Mr Talbot Thompson'.

Dolly was frightened by Mr Talbot Thompson's impenetrable eyes; but Lady Kelly was clearly fascinated. Had he been the Marquis of Zetland, he could not have expected a more effusive greeting. Lady Kelly's weekly gatherings were chronically short of males. The few bachelors she knew were in constant requisition, and possession of a pair of trousers was a sufficient recommendation for her at-homes, provided social antecedents (or their equivalent) did not fall below her not very exacting standard. The meek, middle-aged men whom Dolly was accustomed to meet would certainly be reduced to insignificance if Mr Talbot Thompson appeared at Merrion Square. If he failed to appear, it was not going to be Lady Kelly's fault; she fell at once into an account of the show in the first year of Lord Zetland's vice-royalty; and as they were going in the same direction, Mr Talbot Thompson heard this at her elbow. Uncle Joe and Dolly walked behind. Dolly blushed when her uncle gave a wink at the pair in front. "I had a letter from Milly," he said. "I was telling T. T. about her. He is very influential, and it would be well worth your mother's while to cultivate him."

Dolly shivered.

"Are you cold? That's a very thin dress you're wearing," her uncle said.

But Dolly had shivered at the idea of Milly being beholden to Mr Talbot Thompson. His appearance alarmed her.

"He has connections everywhere, in the city especially. And he is a complete cosmopolitan. Look at your friend. She is eating out of his hand. She is setting her cap at him already."

Mr Talbot Thompson suddenly halted and made a bow, first to Lady Kelly and then to Dolly. His gestures were florid and emphatic; this one was a signal to move on at a parting of the ways.

Lady Kelly obeyed, but first asked Uncle Joe, whom she had never invited to her house before, to be sure to bring his friend to tea on next Saturday afternoon. Uncle Joe promised in the solemn tone he reserved for Lady Kelly. It made Dolly want to giggle. Mr Talbot Thompson bowed his acquiescence, and the ladies went on.

Dolly, looking back, saw the men disappearing into the bar.

"What a distinguished man! A perfect gentleman!" Lady Kelly rhapsodised. "I must give you a new pair of gloves."

Dolly's had certainly been washed very often. She knew that her patron only made these impulsive offers when she was really pleased. But Dolly's satisfaction was impaired by Uncle Joe's reference to Milly. Uncle Joe was connected in her mind with doubtful practices. On the day after her father's death he had borrowed ten pounds from her mother. Like all his borrowings it was a gift by another name. She did not easily feel resentment; but that was so callous that it made her dislike her uncle at the time. She had never got over the disagreeable impression, although she tried to forget it. And yet when he was with her she couldn't resist his charm although it was not a first-class article. But then, she saw very little of men.

If Mr Talbot Thompson had been launched under Uncle Joe's exclusive auspices he would never have arrived, even at Buttercup Square. Carrie had learnt to put up with her brother, but she drew the line at his friends; and even one so untypical and pompous would have been regarded with a suspicion bred by experience. Keeping up with friends had been one of Joe's first excuses for extravagance. Like many Irish Catholics he had an inbred uncertainty about his social standing in a country in which the great landowners were almost exclusively Protestant. It made him overanxious to cut a dash. He had joined a fashionable regiment, hunted, played polo and kept up the appearance of the heir to a fortune. His mother nearly beggared herself to allow him a sufficient income, and twice she had to sell property to pay his debts. When he came home to persuade her to raise £1,000 to save him from being cashiered from his regiment and found her reduced to keeping a shop in their town house in Mountmellick—she had sold two farms—his indignation at her social suicide took the form of violent abuse. He could no longer, he said, hold his head up in the county. If the news reached his regiment he was ruined. She was abject; but how was she to live? He went off in a rage to blow up the solicitor in the town, who had plotted his downfall. This was a mistake.

As a result, his demands were refused for the first time. He was posted as a defaulter and had to resign his commission. Like others in the same case he then went to Canada, and returned after his mother died. She had made a will which provided him with a small income but gave him no estate to pawn or use as security for a mortgage. He resented the arrangement, and accused the lawyer to his face of having conspired to rob him. If anyone was robbed it was his sister; she got nothing from her mother. Her fortune when she married was used by her husband to buy the house in Merrion Square.

Joe scrounged occasional mounts, and fished and shot whenever he could find a host not too particular about his antecedents. He was a believer in nepotism and was forever soliciting the influence of anyone in authority to whom he could obtain an introduction. Nothing very much ever came of it; but he was conspicuous in the organisation of balls for charity and was for short periods secretary to various enterprises. Nothing ever lasted with Joe.

Mr Talbot Thompson was a new and unexplained discovery. Carrie met him at Lady Kelly's, and was impressed by his portentousness. He said very little and behaved rather like an Eastern potentate, with an interpreter in attendance. Uncle Joe was the interpreter.

According to Uncle Joe, Talbot Thompson had decided to settle in Ireland if he could find a place that came up to his exacting standards. T. T. was considering the establishment of a newspaper and Joe was studying the ground. T. T. intended to go into parliament as soon as he had established a base.

For the present he was living in lodgings booked by Uncle Joe and hardly on a scale with his pretensions. His age was as much a matter of conjecture as everything else about him. "A fine-looking man" was Carrie's verdict. Rather stout, his height saved him from being merely a fat man. 'Portly' was the word she settled on. He was possibly forty, but could have been older.

His conversation, if sparse, was unexceptionable so far as Lady Kelly and her friends were concerned. He confined himself to short and rather violent denunciations of nationalistic tendencies. He was an out-and-out Conservative and would not go along with the reforming policy of the Balfour administration. 'Killing Home Rule by kindness' was the description of the policy. Mr Talbot Thompson deplored it.

"I'll write to Arthur," he said; and it was believed in Lady Kelly's drawing-room that the Prime Minister would think twice before he ignored Mr Talbot Thompson's strictures.

His manners were very ceremonious and un-English. He did a certain amount of hand-kissing; this was put down to extensive foreign travel. He sometimes used French expressions. Uncle Joe said that a dinner was being given in his honour by the Viceroy; but could not be precise about details. A delay had to be expected until there was a certainty of a sufficiently distinguished gathering. Lord Dudley was not going to give so distinguished a visitor his run-of-the-mill entertainment, lavish though it was.

Mr Talbot Thompson left Dublin rather suddenly, and Uncle Joe disappeared at the same time; but Lady Kelly continued to enquire for him, and Dolly had to conceal her relief at their departure. Her thoughts were concentrated on Milly's return. She was looking forward to it with unaffected pleasure. She loved her sister as she loved everyone she ought to love, but in Milly's case with a certain hero-worship because she was so much stronger, more enterprising and better-looking than she herself was. Dolly was not jealous. But her love did not soothe her anxiety. Milly would not accept their lot as she did. Milly would make trouble unless she married soon. Whatever happened, Lady Kelly must not be annoyed. She had promised to give a ball, and that might solve Milly's problems.

IV

Rows BEGAN WHEN Milly came home. She had offered to teach; and her mother had consulted Lady Kelly on the subject. As a result she was engaged at ten shillings a week to look after the children of the French consul in the mornings. This had not been Milly's idea. "I shan't be a governess; and I don't care if Lady Kelly is put out," she announced when the arrangement was made known to her. She answered an advertisement and went out mysteriously, watched by Carrie from the window, and was jubilant on her return. She had arranged with a college to coach backward girls for two shillings an hour.

She went once to Lady Kelly's, was heavily patronised, and declined to go again. But she was not averse to amusement; and one day when Dolly returned from her stint in Merrion Square she found her mother in a state of horror.

"Come in here, dear. I've something dreadful to tell you."

Dolly followed her mother into the poky drawing-room, in which the remnants of Merrion Square grandeur—Arthur Preston had invested in solid mahogany—looked uneasy.

"Where's Milly?" Dolly scented at once that the crisis involved her.

"Up in her room. Let me tell you what has happened: after keeping those awful people next door at bay for nearly two years, the mother called this morning, when I was out at the chemist, to ask Milly to a party, if you please. Milly received her and accepted on the spot without even saying that she would have to consult me. I am sure the woman waited until she saw me go out to catch Milly alone. She's unbelievably pushing, and won't be put in her place. At first I made light of it. Milly is still a child—in my eyes at least. I thought that I had only to explain the position and she would understand and solve the problem with a diplomatic illness. But she's quite determined to go. Apparently she has struck up an acquaintance with the younger boy, the one in the Bank, and the mother's calling was a mere formality. It was all arranged between them. Milly was dreadfully obstinate, and said very hurtful things. I don't know what's got into her. I never thought I'd live to hear my own daughter say 'Beggars can't be choosers'."

"Don't cry, mother. I'll talk to Milly."

But Dolly had no success at all. From the opening of the interview she was painfully conscious of how weak she was in comparison with her sister.

"What's wrong with the Terrys?"

"Their father owns a shop."

"What if he does? Grandmother had a shop in Mountmellick."

"You know very well how that came about. Uncle Joe drove her to it."

"Perhaps Mr Terry was driven to it. How do we know?"

"That's being naughty. You know how hard Mama has struggled to keep our end up since Papa died. She doesn't want us to have to mix with common people. It does take an effort; and if you start to mix with the Terrys, the friends you want to have won't know you. They'll judge you by the company you keep."

"Where are these friends? We don't seem to know anyone."

"You're exaggerating. Mama has visitors on every second Friday."

"What use are they to us? Old fuddy duddies with nowhere better to go. How many balls did you get to last year?"

"Three."

This in a gay city was a miserable quota. Poor Dolly knew it, and tears came into her eyes. She knew that at at least one of the dances she owed her presence to Lady Kelly writing for an invitation for her.

"If we were young men, we'd be in demand," Milly said.

"You will find everything will be all right if you are patient. Mama is thinking of selling some capital to bring you out. I think she has lost a little faith in Lady Kelly. There! I promised not to tell you; but I think you ought to know before you go and get mixed up with those people next door."

Dolly broke faith as a last resort. She expected Milly to be overcome by her good fortune and to go in tears to beg her mother's pardon. But Milly always confounded expectations.

"I'm not going to let Mama spend one penny of capital on parties for me. Do you think I could enjoy myself knowing that it cost her any part of her few pennies? What do you both take me for? I'd rather go out as a parlourmaid and be beholden to nobody.

I hate this belief in a marriage market. If we are poor, let's accept the fact. From what I can see, the Terrys have a very jolly time. They are always getting up card parties and hops. The piano is never quiet. Our lugubrious respectability seems to me to be a bad bargain. And Charley Terry is very handsome. I didn't see anyone to touch him at Lady Kelly's. They were all octogenarians there or silly boys on their mothers' leading-strings. None of them would look at us, Dolly."

"You don't realise how pretty you are, Milly. Your face is your fortune."

"Fudge."

"Milly! I asked you not to say that."

"Fudge. I'll say it as often as I please."

Next morning Mrs Preston had a long conference with her elder daughter. What steps was she entitled to take to restrain Milly? Could she lock her in her room? Milly was quite capable of breaking out. And at nineteen, she was no longer a child.

Dolly had nothing to say. She was frightened, not only on account of this single act of rebellion, but for the future. If she was passive and biddable, she was also intelligent. She could see oncoming disasters that she could do nothing to avoid.

In the end Carrie decided to refer the matter to Lady Kelly. Perhaps it would provide the necessary stimulus to develop the idea of a dance for Milly. Carrie, like other good mothers, was not above little calculations of this kind.

She was well-known to the staff at Merrion Square; and on the way upstairs to the drawing-room answered a stream of enquiries after the well-being of 'Miss Dolly' (on view every day) and 'Miss Milly' (a considerable rarity).

Lady Kelly was laid out on the sofa, from which she did not rise at Carrie's entrance. "A chair for Mrs Preston," she said in her dowager voice, indicating with a much be-ringed finger the exact place on the carpet where it was to be set down.

Both women were widows, but they wore their rue with a difference. Carrie's black had a more totally defeated appearance than Lady Kelly's, which shone, and was relieved by ornaments. Carrie wore a hat and veil, Lady Kelly had an elaborate coiffure. But what separated them most was their manner. One so meek, the other resplendent. Lady Kelly puffed out condescension with every breath. Carrie was suppliant. She had small features; the other woman's were large and, as often the case in Ireland, Jewish-looking. Her great nose and thick lips were set off by small, very shrewd eyes. Carrie's eyes were large and plaintive.

"I hate," Carrie said, after they had gone through conventional formalities, "bringing you my troubles."

"What else have you to bring?" Lady Kelly decided that her thought needed elaboration. "If you can't do that, my dear, what use is my friendship?"

"But we are so beholden to you as it is. Your goodness to Dolly—"

Lady Kelly made a gesture of refusal. "I always say that we should be grateful for the opportunities we get to do good. Besides I am very fond of Dolly, very fond."

She is going to leave Dolly all her money, was the thought that rushed unbidden into Carrie's mind. Lady Kelly had a way of raising expectations by her use of emphasis.

She listened very carefully to Carrie's tale, and the grave nodding of her head at its conclusion concealed an element of disappointment at the absence of scandal. She regarded herself as having exhausted all claims on her benevolence by her attentions to the elder sister, and she would have welcomed any details that would justify a total repudiation of the younger. Being herself insensitive, she could not understand why Carrie hadn't dealt with her problem by issuing an ultimatum to the offending neighbours. She would have enjoyed nothing better than composing an epistle in the third person refusing to allow a daughter of hers to consort with unsuitable companions. Presumption deserved to meet emphatic discouragement; but she couldn't express her irritation with Carrie (whom she rather despised) since that poor thing had at least shown appreciation of her inferiority by asking for advice. And it was not her way to treat anything lightly. The fact that a topic had been submitted to her consideration automatically lent it weight.

So she appeared to be thinking deeply and giving Carrie value when in fact she was wondering how much she had paid for her hat.

At length she spoke.

"If you don't want to write to these people, which would be the course I'd follow, I think you should tell Milly that you had to consult me and that I was deeply shocked to hear that she wasn't taking your advice or obeying you simply as a daughter should. Strange after those years in convents that she shouldn't have acquired the virtue of implicit obedience. But I notice on every side a total break-down in parental discipline. I attribute it to too much familiarity. I saw very little of my dear mother when I was a child, and my father was as remote as a stranger. I lived in awe of him."

Tears came into Carrie's eyes. Did she not attribute all her misfortunes to the absence of a husband and a father for her children?

"My father never spoke to us children," Lady Kelly continued, "his wishes were conveyed to us. That was all that was necessary. His word was law. 'Children should be seen, not heard', he used to say."

Carrie nodded to be agreeable, but she was beginning to feel that her journey was for nothing. Milly had made all too clear the value that she set on Lady Kelly's advice. Carrie had hoped for aid of a more practical nature. If Lady Kelly agitated herself she could get some of her friends to include Milly in their entertainments. She was unusually if not conventionally attractive. Nordic-looking, with slanting big blue eyes; long-limbed; high cheek bones; not a submissive type, not perhaps every man's idea of a pretty girl. Not cuddlesome, to use Uncle Joe's unfortunate expression.

"I'm sorry for her," Carrie began—hurrying to get past a frown at the threshold. She had not been asked for her opinion. "After all, she's young, and she has had no amusement in her life. Dolly is the best in the world; but she can't provide any distraction. And what use am I? Milly has not been idling. She gives a great deal of time to her teaching. It's hard to blame her if she wants to be with young people. Our house, I'm afraid, is dull for her."

"Dull, my dear! I would never allow a daughter of mine to deem the house I provided for her dull."

Carrie had almost said, 'But you never had a daughter', when she checked herself in time. The narrowness of her escape made her hurry even faster. "I hope you won't think I'm dreadfully extravagant; but I've decided to sell a little of my capital and give a ball for her during the season. I was going to consult you about it. Our tiny house won't do. If you don't disapprove—and I hope you won't—I should be most grateful for your advice."

That Merrion Square should be put at her disposal for the event was in Carrie's mind, and Lady Kelly was well aware of it. She knew the world; and she did not condemn the idea of the dance out of hand. Carrie had two daughters to get off her hands and entertaining was an approved method. While she was tempted to squash the idea of aid from her at the outset, Lady Kelly was aware that she had used a form of words which might have been construed as an intention to give a ball herself for Milly. And in an ideal set of circumstances she could still conceive the possibility. Here was a chance to clear off any commitment. By lending her house she would give the Prestons an inestimable advantage. But she was determined to raise the value of the concession to the utmost. An impulsive offer would discount the value of her gesture. And she hadn't decided, and wouldn't decide. There was nothing she so much disliked as a commitment. Where only her own interests were at stake she was fast-moving and decisive.

Carrie was therefore to a certain extent on trial. If she did not acquit herself favourably she would not be offered the house. By expecting it, she started under a disadvantage, even though she had said nothing to imply that she had any hopes.

"I'm not sure," Lady Kelly went on, "whether a season for Milly isn't a mistake. It will arouse expectations, and she may be sadly disappointed. I'm a blunt person. I believe in facing facts, and I consider that nothing is more salutary for the young than to let them see quite plainly on which side their bread is buttered."

"I was only hoping to put a little butter on Milly's bread. Neither side has had any on it up to now, poor child."

"You may do her incalculable harm if you start her off at a pace she can't keep up."

"Who else is to do it? I can only try to do my best for her."

Lady Kelly's stays creaked. There was something in the sound, like any unknown noise at night, that aroused awe. The role of patron was pleasing to her; and she did not choose to seem to have abandoned it. "I'm not saying the child should be deprived of amusement. All work and no play, my father used to say, makes Jack a dull boy. And nobody is more anxious than I am to give her any little assistance in that way that I can. But I am very strictly fair; and Dolly has first claims on me. I'm not going to neglect my pet even to advance her little sister. If only I could get Dolly settled I'd be able to give all my attention to Milly. The little season I arranged for Dolly didn't achieve quite what I hoped; but I am not giving up. I've put my shoulder to the wheel, and if Dolly is not settled eventually, it will not be through any neglect of mine. Which reminds me: will you ask her to call at Switzer's and see if the material I ordered has come in yet. She's very good at running little messages for me. Dolly is grateful. I wish she was just that little bit more lively. When people are here, I want to shake her sometimes. She's so backward at coming forward. You expect that sort of thing in a debutante, but Dolly's getting on. She is no longer a slip of a girl. She is developing quite a figure, I think it improves her."

Once again Carrie found herself playing with the thought that Dolly's future was assured whether she married or not. There was comfort in the thought. But the sound of the grandfather-clock in the hall striking twelve brought her back to the purpose of her visit.

"I won't feel so bad if I put my foot down about the Terrys when I can tell Milly she is going to have a ball. We have all grown so accustomed to consulting you about our family plans, I didn't want to take the step without first telling you what I had in mind."

Carrie, her mentor did not fail to notice, was now pretending that she had merely given notice of intent. When she called it was to ask for Lady Kelly's permission.

"I wonder if you are wise. I don't think you should have to bribe the child. It will make a precedent; and then, as regards the ball, you said yourself you have nowhere to give it. I don't altogether approve of hiring rooms. It's not at all the same thing as a dance in a private house, quite apart from the additional expense."

"Well, one is saved the disturbance to the house. I remember when we used to give dances in Mountmellick it took a week to get the house into order afterwards."

Lady Kelly frowned. She did not want to hear about country dances or Carrie's uninteresting history.

"I wish I could offer you the use of this house."

Carrie gave a half-suppressed gasp. "That would be far too much to expect. I wouldn't dream of it."

Lady Kelly nodded as if to say that her magnanimity could even stretch so far.

"I quite agree with what you say about hired rooms; but we must make the best of them. Beggars can't be choosers."

"I wouldn't rush into anything. I'd like to do it for your sake, Carrie. If it were at all possible without disturbing the staff—I have to consider them—I'd say 'take this house' right away. But I haven't only myself to consider. And when I gave the dance for Dolly I decided that it would be my last effort of that kind."

"That was for your niece. Arthur and I . . .'"

"My niece, my sister's child, is on a rather different footing to the children of even my dearest friend."

Carrie blushed with embarrassment. She was being reproved. She hated that. She hated Lady Kelly, she decided; but she owed it to Dolly to dissemble. Lady Kelly was all the provision she had been able to make for her.

Lady Kelly, at that moment, disliked the widow. This was the second time she had taken her up. She didn't wish to be taken up. One set a tone, and expected it to be accepted. Things had come to a pretty pass if one was to be subjected to a legal cross-examination. After all, she had nothing to get and everything to give, why should she be vexed by anyone? Her kindness to Dolly was being taken for granted, her good nature played upon. She would have to give Carrie a sharp rap on the knuckles before she left, for her own good. The opportunity came sooner than she expected. Carrie rose to go, convinced that nothing would be pushed to a conclusion at this visit. With a sense of failure she said, "I'll think over what you said; but if Milly insists on going to these people, I can't lock her up in her room."

"You can hold up her uncle to her as a warning," Lady Kelly said.

"I don't think I understand what you mean."

Carrie had taken a great deal from this pompous woman, but if she was going to start throwing her relations in her face, a point had been reached where even her meekness was not proof against pride.

Lady Kelly, realising that she had gone too far, checked herself in ringing the bell and accompanied her visitor to the hall door. She rather liked her for her show of spirit. There is very little satisfaction to be got from punching a pillow.

V

CARRIE REFUSED TO allow her patron to send out for a cab. She walked to the Rathgar tram stop at the corner of Dawson Street. Not the least of Buttercup Square's advantages was that it was well served by public transport. Carrie had learned to make use of trams by day and had struck up a friendly acquaintance with some of the conductors. They handed her down when she alighted, with natural good manners. This always pleased her. She was young to have to live like an ornament on a fireplace; and because she was a widow, notoriously hard-up, she could expect no other attentions than these. She had been surprised to find how quickly most of her husband's colleagues had drifted away after a vast expense of emotion when he died. Some were faithful; but their attention took the form of invitations from their wives to afternoon tea on days when nobody amusing was present. She had been cast for the role of a widow and would be expected to play it for the rest of her existence.

"Are ye right now, ma'am?" the conductor said to her today as she got down; and as she smiled back assurance she thought how healthy and cheerful he looked. It made her think more gently of poor Milly, who had been the subject of so much debate. Of course, she wanted Milly to have a good time. There was nothing she wouldn't do if she was sure it would bring pleasure into her restricted life; but she had to exercise prudence. All they had was respectability. That was the one slender connection with the world from which Arthur's death had not so much ejected her as switched her and left her in a siding. She could never herself hope to get on to the main line again, but she might manage for one or both her daughters—if a suitable connection were made. There was so little that could positively be done; but the possibility of error was enormous. Any attempt at gaiety so easily became flightiness; the lure of money led to vulgarity; how narrow the line separating pull from push. Even a perfectly harmless hope of fun, such as the next-door neighbours offered, was fraught with dangerous consequences. Involvement with impossible people; and in the attempt to extricate oneself the unpleasant necessity of appearing cold and ungrateful. One must not get involved.

If only Joe could be depended upon. He was a man about the house; and he could be such an amusing companion. Their two small incomes together would be enough to provide little luxuries and amusements that were out of the question now; and the house would be livened up. It would attract people. Who wants to visit a widow in the dumps with two daughters on her hands?

These were her thoughts; she could share them with Dolly, but not Milly; and it was towards Milly she yearned, detecting there some force which had also been in Arthur, whom, she was the first to admit, although married to him for eighteen years, she never understood. There were aspects of him she knew; some of them used to frighten her; but she came to regard them as weaknesses which he shared with his sex. She saw him as the victim of pleasure and prayed for him in the night. Insofar as she could she was ready to act as an insulator; but she came across occasional evidence that his voltage exceeded her capacity to contain it; and when he sat laughing over wine, after a consultation with colleagues, she trembled upstairs in their enormous bed at the images the mysterious male laughter evoked of areas of experience that she had never shared with him. When she saw him dead her first thought was: this is the Arthur I never knew. It was not for days afterwards, induced by the associations of countless and often trivial objects, that her Arthur came back, but never whole, always fragmented, like the pieces of a puzzle.

There was nothing of Arthur in Dolly, and nothing whatever in her own family had gone to the making of Joe. These strains had found their way into Milly, so that she knew instinctively what her mother could only timidly guess. This fascinated and frightened Carrie. Getting close to Milly was like approaching the edge of a great cliff: the temptation to peep over, followed at once by the scramble to draw back. Down below the scene was quite calm; the terror was only in the distance. Milly, her mother knew perfectly well, had no feelings of menace or mystery in her recently-developed bosom. She was simply bored.

Carrie had forgotten her latch-key. She knocked and was let in by Mary, who was called 'cook', but did not confine her erratic attention to the kitchen. She had come up from the country in more spacious days to start life at the bottom of the ladder on six pounds a year. After the dispersal of the Prestons' staff she had remained, like the boy on the burning deck, devoted to Carrie, and determined to die in her service. An incorrigible china-breaker, name-muddler, message-mixer, hider-away-and-loser, she had nothing to recommend her but her heart; the only thing about her that was ever in the right place. But it made up for all her deficiencies, and she provided mild comic relief to the bleakness of life.

"Is it yourself, ma'am? I was wondering what was the matter wid you. Did Lady Kelly not drive you home? Did you have to come by the tram itself?"

Her questions did not call for answers; they were oblique criticisms. Carrie, taking off her bonnet, asked where Dolly and Milly were.

"Miss Dolly went out to do some errand for her ould one."

"Mary, you must not talk about Lady Kelly like that."

"I'm sorry; it slipped out. I can't help meself. I haven't seen sight nor sign of Miss Milly since breakfast-time. But you missed something I'd have given me right hand for you to have seen. Who was here but Mr Joe and that friend of his, Mr Talker Robinson—or whatever his name is—in a grand red motor-car with a brass horn on it like an angel's trumpet. They were going down to the country, Mr Joe said, and had only called to bid you the time of day. But I can tell you their contraption brought the Square to its windows. There was a crowd of chislers round them like sparrows, wild with excitement, and when they went off they got a cheer as if it was the Lord Lieutenant himself had come to call. It will take the sight out of the eyes of them Terrys next door."

Carrie was superstitious; and it struck her as ominous that Joe should turn up again when she was thinking about him. Prosperous, apparently, on this occasion; nevertheless, her brother's visits inevitably aroused apprehension. Someone had always to pay for his good times as well as his bad. The motor-car, of course, was not his, and Mr Talker Robinson was Mary's approximation to Mr Talbot Thompson. That gentleman's eminent silence was just what would have suggested the other name. Under Mary's vagueness lurked an element of caricature, apparently unconscious.

Joe was a slender reed; but Carrie's heart, apprehensive or not, was lifted at the picture of prosperity at her door-step. Her universe was a world of men; she would always incline to trust any of that sex before her own, and Joe's remark that Mr Talbot Thompson could do something for Milly had lodged itself somewhere in her memory. It was an irrational impulse all that mysterious man seemed to offer on this occasion was a jaunt in a motor-car, for which Milly lacked the appropriate costume. But she would have leaped at the chance; and, perhaps, a drive in a motor-car might have done as a consolation for not going to the hop next door.

Now the chance had gone. Milly came in at six, looking tired; she had been giving lessons all morning and in the afternoon had gone exploring on the Quays, where she had discovered another source of income: an Italian manufacturer of holy statues was prepared to pay her for painting them by hand. She had seen an advertisement on his window and had demonstrated her skill. Small ones could be done at home; but she would have to paint the others on Mr Mantovani's premises.

"You are wonderful," Dolly said, with perfect sincerity, but she anticipated her mother's inevitable "What sort of place is it? The Quays are not suitable for a girl. I must see this Mantovani man. Is it the sort of work you ought to be doing, Milly?" She couldn't help herself. The objections to every course of action presented themselves so plainly. And underneath was a simple misery at the tired look on her pretty daughter's face. Milly left the room, and the opportunity was lost to talk about Joe and Mr Talbot Thompson's motor-car. Something cheerful for a change.

She heard Milly telling Mary to be sure to heat up the oven. That meant she was going to have a bath.

"Dolly; have you explained about the party to Milly? I don't want her to regard me as a sort of ogre. You do see my point, dear. God knows I want to do what I can for you both."

"I'm afraid she might go even if you were to send in an excuse. She told me so. That would be utterly humiliating. We could never look those people in the face again if they knew she defied you."

"What has got into Milly?"

"She feels desperate. She's not like me. I know how things are, and how it all can't be helped. I'm satisfied with very little. But Milly's very clever, and so sure of herself. She said the other day that Nell Gwyn was only an orange seller, and see where she got to without any help from Lady Kelly."

"She couldn't have helped her. She wasn't alive."

"That's what I said to Milly."

"It was just childish talk."

"No, it wasn't. Milly said she had three assets: youth was one of them, and she wasn't going to waste that. She keeps on at me about Lady Kelly. She says I'd be better off working in a bun shop. I don't think respectability means anything to Milly. In fact I know it doesn't. She said the other night that we were like a ship-wrecked crew on a raft, too genteel to cry for help. We preferred to drown with dignity. She remembers what Papa used to say about Lady Kelly; and she says he would prefer to see her riding bare-back in a circus than waiting on that old faggot."

"Did she call her a faggot? Where does she get these expressions?"

"The awful thing, Mama, is that I can't feel shocked by Milly. In a way she's right. When I look at Lady Kelly's tea-parties and think that I'm only twenty, and these are my companions, it makes me quite wild. I want to throw all the muffin dishes up in the air. But I haven't Milly's brains and I haven't her courage. I'd rather go on as I am at Merrion Square than look for work on the Quays and hear dockers use dreadful language and pick my way between spits."

"Dolly, dear!"

"Milly mentioned it. I don't think she liked Mr Mantovani either. She said he made sheep's eyes at her."

"I don't want to hear any more. Do you think there's any use my appealing to her at the eleventh hour about this evening?"

"I don't, Mama. We can only hope it will cure her."

"It's the beginning of the end," Carrie said, and putting her face between her hands she sobbed.

It was a very long time since Dolly had seen her mother cry. She stroked her shoulders gently, trying to comfort her. She wanted to tell her not to worry. She was resigned; and Milly was more powerful than either of them. They couldn't hope to control her and they had no help to give her.

"God is good," was what Dolly found eventually to say.

Milly came down the stairs with a very firm tread; she was not going to sneak out of the house: for some time cabs had been drawing up outside and the Terrys' door opened and shut, letting out into the night sounds of revelry within.

As Milly turned the latch, her mother raised her head and cried

39

out, "Let Mary see you round." The door closed; Milly gave no sign that she heard.

"She is walking in off the street," Carrie said.

The appearance of Mary as a duenna would not have impressed the Terrys. Dolly held her peace. In her heart she envied Milly—a little.

VI

IF CARRIE HAD known how much anxiety lay behind the invitation to Milly, her heart might have softened. It was a desperate throw; none of the family—not even Charley—believed there was the least possibility of her accepting. But she had. It was a miracle. Her admirer had taken no part in the festivities so far, and stayed in his bedroom (shared with brother Reggie) because the window commanded a view of the front. He could see Milly set out and be at the door to greet her when she arrived. It was unfashionable, he knew, to arrive punctually; and Milly would not do anything unfashionable; but he wished she would compromise and not keep him waiting so long. Nor could he be absolutely certain that she would come until she appeared. What if Mrs Preston blocked the plan at the last moment!

He had been reading *Maud*, and if Milly showed leanings in that direction he had decided to give her Tennyson's poems. Perhaps she might see the significance.

> All night have the roses heard
> The flute, violin, bassoon;
> All night has the casement jessamine stirr'd
> To the dancers dancing in tune.

There were no roses in Buttercup Square; each house had its patch of green beside the gravel path; but if there had been roses outside they would have distinctly heard Mr Clarke Barry at the keyboard, and his accompanying violinist extracting the last ounce of melody from his fiddle, every time the door opened to let in new arrivals.

'The soul of the rose' went into Charley's blood as he watched while 'the music clash'd in the hall'. From his window he saw the Bradleys arrive. He had been mildly attracted by Phyllis Bradley at Christmas, and she had been very stiff with him. It was almost impossible to believe that he had ever been impressed by such an ordinary-looking girl. Wait till she saw Milly!

> Queen rose of the rosebud garden of girls
> Come hither, the dances are done.

The hero of *Maud* was waiting 'at the gate alone' for her to come to him after a ball. The reverse of the present position, but not emotionally. So far as anxious expectation went their situations were identical. As Phyllis Bradley's escort raised the knocker and Phyllis gave a reassuring pat to her hair, her former admirer remembered that it was she who had originally inspired his mania for *Maud*. It poured alloy into the pure gold of his present exaltation to remember that. Tomorrow he would be fired to compose verses of his own for Milly, and not have to use ready-to-wear ones for her. But until the wretched Phyllis hove into view *Maud* had exactly answered. And rapturously it answered now as the door of number seven slammed and Milly stood, etched in moonlight, on the steps. She was thinking of something.

> There has fallen a splendid tear
> From the passion-flower at the gate.
> She is coming, my dove, my dear;
> She is coming, my life, my fate . . .

Why that moment of hesitation? Charley interpreted it at once as an inward struggle of which he was the centre. In fact, Milly, determined to drown her mother's last cry, had closed the door before making sure she had the latch-key. And now she realised that she had forgotten it and would have to tap on Mary's window in the basement when she came home. That decided upon, she strode down one little path and up another. To less infatuated eyes than her lover's there was nothing Maud-like in her determined walk. Her dress, borrowed from Dolly, gave out little squeaks as if it were being punished. This was not like a young girl, dewy-eyed, going to her first dance. Milly, as she put her slipper firmly on the first of the Terry steps, was mounting the barricades. Charley never once entered her mind. He was 'the boy next door'. Their conversations—engraved for ever on his memory—had made no impression on her. She was used to being stared at by men, and all that she had decided about Charley was that he had a sensitive appearance. 'Those Terrys' had been an inclusive term that left no room for discrimination. When dismissing her neighbours in the phrase,

Carrie bethought her of a fly plague or some other wholesale nuisance. Milly had done no more than distinguish one from another.

Mr Terry was small and red and round. He wore a frock-coat and a hat bought at Troy's for five shillings. Mrs Terry was larger than her spouse and 'very dressy'. On Sundays she might be observed out walking on the Donnybrook Road or the East Pier at Kingstown. The elder Miss Terry taught dancing, the younger was still at the Loreto Convent in St Stephen's Green. Reggie Terry, the elder boy, worked in an accountant's office; Charley was in the National Bank.

Reggie was a 'knut'. A large part of his earnings was spent on the embellishment of his person, which was meagre. Charley envied his brother's confidence in his own charm but reprehended his lack of feeling. He spoke of girls disrespectfully and as if he had only to whistle to attract them. His female companions when he showed himself abroad on piers (and at Ballsbridge during Horse Show week) were rather flashy. Charley looked with apprehension at the guest list, fearing that Milly would get evidence to support her mother's prejudices. Prejudices that were understood by the Terrys and not resented. Mr Terry was pleased to claim Mrs Preston as a neighbour and never aspired to greater intimacy. Mrs Terry saw advantage from it and cheerfully decided to keep up a gentle pressure. Only Reggie was moved to sarcasm. He had no regard for lights hidden under bushels. And even if there were communications between the families he would never, he said, have offered to squire Dolly. He liked, he said, to get value for his money. He had made familiar references to Milly, but decided to spare her as she was 'just a kid'. Charley's indignation at this light talk revealed the state of his feelings: and he had to endure his brother's gibes with his other sufferings.

Rushing downstairs to greet Milly he nearly overturned Phyllis, 'settling herself' for her entry. She took his clumsiness amiss, and he had to apologise abjectly while, over the boom of the band and swish of feet on the floor of the back parlour, he heard Bridget, their retainer, greet Milly at the door.

"Come in out of the cold, Miss Milly. There's them here will be delighted to see you."

Charley, cursing Miss Bradley, who was determined not to make little of the fracas on the stairs, blushed to hear Bridget's allusion to his passion. Milly, not thinking of him even now, was taking in her surroundings—the enormous hat-stand and looking-glass combined, which took up most of the narrow hall, the red velveteen curtains at the end, bound back to admit passage to the stairway on the left, and a conservatory built on to the back of the house, hung tonight with Japanese lanterns on the ferns. You passed this on the way downstairs where the refreshments were. Doors on the left led into the front and back parlours, the scene of the dance.

The host, at first concealed by the red curtain, met Milly half way.

"It's Miss Milly," Bridget said, making no attempt to disguise her pleasure.

Mr Terry, whose eyes were watery, pressed her hand.

"How is your mother? Will you please tell her I was inquiring for her."

The solicitude for an ancient enemy threw Milly off balance. She expected to be greeted as a spy or a seceder, even a notable seceder, but not as an envoy. Mrs Terry, who had posted her husband in the hall, still kept an eye in that direction; now she came from her place inside the parlour to greet Milly with both arms extended.

"Milly—may I call you Milly? Haven't I known you since you were a child! You are very welcome. Charley, will you look at who's arrived and get her some refreshment and not stand there gawking at her as if she had seven heads."

Mrs Terry gave Milly a wink, as from one woman to another. Like all the allusions to Charley's passion, this passed over Milly's head. In Rome do as the Romans do. She was determined not to behave in the consciously dignified way she knew her mother would expect of her even though she had exposed herself voluntarily to these surroundings. But she couldn't identify herself at such short notice with Mrs Terry. She couldn't wink back.

Charley was making vague gestures towards the stairs. He was not sure whether he ought to lead or follow and hoped Milly knew and would take the initiative. The sound of giggles, from behind a screen in the conservatory off the mezzanine, caused Mrs Terry to wink again; but Charley became so embarrassed that an impulse to succour him turned Milly in his direction; and he, gratefully, took flight from his mother.

"It's Reggie and his friends. I hope you don't mind—" He hesitated, she noticed, to use her name. And this did not touch her

44

at all but seemed servile. She had no inkling of the state of his feelings.

"At school there were always some girls who giggled. They were usually fat and they hunted in couples," she said.

Charley brooded over this. It seemed to miss the point; but, at least, was an acknowledgment that she had had similar experiences. What he had dreaded was that his brother's friends would give Milly a wrong idea about the family as a whole.

Downstairs, the dining-room had been converted into a buffet. There was a huge soup tureen in the centre of the table, laid out with cold meats and salads. Some chairs were pushed against the wall, but these were occupied by more elderly guests. The young people balanced their food on plates and stood in tongue-tied groups trying to eat with grace.

Charley disappeared for a moment and returned with a chair. He had kept it especially for Milly; had she known, she might have accepted it less as a matter of course. She had had very little to eat all day and the appearance of food brought on an enormous appetite. It was just as well. Conversation languished.

"Are you fond of Kipling?" he began when Milly was ensconced in a corner with a large bowl of soup in her lap.

"Not particularly."

"Some people say he is the greatest poet of the day."

"I haven't read much. You see, I lived in Holland."

"Have you read W. B. Yeats?"

Milly puckered her brow. The name was familiar certainly; but that might only be because the optician at which Dolly called for Lady Kelly's reading spectacles had the same name.

"At school we were taught only a few selected poets. There was much more French and German than English."

Milly was trying to extricate herself from a position in which she would have to spend the evening confessing her ignorance; but Charley, who saw her in a golden light, was only abashed. His knowledge was limited and confined to English. He must cut a pathetic figure in the eyes of a girl with a European education. A pause fell between them while he was deciding how to pronounce 'Goethe'. After a time he abandoned the project, and, at a loss for an opening to make himself interesting, he suggested a second bowl of soup.

His sister, the dancing teacher, Mabel, who had been making

faces at him for some time, came over on her own account with her partner, whom she introduced to Milly as 'Mr Casey'.

Milly, glad to escape from seriousness, asked Mr Casey with some animation what he did. He was 'in the law', he said. So, she said, had her father been. Mr Casey was interested to hear this, and when he discovered who her father was expressed his grief that one so well-considered in the profession should have 'passed over' so soon. He was not himself in that branch of the profession, he explained; and then he offered to do a ventriloquist trick if Milly approved. Then and there he made a very fair representation of a Mynah bird saying 'Keep your hair on', startling everybody in the room.

Milly was delighted, but Mabel refused to join in the applause and gave her side-long looks of deep significance. Milly noticed these; but she had not learned the sign language of her hosts, and she was at a loss to understand Mabel's disapproval. Charley's, she did understand. When he came back with the soup and found her being entertained by the ventriloquist, he looked quite woe-begone. The shriek of the Mynah bird had made them the centre of the gathering. Mr Casey had revealed himself as an entertainer and everyone turned to him with relief.

"Have you seen *Tan Toy*?" he said to Milly.

Milly said 'no'; but she was tempted to lie.

"It was goodish; not the full London company. Better than *The Country Girl*, I thought. Did you see that?"

"I've only recently come back to Dublin."

"Where were you? In Paree?"

"At school, in Holland."

"Ah! Holland. Then you missed Martin Harvey in *The Only Way*. He was over in Horse Show Week. What an artist! There wasn't a dry eye in the house. And that included yours truly. Do you know what a hen sounds like when she hatches duck eggs and sees her chicks take to water?"

Mr Casey proceeded to imitate a hen running up and down a river bank, cackling with fear. It was very lifelike; but Milly's enjoyment was curtailed by Mabel, who came very close and hissed in her ear, "You keep off the grass."

The noise in the dining-room brought down Mrs Terry; when she saw what was in progress, she insisted that Mr Casey should come upstairs and give the guests in the parlour an example of his skill. He seemed reluctant to leave where he was, but Mabel and Charley combined to persuade him. Mrs Terry, alive to the situation, gave Milly a wink. The company trooped upstairs.

There was now plenty of room, and Charley suggested that he and Milly should move into a corner where they could talk with less danger of interruption. Milly, bewildered, did as she was told, and was rewarded with a plate of cold beef and pickles.

"Don't mind Mabel," Charley began. "She's temperamental. There's a musical strain in our family on our mother's side. Mabel's been going steady with Billy Casey for some time. She is a very reserved type; and he is extremely sociable. You saw that for yourself. I wonder if they are really suited. Do you believe that people should look for their opposites? or for soul-mates?"

"It depends, I suppose, on what attracts them. I seemed to make your sister angry by something I did. I'm very sorry."

"Don't you mind our Mabel. She goes for anyone when Billy performs for them. She means no harm; and she told me that you had a stylish appearance. That's high praise from Mabel. She helps Mr Legget Byrne in his establishment: all the best people go there. I was going to say that Mabel would give you dancing lessons half-price if you wanted them."

Milly had been so deeply engaged in the conflict with her mother that she had not given any thought to the fact that she didn't know how to dance except for what little the girls did among themselves at school. Lessons were to have been arranged; but they were among the blessings to flow from Lady Kelly and, like others, had been indefinitely deferred.

When Charley said that he would much prefer to sit and talk she felt relief; but when he began on poetry again she wondered whether it wouldn't have been better to have taken a chance on the dance floor.

"There are poems by Yeats you must read," he went on. "*He bids his Beloved to be at peace* is very beautiful; and so is *He thinks of Those who have spoken Evil of his Beloved*. But my favourites are *He wishes for the Cloths of Heaven* and *He wishes his Beloved were Dead*. I could recite that for you, if you like."

"It sounds rather morbid."

"Yeats understands the unhappiness of love. His lovers are always unhappy. That sounds morbid, I suppose. But he speaks from the depth of experience."

47

"What else do you do as well as reading poetry?"

"I'm in the Bank, the Baggot Street branch."

"I don't think I'd like to work in a bank if I were a man."

"You despise it."

"Despise is too strong a word. It isn't very adventurous."

"That's true. I should have joined the Army; but you can't live on that. It's hard to know what to do. My brother, Reggie, works in an accountant's office."

"Does he find that adventurous?"

"Not so much adventurous as interesting. He says he is learning how people make money and he is going to profit by it. You haven't met my brother?"

"He's the one with the moustache. I see him sometimes. He doesn't in the least resemble you. Is he fond of poetry, too?"

"He despises it. He has very cynical views. We don't hit it off very well. It's a question of idols. His, as Bacon says, are of the market place."

"I haven't seen him this evening."

"He has been in the conservatory with Kitty Hopkins. He likes girls like that. I've something I'd like to give you."

Charley blushed crimson as he said this, and a profane thought entered Milly's mind, but she dismissed it.

"You mustn't give me anything," she said.

"It's a copy of Tennyson's poems. I've marked the ones I like."

Milly found it hard not to laugh. Charley's devotion was evident to her by now; but it seemed to be pregnant with boring possibilities. Even his brother, upstairs with Miss Hopkins, offered a prospect of low-life adventure. Was she to be kept prisoner down here?

"I'll only take it if you will let me give you a book in exchange," she said.

"Oh, Milly! I would treasure it," he said.

How to get away politely was her sole aim now. From upstairs Mr Casey's imitation of a fog horn gave the opportunity.

"Let's go and see what's happening," she said.

Charley accompanied her, looking very depressed. He had failed, he thought. She tried not to glance in the direction of the conservatory, but saw in passing a foot sticking out from behind the screen. Mr Reggie Terry was still with Miss Hopkins.

The musicians turned to Strauss when Mr Casey's fog horn

subsided. And when Milly arrived at the top of the stairs, the ventriloquist was mopping his brow, red in the face after his exertion. He beamed when he saw Milly.

"Will you take a turn with me?"

She nodded, and was swept away, uncertain at first, but soon at ease, and for the first time, for longer than she could remember, enjoying herself. She knew the rudiments of the waltz; and Mr Casey, like many fat men, had a rhythmical sense. It was like dancing with a large tennis ball. Over the top of his head, circling round in a slight mist, she saw the hot faces of other dancers, heavy coils of girls' hair on bare shoulders, the busy fingers of Mr Clarke Barry, or his face when he turned round encouragingly to see how the dancers were faring, and, in different corners, unattended, looking lugubrious, Charley and his sister Mabel.

When the music stopped Mr Casey pressed Milly quietly against his damp shirt-front. As she wanted to express gratitude for being made to feel that she was alive and not an exhibit in a raree show, she did not resent the familiarity. But Mabel did; she advanced towards them, eyes bulging; then turned and ran out of the room.

"Oh, dear!" Mr Casey said. "Mabel's taken to her tantrums."

Busy mopping his brow, he did not pursue his beloved. In his eyes Milly saw the look of a dog that is used to being beaten. Having no experience of the ways of lovers, she could not understand this romance. Mr Casey ought to be more ardent to fulfil her idea of what a lover should be. He was debating with himself whether to follow Mabel or to rebel when, over the room's chatter, the loud sound of a slap in the conservatory attracted general attention. From behind one of the screens Mr Reggie Terry emerged, twisting the ends of his waxed moustache. He was very thin and very pale, with dark hair brushed back from his forehead. Across his cheek flamed evidence of the recent disturbance. Reggie looked mocking and defiant. From the other side of the screen Miss Hopkins came into view. Her hair was red and curly, her bosom low, and all the flesh on view was richly freckled. Her dress, originally fussy, now looked as if she had been pulled through a hedge. By some happy instinct the band struck up again; and while Milly was still taking stock of Miss Hopkins's condition, a voice beside her said "Can you do the cake walk?" and she was being led on to the floor. She could not, as she demonstrated at once; but Reggie, evidently in the best of spirits, turned it all into a joke and tried to show her how. On the soon crowded floor this was difficult, and the blocking of traffic was the cause of much merriment. Mr Casey went past with his hostess, the liveliest of all the family.

"I've been given my marching orders," he said to Milly, nodding in the direction of upstairs where Mabel presumably was sulking in her tent. His tone was rueful but not tragic.

Reggie, when the music stopped, led Milly to the conservatory and installed her in the chair still warm from Miss Hopkins's pressure.

"Would you like a fag?" he said, winking mother-fashion. Milly trembled a little; she had never expected to go so far.

"I'd like to try," she said.

Her partner took a cautious peep round the screen, and then produced his cigarettes.

"You've never done this before? Let me show you. I'll put this in your mouth as if I was the Doc taking your temperature. You keep sucking it, mind, and I'll do this." He struck a match on the seat of his trousers and applied it to the end of Milly's cigarette. She was sucking as directed, awaiting she was not sure what sensation, any but the one that common sense suggested. Her throat and nose and eyes filled with smoke. She fought for breath.

"You'll learn," Reggie assured her. "Take another pull, and keep your eyes shut this time."

Milly did as she was told and once more found herself suffocating.

"I'm afraid I can't manage," she said, looking round for somewhere to put the cigarette; but Reggie took it from her and stubbed it carefully on his heel.

"I'm going to enjoy that one, I tell you," he said and brought his eyes very close to hers. She could smell the oil on his hair. Seated on a slender cane chair, she lacked freedom of movement. She could only lean away a certain distance from fear of falling over. Her partner was equally aware of this and put his arm round the back of her chair. She sat bolt upright, pretending not to notice.

"The kid brother would be upset, I'd say, if he were to see us now." He bent his face towards her again.

"You still have that mark on your face," she said. It was the first thing that occurred to her, and it achieved its purpose. He sat up and put his hand to his cheek. "You heard it, did you? Kitty is unpredictable. All love and kisses one minute and then—whack! I hope Mabel didn't notice anything. She was mad with me for inviting Kitty, on your account."

"Why on *my* account?"

"Well you know how starchy your family is—we nearly went through the ground when you said you'd cross the Terry threshold —and Mabel was vexed with me for giving you a bad impression. She has become ever so genteel since she started to teach at Legget Byrne's. All the swells go there, you know. And she doesn't think Kitty is good enough any more. I don't like that sort of thing. Kitty may not be class exactly, but she is good fun at a party. Mabel wants us all to behave as if we were at a funeral. She was giving out to poor Billy just now for imitating a Mynah bird. If Mabel is not careful, she'll lose the same Billy. And she can't afford to. Mabel's getting on, and she's not a beaut, not by a long chalk. What made you come tonight? Struck by brother Charley's manly devotion? You have put your spell over that young man, and no mistake. We tease the life out of him over you."

Charley's devotion was so recent, Milly rather resented the idea of its being included in the Terrys' private jokes. She decided to ignore the remark and to wait an opportunity to put Mr Terry in his place.

"I think I saw you on a motor-cycle the other day."

"You did. A Singer, a fellow wants me to buy it; but I'm not biting. I'll tell you something, but it's a secret, mind! I'm out for blood, after the real thing. Look at this."

He took from a pocket-book a piece of newspaper and handed it with self-conscious pride to Milly. She read:

'F.N.'
Double cylinder, water-cooled engine
£150.

"I don't understand. What does 'F.N.' mean?"

"It's a make of motor-car, of course. Where have you been, miss? I tell you what. If I manage to buy it, I'll bring you out for a drive. That will change the colour in Miss Hopkins's orbs."

"Her what?"

"Orbs. Eyes. The brother is not the only poet in the family. You must try me sometime. But I'm a believer in action. I don't hold with sitting still. The world has begun to move very fast, Milly. Old

Queen Vic is dead, and Teddy is a different proposition. Are you quite sure you're comfortable?"

Milly had leaned back as Reggie's moustache, which he continued to move with an action resembling the paddle of a canoe, advanced closer and closer. Now he transferred his hand from the chair to her waist. She was not in the least alarmed. For one thing she was very strong, and Reggie was meanly-built and undernourished-looking. And her curiosity was extreme. Nor was there any basic difference between Reggie's approach and that of the Italian statue-maker to whom she had applied for work. She felt quite competent to deal with either if he became a nuisance; at the same time she was interested to see the effect she was making. Charley's love-sick approach was more of a trial because it demanded tenderness; it would be cruel to hurt it. But Reggie in his way was a pirate, a cardboard pirate, and she—she had told herself long since—was a pirate too.

"Please get me an ice," she said.

"You want something to cool you?" His moustache did a rapid see-saw across his face.

"I merely want an ice. If you don't want to get one for me, I shall go and get one for myself."

"I'd go like a shot but I'd be afraid Kitty might capture me. She must be hopping mad at this moment, wondering what's going on behind here. Little she knows."

"Perhaps you ought to go. Are you engaged to her?"

"Engaged! I'm too smart for that. Engaged, did I hear you say? You're a caution."

Reggie laughed, rather shrilly.

"I don't see why your friend should be so much afraid if there is no understanding between you. But that is not my business."

"Ask me anything you like. I'm fair and open. I have a lot to offer a girl; but not marriage. No, ma'am. I have my fortune to make, and I intend to make it. In the meanwhile I am as ready as anyone to entertain a young lady. I take Kitty to the practice dances at Legget Byrne's on Saturday evenings. She likes that. It's class. I don't bring her to the theatre, though. She can't stop giggling, and it attracts undesirable attention. I have to think of my position. I brought her to the *Myrioama* at the Rotunda. The Boer generals. Nothing like keeping up with the times."

"What's the *Myrioama*?"

"Where have you been all these years?"

"In Holland, in a convent."

"I've heard about foreign convents. I believe things go on in them that are not fit to publish in the papers."

"I wonder what gave you that impression."

"I'm pretty well up, Milly, as you'll find if you see a little more of me. But what are we going to do with brother Charley? We'll have to give him the slip. I wish you had been here for the Horse Show. You're the sort of girl I'd like to take to the Horse Show."

"Dolly went. My sister. But I couldn't afford it. Five shillings is a lot of money."

"Granted; but I regard it as important to my career to be seen in the right places. If you're good I'll invite you to Jammet's. That will set the town talking."

"What's Jammet's?"

"You *are* a daisy. It's the smartest place to eat in town. The French restaurant opened by Lord Cadogan's chef. He stayed behind when his Lordship left the Viceregal, you know. I haven't actually patronised it yet. But I intend to. Don't mention it to Kitty Hopkins, or she'll have your life."

Silence fell upon them then. Milly wished she knew how to conduct a conversation with a stranger. It was rude to ask questions, she had been brought up to think. One was supposed to draw out the other person, she had also been told. In one sense Reggie Terry needed to be put back rather than drawn out; but there was, she told herself, some way of getting him on to general topics. She must read the newspaper in future, she decided. When her mother's friends gathered in her drawing-room they talked about the King's operation, or Mr George Wyndham's proposals to landlords, or the theatre. If she asked Reggie about the theatre, it wouldn't give him an excuse to push his moustache into her face as he did whenever he held out hopes of future entertainment. So she tried.

Had he seen Mr Martin Harvey? Her sister said he made everyone in the theatre cry. Nothing would make her cry. She supposed she was hard.

"Not hard, my dear. Not hard. You are an unopened flower, in Reggie's opinion, a rose in the bud. You need to be shown the sun. That's all. What about coming to the rink? Can you skate?"

"Mama has forbidden us to go to the rink."

"So that is the tune the band is playing, is it? Well, what about a turn on the East Pier on Sunday?"

"I don't know what plans Mama has made for Sunday."

"That's right. Ask Mama."

Without any warning Reggie pulled her towards him and his moustache was now working like a metronome. The smell of oil from his hair was strong, and it mixed with sherry on his breath. Across her mind flashed the image of Kitty Hopkins when she came out from behind the same screen, and the sound of Kitty's slap. She exerted all the strength of her free arm against Reggie's shirt-front.

The fragile chairs were unable to sustain the weight of the combined operations; and as they fell back they brought the screen with them. Milly remembered nothing after that until she opened her eyes and saw Mrs Terry staring at her anxiously. She was dabbing Milly's forehead with a handkerchief that smelt strongly of Eau de Cologne. They were alone in the conservatory, from which the screen had disappeared, and Milly was lying on a sofa.

"Don't try to talk, dear. The doctor is coming to see you."

Except for a headache, Milly felt quite all right; and she was at a loss to understand her situation. But Mrs Terry was even more anxious to avoid conversation, and she kept up her ministrations, begging Milly to keep silent. The door of the dance room was closed, and the orchestra was playing on a subdued note in deference to her illness. Milly remembered the tussle with Reggie. It seemed to have taken place in another decade. How exactly had it ended?

The doctor, roused from sleep, needing a shave, was shown in by the maid, who took an awed glance at Milly before she withdrew.

"This is the patient," Mrs Terry said. She cast an appealing glance at Milly. "She knocked her head against that table."

"Where does it hurt?"

Milly pointed to the place.

"I see the lump," he said, and opened his little black bag.

Milly had only sustained a bruise; but convention demanded that a young lady should spend at least a day in bed after any injury, and Mrs Terry realised that there was no hope of escaping a disclosure to Milly's mother. The family had already taken sides in the affair—Mr Terry, alone, professing neutrality. He was already composing in his mind the form in which he would cast his enquiry after Milly's health when she went home. His obituarial gift would have earned him a living on a newspaper if he hadn't had his shop to look after. Reggie, the culprit, had been vague and defiant, and had returned to the dance floor as soon as his mother came to the rescue. Mr Casey's solicitude had been misinterpreted by Mabel, who did not hesitate to call Milly the author of her own misfortune for not behaving like a lady. Charley, overwrought, had retired to his bedroom, leaving the maid to go across the square to fetch the doctor. She, like her mistress, felt the blow to the family honour; and had given so garbled and misleading an account of the young lady's having taken faint all of a sudden, that the doctor had not ruled out the possibility of pregnancy when he arrived.

Milly made light of her injury, only wanted to go home, and was as anxious as Mrs Terry to conceal the facts. It was decided in the end to send for Dolly and to say Milly had slipped and struck her head.

"How did you slip?" Dolly enquired next day.

"I didn't slip. I fell."

"How did you fall?"

"How does anyone fall? I came down."

"Did you trip over something?"

"I suppose I must have."

There was something about the surrounding circumstances that both Dolly and her mother found unconvincing; nor were their doubts set at rest by Mr Terry's oratory or Mrs Terry's parcel of fruit. They thought in the days to come that they detected a furtiveness in the movements of the family which was unlike the flounce of the past, in which there had been an underlying aggressiveness.

But Milly, luxuriously in bed, gave nothing away. Yesterday had been highly educative even if it had had an undignified end. It was not her fault that Reggie Terry had made advances. She hadn't flirted with him. She could swear to that on a bible. It was, therefore, quite unjust that any shadow of blame should attach to her, and yet she guessed that there would be a tendency next door to put all the blame on her.

Clear-cut among her confused memories were the disapproving faces of Charley and Mabel; and when she had seen what Kitty Hopkins looked like when she came out from behind the screen, why had she agreed to go behind it with Reggie? Not, certainly, to be kissed by him. He was a ridiculous person. But she had been curious. And, then, her mother had been justified in the event. It was, therefore, important not to let her know what had happened, whatever her suspicions were—and Milly saw in her eye a closer approximation to the truth than the agreed explanation. She must be more careful in future; but it was exciting to discover in the course of a single day that she could excite Mr Mantovani, the maker of holy statues, and Mr Billy Casey (a little), and Mr Reggie Terry. None of them conquests to boast of; but the accumulation was impressive. Charley Terry's passion was of another order, more flattering (if he wasn't such an owl), but pregnant with possibilities of boredom. The trouble with him was she would have to avoid being cruel. But his disembodied passion was further proof of her power; and she couldn't help glorying in it a little.

VII

S HE, M I L L Y, H A D power over men as she had had power over
girls at school. Sœur Dominique, in one of their talks, had given
her a lecture on the nature of love. It was, she said, a movement of
the soul towards an object: it asked for no return: its value was not
to be measured by the worth of the object but by itself, because
human love was a reflection of God's love for all his creatures.

But God, Milly had argued then, demanded a return. If He was
prepared to love you, however worthless you were, He had punishments, and eternal punishments, in pickle if you didn't love Him in
return. Was that disinterested? In human love it was possible to go
on loving and get no love, but only bad treatment, in return. Sœur
Dominique had answers to give. God does not reject us: we reject
Him. His law is love; if we choose to belong to the devil's party
God is grieved, but it is the price He paid when He gave us free
will. We don't know anything about Hell except that it is Satan's
kingdom and we only go there of our own free will. As to human
love: what Milly described was often only a selfish obsession,
comparable to a drunkard's addiction to the bottle. The fact that it
persisted or was incurable was no indication of its purity. The great
lovers were the saints, who embraced all mankind for the love of
God. They avoided any close involvement with individuals. There
temptation lay.

There was an incident in Saint Teresa's life which illustrated
this, when she became too intimate with a priest and discovered
only just in time that their religious conversations were being used
by Satan for his wicked purposes.

Sœur Dominique agreed that a wife must love her husband
above everyone, and always; but this was in accordance with God's
law. He blessed the union. It was a stage on the road to Heaven,
where there were no marriages.

Milly had reflected much on these matters. She had cried in the
train, reading Sœur Dominique's present, *The Imitation of Christ*.
A little, perhaps, because she sensed under the nun's austerity an
affection which she never displayed for any of the other girls; but

largely because she was aware that what Thomas à Kempis laid down as a life of perfection was not for her and involved retirement from the world in preparation for Heaven. She knew of both only by hearsay, and she was quite determined to enjoy them in their proper order. The 'higher' side of her nature agreed with Sœur Dominique and à Kempis; but at the moment she was not prepared to withdraw herself 'from all solace of creatures, so much the sweeter and more powerful consolations shalt thou find in Me'.

Was Sœur Dominique happy? She longed to inquire but never could; in the nun's relation with her she had sensed a yearning for something left behind in the world, coupled with an anxiety for Milly if she went in pursuit of it. In the end, the good nun must have resolved the conflict for herself when, in their brief parting, she said she would pray for Milly's early marriage to a good man.

Sœur Dominique's perplexities had engaged Milly's 'higher' side; but she had not lacked evidence of the effects of love divorced from its spiritual context and best represented by the sweet Gertrude produced from her drawers. Gertrude was not the only girl who sighed for her; but she had only once experienced similar feelings. She had had a tremendous crush on a nun, who came only for a time, and left the convent after a few weeks to die, so Milly learned afterwards, in Switzerland. Milly had never even spoken to this Sister, whose handkerchief she had stolen; and for a week after she left, she cried herself to sleep. But, strangely, when she heard that she was dead it hardly moved her at all.

Only someone very remarkable would ever make her fall in love; perhaps the world did not contain him. What then was she to do? If she inspired love and never felt it, she would become a monster; but in the meanwhile there were certain advantages. Even though her head still ached she felt the sap rising and a surge of delicious strength through her veins. It was good to be alive.

Then Dolly came in with *The Illustrated News* from last week and a cup of Bovril. It struck her suddenly that Milly was 'awfully attractive' in her white flannelette night-dress, sitting up, flushed, her eyes looking larger and more vividly blue than she had ever seen them before, her hair glittering in the sun-light.

"Dolly, have you ever kissed a man?"

"What a question!"

"Well, have you?"

"Not exactly."

"What do you mean by 'not exactly'? Either you have or you haven't."

"It's not the sort of thing one talks about."

"Fudge!"

"That's a horrible word."

"It isn't. It's merely expressive."

"Mama told you not to use it."

"We are not with Mama now. Are you going to live in the nursery all your life, Dolly?"

"It isn't a question of living in the nursery. It's doing what's right. Look at you. Look what happens when you decide you know best. Did one of those awful Terrys kiss you, Milly? Don't tell me you let him."

"Well, I won't tell you."

"Milly, what's going to become of you?"

"I don't know, but whatever it is, I'm determined to have a hand in it."

"But if you start to go to parties in Buttercup Square and kiss people and knock your head, you'll become a pariah."

"A what?"

"A pariah."

"Like Nell Gwyn, you mean."

"You have Nell Gwyn on the brain."

"I'd like to have had Charles II as a lover, wouldn't you?"

"Milly, this is bad talk. You know it is."

"But I think we ought to know the truth about ourselves. I won't damn my soul for anyone I met at the Terrys' party; but I might for Charles II."

"You wouldn't if it came to the point. Your better nature would assert itself. But you shouldn't think of these things. It's wrong. I know it's wrong."

"But you must sometimes think about being kissed, Dolly. It's only natural."

"That all comes when you meet the person you are going to marry. It's all right then."

"Fudge."

"Milly, I hate that word."

"It says exactly what I think. You don't mean to tell me that nobody kisses anybody unless they are going to get married. If that were the case, there would be very little kissing in the world.

Wouldn't you like Mr Martin Harvey to kiss you? Be honest."

"He would be too much of a gentleman even to think of doing such a thing. This comes from mixing with the wrong kind of people. What *did* go on there last night?"

"If you really want to know, the young one idolises me and wants to give me poetry books; and the elder one, with the silly moustache, tried to kiss me. I didn't let him because I didn't want to; but if I had wanted to I'd have let him, just as you'd have let Martin Harvey."

"Martin Harvey's married, for one thing."

"So was Charles II."

"I don't know what's come over you. If this is the result of one night at the Terrys', Mama was right not to want you to go."

"Don't worry, Dolly dear. I shan't go again. They are the most awfully boring set really. I'll make eyes at Mr Talbot Thompson instead; then, perhaps, he will take me for a drive in his motor-car. That will make them envious next door. The horrible Reggie has plans to buy a second-hand car to drive the careless Kitty in. I'll show them."

"Have you got a temperature, I wonder? You look rather flushed."

Dolly made her mind comfortable by a sudden conviction that her little sister was raving. It explained everything.

VIII

IF THERE WAS one person in the world who would understand her present predicament, Milly thought it would be her Uncle Joe. All the rest of her family were on the side of the angels, but he would see her point of view. It was, therefore, an overwhelming shock when he arrived a few days after her accident, without Mr Talbot Thompson or the motor-car, and having heard the different versions of Milly's mishap launched a ferocious diatribe at her. He did not need to be told that young Terry had been up to the tricks of his kind and expressed a determination to horsewhip him. Rheumatism in the shoulder and Carrie's entreaties persuaded him eventually to call off the project.

"It would lead to such trouble, Joe. Besides, we have accepted their explanations and apologies. Mr Terry made a long and ridiculous speech to me across the hedge, I might have been the Queen; and Mrs Terry embarrassed me by sending in fruit in brown paper bags. We could open a shop on the strength of it. The young boy has given Milly a copy of *Paradise Lost*. True, the older one is too much ashamed of himself, I presume, to show his face; and the girl walks past with her nose in the air. But the family as a whole have shown how well aware they are of their disgrace. I think we should leave it at that. Milly has learnt her lesson."

"I hope so," said Uncle Joe. "Don't let the old Marchioness in Merrion Square get wind of it. She will make capital of it, I'm sure; and I like to be able to bring T. T. to her gatherings. Like most Englishmen he takes dullness in society for granted, and he can't see what a bore her awful entertainments are. She doesn't know anybody. It's pathetic, really. He's impressed by the title. I told him that Dublin was called the City of Dreadful Knights, and my name for her ladyship's mansion is Apothecary's Hall; but I could see he didn't relish the joke. I rather think a knighthood is in his own plans, if not a baronetcy. He's a power in the land. We looked at a place in Westmeath where he might settle; and if he does, I think Milly will find it a pretty useful base. She will meet the County T. T. will entertain in a big way; and he was struck by Milly. I could see that. She could do worse."

"Oh, Joe! He's as old as a bush."

"Not all that old. She's a girl who will need a firm hand over her. Don't put her off T. T. Remember I have expectations there. He doesn't seem to be able to move a foot in this country without my advice. Between ourselves, he is talking of taking over the hounds and standing for the county; of course he must first see that the county stands for him, and that's where I come in. If he takes on the hounds I'll have to hunt them for him, and as he won't get into Parliament as a Nationalist, he'll have to put me up. Time was when a man from Liverpool or Manchester, prepared to put down solid brass, could make it, but those days are over."

"Joe, are you out of your mind? Since when have you become a Nationalist?"

"I've never committed myself; and there's no swimming against the tide. At the moment we are supposed to love a Unionist Government and what is this fellow Wyndham doing? He's arranging to sell up the landlords. It's an act of social bankruptcy; but it's at times like this, if one keeps one's ear to the ground and one's eyes open, opportunities crop up. It's not the time for my nieces to be making public exhibitions of themselves. I shan't forget you, Carrie, or your children, if my ship comes home."

This conversation took place in the dining-room. Joe had a way of dropping in unannounced, declining a meal, and saying he was prepared to take 'pot luck'. With Carrie's careful system of economy, that meant being eaten out of house and home.

"That's very tender beef, Carrie; try and tempt me with another slice or two, and if that's whiskey on the sideboard I could do with a thimbleful." He always helped himself.

After the beef had disappeared, and when the bottle was empty, he waxed eloquent about Milly. She had had the benefit of his abuse earlier and had kept silent at the little meal, served at seven, which Carrie insisted on describing as dinner. The Terrys, next door, had dinner in the middle of the day. Joe, out on some errand and purporting not to want dinner, arrived when it was over and took 'pot luck', with Carrie in rueful attendance.

He pushed back his chair and rubbed his face with his napkin.

"This is no place for you, Carrie. I'll get you out of this. There may be a small house on T. T.'s demesne which would do for you and the girls. I want to put the family back where it belonged. I may not be a model in some ways; but I have my share of family pride. That's why I feel like thrashing Milly. If she were my daughter, I'd have laid my hands on her in a way that she wouldn't forget."

"She'd have left home if you did, Joe. You don't know Milly. Besides, we may be making a mountain out of a molehill. After all, what has the girl done? Gone to an informal party at a neighbour's."

"And as good as had herself raped in the process."

"Joe, you've drunk too much. How dare you say such a thing! If you are going to talk like that you may take yourself out of this house. I won't stand for it."

"Sorry, old girl. My temper got the better of me. I have a great admiration for Milly. It riles me to think of some counter-jumper putting his dirty hands near her."

"Well I think we've had enough of that subject; but tell me why you think your friend would put you up as a Nationalist. He doesn't talk very much; but he sounds almost excessively conservative; he might be Lord Salisbury."

"T. T. has his head screwed on. That's his tune at the moment; but he would sing another if he thought it would pay better."

"He sounds like a proper scoundrel to me."

"He's a self-made man. That's between ourselves. A fellow like that can't afford the delicacy of political principles. But he's sound at bottom. He has been a good friend to me."

Carrie glanced at her brother, his thin face illuminated by candle-light was a silver moon in the dusk of the little room. He had the delicacy and swiftness of a hare without that animal's passion for privacy. His hands, when he lifted them to his chin, were spectrally thin; and his voice, a light tenor, would not have sounded out of place in the Angelic Choir.

He was not, Carrie reflected, sound at bottom. And what had his friend's goodness amounted to? Nothing, she could attest, that Joe had been disposed to share. She did not need to ask. What Joe got were what he described as 'pickings'. By relentless time-serving he could contrive to get his way paid, journeys in spectacular motor-cars, visits to the Horse Show. More tangible benefits still lay in the realm of hope, the domain in which Joe was at home. His expression of silent rapture, in candle-light, to which the smoke of a cheroot added an illusion of incense, was probably induced by dreams of a future secure in bliss. "T. T. will turn up trumps," he said at length.

Because he was her brother, and she had come to accept him as part of the divine plan, Carrie never felt for long either the fascination or fear that he aroused in her simultaneously. Fascination was always tempered by the recollection of his enormities; and fear by fascination. The fascination was partly in the way he looked at you, always half-smiling, always inviting you to share the joke, always enlisting you against the enemy, be he only a bore. And then, his voice and appearance were all in his favour, if you were a woman. If you were a man, you saw through him, unless you were in a hurry; but a certain kind of man would use him. He was a Madame Tussaud exhibit come to life, and only in that respect more credible. He moved and talked.

He had ruined her mother, Carrie reflected, and had never once had the grace even to admit it. Were it not for his extravagance (and worse), she herself would now be comfortably off. Why did she not hate him? Why did she entertain, even for a second, faith in his schemes for the future? Perhaps she shared some of his nature. He was like a horse he had once owned, when he was trying to impress the county: it was a marvellously handsome beast but difficult to ride, and was for ever going to make its owner's fortune. But it could only run second: whatever the race, the class of its opponents, the distance, the state of the going. Each time there was a different excuse. Finally the trainer said the flaw was in the horse's nature. It could never accept a challenge. It always quitted at the post. Joe backed the animal in its first race at Phoenix Park (which it was predicted it would run away with) and kept on backing it until it failed finally in the Cambridgeshire two years later. Then he shot it. That sudden violent act was very typical of Joe, so were the tears he shed over his 'lovely grey'. Now his lovely grey was Mr Talbot Thompson. Carrie could not find it in her heart to rule out the possibilities of that personage, not until he had been given as much opportunity to prove himself as the ill-fated horse. But he wouldn't carry any of her fortune; and she, certainly, wasn't going to invest Milly in any of Joe's outsiders.

When they went upstairs, Milly was sewing. Carrie glanced quickly at her brother, and he showed that he understood her by sitting at Milly's feet and talking to her as he used to do when she was a child. She had been shaken by his vehemence. On such an occasion she expected him to take her side; and when he didn't, she lost confidence. For all her faith in herself, she was very young and it was hard to carry on with the whole world against you.

At first she was resentful and suspicious, but by degrees the old conspiratorial relationship was established. On going he gave her two sovereigns.

"I forgot the birthday, old girl," he said.

The birthday was so far past that its successor was already looming up; but Milly was too astonished to argue and could only stare at the money as if it were Jove, dropped from the ceiling.

"You're much too kind, Uncle Joe."

"I hope I'll be able to do a great deal more for you. Now, a kiss for your uncle."

It may have been because her mind had been directed to the subject recently and had run on it too much, but she was disconcerted by the vigour of her uncle's kiss. It was a shade too enthusiastic and full on the lips. He had, of course, been taking whiskey. But, even so, it disconcerted her. She was learning a great deal in a short time about men: she decided that she didn't like them.

"It's bread and butter, girls, until Wednesday," Carrie said as she closed the door on her brother. Uncle Joe, mysteriously, did not need a bed that night.

IX

MILLY'S RATE OF pay with Mr Mantovani was three pence for small statues and five shillings for life-size ones. She came to work at ten o'clock, getting off the tram at the Ballast Office and walking up the Quays to Usher's Island, where her employer's premises were, in a yard at the back. If there was enough work she sometimes stayed until after lunch and then walked slowly along the Quays, looking into the second-hand shops at furniture, books and pictures. Everything interested her. Then at four o'clock she went to the college in Stephen's Green where there were always a few backward pupils ready to pay for coaching. Sometimes she worked until seven o'clock.

At the end of the week she gave Carrie a pound; but kept her counsel as to what she was earning 'in that dreadful place with that dreadful man', as Carrie put it.

Milly's employment shocked her mother. She saw it as only one degree above a nursemaid's, and two, if that, above prostitution. It was never mentioned. On no account was Lady Kelly to hear of it. She had never recovered from the ingratitude of Milly's refusal to act as governess to the French consul's children, and concealed her curiosity under a fine show of indifference. "Milly is well, I hope."

"I don't know how you can do it, Milly," Dolly told her after she had accompanied her mother on a surprise visit to Milly's studio. Milly was angry; but Carrie stood her ground. It was her duty to see the circumstances in which her daughter was working; it was also essential that the dreadful Italian should be apprised of the fact that Milly had a mother, and a mother of a kind to be reckoned with. They arrived unexpected, and stood in the yard looking like hibernating birds that had just landed and had not yet found their bearings. Carrie, smaller than Dolly, stood her ground better. Dolly wavered and hovered, five feet seven of apology. Carrie, nose in air, looked round. Milly saw them come in, was surprised, annoyed, and in no hurry to disclose her hiding-place. Mr Mantovani's workshop was what met you when you came into the yard. He was covered in plaster; but he put down the mould on which he was working and came out politely to attend to his callers.

"Good-morning," Carrie said. Dolly smiled and swayed.

"Buon giorno," said Mr Mantovani, looking past Carrie at Dolly and deciding she was a virgin.

"I want to see Miss Preston, my daughter. I happened to be passing. Are you her employer?"

Mr Mantovani had never had time to master the language, but he had gathered that this was Milly's mother and, presumably, her sister. He had always been surprised that Milly wanted to work for him, and he assumed that her family were calling to take her away. She was turning out statues at a prodigious rate; and if this was a deputation to demand better terms he was ready to capitulate. His conscience was easy. He had treated Milly with the respect due to the Madonna even if she was beginning to interfere with his concentration.

"Miss Preston," he said, pointing to a ladder. "Miss Preston up there." He was in a dilemma induced by natural politeness. His respect for all three ladies left nothing to be desired; but Milly's force of character had always subdued him and he hesitated to call her down. At the same time it was wrong to send her mother up a ladder after her. He decided to lead the way.

"We can manage," Carrie said. "Hold the ladder, Dolly."

At this point Milly emerged. The studio was once a hay loft over stables. Dolly got up in two bounds; but her mother, holding her skirts appropriately, took longer. She looked round, contracting her nostrils, exuding disapproval. Dolly's interest was more cheerfully expressed. The loft was crowded with white figures, standing in rows, like a Greek chorus; on a trestle table there were scores of smaller ones; Milly's paints were on a smaller table at a north window. She was finishing the sandals on a life-sized St Anthony.

Carrie shivered. "You will get your death of cold here."

"There's a fire in the grate," Dolly said, earning a frown from her mother for her pains.

"I'm not cold," Milly said.

"We were shopping at McBirney's, looking for blankets for the spare bed. We thought you might like us to pay you a visit," Carrie said.

Milly said nothing.

Carrie looked round disapprovingly. "What happens," she said at length, echoing the thought in Dolly's mind, "when you want to go to the W.C.?"

"I go across to the hotel. In an emergency the Mantovanis have a place in the yard." Carrie shivered and Dolly blushed.

"It's primitive, but it's clean. They have the sweetest little children, tons of them. I've lost count. I wish you had told me you were coming. I'd have warned them. Mr Mantovani would have put on his best trousers."

Dolly blushed again. She had noticed Mr Mantovani's trousers.

"I bought you some fruit. It's good for you," Carrie said. "Dolly, we had better be on the move. I have an appointment with Prost for twelve o'clock."

"There's nothing very much to see," Milly said, "unless you would like to meet Mrs Mantovani. I'm sure they would like you to admire the family."

"I haven't sweets for them or anything," Carrie said helplessly. She had a feeling of defeat, of having walked up to the walls of a fortress, and then retreated without giving battle. Milly was too much for her, and Dolly as effective an ally as a blade of grass.

But Milly was right. Mr Mantovani had gone indoors, and when the ladies came down the ladder they found Mrs Mantovani in an advanced state of pregnancy at the foot surrounded by a flock of black-haired, white-faced, black-eyed little Mantovanis, chattering like sparrows. Mrs Mantovani, like her husband, had no proficiency in English; but she was eloquent in her Neapolitan greetings to the mother and sister of the hen that was laying eggs of gold. Carrie and Dolly were wafted indoors. Coffee was magically produced and sweet biscuits. One little Mantovani threw up. Another disgraced himself. Mr Mantovani was equally delighted by both.

"It's a frightful come-down. I don't know how she can do it."

Carrie, returned from her visit to Prost's, was sitting with Dolly over their luncheon—brown bread, butter, a slice of ham each, and coffee; with coffee, as a treat, they had Marie biscuits.

"I suppose she's making lots of money," Dolly replied, defending her sister and tremulously envious. It was depressing never to have any. It made you feel so completely powerless and at the mercy of anyone who chose to pay.

"She never tells me a thing. I might be a stranger, instead of her mother."

"She does pay a pound towards the house. I wish I could. I'm useless."

"What would I do without you, Dolly dear? And Fanny Kelly doesn't seem to be able to spare you either. You know—it's very wrong of me—but I sometimes wonder whether she doesn't take advantage of you. Youth is very precious. It doesn't last; in fact, it flies. I keep hoping that she will do something for you, Dolly—she keeps hinting—but really she seems to me to be making use of you. I wish I could think of some alternative. If your Uncle Joe were any help . . ."

"Don't worry about me, Mama. I'm perfectly content. I'd much rather have the life I have than be poor Mrs Mantovani with all those children."

Carrie, at this, glanced shrewdly at her daughter. Was it true? If she were herself unmarried, trying to keep house for Joe, without the children to worry over, would she feel that she had missed something? Marriage was a woman's role. She wished she could get Dolly settled. If only she had a little of Milly's devil. Men were sometimes slow to recognise the advantages of an angel without private means. If Mr Talbot Thompson were thinking of a wife, Dolly would be much more suitable than Milly. Dolly was the sort of girl who tended to marry men much older than herself. She wouldn't feel the weight of it. Look at that old Marquis of Donegal, over eighty, marrying a rich Canadian of thirty. Disgusting. Mr Talbot Thompson was still in his forties, or very near them. If a nobleman of over eighty were to ask her to marry, even at her age, the prospect would appal her. But she would do it, she supposed, for the sake of the children.

"Lady Kelly has become very curious about Milly," Dolly broke in on her mother's reverie. "She keeps asking me what she is doing and I try not to fib, but it's very difficult. She is under the impression that Milly is teaching all the time."

"Tell her she is taking art lessons in the morning. It's true, in a way. The Italian showed me a figure she made. I was astonished at how lifelike it was; and I have seen pictures in her room, drawings she had made; they are really quite professional-looking. Of course, that nun in Holland, who took an interest in her, said Milly could do anything if she put her mind to it."

"I needn't say she gets paid. That's what Lady Kelly would object to. But I'm afraid she might want to know who her teacher was and so on. In the end it would be awful if she were to find out the truth and learn about the deception. She has a way of finding everything out."

"She's a nosey woman. I really don't see that it's any of her business."

"You know how she thinks everything to do with us is her business. I don't want her to talk about Milly. If she gets her knife into anyone she won't let them be; and she has never forgiven her for turning down that job. She hates people not to fall in with her arrangements."

But Carrie wasn't listening. She had an idea. Why not make the fib come true? Milly obviously had talent; why not get her lessons? It would be a worthwhile expenditure, better even than a ball. She became suddenly animated and, in the process, shed years. Nobody, were it not for her weeds, would doubt they were sisters at that moment. She turned eagerly to Dolly.

"Here's where Fanny Kelly could do something. She is always talking about Mr Catterson Smith and young Mr Lane, who is so clever and knows everybody. She can find out from them where Milly ought to train, and she can help to get her commissions when she's ready for them. I think this is a brilliant idea."

Lady Kelly preferred to propose benefactions than to be solicited. She could be as much offended by a request for help as she was unforgiving when her gratuitous benevolence was not gratefully accepted. Dolly knew this and did not resent it. Everyone, as she put it to herself, has his own little ways. So she bided her time, and when her patron made a routine enquiry after Milly, not listening to her satisfactory-sounding reply, Dolly put on her asking-for-advice air, which was always certain of the closest attention.

"Mama and I are both so anxious to consult you about Milly's future," she began, and then hurried because she saw her listener brace herself in her stays, an action equivalent to the manning of the walls of a fort against an expected assault.

"I haven't wanted to add to your own problems, but you have taken such interest in us all, I think it would be wrong to take this decision without your approval."

The stays creaked. Lady Kelly relaxed. She had anticipated a covert reference to entertainment and was not to have her good-nature laid to tribute; but this sounded like something in another province than amusement; she was being consulted as a judge, not an almoner. That was as it should be.

"My dear Dolly, I don't know how often I have told you and your dear mother that I am always at your disposal where Milly is concerned. She's what my father used to call 'a handful', I fear. I am very glad that I did not rush into a ball for her. It would have gone to her head. For the time being that young lady needs a tight rein; and, to be quite honest with you, my dear, I don't think your mother capable of holding it."

As always Dolly found herself disliking Lady Kelly and tempted to take Milly's part.

"She is working very hard; too hard, in fact."

"Well, my dear, who is to blame for that? If all the trouble I went to to get her suitable employment is thrown back in my face, I am too human not to get some satisfaction from finding that I knew better all along."

"I have to tell you a secret," Dolly persevered while Lady Kelly held her breath. "As well as working (well, *that* was true) for money, Milly has been studying on her own account."

"And will you be good enough to tell me what she has been studying?"

Lady Kelly was always quick to put down presumption. Dolly regretted now the unnecessary reference to 'a secret'.

"Art."

"Art!"

"Modelling and drawing."

"And for how long, pray, has this been going on?"

"Since—" Dolly hesitated. She had almost let slip about Mr Mantovani's statues.

The hesitation had not gone unobserved. A wave of exasperation passed over Lady Kelly's vast acreage of face. Why should she be for ever troubling herself with the concerns of these insignificant people? They were merely a drag on her time and patience. And Dolly was looking signally plain today with that cold in her nose. What were they keeping back from her?

"*Since?* Out with it, Dolly. If there's one thing I hate, it's shuffling."

"I'm not shuffling. I was trying to think. Milly doesn't tell me everything. Since before Christmas. She gets lessons from an Italian; but I don't think he is a suitable teacher."

"And who, may I ask, pays for the lessons?"

"Milly."

"Milly? But I thought you said Milly gave all she earned to her mother? I don't know what I'm going to do with you, Dolly, if you begin to deceive me in little ways. I've noticed it lately. Don't let the habit grow on you. 'Tell the truth and shame the devil', as my grandfather used always to say." (It was one of Lady Kelly's peculiarities to attribute all the copy-book maxims, including Shakespeare's, to members of her family.)

Dolly fought against tears. "I don't think that's fair. If you feel like that about me, I had better go away. I hate dishonesty."

"Who said anything about dishonesty? Pull yourself together, child. You must learn to take a little correction from the people who love you. The world will use its own rods. Believe you me. My father—"

But Dolly was determined not to hear what her father had to say on the subject. She was beginning to wish she had never involved herself in this project and allowed Milly to go her own way. Steadying her voice, she began again; and her tormentress nodded approval.

"Milly does something in return for her lessons."

Lady Kelly's eyebrows shot up.

"What did you say he was—an Italian?"

"He sells church decorations. Milly is very good at that sort of thing. She learned it at school."

'Church decoration' was a happy inspiration. It drew Lady Kelly completely off the scent, conjuring up pictures of the Sistine Chapel and the Rose window at Chartres. She was not herself quite certain what the term might denote in the present context, but she never showed ignorance even though she liked to ask questions.

"Church decoration has a great deal to be said for it, but requires more training than I should think Milly has had. Her employer, I take it, is in a small way."

"Yes. I believe so."

Lady Kelly nodded. She was right. She was always right. But the recollection of visits abroad with Sir Patrick—the year of the private audience with the Pope, the glimpse of King Leopold in the Champs Elysées—accidently conjured up, so vivid, were not to be dispelled. And a half-formed notion that she and Dolly were at cross-purposes encouraged her to act at once. She always arranged other people's affairs with a bland disregard of their desires. Milly wanted to study art. She knew what that meant—bohemianism, nude models, cigarettes—but 'church decoration' had been mentioned. Here was a chance to take over and upset Milly's plans while purporting to forward them.

"I'm very glad you spoke to me. This afternoon I'm going to the Hospital linen guild. I never miss it, for Sir Patrick's sake. His Grace will be there. I'll discuss the matter with him. I find him a wonderful friend, and on a subject like this where better could we turn for suitable advice."

"I don't want you to bother Dr Walsh on Milly's account."

"No bother, my dear. Write down the name of the church decorator she is working for. His Grace will know at once what his standing is. I wouldn't put it past poor Milly to have picked the wrong person. Why didn't she refer to me in the first place? How often have I to say I'm here at all times ready to be consulted, and delighted to be of help where I can."

Dolly cursed herself. How could she have foreseen that Milly's art lessons would end up in an entanglement with the Archbishop of Dublin. Whatever he suggested to get rid of Lady Kelly—but one of the many idle women who forced themselves upon his notice—would be handed down as if it was the decalogue. The French consul was nothing in comparison with this: if his Grace's recommendation was ignored she might as well leave Lady Kelly. Life would not be worth living with her. And she would say she had put her own soul in jeopardy if she did not insist on seeing that the Archbishop's recommendations were obeyed to the letter.

Dolly postponed the inevitable by pretending not to know Mr Mantovani's name. Then she hurried home as soon as tea was over—Lady Kelly was going to the theatre and did not require her attendance.

Carrie listened to her breathless account.

"You are too conscientious, dear child. I think I know how to cook that woman's goose."

Carrie, at home, was increasingly throwing off even a show of awe for her daughter's employer. Joe never ceased to remind her that she had been diddled over the letting of Merrion Square. Having signed a ten year lease Lady Kelly could afford to snap her fingers. Carrie hadn't had the courage to admit this to Joe, whom she left under the impression that she had the matter in hand. She often intended to call on her solicitor, who arranged it all, but could never summon up the courage. He, in his pompous, kindly way, made her feel an imbecile, and she could not forget that it was in such a light that she had presented herself after Arthur's fatal accident. It seemed, at the time, the correct way for a young widow to behave. It would have been very common to have shown herself indecently anxious for information.

There was after all a little of Joe in Carrie. It came out in the letter she decided to post so that it would be digested before Dolly appeared. But she let Dolly see it.

My dear Fanny,

Dolly tells me that you have been good enough to offer to interest the Archbishop in Milly's career. Please do not put yourself to that trouble. Milly intends to become a professional artist; and I hope that if she shows promise you will help to spread her fame. A word from you always goes a long way.

I hope that my brother Joe's friend, Mr Talbot Thompson, will be able to procure Milly an opening in an art school in London. The idea of Paris or anywhere abroad, is, of course, out of the question.

Yours affectionately,

Carrie Preston.

"But has Uncle Joe been consulted?"

"Of course not; but it suddenly struck me that if I said this, Fanny Kelly will at once try to checkmate him by approaching someone even more important. It would kill her to think we were not beholden to her. Just you wait and see."

By one of those coincidences which convinced Carrie that Providence was never sleeping where her affairs were concerned, her letter arrived when Lady Kelly was studying a social column. Her attention had been attracted by a paragraph which said that the fashionable thing to do at the moment was to give a reception in the premises of the Royal Hibernian Academy in Abbey Street where there was an old masters' exhibition arranged by Mr Hugh Lane. Mr Lane was one of the many interesting people that Lady Kelly did not know; but she could claim acquaintance with the secretary of the Academy, and she decided to hold a reception there and persuade him to enlist some of the people connected with the

74

exhibition. She had a picture in the library which her late husband had prized. What about asking Mr Lane to come and look at it? He did that sort of thing, she heard. After that it would seem quite natural to ask him to the reception. If he accepted she could use his name to rally otherwise reluctant guests.

Carrie's letter reinforced her decision. It gave her another topic. Milly's talent could be used as a bait. She would have to buy the girl a dress. But she was undoubtedly attractive-looking, and the favourite, how did it go? "They call me Mimi, but my name is Lucia."

Her imagination, fired beyond its wont, conjured up a picture of Milly dying of consumption in the arms of Mr Lane during the reception.

She was making a conscious effort to forget that the Archbishop had been extremely—and unwarrantably—short with her yesterday. The proceedings of the linen guild seemed to bore him; and when she introduced the subject of church decoration over the tea and biscuits afterwards, he said he knew nobody who went in for that sort of thing and referred her to the College of Art. There were people who said the Archbishop was too nationalistic in his politics for a man in his position. She was afraid there might be something in it.

However, the unpleasantness of yesterday was quite washed out by the prospects ahead. She would have telephoned Carrie then and there to come and see her, but the poor dear had not installed a telephone. She couldn't afford it. Lady Kelly was absurdly proud of hers. Her husband had been one of the first to invest in one. She remembered all his triumphs.

A letter posted early in the morning was delivered during the afternoon. Having ascertained Mr Lane's address by telephone, Lady Kelly sat down after breakfast to start—as she told herself, her brother used to say—the ball rolling. Writing a letter, however brief or however commonplace the occasion, was always a solemn affair with her. She treated her every note as if it were a state paper that she had to prepare as well as sign, lending her the consequence of Prime Minister and monarch at the same time.

Her paper retained a narrow black edge, although Sir Patrick had been laid to rest seven years ago, and it was scented with lavender. Having arranged herself Lady Kelly sat with the point of the pen in her chin as an aid to thought. Not until she had the whole composed, down to the last full stop, did she poise herself to write.

Dear Mr Lane,

My friends in the Academy tell me that you are interested in seeing pictures of note that are not on public view. I have here a large landscape which my husband thought highly of; but I am not sufficiently a connoisseur to know whether it is suitable for display in a public gallery. Sir Patrick would, I am sure, have wished me to leave it to the National collection; and as I am in the process of settling my affairs I should be very grateful, if you could spare the time, to call and inspect it. I shall be guided by your advice in every particular.

May I take the opportunity to congratulate you on your Exhibition at the Academy? I hope in the near future to make my own small contribution to its continued success.

Should she say 'yours sincerely'? She had never met her correspondent, and he had yet to discover that he was already on her invitation list. On consideration she decided to say 'yours gratefully'. He might be intrigued by that.

The letter duly folded and put in its envelope needed only to be carried to the pillar box. If only Dolly would get up and come in early, she would have been here to post it. It was not a letter to entrust to a servant. Complaining to herself about Dolly's ingratitude, she wrapped herself up and walked her Pomeranian to the corner; as her father used to say, she was killing two birds with one stone.

When Dolly came in at her usual and arranged time, her patron was taking tea, but did not offer her a cup. This was a signal, conveying disapproval or that she had benefited in some way and was not to be put under too great a load of obligation. Today it meant both.

"You find me a little rushed, dear, slightly tired. I had a letter from your mother—how is she, by the way?—hinting that I ought to help Milly in her artistic career. I wrote at once—you know me—to young Mr Lane. I was sorry you were not here to post the letter—Sir Francis has begged me not to go out in the cold—but I felt that I must get it off by first post. I am never at ease when I hear a call until I have answered it. Would you be so good as to close the window or ring for Sarah. The draught is killing me."

Dolly went to close the window; but Lady Kelly stopped her. There was a want of dignity in doing these tasks for which servants were employed. Dolly was apt to be casual; and it was wrong to let her acquire little habits that in impoverished people were all too often attributed to lack of breeding. "Ring for Sarah, dear."

"It's no trouble."

"I said 'Ring for Sarah'. It's not a question of trouble. In doing what is one's duty one should go to no end of trouble. My poor sister, whom you never knew, used to say 'what is worth doing is worth doing well'. I remembered it this morning when I wrote to Mr Lane on Milly's account and went out and posted the letter. I never encountered such an east wind. It would skin a crocodile. I wouldn't entrust a letter like that to Sarah. I was sorry you were not here; but I did it myself. I regarded it as my duty. I think one can't be too particular about these matters. It is painfully easy to slip into unbecoming ways. Ring for Sarah."

Dolly rang; but the bell was out of order. The point now to be determined was whether Dolly should go in search of a servant or attend to the matter herself. Lady Kelly, in the role of Solomon, decided she should tell John to have the matter of the bell attended to and at the same time ask him to send Sarah if she were not to be seen.

"You will be killing two birds with one stone, as my poor father used to say."

Dolly was used to these dilemmas, and waited for final instructions. She was inwardly smiling at her mother's machiavellianism. Carrie, under the stress of life, was developing into quite a formidable figure under her meek exterior.

But there was a problem; how to break the news to Milly. She had so jealously paddled her own canoe that she might resent her mother's interference, although Dolly thought that the manner in which she had accomplished her designs might amuse Milly.

It was decided between them that Dolly should break the news, and she chose the time when Milly was at her meekest, when she was drying her hair. It is impossible to kneel before a fireplace with one's hair hanging over one's face, like a Magdalen, and be other than submissive.

"Mama has played a very naughty trick on Lady Kelly," Dolly

began. Milly perceptibly stiffened under her wrap: a bad sign. Dolly began again.

"You mustn't be angry with Mama. She is so anxious to help you—" Milly's head reared up again. Dolly made a new approach.

"We think you are doing wonders and we want to help if we can. Mama thought that Mr Lane, or someone like that, might be able to get you proper training. Mama has her mind made up that you are going to be a famous artist."

"Mama doesn't know Mr Lane."

"Lady Kelly does, or at least she knows how to get hold of him." Milly sat up on her heels.

"Dolly, Mama hasn't asked that woman to help, has she? I can't stand it. I'd rather beg from door to door than be beholden to that, that—"

"Mama asked her for nothing. Lady Kelly wanted the Archbishop to take an interest in your career, and Mama said she had plans of her own to send you to London. That's where Mr Lane comes in. Lady Kelly wrote at once to him. Mama knew she would. She can't keep her finger out of anyone's pie."

"I wish she'd keep it out of mine. I don't know why you should all be plotting and planning behind my back. It's not straight. It's so typical of everything in Dublin. I hate the place. I hate its littleness and its smugness and its snobberies. And if you and Mama start to interfere, I'll hate you as well. I've a good mind to go to London at once. I can afford to—very nearly."

"Can't you see that we were only anxious to help? Mama was upset to find you in such an unsuitable place. If you must be an artist, at least you can try to do it like a lady."

"Such bosh."

"It's not bosh. We want to help you."

"Don't mix me up with Lady Kelly. She's your pigeon. All that woman wants is power. She is a tyrant."

"Underneath it all, she has a kind heart, Milly. I'm sure she has. It's just that she is—"

"A bully. Don't tremble like that. She is a bully, and you want someone to bully you. You are one of the meek, who will inherit the earth. I'm not. I'm a Lady Kelly in my own right. But I've brains and she has only her title and her pomposity."

"I hate to hear you talk like that, Milly. I wish you could hear yourself. You'd give it up. All that is going to happen is Lady Kelly will give a party at the Academy and we shall be there and you can meet Mr Lane. What objection do you see to that?"

"Well, for one thing, I'm sure Mr Lane is a sensible man and he will see through Lady Kelly at once. For another, how is he to know from meeting me whether I have any talent or not?"

"Mama thought you might have some of your drawings with you. What does it matter whether he sees through Lady Kelly or not? It's you that matters."

"I hate this roundabout approach. What's to prevent me calling on Mr Lane and showing him my drawings? That would be more honest; and if he is a sensible man I'm sure he'd prefer it."

"You can't call on a man like that. You know you can't."

"Dolly dear. This is the twentieth century. The crinoline is out. Lady Kelly lives in the past. Nothing could be so stupid as the little world of gentility she moves in. I'm sure Mr Lane would be more impressed by me if he didn't meet me under her wing, with Mama in attendance. You don't think he will try to make love to me, do you?"

Dolly dropped the brush with which she was gently stroking her sister's hair. When Milly said things like that she felt a pain inside. It made her sweat. She couldn't bear it. Where did she get that coarse streak from?

"Don't act, Dolly. If you make so much fuss about me going to see a young man on my own, you must have a reason for it."

"It's not done, Milly."

"But if it's not done it must be for a good reason. I am giving you the only one I can think of."

"That's because you enjoy shocking me. The reason is very plain: the sort of girl who calls on men alone hasn't any regard for her reputation. Nice men won't want to know her."

"If they were nice, what harm could she come to? Your idea is that men are not nice. If they find a girl unprotected, they attack her."

"Nonsense."

"If it were not the truth, why should they disapprove of her calling on them?"

"It's a question of appearances. Why doesn't Mama wash the front steps?"

"Because it would be telling the world the truth, that she can't afford to pay a servant to do it for her."

"There's a question of dignity involved."

"I don't propose to wash Mr Lane's front steps. I shall ring the bell and ask if he's at home. Then, if he is, I'll introduce myself and show him my pictures. No, I shan't do that. I'll write to him in the first place."

"He'll think you are a designing woman. He'll tell his servants to say he's not at home."

"Then you think I ought to surprise him in his den?"

"I think nothing of the kind. I'd do what Mama has been so clever and thoughtful to arrange. I'd wear a new hat. I'd charm him if I were you. You can look so charming, Milly, when you don't frown and pout."

"Wouldn't it be fun to go to Lady Kelly's silly old party and disgrace her, pretend to get drunk on the meagre drop of sherry, show too much leg, ogle Mr Lane, and smoke cigarettes. I would just love to do it, and say 'damn' at least twice, rather loud."

But the prospect was too much for Dolly. She went to bed feeling unhappy. There was a bad drop in Milly; there was no point in shutting one's eyes to it. Uncle Joe was only a symptom. There was a taint in the blood. And she seemed to take a positive delight in giving pain.

X

ON THE MORNING after her triumphant intrigue, Carrie received an attractive-looking envelope. Envelopes betray their contents. This one seemed to shout 'Open me', and Carrie found she was trembling as she opened it to see if it would live up to its appearance. It contained an invitation to a ball, addressed to Dolly and Milly, inside a letter to herself pressing her to come with them. The occasion was the 'coming-out' of a daughter of a judge, a recent appointment, a contemporary of Arthur's. No doubt the same thought prompted the letter that had occurred to Carrie when she read of his elevation, that if Arthur were alive, the promotion would have been his.

His colleagues had been very attentive to the widow after Arthur died, but by degrees their ardour cooled—they had their profession to attend to. And their wives, with a few exceptions, had begun to forget her. Buttercup Square was socially speaking in the desert.

Mrs Day wrote the warmest, friendliest letter. The world was smiling on her, and she remembered that it had once turned its kinder face towards Carrie too.

She did not in the least want to dress up and go to an evening party; but, for the girls' sake, she was determined to, and she had an affectionately melancholy curiosity to see Arthur's associates and their children. The social division between Protestants and Catholics existed even in the professions. Arthur was on good terms with other barristers, but most of his close friends were Catholics. The new judge was an exception. He was notoriously liberal in these matters. Some of the guests would be drawn from her circle, on the very periphery of which she now nervously hung, who had once been in the confident centre. To them she was 'Carrie Preston'; to the Protestant bar 'Poor Preston's widow'.

For once Carrie had news that pleased everybody, everybody that mattered to her. Lady Kelly, needless to say, did her best to dampen Dolly's ardour. The rooms in Herbert Street (where the Days lived) were not, in her opinion, large enough for a suitable entertainment. She thought Dolly was looking anaemic and was better advised not to stay up late. Milly's work would make her so tired-looking that she could hardly expect to do justice to herself at a party. Carrie would be made miserable by the recollection of vanished splendour. They would know none of the guests. Then there was the expense of it all. And how were they to go? She would not ask her driver to stay up late and fetch them unless they were prepared to leave before supper. On the whole, she decided, that was the best plan.

But her offer was refused; and her order that Milly was to wear a cast-off dress of Dolly's, and on no account to put her mother to the expense of a new gown, was also ignored.

"Carrie Preston is a fool, and her younger daughter a great trial to me," she confided in a friend. "Dolly means well. I do what I can for her; but she will never set the Thames on fire, as my mother used to say."

Milly was looking forward to the ball, relieved that for once it was not an engineered entertainment and delighted that Dolly and her mother were both going to get pleasure from it. Carrie's eyes brightened; she threw herself into the task of providing clothes that would do them credit.

"I feel that I'm doing it for Arthur," she told herself. She chose materials and took a large part in making them. Milly was quite expert. Dolly did minor tasks, sewing buttons, attaching ribbons. Milly insisted on paying for her own materials.

A cab was ordered, and Mary stood in the window of the drawing-room, waving good-bye.

"You'll be the belle of the ball," she said to Carrie, who was looking attractive and young, and tiny beside her tall daughters. Milly she described as 'like an angel from Heaven', and Dolly, she said, 'would do'.

Dolly, expecting least, was the calmest of the three women, and, forgetful of herself, was admiring the others. Even though, in the role of chaperone, her mother going to a dance was a new and different sort of person, in the bad light in the cab she looked a contemporary; and Dolly thought how bright and attractive her eyes were (Dolly's were rather pale). Carrie in her excitement couldn't stop talking and she kept on fussing over her daughters' clothes.

"I remember my own poor mother advising me before my first dance," she babbled. "Don't dance more than three times with the same partner; don't sit on the top step of the stairs; and see that there is someone to take your chaperone to supper. Now I let you off the third condition. I have always been able to forage."

"And nobody is likely to ask me to dance more than three times," Dolly said.

Recollections of Milly's evening at the Terrys now came over everyone. A slight air of constraint had been induced by Carrie's not tactful reminiscence.

"What is one supposed to do if one's programme is empty?" Dolly asked.

"Yours won't be, Dolly. At a well-run entertainment the hosts see that girls are not left without partners."

Milly did not join in the conversation. Inside she felt tense, as if she were going into battle. She had had very little social life, and her idea of balls were still governed by early reading of *Cinderella*.

"Milly's not talking," Dolly said.

"She's thinking," Carrie suggested.

Cabs were debouching from Herbert Street into Baggot Street, and there was quite a crowd gathered round the door to watch the guests arrive.

Their own cab was a local enterprise to which Carrie had resort on great occasions. The driver and proprietor, Mr Wright, handed down his passengers very handsomely and agreed to return at two o'clock. There had been a great deal of argument on this subject: duty and inclination being at war. Carrie had pictured herself half-asleep among the duennas. Milly suggested she should go home after supper and leave them to fend for themselves; but Dolly said that this would be unfavourably noticed.

They were ushered up to a bedroom to deposit their cloaks, and then came down to the first floor where dancing was to take place in the double drawing-room. Programmes were lying in a bowl at the door where a footman was announcing the guests in a voice that frightened Dolly, embarrassed Carrie, and irritated Milly.

The hosts were a comfortable smiling couple, who greeted Carrie with enthusiasm and looked with interest at her girls, whom they half-expected might look like waifs. Their own daughter, for whom the dance was being given, was a pretty little thing, whose light Milly dimmed at once.

There were chairs everywhere: and Carrie sat down, a daughter on each side of her, awaiting their fate. Polite young men were brought up, shook hands with Carrie and invited each of the girls to dance. Milly showed the first her empty page; but Dolly pretended to have to look for gaps in hers.

It all passed off very easily, because Carrie's old acquaintances, relieved to see her looking so prosperous, tumbled over one another to be obliging. All the young men wanted to dance with Milly. Dolly benefited by this. Having invited the attractive sister, they were constrained to pay attention to the plainer one. Compared with the Terrys' party it was very grand and very formal. Nobody tried to imitate a Mynah bird; and if flirtation was in the air, it had not as yet assumed the bold front favoured by Reggie Terry.

A studious-looking young man came over and greeted them. This was Bernard Roche, Dolly's erstwhile admirer. He had a rather pompous manner; but to Dolly's delight asked her for three dances, the maximum, according to Carrie's mother. He then asked Milly for one. He had been invited from policy and knew nobody else. She thought him unattractive and would have liked to be able to say she had no dance left; but it was not the case. What happened, she wondered, if there was someone you wanted to dance with all the time? Did you have to limit yourself to three? How was it possible? She saw some young men who looked more romantic than Bernard Roche, and what was to happen if, when one of these was introduced to her, she had no dances available? She decided that it was a gamble like so much in life. She would put down imaginary names in the last half of her programme; these could be used as a safeguard against bores and made available for more promising material.

Carrie looked up more than once with surprise when she heard Milly say that she was engaged. The dancing had begun; the position was becoming more desperate. Milly's partner was a student in Trinity. His only topic was himself; and when they went to sit on the stairs after the dance, he complained about the unfair advantage Army officers had over civilians. The —— Regiment was stationed in Dublin then. The officers were invited to a dance like this, and just took the cream of the girls.

"Why don't you challenge one of them to a duel?"

"That's out of date," the young man said, picking at a pimple.

Milly had met no officers, but she reflected that from a girl's point of view they might offer advantages over her partner.

He was studying for the church, he said; but the profession was overcrowded. Gladstone had ruined it by the disestablishment. Milly had never heard of the disestablishment. Her partner explained it to her with a melancholy zest.

"This is awful," she told herself. When the band struck up, she leaped to her feet, not waiting to hear about the final debate on the iniquitous Bill.

"She has a dance engaged with an officer," the embryonic divine told himself. Although he had done nothing to let her know about it, he thought her decidedly pretty if, perhaps, flighty. And he had failed to impress her. He was looking for a girl he could impress; it was his test of the sex.

In the crowd going back, she saw Dolly, looking animated for her, and saw that the cause of the excitement was Bernard Roche, who was claiming his dance, looking like a creditor in a bankruptcy petition, filing his claim. At almost the same moment she found herself looking into a pair of large brown eyes. They were fixed on her; and by turning suddenly she surprised the starer. He blushed, and she felt a sensation as if some part of her inside had dropped, at the same time she experienced a slight weakness at the knees. She had to make an effort to look away, and as she walked towards where Carrie was sitting to wait for her next partner, she felt those eyes on her back.

"What's the matter, child?"

"Nothing."

"You've lost colour."

"It's very hot."

"That makes one red not white."

"I'm peculiar, I suppose."

Milly, annoyed with herself for having shown her feelings to her mother, concentrated on her programme. The last ten dances had been filled in with the names of Rembrandt, Beethoven, Mozart, Bonnie Prince Charlie, General Gordon, Lewis Waller, Kitchener, Lord Roberts, Nelson and Hereward the Wake. She saw the names through a slight fog. Her surroundings had become suddenly unreal. She hoped her partner for the dance that had just begun, who should have appeared by now, would forget their engagement. She didn't want to dance with anyone. The music, a Strauss waltz, seemed to come from a hundred miles away; and her mother's voice beside her was like a voice in a dream.

She was brought back to consciousness by a prim voice immediately in front of her. "I think this is our dance."

She looked up and recognised one of the young men she had been introduced to. Her programme said his name was Miller. He was standing up; she was sitting down; hence she could not make out a figure behind him, nor did she pay much attention when Mr Miller introduced whoever it was to Carrie. Then he said without enthusiasm, "Miss Preston, may I introduce Mr Alan Harvey?"

She looked up and into the dark brown eyes.

She heard as through a gale at sea a silver voice asking her if she had a dance to give him, and she found herself, like Dolly, pretending to consult her programme.

She expected his eyes to look haughty, but they were imploring. If it could be true, she would say 'Take as many as you want'.

"Have you the next?" he said. "No. Bother. I've booked that. What about the one after?"

"I'm sorry."

"The next?"

"I'm sorry."

Would he persist? Could she not show him? Mr Miller coughed. He wasn't enjoying the delay. He had made it clear that he took no particular pleasure in introducing his friend. He had been importuned. Carrie, sensing something, asked Miller a question. His attention was diverted. It was one of those historic moments in a life. Milly handed Alan her programme.

"You can see how it is."

At first he winced, seeing a name on every line. Enemies all. He stared. Mozart. Nelson. It was Lewis Waller who gave the show away. That matinee idol would have had the room in a swoon.

"Those are free," Milly said. He said nothing but handed her his own. She saw that there were relatively few spaces; and the names on the list had a horribly real look: Miss Parsons, Diana Vereker, Miss Trumbull. Nothing like Boadicea, Ellen Terry, Deirdre of the Sorrows. Mr Harvey hadn't had to play games. She saw him putting crosses here and there through her list. Mozart was covered with an 'A'. So were Lord Roberts, Nelson, and Hereward the Wake. Then he gave the card back and bowed. She followed Mr Miller in a dream. A gawky young man, he was clothed in the grace of an angel of the Lord.

"I say, you waltz rippingly."

Those were his very words uttered when the music stopped. They had not talked as they danced. Milly tried not to look for her partner to be. She was afraid to encounter his gaze. She followed her present attendant to a small sofa, where she heard him say, when they sat down:

"Harvey asked to be introduced to you. I hope you didn't mind."

"Not at all."

"I hardly know him. He's very junior to me. I thought it was rather cheek."

"What does he do?"

"He's a student at the Inns."

"You are going to become barristers."

"I was called last year."

"I'm sorry. I should have known."

"I hope I don't strike you as having the air of a student. I'm devilling for Horace Porter. I got a brief on my own account yesterday. It was a trespass case; a tree that grew out of a garden into my client's garden, and he decided to lop the overhanging branches. But in order to do this he had to climb on the wall that bounded the two properties. The question was who owned the wall? And even if, as it was alleged, the wall was not a party wall, had not my client the right to climb on it to cut the branches that were overhanging his property. Had he not the right to enter the property of the owner of the tree? If he had, it followed he could climb on his wall. Unfortunately the position was complicated by the fact that the wall was in a state of disrepair, and a large part of it fell in, breaking glass cloches that were covering strawberry plants in the owner's garden. At the same time my client fell and did himself considerable injury. I argued that we might proceed by letting them claim for trespass and putting in a counter-claim with our defence. Mr Porter, with whom I had a word in the Library, advised that we should proceed and let them put in the counter-claim if they wanted to. I hope I'm not boring you."

Milly, hearing only a babble of uninteresting sound, was brought back to earth by the question.

"It's very interesting," she said, noticing for the first time that Mr Miller's ears stood out like a bat's.

She had resources now that made her impervious to boredom, a glow within; outside she knew the sky was brilliant with stars. Tomorrow all the earth would be beautiful. She smiled on

Mr Miller, dazzling him. His writ had been issued, and he was anticipating the defence that would be offered to it.

"Is Mr Harvey clever?" she asked.

"I really don't know. He is so very much junior to me."

"He doesn't look so very young."

"I suppose he's twenty-two. I'm twenty-six. Or, rather, I am going to be twenty-six in March."

"Where does he live?"

"His people have a place in the country. He is rather stuck-up. I believe his parents are dead. They were killed in an earthquake in India. He lives with two old aunts."

"Poor boy."

"I think the aunts are very rich."

"To lose his parents, I mean."

"Yes. It was rough luck. I never told you what happened when we got in their defence."

"I don't think you ought to. I think you should rest your brain and try to forget your work when you're supposed to be enjoying yourself. Do you go to many dances?"

"Crowds. But I think you will be interested to hear how we dealt with the point about the cloches."

"Do tell me."

I could be brutal, Milly told herself. I could tell him to tumble into his old cloches. I could tell him that he is a young fogey and that he will soon be an old fogey. I could extinguish him; but I don't choose to. And yet why should I have to put up with him? Why should I not shut him up and bore him? I don't want to. My thoughts are too precious to waste them. They would be contaminated. It would be sacrilege. We could sit in silence. But that wouldn't be playing the game. If I hadn't met Mr Harvey tonight I'd have had the most excruciating boredom with Mr Miller and Mr Roche.

But she saw Dolly on the stairs listening to Mr Roche lecturing her. And Dolly was smiling as she leant towards him like corn in a breeze. Perhaps because she was self-conscious about her height, Dolly was for ever in motion, swaying and drooping.

Mr Roche was dancing with Milly now. She would never hear what happened in the end about the tree, any more than she would ever know the full extent of Gladstone's disestablishing depravity. And yet another dance would begin before she had heard Mr Roche's plans for the future. He had recently purchased a solicitor's practice in Waterford. It was a golden opportunity. His father had connections there. He was very lucky. In the ordinary course he would have had to wait in his father's office to fall eventually into a dead man's shoes. Now he could settle down. Milly saw that Dolly was on his card for the supper dance. Did she find him a complacent horror? Evidently not. Dolly had never looked so approximately gay, so approximately pretty. It was a night of marvels. Even Carrie had found an unexpected friend. A barrister who had gone on circuit with Arthur, god-father to the child whose party it was, had heard Carrie was present and introduced himself. He insisted on taking her down to supper. He talked about things that recalled the old days. How the world had disimproved since then, Carrie thought. What memories this nice man brought back of good times before everyone was rushing about in motor-cars, calling up on telephones, reading penny papers.

She inquired tactfully about his circumstances and let him disclose that he was the saddest sort of widower—his wife was in a mental home. They had no children.

"You must come and see us," she said, and blushed at her temerity.

When Milly felt rather than saw Alan beside her to claim his first dance with her the rest of her family were fully occupied with their partners. Dolly was looking ravished on what an eaves-dropper might have thought indifferent fare: "Someone in my position must consider every step. I am on what is called the threshold of my career. I must create the right impression . . ." Mr Roche was not a dashing young man; but Dolly glowed gently in the light of his plans as an attorney in Waterford.

Milly found herself dancing; waltzing came easily to her, but it had never been like this; she was floating; they were in another element. Inside her she hugged happiness that for the first time in her existence had taken palpable shape. The band must not stop: the spell must not be broken. When their eyes met his smile matched hers; but she preferred to feel the support of his arm and to nurse her joy. When the music stopped his gloved hand pressed hers for a moment, an electric current ran between them. She followed him as he looked for somewhere to sit. There was a conspiracy, it seemed, to thwart them. Hearty voices and soulless laughs came from every corner. They went down to the hall.

"This will do." She raised herself on her hands and sat with feet dangling from a high marble table. He came beside her. Some disapproving glances were cast in their direction, and the grapevine passed along its message that the younger Preston girl was rather fast.

He told her about himself; he lived with aunts who obviously adored him. He had been to school in England and recently left Oxford. He hunted on Saturdays. As he went on he became in Milly's eyes increasingly like a prince in a fairy tale; but his good fortune did not make him remote, and his orphan state lent him pathos. He assumed that she did nothing. All the girls he knew did nothing, except a few blue-stockings. He hoped she was not a blue-stocking. Milly had been ashamed at her backwardness in reading; and ever since she came home had been reading avidly. She had a mind and it required nourishment. But now she had misgivings. She must conceal her studious leanings from him. He said she must come riding with him, and she didn't say that she had nothing to wear. There was nothing in her appearance to suggest that she didn't command the resources of Rothschild's bank. The simplicity of her dress was exactly right for a girl of her age. The absence of jewellery showed good taste.

He wanted to know if she had been presented yet; and when she said 'no' he glanced at her to estimate her age, and decided that she was even younger than he had thought when he first saw her, when his stomach dropped and he had gone weak at the knees, and had difficulty in controlling his voice when he asked Miller—who put on such nonsensical side—to introduce him.

"I suppose you will be when the King comes in July. That's going to be an awful scrum."

What would he think if she told the truth about herself? She couldn't take a risk. She was holding the most fragile and precious porcelain in her trembling grasp. She must handle it tenderly. It was too precious to risk. It might crumble into tiny pieces. She must be whatever he wanted her to be. How beautiful his hands were. And that wavy chestnut hair. When he was speaking his mouth moved in a way that fascinated her. She wished they could start to dance again; somehow she felt safer then. When they talked she was afraid; the world pressed in.

"I should be looking for my partner," he said, without moving. "Who are you dancing with? You never told me why you put down those other names."

She couldn't say 'I must have known you were coming'.

"I didn't want," she said at length, "to waste them."

"What will you do now?"

"I'll be perfectly happy. Our dance will come soon."

"I really ought to go. Who is it I am engaged to? Miss Moran. Who is Miss Moran? Why is Miss Moran? Where is Miss Moran?"

"Upstairs waiting for you."

"Do you think someone else might capture her?"

"She won't let them. She will wait for you."

"I suppose I *must* go."

"Don't ask me to tell you your duty."

"And who is your next with—Beethoven?"

"No I've had that. Bonnie Prince Charlie. I hope he's sober."

They slid down to the ground. He took her hand. Once again she felt the electric current. Suddenly all the faces of the people on the stairs became beautiful. She loved and pitied the whole world.

"Why are you not dancing? I heard you say you were engaged for every dance," Carrie enquired when she came back to her.

"I was making excuses."

"But now the young men will see you are not dancing."

Carrie was feeling guilty. She had been enjoying herself; and was afraid that she had been neglecting her duty.

But Milly was not left unpartnered for long; and she was glad, not on her own account—she hardly listened to, or looked at, her partners—but because it made her feel worthier of him. He would see that she was in demand.

She needed no encouragement if he felt about her as she did about him. It seemed that he did. But it was unbelievable. She was afraid to ask herself if it could be true. She would watch every word, every nuance. It would be fatal to let him know how she felt. Unconventional as she was, she believed this. Ever since she laid eyes on Alan Harvey, she was surprised to find an unsuspected lair of conventionality in her make-up. She was deplorably anxious to live up to whatever ideal he had for women. She couldn't afford to say to him as she intended to say to the world that she must be accepted on her own terms.

His conversation seemed to her to be brilliant and his wit striking. In retrospect there was very little evidence of this; she could produce none if she had to go to court; but it was implicit in all he said. He was unique and splendid. It was incredible how the other girls in the room could be talking and flirting with their commonplace partners with such a paragon in their midst. Or were they blind? Miss Moran was a handsome girl; and Milly watched their dance with dread. Whenever Alan smiled or looked up into his partner's face, she was sure Miss Moran would put a spell on him. When he wasn't dancing with her she wanted him to dance only with decent dull girls.

After a hundred years their next dance came. Now he began to ask her more about herself. He wanted to know where she lived. He would call. He would ask his aunts to call on her mother. They lived in Dublin for his sake, in a house in Blackrock; but they came from the country. Did she play tennis? They had a court. She must come in the summer and learn to play. In Holland, she explained, the girls did not play proper games at school, only childish games, at which they cheated.

He took the same absorbed interest in what she told him as she had taken in his personal history.

At their third dance she let him know the truth. She worked; she was poor. Tears came into his eyes. He took careful note of Mr Mantovani's address. It was very near to the Four Courts and not far from the King's Inns. He was very fond of sketching; perhaps he could help her with her work. He wanted to know about Mr Mantovani. It seemed to him that her plight was pitiable, and he must rescue her.

She was glad she had let him know the truth; and so far from putting him off, it had made him almost reckless. She had become infinitely more romantic than if she were a mere girl in good society. He told her so.

The party was coming to an end. Upstairs the floor was heaving and creaking to the final dance—a gallop. Everyone was joining in except Alan and Milly. They had been in the dining-room where the remnants of the buffet lay sadly on untidy plates and tired waiters covertly helped themselves.

They came out into the hall and stood listening to the pandemonium upstairs. Then they turned to one another and he kissed her, on the lips.

She trembled, and he misunderstood.

"I say, I am terribly sorry," he said.

"Let's dance." She ran upstairs, and he, still not understanding, followed her and they pranced round the room, he looking as if the world had ended, she as if it had just begun.

When at last the music stopped, he gave her a contrite look and disappeared.

On the way home Carrie couldn't stop talking. Dolly and Milly lay back in their corners of the cab, eyes closed, smiling.

"I must say I never came across such a pair of girls," their mother said at last. "You might as well have been at a funeral."

"It was great fun," Dolly said.

"And what about you, Milly? I thought I saw you dancing rather a lot with that pasty-faced boy."

"He was nice-looking, rather delicate," Dolly said. "He was very attentive."

"Who are you talking about?" Milly snapped.

"Alan something or other," Carrie said.

"Oh, him."

Milly was satisfied. She had only wanted to hear his name. She could not have trusted herself to pronounce it.

There was a letter for her next morning.

Dear Miss Preston,

If you can forgive me for what happened last night and are prepared to see me again, I shall be more grateful than I can say.

I haven't slept all night. You have every reason to be angry with me. Please send me a line to say that you will see me again. I shall be

Your ever grateful,

Alan Harvey.

XI

MILLY CARRIED THE letter in to work, and by the time she had her apron on and was beginning to put the blue paint on her current Virgin's robe, it was almost worn out from being opened, read and folded. His handwriting was graceful, like everything about him, but not forceful; and if she thought it was beautifully sensitive of him to take on so about having kissed her—a contrast to Mr Reggie Terry—there was in her something that wished he had not thought he ought to apologise for having given her the moment of greatest rapture in her life. They had proved that there was after all such a thing as love at first sight, and therefore the caution, and feeling their way that ordinary lovers had to employ, who neither knew at once the state of their own feelings much less that of the other, did not apply to them. They were like Romeo and Juliet, who didn't so far as she could recall apologise to one another for giving way to their emotions.

The kiss had been a miracle for her; it told her that he shared all her feelings. Why could he not have left it at that? Now he was as good as saying that he expected her to be outraged; and perhaps he would be disappointed if she seemed to take it for granted that, so far as kissing was concerned, they had crossed the Rubicon. Now he was forcing her to retreat and to be ashamed of her own feelings. The new woman, a species to which she had decided to belong, had no time for this nonsense. She believed in free love. That was out of the question in Dublin where the new woman would be stoned in the street, but, at least, lovers kissed. And Alan had been at Oxford, and ought to know the ways of the world.

The Romeo and Juliet idea took possession of her. In her loft she was at exactly the height of Juliet's chamber in a stage set. She even got up and went to the window to see if Alan was looking up from below. Mr Mantovani, covered in plaster, blew her a kiss from his workshop.

She began a statue by painting the robes, then the face, then the feet, leaving until the end the detail. Today she was at work on the Virgin's crown when a shadow crossed the light coming from the glass door. Usually Mr Mantovani paid her a visit and marvelled at her progress; sometimes he offered her sweets or chocolates. The Mantovanis had a passion for these. As she was at a part where precision was required, Milly didn't look up. She was on such easy terms with her employer that he came and went without any formality. She knew he would stand there, admiring her work—herself, in fact—until she was ready to give him her attention.

"There. We must get more gold leaf. I'm down to the very end of the last lot."

Getting no reply, she looked up.

"Mr Harvey!"

"Miss Preston."

"Alan."

"I had to come."

"I'm so glad you did."

"You got my letter?"

"It wasn't necessary."

"I'm forgiven?"

"There was nothing to forgive."

The second kiss lasted longer than the first, and when it was over, she felt dizzy and sat down. He knelt beside her, holding her hand, his head buried in her hair.

"I can't believe it," he said.

"Nor I."

"I've read about it."

"Oh, books!"

"But they are right. It's true. When did you realise you were in love with me?"

"When did you? I mean, when did you know you loved me?"

"When I saw you. The moment I saw you. It was as if what I had waited for all my life had come true."

"I loved you, I think, the moment I saw you."

"Why do you only *think*?"

"I don't want to deceive myself. I think I loved you then. I knew—"

"When did you know?"

"When you kissed me. A girl never really knows whether she loves a man or not until he kisses her."

"Then Beatrice didn't love Dante."

"I'm not going to bother my head about them. Promise you won't give me Tennyson's poems."

"I promise. Of course. What have you against them particularly?"

"Nothing, really. If you do want to give them to me I'd accept them gladly from you."

"I don't know very much poetry. I've wasted a great deal of my time; but I know a line, I think it's from Meredith, that is always in my head. When I left you last night I wrote it down a dozen times. I wanted to send it to you, but I thought then that you would never speak to me again."

"Silly boy."

"May I give it to you now?"

"Oh, do!"

He felt in his pocket and then produced a letter.

Milly, dearest, dearest Milly. I have written this down as it says what I feel so much better than I can hope to.

> She is what my heart first awakening
> Whisper'd the world was: morning light is she.

And now it is morning.

Alan.

She held her face close to the letter and then for the first time she kissed him.

"I wish you had sent that letter instead. But if you had I would have read it then instead of now and you might not be here now. So all is for the best. What's the rest of the verse? Can you remember it? I have always thought of Meredith as someone hopelessly complicated and unreadable. Why are you blushing?"

"I am not blushing. Men don't blush."

He had no head for quotations; but he did remember that he had had to start the line in the middle, as what went before was: 'Brave is her shape, and sweeter unpossess'd'.

"That line is all I can remember."

"You must show me the poem."

Then he kissed her again, but she raised her head and whispered, "Up, up, up."

Mr Mantovani's feet were on the ladder. When he came in Alan was brushing his knees. Mr Mantovani rushed over and began to assist.

"It's dusty up here," Alan said. Milly gave a final touch to the Virgin's eyebrows.

"You buy something?" Mr Mantovani said.

Alan took an alarmed look at a shelf of saints and chose the Infant of Prague.

"Ah! Ch'è bello il Bambino. Molto bello!" He proceeded to wrap the statue up in newspaper.

"Seven shillings and sixpence, please."

"It's cheaper than it would be in a shop," Milly said. "Are you sure you wouldn't like to buy a lifesize St Anthony of Padua."

"Not today," Alan said.

He was waiting for Mr Mantovani to go; but Mr Mantovani had no intention of leaving. He had been out of the yard when Alan arrived. It was the watchful eye of Mrs Mantovani from the kitchen window who saw a young man go up to the studio. She sent her husband up in the interests of propriety; and he had employed tact in handling the incident.

"Will you come to luncheon on Sunday. My aunts will be delighted to see you."

"If they invite me."

"I'll get one of them to write. I had better go now."

"Thank you for coming; and if you are not perfectly satisfied with the Infant of Prague, Mr Mantovani will make an exchange provided you don't chip the statue in the meanwhile."

Mr Mantovani bowed Alan off the premises. The studio, he made clear, was not to be used as a rendezvous. But Alan was too happy to care. His only concern was to dispose of the Infant of Prague before he was seen by a colleague. He gave it to the first woman in the street to address him as 'Yer honour', and because it seemed like cheating, handed her sixpence as well.

Because he was happy it came as a painful disappointment to find that his adoring aunts refused to enter into his Sunday plans with any enthusiasm. Miss Susan and Miss Jane Harvey were known in their circle as Sweet and Sour. Susan was feminine and had once been pretty, Jane looked and talked like a man, a rather fierce man. Susan went in for flowers and china; Jane kept dogs. Susan was an excellent cook; Jane kept abreast of the news. Susan played the piano; Jane smoked cigarettes. Whenever he wanted to wheedle one of them, it was to Jane he went. Susan looked sweet and acted sweet, but she got her own way; Jane cursed and swore, but she made great-hearted gestures. Beggars went to Jane. It was Jane who had taught him to ride and when he went to school, Jane used to stuff a five pound note into his pocket. Susan kissed him and cried.

"I met such a corking girl," he told both his aunts. "One of you must write and ask her to lunch with us on Sunday. She won't come on my invitation."

"Naturally," Jane said.

"Dean Dickenson said something about their coming on Sunday," Susan remembered. "One more won't make any difference."

"We've too many damn women as it is," Jane said.

"What do you know about this girl? I'm sure she's awfully sweet. But do we know anything about her? Who are her parents? Where does she live?"

Susan had a plaintive way of speaking, as if she was always being put upon.

"She sounds a forward piece to me," Jane said when Alan had finished.

"She's delightful. Her father was a barrister. He died tragically young. I'm awfully sorry for them."

"And what does 'them' consist of?" said Jane darkly. She smelled a conspiracy, and the mention of misfortune only thickened the atmosphere.

"I wish you wouldn't call her 'she'. Milly is her name."

"Milly what? Pray."

"Who, Susan, Not 'what'."

"Milly who, then? I can't see that it signifies."

"Preston."

"Preston," said Jane, "could be anything."

"She's a lady, if that's what you are driving at."

"Don't get so violent, dear. I'm sure Miss—what did you say her name was?—is everything she ought to be. My only objection to her coming is that the Dickensons will be here, and they won't know her, and the poor girl will be all thumbs."

"We're not sure about the Dickensons," Jane said. She was no keener on the idea of the girl than her sister, but she never let her get away with anything, even in a good cause.

"If neither of you will invite Milly, I shan't stay in for luncheon. I'll go to the George."

"On a *Sunday*, Alan? It will look as if you had no home."

"I told Milly you would invite her," he said.

"You damn well shouldn't have," said Jane.

"I do think you might have consulted us beforehand," her sister agreed.

"It never occurred to me for a moment that you'd raise objections. If I can't have my friends to lunch occasionally, I had better see about getting myself bachelor quarters. After all, I'm nearly qualified."

"You know damn well that you ask your friends whenever you like," said Jane.

"It's only that we don't know this girl or anything about her, and we naturally object to writing to her before we are sure that she is someone whom we ought to entertain. Now, that's reasonable, is it not?"

Susan smiled very sweetly, always a sign that she had her heels dug in. Jane, who had been brooding, said:

"Well, I'll write to her. It doesn't involve us in anything: but I'd be wary of widows with unmarried daughters, Alan. I think you make a mistake accepting invitations from here, there and everywhere. I know Jack nowadays is as good as his master; but, believe you me, if there's one sure way of getting into trouble, it's mixing with the wrong set."

"You know that Jane and I only want what's best for you, Alan. We both think you should try and go into the country more in the week-end. When you are called and have a place of your own, we will open Lingfield again. It will take you out of Dublin and away from awful friends."

"My friends are not awful, Aunt Jane. I do resent that."

"Jane doesn't mean awful, dear. She means that you shouldn't make yourself cheap."

"I said 'awful', and I meant 'awful'. I can't stand Dublin. Every Tom, Dick and Harry shoves a foot in the door. I wish my advice had been taken. Alan would have been called in England and come here to us in the holidays. This Dublin idea was a foolish compromise, in my opinion."

When Jane was downright like this, Susan took refuge in tears. She preferred town to country and made only an apparent sacrifice when she suggested that the sisters should close up their family house in the country and rent a suburban house while their nephew was a student. They were his guardians and controlled his money until he was twenty-five. Until then he was beholden to them for everything. His father, like many men who had been wild in youth, had made a very rigid will, anticipating profligacy, although Alan, aged two, had the general reputation of having inherited his mother's angelic disposition.

Alan gazed on his aunts with unconcealed irritation. As a rule they spoilt him, and he had very little reason to chafe under the restrictions of his father's will; but they were jealous and suspicious of womenfolk, seeing in every girl a designing hussy. Plainness was the best recommendation, something told them Milly was not plain. Nothing more was said; but in the morning Susan—after her sister had argued in favour of it ('he will see her for what she is in his own house. It will restore him to his senses')—approached Alan in a meek way that, experience told him, boded no good.

"What is the name and address of your friend, Alan? I forget it. I want to invite her to lunch on Sunday. Even if the Dickensons do come, I'm sure we can always squeeze her in." (The dining-room table sat fourteen.)

Alan resented his aunts' behaviour, but he never doubted that he would get his way. Not being inclined to sulk, he said—as if there had been no dispute,

"Milly—I suppose it should be Millicent on an envelope— Preston, No 7, Buttercup Square, Rathmines."

"Did I hear you aright, dear? Did you say Buttercup?"

"Yes. It's a silly name."

"Buttercup Square! Who'd believe it?"

"Well, London has Primrose Hill."

"I daresay."

No more was said. Alan departed for Dublin carrying the letter. He decided to leave it on his way home. He would pay a formal call.

Carrie was laid out for callers in the afternoon. Mary was always in a fresh apron, and scones were made in preparation, backed by fruit cake and sponge cake. Callers were few and far between, and, more often than not, the girls ate up the sponge cake before it went stale; but Carrie, unless she was out, prepared herself for callers as an army in enemy territory kept a look-out for sudden assaults on its rear.

Mary's face showed infinite gratification when she announced

Alan. She had got herself into trouble for familiarity when she described Mr Roche as an 'all buttoned-up little bit of a fellow', and she regarded the appearance of this stranger as a vindication of her opinion. "He will be after Miss Milly," she told herself. She drew a clear distinction between the sisters.

Carrie did not fail to observe Alan's concern that the invitation to Milly should be sure to be put in her hands. He went into detail about how to reach his aunts' house, but Carrie assured him that Milly would think nothing of taking the tram to Blackrock.

"If she catches the one that leaves the Pillar at a quarter past twelve I will meet her at the end of Merrion Avenue. There is about two hundred yards to walk after that."

"Milly is well able for that."

"If it is wet, please see that she comes by cab. When it comes to a risk of catching cold, I think small economies are a penny wise pound foolish policy."

"I'll tell her you said that. We have a cab at hand for emergencies. The one we came to the dance in. It's very shabby, I fear. I don't know how a cabby lives and feeds his horse."

Alan didn't like to think of poverty. He found it hard to believe that anyone he knew could be poor, and it required an effort of imagination to realise that a cab out to Blackrock might be a strain on the Prestons' resources. Because this was Milly's house it shone with peculiar glory; but he could not help wishing that she lived in a more attractive square. These little red-brick houses with their bow-windows and horse-shoe porches were altogether unworthy of her. None of the furniture in the room offended his taste; but its proportions were mean and the fireplace hideous.

Carrie, he liked immensely. If he could persuade his aunts to call they would like her, he was sure, and they would see that she was a lady, although the house would depress them. It was a bore that Milly had to have the handicap of these surroundings. When he heard her story it appealed to all that was chivalrous in him; but his common-sense told him that it would be much better for everyone if she was not a picturesque orphan.

He listened enchanted while Carrie told him stories of Milly's childhood. The topic had inexhaustible charm. He hoped, if he stayed, she would come in; but he dined at seven, and it would take at least an hour to get home. Milly had not come in at six, so he rose to go and repeated his instructions. Carrie listened carefully.

"I'll see she leaves in time. We can go to Mass at eleven. That will fit in perfectly."

The look of shock that passed over Alan's face was put down to his touching anxiety on Milly's behalf; but he could hardly get out of the house quick enough to be by himself and think out the implications of what he had heard. He wanted to believe that Carrie's reference to 'Mass' meant something other than a confession that the family were Catholics. That they were poor was a misfortune which would have been fatal if he was not so well-to-do. So long as Milly was a lady, her poverty hardly mattered. And he was quite sure that she was a lady. One knew. But the idea that she might be a Catholic was one that never entered his head. Some Catholics were all right socially; but no member of his family had ever married one. It would be like marrying the cook. If Milly belonged to one of the landed Catholic families it would be a snag, but it might be got over; but a Catholic from Buttercup Square— the picture was a sordid one. It would confirm his aunts' suspicions. In fact he did not have the courage to break it to them. What would happen if Milly were to make a casual reference to Mass during luncheon on Sunday? It would fall like some hideous obscenity. He would require heroic resources to stand up against what it would not require his aunts to tell him would be a death blow to the family. Had he that courage? Could he brave it out? A small mean voice inside him urged him to escape while he could. But whenever he listened to that voice and then thought of Milly, the scent of her hair, the sweetness of her lips, came back to him and he told himself that life without her would be drab and dull and empty. Life without her was unthinkable.

Braced, he would step out cheerfully, but the closer to home, night fears came on. He was not a fighter. He never had to fight. Life fell into his lap. This evening Sweet and Sour seemed to sense that there was a threat in the air. Jane had had a letter from a friend in the country explaining the effect of Wyndham's bill. The tenants would be given money by the Government to buy out their landlords. The country was going to be given to the peasantry. There was talk about Trinity College building a chapel for Catholic students. Everywhere one turned the signs were of an impending crack-up, a loss of nerve, capitulation to the enemy. The prospect was grim. It was not the moment to tell the aunts that Milly Preston of Buttercup Square was an R.C.

When Sunday came, Dolly suggested that the family should go to half past eleven Mass at Newman's chapel in St Stephen's Green. Then they could have a pleasant stroll across the Green afterwards and see Milly into her tram.

The congregation in the University Church was more glamorous than in the parish that included Buttercup Square; Carrie was pleased at the idea, Milly didn't care. She had so utterly changed that her mother had become nervous, no longer because she was difficult and unaccountable, but because Carrie had learned from life that too much was not to be expected of it. Milly happy was in a way more alarming than a discontented Milly. There was a great deal to be said for a less brilliant child such as Dolly. Her expectations were modest, and she was less likely to be disappointed.

There was a world of difference between Bernard Roche and Alan Harvey; any girl would fall in love with Alan but Bernard was a safer bet. Carrie's experience of men had necessarily been limited, her possibilities had never been explored, and she had an instinctive knowledge. She had been taught and she taught one thing; what she knew, she kept to herself. Arthur Preston was the sort of man who put his wife into a special category. There was a side of him that he would show to other women, not to her. Carrie divined that side, and accepted the idea that her dignity was of more importance than her passions. Of these she had felt ashamed.

Alan Harvey, she could see, would be a prey to women. She would have fallen in love with him herself. She sympathised with Milly. But her knowledge of the world told her that a young man with so much freedom of choice was probably a philanderer. That type tended to marry with its own kind. Every pressure would be brought to bear on him not to involve himself with a penniless papist. And yet, where in the world would he find another girl who combined Milly's intelligence, good looks and strong character? His relations might see this if he persisted. But would he? She was too romantic not to support Milly; but she was anxious for her.

Dolly's object was made plain after Mass when the three women found themselves shaking hands with Bernard Roche and his parents. Carrie knew them of old, and recognised in the portly father and wizened mother the outstanding characteristics of the pompous little son.

The Roches were also in favour of a walk across the Green. The party set out with Bernard and Dolly in front, all eyes trained on them. Although the smaller of the two, Bernard seemed to displace more air. He had a consequential manner, even from the back. Dolly bent over him, gently, like the bough of a willow.

The Roches regarded their son with undisguised approval. He was the result of long trying and hope endlessly deferred. Dolly was included in their benevolence, as was anything associated with their son. If he wanted her, she was desirable. He was incapable of error.

Perhaps it was unconscious fear which led Carrie to announce that Milly was on her way to Blackrock to lunch with the Miss Harveys of Lingfield in Carlow; their nephew came into the place when he was twenty-five. He was going to be called to the Bar and had won a half-blue at Oxford for tennis. His grandfather had been Master of the hunt in her young days. She remembered him as a child. Very handsome, as was his son who married a cousin of Lord Castleton, a lovely girl. They had been killed in that awful earthquake at Quetta.

Milly felt her face scarlet and she nudged her mother; but Carrie seemed oblivious to decency. What possessed her? Did she want to make the Roches realise how lucky their son would be if he could make such desirable connections?

What would Alan think if he heard her talk like this, as if the Harveys were close acquaintances. She was surprised to learn her mother knew so much about them.

Neither of the Roches seemed to be as interested in what Carrie had to say as in the spectacle before their eyes. Mr Roche remarked to his wife that Bernard had spread out across the shoulders lately, and Mrs Roche said he had taken the words out of her mouth.

Carrie should have taken the hint; but instead she launched out into a monologue about the sacrifice made by the Harvey aunts in leaving Lingfield—one of the finest places in Carlow—to live in a house in Blackrock, not that those houses in Merrion Avenue were small as surburban houses go, but still.

Mr Roche then said that he seemed to remember coming across a Harvey, a protestant bishop, but he couldn't remember the circumstances. This was his way of deflating Carrie. He was not a family solicitor for nothing; he saw Milly's prospects with a professional eye; he understood Carrie's hopes; he had met people like the Harveys in his business; he knew the world that was written in parchment, tied up in red tape, and kept in tin boxes. He regarded himself as magnanimous—but luckily he could afford to be magnanimous—in not holding Dolly's lack of fortune against her. Well brought up, a barrister's daughter, a Catholic—she was in many ways suitable for his son. But all the concessions were being made on his side; he was not going to let Carrie give herself airs.

He hit Carrie where it hurt. She had allowed her euphoria to disguise the awful difficulty of religion. Mr Roche had brought this home. He also brought it home to Milly. Not until she heard the family talked of in a prosaic way had she thought of difficulties in the path, if Alan loved her. If he really loved her he would surmount every difficulty; but the Roches reminded her what the world looked like when Alan wasn't there. There was a cloud over the sun. She felt afraid.

Aunt Susan was particularly sweet at breakfast. The Dickensons were not coming after all, and she proposed not to open a bottle of wine if there was only the Patterson girl for luncheon. Aunt Jane for the first time for weeks insisted on going to church. She liked hymn-singing. It did her good, she thought. But she had a particular contempt for the local parson and was always infuriated by his sermons. She would certainly be in a vile temper when she came back.

Aunt Susan gave directions that the best silver and plate were not to be used as the Dean wasn't coming. Alan kept his temper. "Don't call Milly Miss Patterson, Aunt, please. Her name is Preston."

"I'll try not to, dear; but I'm wholly forgetful about names."

Unable to bear it any more, Alan set out too early. It was cold waiting for the tram; and it came five minutes late. He began to fret. He could not wholly acquit Milly for responsibility for the delay any more than he could avoid wishing she had been someone whom his aunts would like to know. He was enduring a great deal for Milly. She could never know; but it lent the smallest touch of condescension to his devotion. Loving her meant putting up with no end of disturbance to his peace of mind. The aunts were bad enough; but there was his uncle, Bishop Harvey, his godfather. He was a formidable old stick at the best of times. With no children, he regarded Alan as his heir.

On his mother's side there were some sticky relations. Up to now he had managed very well. Everybody liked him. He could rely on a gun at any shoot and a mount at any hunt where he had a relation;

it would be a black-out if they were all to ostracise him. Not that Milly wasn't worth it all. But why was she so late?

When she stepped off the tram and came towards him, looking radiantly happy and utterly trusting, he forgot all his misgivings. His eyes answered the rapture in hers. He would have embraced her then and there; but there was a policeman at the corner.

They both started to talk at once: there were so many things that it seemed so urgent to say. Everything about each of them had such transcendental importance. It was absurd to think that ordinary people in the workaday world could be considered capable of putting obstacles in the way of love that flew on wings like these.

There was a clump of laurels on the turn in the drive when they passed the lodge gate. Alan took Milly's hand and pulled her gently in.

Their kiss seemed to last for ever. She felt as if he had drunk all her strength and she made an ineffective gesture with her hands to free herself. Their kisses had lost their morning sweetness; the shining pool in which they first waded had become a river in which she was powerless to swim. It swept her on towards deeps which fascinated her. In the beginning she had let him lead her, now her instinct told her that strength must come from her. Her feeble push against his chest became more urgent. She pulled her mouth away and turned her cheek towards him. They were both very pale, and when she took his hand she felt it trembling. There was something about him today which was different; not, exactly, more masterful than before; she thought she sensed an inner desperation. It lay at the back of his eyes. She attributed it to her breaking away and felt compassionate.

"I am not fit to be seen," she said, settling her blouse. Her Sunday hat had fallen back and rested on her hair, which she wore in a large bun at the back of her head.

She felt strengthened for the ordeal ahead even if he had flustered her a little. He had used her like the brandy a man swallows to give him strength. He had lost his unselfconsciousness. He could not tell Milly about his difficulties as yet. He wished he could.

He turned the handle of the door and led her into a bright hall. A maid came out from somewhere at the back and Alan handed Milly over to her. They went upstairs and he put his head into the study where the family always sat on Sundays. There was nobody there. He then looked into the drawing-room. The fire had only recently been lit, and Susan sat beside it, very straight, in a winged chair.

"Why are you not in the study as usual?" he said.

His aunt smiled as one who preferred not to confess to pain. "The study is for when we are only the family."

"But you said yesterday you were going to sit in there."

"That was when I thought the Dickensons were coming."

"But now there's nobody except ourselves and Milly."

Susan raised her eyebrows at the use of a christian name.

"I always regard the Dickensons as if they were one of ourselves."

"But now we are quite on our own."

"Not quite, dear."

The maid opened the door for Milly and Alan went towards her. He was looking vexed, and it threw her off balance.

"You haven't met my aunt, Milly. Aunt Susan, this is Milly."

"How do you do, Miss Patterson."

"Preston," Alan said testily. Milly shook hands.

"Alan will have told you, I'm a perfect ass about names. Won't you sit down?" Milly ignored the invitation.

"Preston? Are you a relation to the Gormanston family? Their name is Preston. I can't think of any other Prestons."

"I don't think I am."

"Of course not. The Gormanstons are R.C.s."

"So are we."

Susan was too well-bred to show the perturbation she felt. She had disliked the sound of this girl and was genuinely alarmed on her nephew's behalf. She had diagnosed a pretty young thing with a designing mother in the background. Utterly unsuitable, possibly dangerous, certainly unscrupulous. They offered a threat that the two women felt it their duty as guardians to their nephew and the principal object of their lives to help him to overcome. That she should be a 'Roman' was a horror that they had not even contemplated. It showed with what class of people Alan had begun to mix in Dublin.

"I've lost my spectacles, Alan, did you see them lying round anywhere?"

It was all she could think of. She was for ever losing her spectacles; and the remark was not so hopelessly a *non sequitur* as it appeared. In effect she was saying that she wanted artificial aid to look at what she had naw to face.

None of this was lost on Milly; she glanced quickly at Alan for support. He was looking at his aunt with a resentful expression on his face; but there was nothing in it to give Milly strength. He seemed to be saying, 'Don't bring that up', as if it were a charge which was being laid at an unfair time. He was resenting the intolerance on his account and not on Milly's. Joy had gone from the morning.

"You might as well sit down," Susan said, leaving unspoken 'as you *are* here.'

"Where's Aunt Jane?" Alan enquired, not with any show of interest, but to break what threatened to be an embarrassing silence.

"She insisted on going to church. I told cook that we would have to wait luncheon."

Milly stared straight ahead, trying to look at ease, Alan frowned, Susan looked like God surveying a field of battle.

"Ah! Jane," Susan said with evident relief when the front door noisily slammed and a dog barked.

"Down, sir. Down," boomed Jane, striding in.

"This is Milly, Aunt Jane," Alan said between his teeth.

"How d'ye do?" Jane said absently then, turning to Susan, "I declare to God I shall go out of my mind if that man preaches again. I can stand anything except gentility. He was going on and on about Hell; I was waiting for him to say it was warm. Do you remember when I asked him how his tea was and he said it was warm enough. 'What d'ye mean by warm, my dear man?' I said. 'Tea is either hot or it's cold.' I put the fear of God into him."

"Don't be so hard on Mr Mills, dear. He means very well."

"I daresay he does. There was some perfect fool at the organ today. We were all ready to begin *Abide with Me* and he boomed out *Rock of Ages*. I hope he didn't hear my 'damn'."

"Not on Sunday, Jane, dear. Thank you, Ellen. Now we may go into luncheon. I'm sure you are starving, Miss Preston. Miss Preston was at Mass at some unearthly hour, Jane. Fancy that."

"I went to half-past eleven. I don't think that's particularly early," Milly said. But nobody joined issue with her.

The announcement had the effect of attracting Jane's attention to her for the first time. She had been far too intent on the sermon to take any notice of any chit of a girl. But the implications of Mass were not lost on her, and she looked at Milly as curiously as if she were a zoological specimen.

"I've often wondered what happens at your Masses," she said to Milly when they sat down. "I've never met anyone I could ask. Do you all shut your eyes at the real presence part and open them again when the priest tells you to. Someone told me that."

"I keep my eyes open," Milly said.

"And what happens?"

"Nothing."

"Well, that is what I would expect, I must say. Take that frown off your face, Alan. What's on your mind?"

"Nothing."

He should, Milly thought, take over the conversation now. The only man among these women. He shouldn't leave me to be picked at. He should show his feathers and rule the roost.

But Alan continued to stare at his plate as if he was looking at his own reflection in the soup. Jane, nothing abashed, by a natural succession of ideas—Catholics, rebels, peasants—switched over to her pet topic, the folly of the Conservative party's Irish policy.

"You can't kill Home Rule with kindness. The English don't understand this country. When the landlords are sold up, and the peasants have the land, they'll feel themselves in the saddle at last and—mark my words—they will want to be in the seats of power. After all, they outnumber us ten to one, and they breed like flies. No offence, Miss—what's your name, my dear? I'm becoming awfully stupid in my old age."

"Preston," Susan said, with a curious emphasis.

"You must be related to the Gormanstons," Jane said hopefully. The girl might be an R.C. and yet by a miracle a lady.

"I don't think so. I don't know them. My father's family came from England originally."

"I never heard of any English Prestons. I never heard of any Prestons except the Gormanstons, come to think of it. Did you, Susan?"

"No," said Susan, tightening her lips.

"My father was a barrister," Milly said. She hated herself for saying it; but it seemed to be a way of stopping further insinuations that she was engaged in a peasants' revolt.

"What are you going to do after luncheon, Alan?" Jane said.

"I thought we might go for a walk."

"I had hoped as we had a fourth for once we might have had a game of bridge. Do you play, Miss Preston?"

"A little."

"Now what precisely do you mean by that? Do you imply that you get little opportunity to play or that you are no damn good at the game?"

"Jane, dear!"

"I believe in being plain about these matters. The parson said he could play bridge, and I took him at his word and never had a more infuriating experience. He hardly knew how to follow suit."

"I don't get much opportunity to play. But I sometimes make a four at home."

"I dare say you will do very well. What do you say to a rubber, Alan?"

"I had planned to take Milly for a walk on the East Pier."

"Pull yourself together, dear boy. Every grocer's curate has his dolly on the East Pier on Sundays. If I were Miss Preston I wouldn't be seen dead in that place. I'm sure you'd rather have a rubber of bridge, my dear, wouldn't you? I'd like to see Mr Mills' face if he caught us at it on a Sunday. He'd give it to us *warm*."

The notion tickled Jane so much she threatened to explode.

Susan looked grim. Her sister was letting the side down. On the day when Alan came to lunch with a Roman it was hardly the thing to make jokes about the rector, whatever they might say among themselves. Jane lacked discretion; and when she wanted to do anything—as in the present instance—had no regard for any consideration other than 'getting on with it', as she described having her own way.

Milly was longing to escape from the old women. She disliked Susan more for looking so fragile and being so tough; the other old thing was probably a more scrupulous opponent, but she was ugly and noisy. Neither of them had shown herself in the least anxious to be kind. How differently her own mother would have acted in the circumstances! She would have thought it ill-bred not to put a guest at her ease. She waited for Alan to put his foot down; but, instead, he looked peevish and said, "Couldn't we have a rubber after tea?"

"I suppose Miss Preston will have to hurry home for Sunday supper; and if there's one thing I can't stand it's getting up in the middle of a rubber. By the time you get back from the pier it will be five o'clock. There's a nip in the wind that will redden the young lady's nose if I'm any judge. I was counting on a rubber if the

Dickensons came. The Dean doesn't mind playing, not with friends. I don't suppose he'd go out on a Sunday to play."

"The Dickensons were meant to be coming," Susan explained. Milly, not knowing them, refused to look interested. She was intent on Alan's face. Here was a challenge. Would he accept it.

"You are such a bully, Aunt Jane. Do you mind playing bridge, Milly, instead of a walk? The day has gone off a bit."

"Of course she doesn't mind, dear boy. I hope Kate has kept an eye on the fire. If there is one thing I like less than another it's being greeted by a cheerless grate."

Alan looked at Milly and shrugged his shoulders. He was giving in; he was signalling his preference was to do what he promised Milly, but his obligations were to his aunt's whim. The girl felt betrayed. Alan should have resented Susan's impertinence. He seemed to suffer it as part of the natural course. If Milly was a Catholic, there was very little he could do to help her. It was like trying to get credit for an undischarged bankrupt in the City.

Going into the study where the card table was, Alan put his hand on Milly's elbow. She dropped her arm and refused to meet his imploring glance. She felt angry now.

Aunt Jane, having got her way, was in a thoroughly good humour. Unlike her sister she refused to take Alan's situation very seriously. Milly was pretty; Alan was a man. Men had their fun. None had ever tried to have his with her—Susan was the one who got a proposal, but the engagement fell through when, after long waiting, her fiancé developed lung trouble and had to go to the South of France—but she had a greater tolerance of men than Susan, and often thought God meant her to be one.

"Don't go making heavy weather," she had said to Susan at the first opportunity. "It's a storm in a tea-cup. He will forget her as soon as he meets someone pretty from our own lot."

Susan, being serious, began to plan for Alan in her mind, and it was fated to ruin her game.

"I am going to play with Alan," Jane said.

"I think we should cut for partners."

He should have said "I want to play with Milly," but he had gone as far as he cared to.

"I don't like playing with Jane. She loses her temper," Susan said.

"Nonsense, woman! Job himself would lose his temper if his

partner said 'no bid' when his hand was black with spades and he had just gone two no trumps."

"You shouldn't have called no trumps if you hadn't a spade in the first place."

"I was pushed into it."

"You never return a lead. That's my objection to you, if we are going to be perfectly candid."

"I'll play with Aunt Jane," Alan said. He meant to spare Milly the possibility of unpleasantness, but she saw it as a further proof of desertion.

She was quite useful at cards, having power of concentration and a good memory. Fate, on this occasion, put every card into her hand.

But she showed no gratitude. Fate was not in her debt today. She won game after game, grimly, keeping the score, showing herself to be formidable. The rout was too complete even for Jane to try to blame her partner.

"I haven't had an honour in my hand all day," she said after the third rubber had gone to Milly and her partner. By now it was beginning to be dark. On a winter afternoon she and Alan would have to go out immediately after lunch. Now the day was spent.

"A cup of tea might change my luck. Ring the bell, dear," Jane said to Alan.

But Milly rose to her feet. "I can't stay for tea. I must go."

"Nonsense, child. You must have afternoon tea," Jane said. She was an honourable if a ruthless foe, and Milly's formidable quality had impressed her, as it confirmed Susan in her belief that Alan was in real danger.

"Thank you very much, but I'm afraid I can't."

"I'll see you to your tram," Alan said.

"Please don't bother."

"It's quite light still," Susan put in.

"You'll miss your tea," Jane added.

"Don't miss tea on my account."

But this time Alan obeyed his own inclination. Milly shook hands very formally with the two old ladies and thanked them in terms of studied moderation. Outside, she said nothing; and Alan looked at her desperately and did not know how to begin. He wasn't going to pull her into the laurels now. A kiss seemed as remote as the North

Pole. Indoors Jane was saying to Susan "Quite a *miss*, if you ask me."

Susan sat down as she always did when she was troubled.

"I think one of us should write to Harry. He is the boy's god-father."

Jane was too bruised in spirit by her recent defeat to argue for long. This was a girl to be reckoned with. Alan couldn't kiss her and pass on to the next flower. She would adhere. The boy's life might be ruined, and on the threshold of his career.

"You write, Susan. You will know how to put it. He thinks I'm too much of a hell-raiser. If he had Alan to stay in the holidays he might talk sense to him. What can a pair of old women do in a case like this?"

Susan said nothing: the letter was composing itself in her anxious mind.

Out of doors Alan broke the suffocating silence.

"I can't tell you how sorry I am. Our day was ruined. Aunt Jane and her wretched bridge. Some day I am going to tell her exactly what I think of her."

"She knows what she wants."

"She's an awful bully, you mean."

"I don't know that I don't prefer people who know their own minds. It saves trouble in the end. One knows where one is with them from the start."

Alan took a little time to digest this. Milly's manner had altogether changed since morning. It had been such a sunny morning for the time of year, and the day had now reverted to type, a late winter Sunday afternoon. One can shut them out and be warm and cosy indoors. Milly was neither warm nor cosy; she, like the day, had shed her patina.

"I could have kicked Aunt Susan. Jane I don't mind really. She always acts the major general, but Susan can be sweet; and she was not at all nice to you. I think the Dickensons not coming put her in the sulks."

"Please don't abuse your aunts, Alan. I'm sure they haven't changed."

"Aunt Susan is not always as nasty as that."

"I'm sure she's not."

"I know you are angry, Milly; and I feel it is my fault; but you know how it is with one's own people. Not that my aunts are like a mother and sister; but they are the only family I've got."

He was playing on her sympathy: the orphan boy. But she was not prepared to capitulate.

"I wish you'd go home to them, Alan. I'm sure they are missing you; and I'm very well able to look after myself."

"If I were to go back now, I wouldn't trust myself not to blow them up. They were really most inhospitable to you."

Milly stopped at this and faced Alan. His features were blurred in the approaching darkness; and she was free of the appeal of his eyes and mouth. She was always drawn by the expression in his eyes; but the attraction of his mouth she found irresistible. Now she wanted to speak her mind uninfluenced by either.

"I don't think a man should run women down. What did your aunts owe me? Why should they like me? I am not a friend of theirs, and they made it quite clear that they didn't think I should be a friend of yours. They are bigoted. But they can't help that."

"I wouldn't say 'bigoted' exactly."

"No. You share their prejudices."

"Milly, how can you say that?"

"You do. You think it's most unfortunate that I'm not a Protestant. Your world is tight and narrow. I don't blame your aunts. They didn't invite me out for the day; why should they bother to entertain me?"

"You imply that I failed you."

"Don't let's discuss it. You were good enough to ask me to your house. And I, certainly, am not going to criticise it."

"Milly, you're unfair. You know it's not my home. I was left in the care of my aunts. They are fond of me in their funny way; and if it wasn't that I am grateful to them I'd have kicked no end of dust up about today's entertainment. I wish we had gone for our walk as we arranged."

"I arranged nothing; and as one of your aunts said, it might have been cold on the pier. It couldn't have been colder—" but now she was breaking into metaphors and tears. She hurried on with Alan a step behind, imploring her forgiveness. The more he went on, the more harm he did himself, the less tearful she felt. "Oh, stop whining."

That stopped him like a smack in the face. He watched her run now—the tram had come clanking along the iron tracks—and she looked as scornful, backview, as she had sounded. He would have given anything to live the day again, to cut a wholly different figure. He played with the idea of following in a later tram and calling on Milly at home. But if he did, how was he to regain all the ground he had lost?

He walked slowly home, cursing his aunts, cursing the fate that left him in their care, cursing his excessive amiability, his dutifulness. They had between them deprived him of the only woman he would ever love. That he had lost Milly he now regarded as certain. And so, when he went into his aunts' house, it was with an overwhelming sense of grievance. For their part, they conducted themselves with unusual and inappropriate cheerfulness. His gloom was the measure of the success of their tactics. They made no reference to Milly, as if to convey her total insignificance. This was also part of the treatment. It would bring home his error of taste; he would see the world in proper perspective. He scowled into his plate and they smiled on him; Susan spoke in her sweetest voice, and Jane put down the soft pedal on her bass. They treated him with the forbearance and gentleness an invalid might expect, making him see that unpleasantness—if there were any in the air—did not emanate from them.

He struggled inwardly, searching for words to describe their unforgivable conduct, their moral assassination; but the words wouldn't come, and the more time passed the more indefinite became the shape of his grievance. All Jane had done was to suggest bridge; and she had taken a trouncing without recrimination, like a good sport. Susan had received a shock to discover Milly was a Catholic. So had he; and now he blamed himself for not having prepared them for it. He had been a coward, and a fool; for the truth was bound to come out.

Instead of anger he began to feel that they were all victims of fate. There they were, his aunts being as nice to a fellow as any woman could be. Of course, they hadn't the least idea what it was like to be in love. They saw Milly as just a pretty girl, and an ineligible one at that. From their point of view a quite reasonable diagnosis.

He would have liked to break through the barrier, to take them into his confidence, to discuss the possibility of Milly's changing her religion. They must see that she was a lady as well as being pretty and intelligent. The lack of means was a pity; but he would be quite well-off, apart from what he might hope to make in his profession. Really, the religious difference was the only obstacle; the aunts could be persuaded to overlook the rest—he had no doubt at all that he wanted to marry Milly. Love and marriage were to him then the two sides of the coin that was his dream of women.

He did not ask himself if it was unreasonable to make religion into an obstacle. It was not as deep a prejudice as if she had been Jewish (not to say coloured. Ha! Ha! Ha! Thank God he had a sense of humour), but it was very deep. Curiously enough, if she came from Europe it would not seem quite the same. An Italian girl of family had, as it were, the right to be a Catholic; it was a continental extravagance, almost as much part of the charm as broken English, but in Ireland the element of charm was entirely absent. One had only to see on one's way to church, where there would be a small and, to an extent, select congregation, the hordes coming out of the Catholic chapel—not bare-footed on a Sunday, but beggarly. One's servants went to chapel—but got up at cock-crow so as not to let their superstition interfere with their household duties—the family went to church, at a suitable hour, before Sunday luncheon. To marry someone who, under pain of Hellfire (think of it!) was obliged to accompany the servants was hard to contemplate. The thought of accompanying her was so extravagant that it was funny. He did laugh aloud—a short laugh; but refused to tell his aunts what had provoked him. They took it as a good sign, and Jane, who had a capacity for large gestures, took out the flask in which she kept a supply of brandy for emergencies and insisted that Alan should drink some with his coffee. She went so far as to pour herself out a tot. Madcap Jane, Susan nodded her head over her. She should really have been a man. And she exuded masculine wholesomeness and confidence afterwards when she stood with her back to the fireplace, her skirts pulled tight to get the maximum impact from the fire, smoking a cigarette. Talk of the new woman! Jane had the Pankhursts knocked for six. And she didn't give 'a tuppenny damn'—to use her own expression—for women's rights. She favoured the horse-whip for suffragettes, and said she would volunteer to administer it if her services were ever required. She was well out to the right of the suffragettes, in league with the men.

Alan at a pinch could get round his aunts; but his uncle, the Bishop, was another proposition. They rarely met; but he had a very special position as the only near relation of his own sex. Not to put a tooth in it, Alan was frightened of his uncle. He had immense authority of manner, with that invaluable asset, a knack of making you feel ashamed not to know people or facts if he knew them, and not less ashamed to have confessed to knowledge if he didn't share it. In relation to him, one was perpetually exposed as lacking either essential knowledge or mature judgment. If his uncle were to hear about Milly he would go berserk; there was no doubt about that. The extent of his power to interfere with Alan was negligible; it was a tribute to his force of character that he seemed to hold his fate in his keeping. His disapproval was somehow too awful to contemplate, worse than God's, because one ran no risk of meeting God anywhere; and one never knew when one might be confronted by the Bishop.

Alan slept wretchedly that night.

Milly sat very stiff and still in the tram. She had gone quite numb. It was as if she had set out full and returned empty. Towards Alan she felt nothing. He had emptied her of himself and there was nothing in the void. She felt impervious now to shock or pain. You might stick needles into her; like a fakir she would feel nothing. That to an observant fellow passenger she looked utterly woe-begone would have surprised her.

She had alighted from the tram and was bracing herself for Carrie's greeting, anticipating her overwhelming affectionate curiosity, and wholly absorbed, when a voice called her name; Charley Terry came out of the shadows. For a moment she didn't recognise him and she hoped she had not revealed it as he walked beside her in the direction of the Square.

"I never see you now. You have never forgiven us for your accident."

"Nonsense. That was my fault. Did you not get my card at Christmas?"

"My parents sent one. I don't believe in greetings of a formal nature."

Milly felt uncomfortable. The Terrys' card had been discussed at length when it arrived—a wonderful business of holly and seasonal snow—and Carrie had been quite adamant that she would neither return nor acknowledge it. After what had happened it smacked of presumption. The Terrys were beyond the pale. They must be kept in their place.

"I've changed," Charley went on in a gloomy voice.

"In what way?"

"I've come to realise that personal happiness is not what counts. We need a cause. Mine is Ireland."

"I don't follow."

"Have you ever heard of Arthur Griffith?"

"Let me see. Hadn't he something to do with Vartry water? Or was that—? No, I'm mixing him up with somebody else. What about him?"

"He is the editor of *The United Irishman*."

"Oh, you mean politics."

"You sound as there was something wrong with them."

"I didn't intend to. I don't know anything about them. That's all."

"You never heard of *The United Irishman*."

"No, I don't believe I did."

"It exposed English perfidy in the war."

"Oh, it's pro-Boer is it? The girls at school were. We were in a minority; but we let them have it."

"By *we*, do you mean Irish girls?"

"English and Irish. In fact, I was the only Irish girl there."

"And you sided with the English. Shame!"

"You wouldn't have me side with the Boers would you?"

"Of course, I would. They were fighting for their freedom as we should be. But Griffith believes we can achieve it without fighting. He wants to restore Grattan's parliament."

Milly, out of her depth, preserved a tactful silence. Charley as a patriot was no less intense than Charley as a poet; he was also more aggressive.

"I didn't believe I could persuade you. My eyes were opened by Ethna Carbery."

Milly, believing that he was boasting of someone who took her former place in his affections, found herself surprisingly on edge.

"Were they, indeed?" she said in a voice that was intended to shut out any more information about the lady.

"You don't know her?"

"I'm afraid not."

"I must lend her to you.

"They are going, going, going, and we cannot bid them stay;

Their fields are now the strangers' where the strangers' cattle stray.
Oh! Kathleen Ni Houlihan, your way's a thorny way!"

"Oh! Poetry."

Milly, for the first time since morning, smiled. Charley had not changed. He was, she had to admit, in any capacity a boring young man. But they were now at their neighbouring gates, and she murmured something about being 'dreadfully late' and made her escape as gracefully as she could.

He watched her up the steps. Why had he yielded to the temptation he had resisted for so long? Why did she make him throb and tremble? He went in and wrote a long poem, in which Ireland was a beautiful maiden, naked, chained to a rock, whom a 'peasant Perseus'—the conceit pleased him—rescued from the dragon (England) with a pike thrust. The maiden's face was Milly's. When the poem was finished he threw himself on his bed, and sleep came only when he had freed himself of the burden of that image.

Milly was met at the door by her mother with a "Well?"—an open invitation to give an exhaustive account of her day; she pretended not to catch the encouraging and inquisitive inflexion; at the same time she was struggling with herself not to disclose her own disappointment. She compromised by inquiring solicitously for Dolly and professed anxiety to hear about Dolly's day. Carrie had had enough of that; glad for Dolly's sake that she seemed to have solved her problems, Carrie could not pretend (except to her) that she was even faintly excited by the approaching engagement. She had an eye for men, and would herself have preferred single blessedness to nights in Bernard Roche's bed. She had asked herself, as a mother, whether she should open up this question. Did Dolly know what she was letting herself in for? Did she even know what Carrie, with a shudder, had heard her husband describe as 'the facts of life'. She herself had not been prepared for her initiation; but, at least, she had been attracted to her husband, and if he frightened her a good deal, nature eventually came to the rescue. Modesty forbade Carrie to visualise Bernard Roche in expectation of what she was sure he would call his 'marital rights'; but even the quickly suppressed picture that flooded on to her brain was so unalluring that it was dismal to think what Dolly had coming to her. But it was woman's lot; and Carrie had resigned herself to a pessimistic view of the human condition. The falling away of the circle that had surrounded her husband had not embittered her, but it taught her on what flimsy foundations social life was built. One was always thrown back on one's own; and Dolly was right to settle for a life that was secure, and if not attractive or brilliant, not lacking in clumsy kindness. She would get three meals a day, and probably good ones. She would have a decent house; she could bring a family up in comfort. She would never know the pangs of financial pressure or the shifts and dishonesties or privations that are thrust upon the impecunious.

But it was much more pleasurable to dwell on Milly's possibilities. She might have all that Dolly was compromising for and an enlarged life, good company, contact with ideas and the main springs of events, all that she was beginning to enjoy when Arthur fell off the jaunting car. Now that seemed to lie in Milly's way unless she did something foolish, which was never out of the question. It was curious how a brilliant child like Milly was always so much more prone to do something wildly foolish than ordinary Dolly who knew so well the pace at which it was safe for her to travel.

Nevertheless, Milly's concerns were of infinitely more interest to Carrie. She had a fancy herself for Alan. He put her in mind of a young man who had danced twice in succession with her at her first hunt ball, the programme for which lay under her pillow for a month. He had been going to kiss her, too; and her heart was fluttering at the prospect when the band struck up *God save the Queen*, and he stood up at once, even though obscured from all eyes by a potted plant.

Milly avoided further questioning by escaping from her mother to her room. When she came down she was no longer a target, Uncle Joe had arrived 'to take pot luck'. He had been drinking, and his voice penetrated every corner of the little house. What he had come to say was that T. T. had bought a place in Westmeath and hoped to be in residence at Easter. There were pickings on the place for the Prestons if the family would be guided by him. Carrie's first reaction was to wonder if, after all, Dolly had been too precipitate. This connection, certainly, could not be helpful to Milly. That something had gone wrong with Milly's day, she did not need to be told. A mother's worst fears never entered her mind, because a visit to a young man's maiden aunts precluded sordid as well as romantic possibilities. She guessed what had happened. There were youthful memories of snubbings still fresh in her own mind: if Arthur Preston, a young barrister on the midland circuit, had not met her by chance, she could not have hoped to marry even into a rich Catholic family, much less once her brother Joe had depleted the family fortune. A local solicitor or doctor was the height of her ambition. She was pretty enough to get by without a fortune. The young man who had been the inspiration of a month's dreaming had never reappeared. When she heard of him again, he was getting married to a landlord's daughter in another county.

Now came Joe, who had ruined his own family, full of bright prospects for hers. T. T. had left the final negotiations to Joe. Joe was to see about staff. Joe was to get horses. Joe was to look to furnishings. Joe was to spy out the land; and when his patron arrived in the spring, Joe was to have all in readiness for his reign to begin as a county magnate. It was a brilliant prospect. But only Carrie was listening. Dolly and Milly were too deep in their own concerns to take more than a passing interest in their uncle. He sensed this and resented it. He liked to impress, and he liked particularly to impress pretty women. It annoyed him to see behind Milly's polite attention no live interest at all. It made him aggressive—he had helped himself to Carrie's whiskey reserve—and his aggression took a form of fantasy.

"He wants you all to spend Easter with him," Uncle Joe said. As he said it he made a gesture with his right hand as if he were sprinkling bird-seed. It was the gesture that told Milly he was lying. This interested her because she had at the same time a sensation of empathy with her uncle, as if it was she who was making the desperate throw. It disturbed her to see through him so plainly and at the same time to recognise so much of herself in what was most flawed in him. It might have served as a warning. This evening she was filled with a gloomy sensation that he mirrored her future.

XII

L ADY KELLY, HAVING sent off her letter to Mr Hugh
Lane, saw to it that her bait would be ready when the fish appeared.
She liked to think that she knew the way of the world, and she
pictured Mr Lane as likely to call on his way home to dress for
dinner. He was much in demand with hostesses she had heard,
being young and quite well-connected and getting on so well.

She always had afternoon tea in perfect readiness for callers; and
if Mr Lane appeared at the appropriate moment he would get
drop-scones, honey and delicious sponge cake. But if, as her
experience taught her, he was unlikely to be available so early, then
sherry was the thing. She had a decanter in readiness on a silver
tray on top of the grand piano.

She dressed herself becomingly, and once—though even her
confessor never heard of this—startled herself with the fancy that
the connoisseur might be bowled over by her own mature charms,
set off by her tact and breeding. She even pictured him in a
blushing moment turning away from the cattle in a landscape and
expressing in action a preference for more palpable attractions.
Nothing like this had ever happened in her life, Sir Patrick's
proposal having been a mere formality: the transaction had already
been settled in detail after consultation with the Very Rev Monsig-
nor Keohane, D.D., and her parents. Her married life had attained
a moral elevation rare, even in Ireland, when Sir Patrick had, in his
own words, 'thrown his hand in'. Age had not withered and custom
had had no opportunity to stale her infinite variety. At fifty-five she
was ready if a man of Mr Lane's distinction were prepared to try
his fortune. As afternoon followed afternoon her fantasies grew, but
Mr Lane had given no indication that he had even received her
letter. At this rate of going the exhibition would have closed and
her party joined other unrealised dreams. She had to do something,
if only to maintain face before the Prestons. It would be too
humiliating for her if they should discover that she was not able to
call on anyone in Dublin. So she had recourse to the telephone. Mr

Catterson Smith promised to remind Mr Lane, who was very enthusiastic and always so busy. That ought to do the trick.

On the day after the very satisfactory telephone talk, Lady Kelly felt a slight disorder, for which her physician had prescribed, come round again with its usual unmentionable symptoms. She asked Dolly to be good enough to call at the chemist's with the prescription and bring back the medicine while she was waiting; she was quite sure *he* would call this afternoon, her powers of divination were, in some matters, extraordinary—she rehearsed their conversation. She was not going to bring him straight to the picture in what used to be Sir Patrick's consulting room, but over sherry she hoped to arouse his interest, if not in herself (one was not vain) at least in her project. She would let him know what Sir Patrick's position had been, in case her friends had not filled in the background; then she would imply that she hoped to act in a modest way as a patron. From there it was a short distance to her plan for a reception in the Academy and a verbal invitation.

She had it all word-perfect, but was bothered by the term 'mutual friend' to describe Mr Catterson Smith. Sir Patrick had once told her that the title of Dickens' novel was a solecism. 'Common Friend' was the correct expression; but, somehow, she would not reconcile herself to its employment. 'Our common friend, Mr Catterson Smith', seemed to her ear to have denigratory implications.

While she was resolving this, deciding eventually to avoid both, in a happy change of phrase, she heard the hall door open, shut, open again, shut and then, after a pause long enough to wind up a clock, open and shut again. By that time she was in such a frenzy that she only avoided the indignity of looking into the hall by a superb effort of self-control. She could only pull at the bell and listen to it jangling in the basement.

Dolly came in before the servant. She had the medicine. Lady Kelly almost dashed it from her hand.

"What's happening? What's going on? Am I entitled to no consideration?"

"I'm sorry, but I was delayed at the chemist's."

"I don't care a button about the chemist. I want to know what all the coming and going downstairs was."

"Mr Lane."

"What do you mean? Mr Lane. Don't be a fool."

"You shouldn't say that. It's too rude. I really must object. I had just come in from the chemist when I heard a knock at the door. So I opened it."

"Why? Don't I employ servants to answer the door?"

"I was *at* the door."

"That's no reason. I'm *at* the fireplace, but I don't put coals on it. I ring for the maid, whose place it is."

"I'm sorry. Anyhow, I did open it; and there was a gentleman who said his name was Lane and he had heard about a picture and wanted to see it. I said that you were upstairs and offered to show him up; but he said he was in a hurry and wouldn't trouble you."

"And?"

"I showed him into the library. 'Where is it?' he said. I pointed it out, but he didn't seem to take any interest."

"Did you not offer him any refreshment?"

"I did. I said you were expecting him to call; but he again said that he was in a hurry, so I had to let him go."

"Damn."

Dolly jumped. That Lady Kelly should swear was so much against the course of nature it really frightened her. If she had stripped herself to her corset the effect would not have been more startling. And she realised this herself. The effect of such a major departure from habitual propriety was cathartic. It even transcended her irritation at Dolly's social incompetence. She saw in the whole incident the hand of God. Perhaps He was punishing her for her wild thoughts. She blushed in retrospect. Perhaps her imaginings were inspired and God had saved her knowing that at the critical moment her sense of occasion might have been too much even for her virtue. There was some profit to be derived even from so miserably muddled a business; and it was better to think of Dolly as the unwitting instrument of Providence than as a silly goose. There was something grand, she felt, about her interpretation. It did her honour. She worked up a smile for Dolly and presented her with a pair of cast-off gloves. In the morning she would ring up Mr Catterson Smith and ask him to enlist Mr Lane for her party. Dolly could write out the invitations. A Saturday would be best.

At such a moment Lady Kelly attained greatness. She was up before eight o'clock the next morning preparing her list, and when

Dolly arrived a letter had already been written to her mother. She was given it to bring home.

My dear Carrie,

I have been wondering for some time what I could do to help you and Milly about the little dear's desire to become an artist. I gather from Dolly that there has been no relaxation in Milly's determination. If that is the case it is the duty of your friends to see that she begins under favourable auspices.

I am, therefore, giving a reception at the Academy on Saturday week at four o'clock. It is very much the thing to do this year. I expect Mr Lane will be there, and it is part of my plan to introduce him to Milly.

I wonder if your brother and his friend Mr Talbot Thompson would care to join us. I think it will be quite a little occasion. On the chance I have included cards for them, which you might send on. I enclose a small contribution towards a dress for Milly. I don't want ever to hear about my little present. Remember.

As ever

Fanny Kelly.

The most significant feature of this letter was the fact that until she sat down to write it, Lady Kelly had forgotten that Milly played any part whatever in her plan. But now she saw her way plain as Milly's patron; and Mr Lane was forgiven for his brusquery yesterday on the understanding that he would redeem himself a week from Saturday. Lady Kelly also wrote a little note to Mr Catterson Smith, lest he should have forgotten their telephone conversation. It was enclosed in an envelope with two invitation cards, one for Mr Lane.

Dolly had not told Lady Kelly about her friendship with Bernard Roche. She was too likely to interfere and she might even disapprove sufficiently to take it on herself to write to his parents, calling them to their senses and their duty. Not until there was a formal engagement would she hear what had been in the wind. It would be a memorable occasion. Milly was the only person in whom Dolly confided, and Milly told her in return about Alan's aunts, leaving out the part he had played in the day's events.

"No. He hasn't spoken," Dolly had to confess. "He could let the whole matter drop if he wanted to. When we were alone yesterday he told me more of his plans. He has determined to buy a new motor-car of an expensive make. Nothing is more likely to impress people, he says. Then he made me nervous by saying what he admired in women. He has almost impossibly high standards. He says he can't help it. I must blame his mother. I must say she never struck me as being such a paragon. She becomes very peevish if she doesn't get her way."

"He is being very careful, and I must say I resent it. You are far too good for him. Why should he go on as if he were the King of Greece or somewhere?"

"You mustn't run him down, Milly. I think his parents are to blame. He wants to make quite sure he does nothing to disappoint them. He's all they have."

Milly said nothing. If she spoke she would make too clear her contempt for Dolly's admirer when her own hero had shown feet of clay; and why was Dolly taking the view that men owed their first duty to their parents instead of to their wives? The Sabines were more flattered by the Romans than were she and Dolly by the men who attempted their capture and sounded out every inch of the ground.

Nevertheless, when Dolly was writing out Lady Kelly's invitations, they included one to Alan, of whom Carrie had boasted.

Milly, busy painting wings on the Angel Gabriel, found all her resentment against Alan had been dissipated. Too much consideration for the old ladies who had brought him up was an amiable weakness: she had expected too much of him. He was essentially a dreamer, not a man of action. His hair, which curled slightly on the neck, his poetic eyes, his long, slender hands, his proud lips, his caressing voice—these dominated her thoughts. She had forgotten the humiliations for which, after all, he was not responsible, even if he should have resented them more on her behalf. It was too soon, perhaps, in their relationship to expect him to enter the lists for her. If he were to come again she knew she would forgive him at once so as to prevent him from pleading. She couldn't bear that. A man should not plead to a woman, particularly when he is in the wrong.

She brought bread, butter and sausages and made herself lunch, lest he might call when she was off the premises. At three, she had to leave to go to her language pupils. She waited until the last moment in the ever-receding hope that he would come. She crossed the river by Queen's Bridge and walked past the Four Courts. She remembered her father coming out through the pillars, looking splendid in a wig. Alan would not be so impressive. He was not really intended by nature to be a lawyer. Perhaps when he came into his property, he would take up one of the arts. She peeped into the great hall under the dome: no sign of him there. At the corner of Capel Street, waiting to cross, she heard her name above the noise of the traffic. She looked about her, saw nobody, and decided that it was an illusion. Crossing the street she heard it again and this time she saw a man leaning out of a cab. Alan, in a top hat. She heard a cabby ask rudely if she knew where she was going when she ran up the line of cabs and carts and jumped in through the door Alan held open for her.

Neither said a word; they fell into each other's arms. His hat slipped off and rolled across the floor. She smothered him in kisses. It was still daylight, and Capel Street was the haunt of attorneys; but to Alan's credit he forgot them. He had been unable to pluck up courage to call on Milly because he had fixed in his mind her arctic remoteness when they last parted. How was he to begin? But when he saw her, looking exquisite, unattended, on the common pavement, he had acted spontaneously. So had she.

"Oh Milly darling, I love you," he said. The words surprised him. He had made a declaration of love. He had thrown in all his reserves. But since Sunday his only fear had been that he had lost Milly. His aunts were positively gloating over the success of their campaign. He hated them for it. If he could recover Milly's affection—he was sure he had lost it—his aunts could go to hell.

It had happened in this miraculous manner.

"Oh Alan, I love you."

They were both overwhelmed by the solemnity of the occasion. Even Milly's taking the initiative in the kissing—it surprised them both when they thought over the meeting—had no ritual significance. But now they had declared their mutual love. For them that was as good as plighting their troth. She felt reborn and awfully solemn; he, ecstatic and alarmed. Even in the most blissful moment of his life, when the girl he loved and thought through his own fault he had lost was telling him that she loved him, at the back of his brain the perils of the sea on which he had launched himself so recklessly began to take shape. But when he put her down in Stephen's Green and told the cabby to drive on, he deliberately put out of his mind all craven fears and basked in his happiness.

When he saw her in the street he asked himself how any man in his senses could have thrown away such a prize? The realisation of his criminal folly would haunt him all his life. Within a few seconds she was in his arms and all his. It was a miracle; and he shut his mind against the prospect of the bill that fate would furnish in due course.

Milly was noticeably absent-minded during the lessons; but when she got home the contrast between her own happiness, her mother's lot and Dolly's meagre hopes, filled her with a desire to make up to them for the unfairness of Providence in the distribution of its favours. She could always make herself attractive; but she was not what anyone would have called a 'sweet' girl. There was some element in her that was too formidable to tuck in with any expression of that order. Her kindness had a deliberate quality. She was not often gay (although she believed that she would be in other circumstances). But that evening she was gay and thoughtful and encouraging, smiling to herself at the thought of owning so prodigious and impenetrable a secret.

She rightly regarded her own intelligence as superior to her mother's or her sister's; and she would have been amazed to hear Carrie, when she was out of the room, say to Dolly, "They must have patched it up," and hear Dolly, quite as a matter of course, reply, "I hope he has been able to get round his awful aunts."

"I don't altogether blame them," Carrie said. "After all, they knew nothing about Milly."

"But they could see at a glance that she was a lady."

"Of course; but even if I don't like Protestant impudence, I don't approve of mixed marriages either. There is so much in an entirely suitable marriage that can go wrong, one doesn't want to add any additional factors. And religion is something very fundamental."

"But is it not largely a question of what Church one has been accustomed to attend? I don't think or talk about matters I don't understand. If my husband were a Protestant I should be able to get on very well, provided he didn't try to make me change my religion."

"And the children?"

Dolly always blushed at that prospect; and Carrie brought the subject to an end—Milly was coming downstairs anyway—by saying, "That is one problem you won't have to face. We should count our blessings."

Dolly blushed again, partly because it seemed indelicate to discuss her marriage as if it were a thing certain, and also because there was an implied acknowledgment of Bernard's short-comings in her mother's consolations.

Lady Kelly's party was the topic of the evening. Dolly told her family about the Lane incident. Carrie laughed. It was good to see her laugh, if only because she had such pretty teeth. Lowering her eyes, Dolly said that an invitation had been sent to Alan.

"How dare she presume to do any such thing? I shall go and tell that poisonous old woman to her face exactly what I think of her."

It took some time to soothe Milly, and it was Carrie who put the whole matter in perspective. She had begun to look at Lady Kelly with less awe-stricken eyes since the possibility that Dolly would soon be quit of her had appeared on the horizon. She could see the pursuit of Mr Lane as a lion hunt, but it might be to Milly's advantage. "Never look a gift horse in the mouth," she said.

"Lady Kelly is very fond of that expression. She attributes it to her uncle, the Canon in Cork," Dolly told them.

Milly's aversion to the scheme and to the impudence of inviting Alan cooled on reflection. Her mother was right: it was a matter to treat lightly. She would even tell Alan to accept the invitation. They might be grateful for the rendezvous.

Mr Lane, approached by Mr Catterson Smith, also agreed to go. He would probably be at the exhibition in any case, he said: at that time of day there was stimulus in tea; and he was glad to hear of people attending an exhibition he had gone to endless trouble to set up.

"Not one refusal," Lady Kelly told Dolly. "Mr Lane, I understand, is immensely grateful. Please explain to your mother, dear, that I have too much on hand at the moment to offer any assistance in buying Milly's frock. She must do that on her own. I won't always be here, you know. A day will come when you must learn to rely on yourselves."

Lady Kelly had never been in such excellent form. She gave Dolly a pair of gloves, admittedly too tight for her, but only worn twice, and the stain hardly showed as it was on the left-hand one.

XIII

IT MIGHT BE said that everyone looked forward to Lady Kelly's party; this made it unique among the many entertainments that she had fostered in her time. Even the elusive young celebrity, Mr Lane, was known to care only for people who supported his enterprises; and in his eyes Lady Kelly was lent a certain grace by encouraging people to look at the pictures he had assembled.

A room in the Academy—the Council chamber in Francis Johnston's fine building in Abbey Street—was set aside for people such as the hostess on this occasion. The caterer got busy in the morning; and as caterers in Dublin were few, the room had a familiar appearance to anyone who was accustomed to Dublin social life.

Nervousness made Lady Kelly difficult to deal with, and she snapped Dolly's head off whether she spoke or was silent, agreed or dared to differ. She will be all right, Dolly told herself, when Mr Lane makes his appearance. That would put the seal on her success. As is always the case on such occasions, the earliest to arrive were those least looked forward to, who owed their invitations to reasons of charity or policy. Their coming solved nothing; they were lucky to be there; their hostess gave them only as much civility as her sense of the proprieties prescribed. Having shaken hands they were glad to scuttle away into corners and whisper among themselves.

Carrie and Milly had been instructed to arrive late. A theatrical sense reared on Victorian melodrama suggested that Mr Lane should be present when Milly came in accompanied by her pretty mother.

"Who is that lovely girl, your ladyship?" he would enquire.

"A little protégée of mine, Milly Preston; she has artistic talent, I believe. I should like you to meet her. The family have fallen on misfortune. I do what I can. Sir Patrick had a regard for the child's father—a brilliant lawyer—died prematurely—an accident—very sad. The mother is quite a lady. I shall present you."

This was what Lady Kelly had rehearsed, and no wonder she was nervous. The effect depended on proper timing as well as punctuality on the part of the principals.

Dolly did not mind her patron's constant rebuffs. She was like one who is borne up by inner resources. These were made plain when the hired footman announced, "Mr and Mrs Roche and Mr Bernard Roche."

Dolly had chosen an inattentive moment to murmur their names when the invitations were rolling off. Lady Kelly said 'of course', not having heard properly. She did not know the Roches. They came now at the moment their hostess had chosen in her mind for Mr Lane's appearance—time was getting on—and she saw them as trespassers on his ground.

"Who are these people? I don't know them from Adam," she said to Dolly, in a tone of outrage.

"The Gerald Roches," Dolly said, trying to convey that they were worth knowing, using Mr Roche's christian name with double-barrelled intent.

Dolly's enthusiasm did not have the desired effect. Her mentor did not regard her social judgment as worth attending to when it operated without her direction. Lady Kelly was not in the least vague, although she assumed a vague manner to suggest she was well-bred. Dolly has slipped these people in. That was her first thought. They had been thrown upon her. She shook hands, but said nothing, thereby making a most agreeable impression and confirming the Roche family in their regard for Dolly for having won favour with such a splendid person. Bernard, ever on the watch, would have seen through any pretence of affability. Dolly, by getting him and his parents to this party, had shown herself to be the kind of wife he wanted—a lady with push.

Soundly snubbed, the Roches withdrew satisfied; and Dolly, mortified, rushed to their assistance. The other snubbed guests were more than ready to make friends, a fellow-feeling making them wondrous kind; all agreeing tacitly not to display their wounds. In a moment the two Roche men were holding forth to groups in different corners, swilling tea.

An expectant hum put the unpleasant incident out of Lady Kelly's mind. She saw a group of men at the door and heard the hired footman announce, "Mr Catterson Smith, Mr Walter Osborne, Mr Hugh Lane."

All eyes were on the scene which young Bernard was well qualified to evaluate. Just as he had been impressed by Lady Kelly frozen, he rejoiced to see her thaw. If not regal, she was massive;

and everything she did partook of her splendid shape. Now she was like an iceberg that the sun's rays had melted. She shone. She gushed. She flowed over.

She had a little speech ready; but for him alone. His entering in the company of two of Dublin's leading artists, one of them the President of the Royal Hibernian Academy, upset her plans. Besides, she had pictured the distinguished collector as standing admiringly in front of her as if she had only recently been discovered in an archaeological dig in Athens. She had anticipated artistic appreciation as his first reaction, followed by more animated behaviour while the animal in the aesthete struggled with the artist in the animal. She saw herself as the star captive in a Roman triumph awaiting a victorious emperor's decision: lions or lust.

"Well, I suppose we had better be getting alone" was the bugle call to which the three men charged in the first place. Mr Catterson Smith had reservations about his hostess; Mr Osborne wondered if she would order a portrait, he needed the money; Mr Lane was thinking about a Corot he had seen in the morning. All three showed themselves to be very shy and likely to drown in the warm current of the melted ice floe.

None did more than nod in reply to her, "What a pleasure", "This is a treat", "Mr Lane, I am honoured"—nodded, bowed and slipped out of the picture, leaving Lady Kelly to greet Carrie and Milly.

They got a very curt welcome, their hostess turning, like a conductor, to the first violin, and finding the place empty. As she had arranged it, Mr Lane should have been at hand for their dialogue, his part, had he known it, already composed and in her mind. But he was in a corner, looking around uneasily, like a trapped hare; at any moment he would make for the door. It wasn't Carrie's fault, nor yet Milly's; but Lady Kelly brought the weight of her disapproval—massive as everything belonging to her—to bear on them.

"There's refreshment over there. I'm afraid you will have to look after yourselves," she said. Once again, she told herself, the Prestons had proved unworthy of her patronage. She couldn't bring herself to lay the blame on Mr Lane; he, as she, was the victim of this family's gaucheries.

Her wrath was like thunder; it was the price paid for summer splendour. And before the bolt had crushed the unoffending

Prestons, they, not less than she, were riveted by the announcement of "Captain Dunne and Mr Talbot Thompson."

Typical of Joe to get his name in first, Carrie thought. She had sent on the invitations as directed, but never expected them to be taken up. Mr Talbot Thompson was not to have arrived in Ireland until Easter. He was in a morning coat with a splendid watch-chain on his waistcoat, from which a gold seal depended. His face was, as always, expressionless. The moustache acted as camouflage for the lower part; in his large oriental eyes the pupils circled like goldfish in a bowl, not so much baffled as resigned.

Whenever Joe called himself 'Captain', it meant that he was dressed to kill. And he certainly looked today as if he had left the best London club after lunch and ridden in the Row before breakfast.

Lady Kelly remembered that she owed this pair of gallants to the Preston connection, and it softened her wrath. After Mr Talbot Thompson had kissed her hand and Uncle Joe made as if to kiss her cheek (but, of course, it was only a trick of manner, nothing could have been more respectful than his behaviour), she made a playful gesture towards Carrie, school-girlish, winsome. "What a handsome family you are," she said and then, seeing Dolly in the corner, raised her eye-brows just a trifle, to indicate that there was always an exception to prove the rule.

Carrie was impervious and oblivious: something told her that the clouds were lifting for her; and she had ceased to regard Lady Kelly as a factor. She saw Dolly being almost fawned upon by the Roches, not what she would have ever fancied herself, but good for her humble, self-depreciatory, undemanding daughter.

Milly was in an alcove with Alan. They were quite unable to conceal their devotion. Being so beautiful, the scene was not lost on others in the room. Mr Lane's last remark before he 'slipped away' was that they would make a more appropriate Romeo and Juliet than the usual stage version with fifty-year-old principals.

Mr Talbot Thompson nudged Joe. "Lucky fellow. I wouldn't mind a helping of that."

"You are speaking of my niece," the Captain replied with appropriate hauteur. It was a God-given chance to prevent T. T. from getting too big for his boots.

"Sorry, old man. No offence. You'll admit yourself she's a nice armful."

He talked as was his wont when alone with the Captain, and could not see why his friend should become so priggish. Joe was taking in the scene and assessing its possibilities. He never let the grass grow under his feet, an expression his hostess could have told him originated with her grandfather.

He walked up to Lane, introducing himself, and offered on Mr Talbot Thompson's behalf to put up a hundred pounds for any project Mr Lane had in mind.

"Get him to sit for Mr John Butler Yeats," he said. "Tell him to buy one of my friend Osborne's paintings. He ought to have a Hone. I will select one for him if he writes to me."

Then he bolted.

Joe went across the room to tell his patron what he had let him in for, and found him staring pensively into Lady Kelly's bodice.

Joe was pleased to tell Lady Kelly what had already been accomplished by her splendid reception, and Mr Talbot Thompson took the opportunity of her distracted attention to take another peep.

"An ample dairy," Joe remarked when they were on their own again, comparing notes.

Mr Talbot Thompson was relieved to find him back in his usual form, and suggested that they ought to talk to Carrie about arrangements for Easter. Since he had seen Milly the idea of the Prestons in residence had recommended itself to him more than when—as he put it—"my fellow in Ireland had been trying to land his relations on top of me."

Carrie was by no means out of place. She was dryly amused to find herself receiving attention from erstwhile friends. When it seemed that she might no longer need support, it was beginning to offer itself.

"We haven't seen you for ages. I've always been meaning to call."

She heard that six times, when she felt rather than saw Mr Talbot Thompson at her side. It coincided with the onset of the three Roches; and when Mr Talbot Thompson in his laconic way spoke of his place in Westmeath and his anxiety to see the Prestons as his guests, Bernard Roche made up his mind. He would propose to Dolly before the afternoon was out. This was exactly such a setting as he would choose for the second most important decision in life (the first was choice of profession).

"You need a good lawyer, T. T.," the Captain said. "I think you should give young Roche an opportunity to win his spurs."

Mr Talbot Thompson thereupon winked at Bernard. It could be a formidable omen.

Within five minutes Dolly, scarlet faced, and bent almost double, as if the wind had at last become altogether too strong, smiling and almost in tears, whispered something in Carrie's ears.

"Dolly's engaged," Carrie told Joe.

"Not to the little—Oh, I see. Well, this is great news. Give your uncle a kiss, Dolly. Felicitations, my dear. He's a lucky fellow. Devilishly so."

Lady Kelly, all ears, even in the cannon's mouth, heard the phrases, caught their meaning and conferred with herself as might a general with no time to waste at the turning point of a battle. Dolly had betrayed her. The sly little thing. This had been going on unbeknownst under her nose when she should have been the first to be consulted. It explained the presence of the Roches. Dolly was not only sly, she was artful. "I won't give her a present." In that simple phrase Lady Kelly packed all her indignation.

But the desire not to be left out of anything, the prospect of 'coming into her own' (her mother's phrase) when wedding preparations begun—these advised the adoption of a watching brief. Perhaps, after all, she might give a small wedding present. Had Dolly put through a courtship under her control and direction, the operation would have necessarily ended with an appropriate gift—a sacrifice.

Now Dolly, by her slyness, had forfeited her rights and relieved her of any serious obligation. For years she had been wondering what to do with the massive plated cruet which a group of famine-relief workers had given Sir Patrick on his first wedding. It was the devil to keep polished, and took up more than its fair share of the sideboard. Now was the chance to jettison it. The silversmith could always change the inscription.

"I wanted you to have it, Dolly. I know how much you have always coveted it." Yes, she *would* say 'covet' instead of 'admired'. It would be a 'word to the wise' (Sir Patrick's favourite expression) that she had seen through Dolly and put the worst construction on her apparently innocent preferences. That the cruet would be Bernard Roche's most treasured possession did not occur to her, and it would be interesting to speculate whether, if it had, she would have been gratified or otherwise.

Now was the time to go; Mr Lane had gone, The Director of the National Gallery, Sir Walter Armstrong, had gone, the Lord Mayor and his spouse had left, so had the Accountant General, Mr Teeling, and the secretary of the Incorporated Law Society and Mrs Wakely, and the secretary of the Landowners' Convention, and Mr and Mrs Walker Waters and their beautiful daughters, and Sir Francis and Lady Cruise, and Surgeon Mac Ardle and Mr T. P. Gill.

"Lovely friends, lovely friends," Lady Kelly murmured to herself, but so as those in her vicinity could hear. She cut off her soliloquy to shake hands with the devoted Roches, to whom a cruet would soon be dispatched.

Milly became suddenly aware that she and Alan had isolated themselves, and now, in the thinned ranks, were too conspicuous.

"When can I see you, Milly?"

"Come back to supper."

He hesitated; it meant ringing up and making an excuse, and he hated doing that. For one thing his aunts had never learned how to use the telephone and were inclined to shout on it as if the human voice travelled by main force. For another, he knew that he would not give his true reason for staying in Dublin, and he would be obliged to roar his lie, because they insisted on holding the instrument in some way that shut off the hearing end. Milly noticed his hesitation.

"I was going to work; but what of it. When shall I come?"

She suggested eight o'clock. They drew away from one another then, Milly joining her mother.

"I wanted you to meet Mr Lane," Lady Kelly said to her reproachfully. She remembered now that the tableau she had designed had never taken place. It would have been the highlight of her afternoon; but there were other compensations. She quite forgot that the whole idea had been to forward Milly's career.

Towards Dolly she showed a coldness such as she read Queen Charlotte exhibited towards Fanny Burney when she wanted to 'bring her up to scratch'.

Dolly attached herself to her mother and cared not at all whether Lady Kelly blew hot or cold. But she felt grateful, good creature that she was, to the woman for having been the unwitting cause of her happiness. Bernard's proposal had had such a ring of conviction—he never thought for a moment that he could be refused—she knew that something about the afternoon had made up his mind. To the extent that Lady Kelly provided a favourable ambience for her, she would remember her kindly in Waterford days.

Milly, happy for herself, was sweetness itself to Dolly. They were fond of one another; but Milly saw quite clearly that Dolly, married to Bernard Roche, would be lost to her. However, her own prospects were too beautiful to allow that to affect her.

Carrie was radiant.

"By God, I'd plump for the mother," Mr Talbot Thompson said to Joe, who was too busy to listen; he had been making contacts all the afternoon, and now was ready to go. As often in his life, he was not quite sure of his next move. T. T. might invite him to dinner, or he might invite T. T., hoping that he would ask for the bill. Alternatively there was the certainty of pot-luck at Carrie's, and Milly to look at. Failing these there was a Mrs Ball who lived in Percy Place, upon whom he called occasionally. She was not as young as she had been, and a visit involved an outlay. All possibilities were weighed while he waited.

Mr Talbot Thompson offered to drive the whole party home; but Carrie objected that neither she nor the girls were equipped for motoring. Alan then offered to take the Prestons in a cab. And so it was decided.

Lady Kelly found herself alone. Her coldness towards Dolly had been intended as reproof, not dismissal; and she wondered what had possessed her to let the girl walk off like that with her family. It was most humiliating to have to come down unattended and give sixpence to the porter to fetch her a cab. While she was waiting, bare-foot urchins gathered round. "Give us a penny, Missus," "Spare us a copper, lady." She took no notice. She would complain to Mr Catterson Smith. He should see that the entrance was kept free of beggars. It was not the way that her day of triumph should have ended.

Mr Talbot Thompson, who had a genius for the unexpected, came up to Joe and said: "You've mentioned a certain party, name of Ball, in Percy Place. What about a reconnaissance? I have a bottle in the boot."

Joe agreed, reluctantly. He kept on planning how he would use T. T.; but as time went on T. T. seemed to grow more and more adept at making use of him.

XIV

"WE WON'T NEED you, Captain," T. T. said to Joe, three hours later. He was ensconced in an arm-chair and Mrs Ball, over whom a fine dust seemed to be spread, was admiring his watch-chain and offering to read his hand.

Mrs Ball showed the Captain down to the door, reciting in genteel accents her admiration for his friend. Joe said nothing. She could make trouble for him; and all he resented was the cool way T. T. took it for granted that he was the one to clear out. Not that he ever wanted Mrs Ball very much unless he had consumed so much whiskey that he found, when she 'forgot herself', that alcohol as an aphrodisiac was a fire made of paper.

"I think he is so interesting, and such a gentleman. I find that I can only be completely at my ease with gentlemen. You were always a perfect gentleman, Joe. You must come and see me and tell me all the news another time. I think Mr Talbot Thompson has something on his mind this evening. You were very kind to introduce him to me. What did you say he did?"

"I didn't say anything. If I were you I'd stay my ground until there was something on the table."

Mrs Ball gave him a playful push. He was not angry with her but his pride rebelled at the thought of his dependence on a third-rate Englishman. It was not any nationalistic fervour. He had none; but an Irishman of T. T.'s type would recognise him as a superior and treat him accordingly. T. T. did not deal with him as an inferior; worse, he accepted him as an equal. "I have the tin," he liked to say, "and you have the time." He saw them as explorers with predatory designs. T. T. was not in search of gold. He had it. He wanted a position in society. Joe was a local guide whom he had hired to show him the way through the jungle. He had been chosen as anxious for reward and, therefore, unlikely to quit, well-informed about the terrain, and fertile in expedients. That Joe was not as well in as he pretended was obvious to his patron. The fact that he was available disclosed that. But it strengthened his hold on Joe to know that he too was socially insecure. They had that in common. Joe regarded his absence of 'tin' as his only disqualification for a place in the County. He forgot that he had ruined his family by trying to buy himself in. T. T.'s more deliberate campaign seemed to bear no relation to his own. In this he was right: his own morbid vanity had driven him on. He wanted to prove himself, to establish that the Dunnes, who had once been princes in Hi Regan, could take their place in an anglicised Ireland. Mr Talbot Thompson had no illusions. His father had begun life in Whitechapel. His mother had no idea where hers began. She gave him his eastern market eyes. She thought that there had been some Bristol blood in her own mother who talked to her about the sea and foreign ships before she went away in one.

Mrs Ball was certainly a poor thing, and she had never been Joe's own because he had never had the wherewithal to establish a monopoly in a going concern. Her mother, she told him once, in confidence, was the offspring of Isaac Butt, father of Home Rule, and much else besides. The circumstances of her birth gave her an interest in politics. She could talk to Mr Talbot Thompson about the prospects of the Unionist party. She knew something. She had friends . . . in the Castle.

Joe stood in the doorway gazing over Huband Bridge at the turret of St Stephen's in Mount Street Crescent. Why 'Mount' he wondered? And then, thinking of Mrs Ball, gave a Rabelaisian laugh, which puzzled her. She had not hurried him away, although she wondered if Mr Talbot Thompson upstairs might be becoming impatient. She was a polite woman, not merely an obliging one. Besides, it was a mistake not to keep all one's options open.

"Tell me," she said, "is not your sister a friend of Lady Kelly? With whom does she arrange the disposal of her clothes? I give excellent terms. Perhaps you would put in a word."

He would put in a word. He would put it in that very evening, he decided, glancing at his watch. If he walked along the canal, he would be in Buttercup Square by nine o'clock, in time for pot luck.

He walked away briskly but slowed down when he crossed the bridge. It was curious, he reflected, and a sign of age and wisdom increasing together, that he didn't give a tinker's curse about leaving that pair together. There was a time when male competitiveness would have made him jealous, if even Mrs Ball were anxious to get rid of him for the sake of another man.

But tonight he preferred the thought of his sister's house, her girls (undamaged goods) and the prevailing atmosphere of cheerful goodness. Often it had been the other way, he had fled from Carrie's respectabilities to Mrs. Ball, who had always some comfort in the cupboard and who could talk to him about a world in which Carrie had no place. Not that Mrs Ball had ever abandoned in her own mind the right to hold up her head. She was to be found where men were and in the seedier political and literary societies. She followed every cult; and of recent years put out that she was skilled in fortune-telling. Dealing in clothes was her regular source of living. Officers' wives in financial difficulties parted with almost new dresses and even jewellery. Joe had mentioned her, cautiously, to Carrie as a source from which she might get party clothes for her girls; but Carrie objected that it would be awkward if they confronted the original owners. Joe saw the sense of that. He never told Carrie where Mrs Ball lived . . . "I know a very decent little woman" . . . and Carrie never enquired. She learned early on not to ask her brother questions. It only encouraged him to tell lies.

By now she would have turned out the light—a stickler for the proprieties—and be in the four-poster with Mr Talbot Thompson.

"I am a pimp," Joe told himself, "a bawd, a whore turned madam, a purveyor to this lump of lard." And he thought of the very short time ago, when he would have thrown T. T.'s pretensions in his face. "Wouldn't have been seen dead in his company." Now he found him women.

Mary opened the door for him. "They're at supper, Mr Joe," she said. She loved his visits, and not for the shillings he sometimes gave her. She knew that he ate them out of house and home, but that was as it should be. Her family, in its small way, was dedicated to the men. They got whatever was going, and the women looked after them and were content to exist on the leavings. Joe's arrival was a signal to her to go to the larder and to cook whatever was in it for 'Mr Joe'. He was never 'the Captain' in his family. That was put on with his overcoat when he went abroad.

"It's Mr Joe," she said, going ahead, nothing in her voice suggesting that the news would not be as welcome in the dining-room as it was to her.

He came into the little room, his head an inch from the ceiling, all twinkles and smiles, still in his hired frock-coat, looking like the man who broke the bank at Monte Carlo, as Carrie remarked to

Dolly, when bed-time came at last, and Dolly was brushing her long hair.

He smiled round the table, showing a gold tooth—on Carrie and Milly and Dolly and their young men, Bernard, whom he found it difficult to greet without aversion, and young Harvey, of whom he had heard, and who had impressed him this afternoon as a young man destined for high places on easy terms. Milly looked radiant. His girl; he couldn't take his eyes off her. He was jealous of any man who was favoured by her; but he knew that he would have to fight this, and glancing from poor Dolly with her make-do betrothed to Milly's young man, he was satisfied that it was as it should be. If anyone were to put his hands on Milly, it must be one of the right sort, one from the world to which she was intended by nature to belong. He was ashamed to think that he had allowed himself to use her as a decoy to T. T. It was a desperate expedient.

Now he had other plans. He talked to Alan as man to man, enquired about his career, went as near to impertinence as his not always fool-proof antennae allowed in collecting information about his background.

Alan was so happy that he was uncritical; and like most men in love, he saw Milly's surroundings and her family in the kindly light of his reflected love. They were sanctified by the connection so long as she approved of them. He did not resent Uncle Joe's familiarity, even welcomed his interest and explained his volume of questions as the natural anxiety of one acting *in loco parentis*. He had, after all, shown his hand pretty plainly. He could not complain if he was regarded as Milly's suitor. Nor did he object. It made her safe for him, put his label on her. She had looked so dazzling that afternoon he was apprehensive whenever he saw her being looked at, even by the artists. They would spread her fame abroad. He wanted to think of her as in a fairy tale, hidden away, living only for his love.

When they got upstairs, Uncle Joe, who had been drinking steadily and was inwardly anxious to throw off a recent episode that weighed on his innocent pleasure in his present surroundings, suggested that they lift the carpet and dance among themselves.

The young men agreed. Carrie sat down to play, and when Milly said it seemed somewhat odd, a dance with only two couples, Joe disappeared and returned with Mary, blushing, protesting, and delighted.

"You'll have me kilt! You'll be the death of me! What's got into you, Mr Joe?"

But she bounded round with wonderful agility, sweat streaming down her face, her hair coming adrift from its pins. She was a born dancer.

Carrie played well, and tonight she felt happier than since she could remember. By shutting her eyes she imagined herself at home when the world was young and there was plenty for everyone and she did not know what trouble was. She remembered her first dance with Arthur Preston. It was a waltz, and his wonderful beard tickled her and made her—as she told him much later—want to sneeze. He had descended on her like a God; and she had worshipped him from the first moment; never—although they had two children born alive and three who preferred to go to Heaven straight—never had she known any more of him than the side he turned to her. He liked to tell her:

> God be thanked, the meanest of his creatures
> Boasts two soul-sides, one to face the world with,
> One to show a woman when he loves her.

And she was grateful for the one he showed to her and grateful for the one he turned away, although sometimes she was curious. Those books on his shelves—what a row there had been when Milly had gone rooting and come up with Balzac (mercifully in French). Arthur went on like Bluebeard, and it had tempted her to explore. So much was in Latin and in French, but there were books in English as well, and when she peeped into one she felt as if she had been exposed naked to the public stare. What strange things men were. What a dreadful world there was from which women like her were protected and one would like to think nice men would keep themselves free of its contamination. How much Arthur knew and thought and felt and never shared. It left her incomplete, a pet, an ornament. My wife, the mother of my children—that was her role and it demanded that she should not seek to live, even vicariously, as he had. Was there a type of woman to whom he would show his whole self? What women had he known? Did he meet women after marriage, without her knowing?

She had a vague presentiment that she had lived in a box of which he kept the key when he roamed the world. It hadn't mattered then—even if there were strange moments when she had brief glimpses into dark places—but it mattered now. He had died and taken away the key. She had seen not the world's foul but its flinty face. It left her bruised but intact. She did not need the key for Dolly, Dolly would stay in the box always; it was for Milly she needed it. There was in Milly a part of the Arthur she never saw, as there was a part of Joe in her. Joe was secretive as all schemers must be, but he was not mysterious. He was all surface, all shallows. Arthur was deep; and so was Milly. It would solve all their problems if this pleasant, handsome, well-bred young man, whom she too obviously adored, was able to marry her. It would not be easy. He would have to quarrel, perhaps to break, with his family. Did he love her sufficiently? Was he strong? She hoped so. But she had doubts. This side of the world she knew.

Dolly was safe. Her life was set on mediocre lines. But she would probably be as happy as most women were.

Carrie broke into a waltz by Chopin. She put her reflections away and looked at the two couples, Milly and Alan, for whom the waltz might have been composed, Dolly, with the grace of youth, lending vestigial romance to her Bernard (he had taken a course of lessons from Mr and Mrs Legget Byrne), and in her mind's eye she was circling round the room with them in Arthur's arms, tickled by Arthur's beard, breathing in the comfort of Arthur's peculiar scent of soap and tobacco.

Chopin was too much for Mary. She broke away and went down to the kitchen to see what she could put a hand to that might add to the gaiety upstairs. She had a light hand with pancakes, and they might be acceptable as a treat. She liked to provide treats. She shared all Carrie's feelings about the evening. This family was hers. What happened to them mattered more to her than her own fate.

"Is it a match do you think?" Joe had asked her, looking at Milly and Alan.

"They'd make a lovely pair," she said. But she knew the lie of the land as well as Carrie who, unlike Joe, thought it *infra dig* to converse with servants. Somehow it wasn't necessary. Mary seemed to know.

The arrival of the pancakes was greeted with sufficient enthusiasm to send her to bed happy and proud. The party sat round the fire and ate them, not talking very much.

Carrie took the opportunity to ask Joe what had been the reason for Mr Talbot Thompson's altering his plans. It was understood that he would not come over until Easter.

Joe, in fact, never knew what his patron's motives were; but he found explanations for his conduct that fitted his own vanity and coincided with his hopes. He had persuaded himself that political ambition was the cause.

"This government is on its last legs and T. T. realises that if he is to get local influence behind him he can't strike too soon. He keeps his nose to the ground, and he tells me that Joe Chamberlain—my screw-making namesake—has ruined the Tories with his schemes. They won't get back. He says he has written to Balfour, but between you and me and the door-post, I think he exaggerates the influence he has in that quarter. My advice is to read the writing on the wall and write off the money invested in the Tories. I've had a look round the constituency and I believe the best bet is to put up a member for the Irish Party. T. T. saw that it was too much to expect them to swallow him, and he seemed to think that I would fit the bill; but I have doubts. I'm not known in Westmeath. It doesn't matter who gets in so long as he's in T. T.'s pocket.

"I wonder if young Harvey would fancy a seat in parliament. I think Redmond would like the cut of his jib. Being a Protestant won't matter. His own lot wouldn't vote for him anyway, and the peasants are always impressed."

Carrie's optimistic strain saw a new hope for Milly if she could offer Alan a parliamentary career. But the thought had hardly found itself when the unlikelihood of Joe's leading anyone to anything but disaster supervened.

She didn't know very much about politics; but she was sure that the idea of Alan in the ranks of the Irish party clamouring for Home Rule would arouse his family to fighting pitch.

But Joe had a glamour for a man so young as Alan, even had he not been Milly's uncle. He was so persuasive that he frequently persuaded himself, and when he told Alan that he could present him with a safe seat in parliament, it seemed to Alan that his love for Milly was shedding a glory over all his life. He was not himself interested in politics; they were not discussed at home; but the Irish Party, which he was being invited to join, was regarded by his aunts as little better than licensed brigandage. They did not fit at Westminster though there were sometimes gentlemen—eccentrics possibly—in their ranks. Redmond was a gentleman in a sort of a way; but he was a Catholic, and, therefore, when it came down to brass tacks, an outsider.

Would his aunts be sufficiently intrigued by the idea of his being in parliament to swallow the means by which he got there? What would his uncle, the Bishop, say?

Alan, a little drunk with all the possibilities sprung on him in Buttercup Square, and under the spell of Uncle Joe, saw himself rising within a year to the position of Parnell—Parnell with a lovely wife at his side.

"The Harveys have a stake in the county. Your family is known and respected. This will be a great accession to the Party and, at this time, your accession will cause no end of a stir. It will be seen as a straw in the wind. Other ambitious young fellows, who would have joined one of the English parties, will now think twice. You will have a chance to emulate Grattan, young man. With T. T.'s money and my experience behind you, there will be no stopping you."

The Preston family liked the picture of Alan in the role of a national leader too much to offer any objection or to throw cold water on it as typical of Uncle Joe in his expansive moments. Bernard Roche, as near ecstasy as he could ever be, had not lost all his customary caution. Even now he had to raise practical difficulties. Having decided, after much thought, to join his fortunes with this family, he saw himself as their adviser and protector. His *amour propre* would have been much offended had they sought any other. Well-disposed towards them all, he had not failed to notice that Uncle Joe was not impressed by him and had shown coolness when he heard Dolly's good fortune. This irked him and, characteristically, caused him to question Uncle Joe's credentials. From Dolly—inclined to gossip about the family—he had picked up enough already to know that Uncle Joe had been a conspicuous failure.

He was sitting now in the centre of the circle, under the lamp, with the face of his listeners half in shadow, lit up only by the fire. Now, Bernard's prematurely elderly countenance was thrust forward. Uncle Joe had to share the limelight, and he did not conceal his displeasure. When his imagination was having a free run—and he had just built up a picture of Alan holding an Irish House of Commons in thrall—he objected to being pulled up in mid-career.

"How do we know the Party will adopt Alan as a candidate?"

"I think I can commit myself on that."

"Are you in their governing body?"

"I am not, sir. I am in favour of dealing only with the man at the top. I am known to John Redmond; and I will make it my business to see him and to bring the recommendations of the leading people in the constituency."

"Have you asked them? The idea only cropped up in conversation this evening."

"It cropped up—as you put it—because it was as plain as the nose on your face to anyone with an eye for political possibilities. Every impecunious barrister wants to be nominated by the Irish party. What chance would any of them have against a man with Alan's background? Talk sense, man."

Bernard did not mind rebuffs. He concentrated on his point.

"It may be as you say, but I don't see how we can regard it as *un fait accompli.*"

"Nobody is regarding it as any such thing; but if we approach a matter of this kind in a miserable, snivelling, sneaking, pettifogging way, we are unlikely to make an impression on anyone. I believe in doing things in style."

"An election costs a great deal."

"T. T. will pay. Don't worry on that score."

"But I overheard Mr Talbot Thompson talking to Lady Kelly. He is an arch-conservative. He favours military government in Ireland and flogging for sedition. I was quite alarmed by the severity of his remedies. He would make the mere mention of Home Rule a criminal offence."

"That's T. T. unbuttoned. But nobody is better aware of what side his bread is buttered on than your man. He could do with a tame member in the House. Anyone with as many irons in the fire as T. T. has never knows when he may need a friend in court. In Britain he would have certain difficulties; but he's not known in Ireland; he can show a loose leg here. I told him a Unionist hasn't a chance in a county constituency, and if he wants to have an interest in parliament he had better change his tune. He took my point. Whatever goes on behind that forehead you are not going to hear any more Jingo talk from T. T."

"He sounds like an unprincipled ruffian," Carrie said. It was her first intervention. Little though she was attracted by her future son-in-law, she had been struck by his solid sense. He would not lose his head as the other boy might. He was as solid as the ground he stood on, and a useful acquisition by a family that could boast only an Uncle Joe as its male member.

"T. T. is a man of the world, Carrie. He will not be the only one to defect from the Tories when the time comes. It's foolish to be hidebound in these matters. What are politics for? Why do people take them up? If you want to become a Trappist monk you go to Mount Melleray."

"I think there is such a thing as political principle," Bernard said thoughtfully. "Monks are a different matter."

"I don't suppose we are concerned with Mr Talbot Thompson's motives if he wants to put Alan into parliament," Carrie compromised.

Dolly's never-sleeping suspicions of her uncle were alerted by her lover's cross-examination. What a fine mind he had! Alan had better be careful if Bernard counselled caution.

Milly suspected Mr Talbot Thompson's integrity because he was connected with Uncle Joe, apart from his enigmatic manner; but the idea of Alan in parliament, and the thought that it would be through her connections he would leap into fame, had gone to her head. She was so happy that she dreaded any threat to her happiness. She must do what she could to safeguard it. Alan's love she was sure of; but Alan had pressures on him which would be exercised when she wasn't there. Would he be as strong as his love? She knew by instinct that she was the stronger of the two, the more ruthless and single-minded. By showing him a way to become independent of his family, by being an influence as well as an inspiration, she was helping him and throwing something as well as love into the scales.

It was getting late but she didn't want the evening to end.

Bernard, sensible Bernard, with work to do on the morrow, broke up the party. He proposed to walk back to his lodgings in Pembroke Street. Joe, invited to stay, hesitated. If T. T. returned to the Dolphin he could rely on him to pay his bill; but T. T. might stay with Mrs Ball. They had not discussed the possibility. Their luggage was with the porter at the Dolphin, an old friend of Joe's. If T. T. left Mrs Ball, and from what Joe had seen his principal business with her would have been accomplished long since, he might get irritated on returning to his hotel to find Joe wasn't there. He was uneasy on his own.

"I'll stroll along with Bernard," Joe said at last. He wanted to win over this new connection, whom he could see had a head on his shoulders. When he left him he would proceed to Percy Place. The fancy had taken him to lie in the sheets warmed by his patron. He would ring and see how the land lay. Mrs Ball kept no staff living in. They poked their noses into her affairs, she said. Someone came in during the day, a discreet body from whom Joe often got useful tips for races. Mrs Ball sometimes accompanied Joe to the meetings near Dublin. An odd flutter with the bookmakers and a glass of port were her only indulgences.

Alan waited to leave until the others had gone; he, too, was walking in their direction, but he did not want them to intrude on his thoughts. Milly came to the gate with him, and they kissed under the soot-laden plane tree. Their kisses had been of different kinds; but tonight's Milly knew she would remember after all but the very first were forgotten. There was such a blessing of renewal in it, such confidence and sweetness, none of the fierceness which was often a cover-up of doubt or despair. Neither mentioned love or murmured a name. Their kiss said everything and put them beyond the need of speech.

Alan, weightless, glided home under the cheerful stars. He was staying with a friend, and he glanced at his door as he made his way to the room assigned to himself. He felt a profound pity for his friend and for all men everywhere who had to live and die without knowing Milly's love, without knowing Milly. How could they reconcile themselves to such a dreary existence?

Joe and Bernard walked along in silence. Bernard had no gifts of casual talk. Joe was feeling his way. On Leeson Street Bridge he asked Bernard to give him his hand, and said that in his long life he had never been so impressed as he had been this evening by Bernard's masterly analysis of Alan's prospects.

Surprised and pleased, Bernard apologised for his apparent suspiciousness and accepted the fervent clasp.

"You were absolutely justified, Bernard—I call you 'Bernard' since you are connecting yourself with our family—I said to myself as I listened to you, 'there's a head that ought to be under a wig'. A wig would suit you, Bernard. Did you ever think of employing your talents on the senior side of the profession?"

Bernard had not; but he was pleased to hear he would look well in a barrister's wig. Dolly's Uncle Joe, if flighty, was certainly an agreeable customer.

On Baggot Street Bridge, Joe offered his hand again, and pledged himself never in future to take a decisive step in life without first obtaining Bernard's blessing.

"We must get T. T.'s business for you, my boy. I have a very high opinion of T. T.'s acumen, but he's as close as an oyster. I've already mentioned your name to him. Perhaps you would come down at Easter with the Prestons and get to know him better. I shall tell him we will need you when my plans for young Harvey mature. We will have a pack of double-dyed ruffians to deal with then, and I don't want T. T. to spring a leak. We must get Alan safe into harbour. Good-night, my boy, pleasant dreams."

With that Joe turned rather abruptly away; and Bernard watching his retreating figure in the dusk, thought there was something vaguely suspicious about it. Had he been a policeman he'd have proceeded cautiously in the same direction. As it was, he did not feel at all sleepy, and instead of turning to the right towards Pembroke Street, he followed Joe in the direction of Mount Street. He saw him cross Huband Bridge into Percy Place and take something white out of his pocket. It was his handkerchief. He wrapped it round the knocker to deaden the sound.

After quite a long delay, the door opened slightly, and a conversation took place. Then Joe went in, and the door closed.

Bernard stepped smartly across the bridge and made a mental note of the number.

XV

UNCLE JOE WOKE up, like Byron on his wedding-night, thinking he was in hell. But it was only the red light of the morning sun coming through a red window blind, and the crackle of a few sticks that Mrs Ball had thrown on the fire when she got up at the rattle of the milkman's pails in Percy Place. Joe shut his eyes again and reached out his hand for comfort. It found none. He opened his eyes slowly and slowly turned his head. The pillow beside him was unoccupied, but there was a dent in it. He closed his eyes again and brooded.

He was worried about Milly. The girl had changed; and she must be demented about this Harvey boy. A good-looker, certainly, but without very much else to recommend him. He had tried to make up to Milly when he was going. Mrs Ball was calling him, as it were, from across the canal. Setting out for Percy Place Joe could not help contrasting Milly's young eyes, shining in her fair face, and the pouchy caverns from which Mona Ball would look into his and the aroma of brandy that always accompanied her experienced caresses. For a moment he had almost asked Carrie for a bed, and let Mona lump it. But he hadn't, he never obeyed that sort of impulse nowadays. Instead he had thought of Milly and of the days when he was entitled to call himself Captain and turned the heads of girls as young and fresh as she. He had been romantic. "I'm an old romantic, at heart, still," he told himself; and it was true that he had known love that kept him from sleeping and drove him to versify. It had never been plain sailing; there were heartbreaks and recriminations, and he had never failed to take any opportunities that offered, but there had once been a morning air to his love. He had walked among roses and listened to bird song; he had dreamed dreams.

Now it was a knock on a door and waiting; the shuffle of slippers over oil-cloth, and a door half-opened on a chain. "Oh, it's you. I wasn't quite sure. I'm afraid the gas is turned off. We may as well go upstairs. Have you a match handy? The draught put out the candle."

They didn't kiss; he followed her upstairs, her hair in curlers. Gone were the days when she was all bangles and bows. They knew one another too well.

She got into the brass bed and resumed a cigarette lying in the saucer of a tea-cup on the commode at her bed side. He undressed slowly, thinking of Milly, not hearing the stream of stale chat from the pillow.

"You have a fine pair of legs on you. I'll say that; and it's more than I can say for your wealthy friend. There's nothing I like less in a gentleman than a big carcase on top of thin pins, like a potato with matches stuck in it."

Later she said that she did not know what had come over her lately but she didn't feel like it this evening. He had turned to her as automatically as he had knocked on the door; and it was only when she raised difficulties that he felt he wanted her. Not her for herself, but as a shattered temple in which he could worship woman. When he went into her he would have to make an effort to leave the face blank and blot out Milly's, haunting him now. Mrs Ball had her own plans. She lit another cigarette and pretended not to notice his impatience.

"You know I can't stand a cat on the bed," he complained. But it wasn't really the cat, who lived on it, that angered him. It was the seediness of his situation. He seemed to want the woman beside him urgently; but it was the urgency of despair. He wanted, in fact, to have her and have done with it. She was one of his bad habits.

"You mustn't be cruel to poor pussy," she said, emphasising 'pussy' with a playful pat on Joe's cheek.

"Oh, God!" he moaned silently; for of all her moods he liked her least when she was playful. It reminded him of her age and of his. Not for that did he come here, but to keep hold, however shabbily, on life.

The staple of her talk was Talbot Thompson. It disgusted Joe to think of him in connection with her, but did not make him jealous. She spoke of the great man without much feeling. The general tenor of her remarks was that she had entertained him to oblige Joe. At that moment Joe saw her corset, salmon-pink, on a chair, and thought of his patron's buggish body; the juxtaposition of ideas was displeasing.

"You'll have to get me a drink, Mona," he said. He didn't say why.

"It never has the required effect, you know that, you cunning old rogue," she said, and gave him a brandy-scented kiss instead.

"If you don't fork out brandy, there will be nothing from yours truly tonight," he threatened.

"Nobody axed you, sir," she said.

The saucy little girl ploy was of all her repertoire the most nauseating.

"I'll bloody well help myself then." He was referring to the brandy. He knew the cupboard; but it was locked. "Give me the key or, by God, I'll kick the door in."

But, naked as a radish, he knew that he could, and would, do nothing of the sort.

She held up the key, then pushed it playfully under the clothes. "Here, give it to me."

"Fetch it for yourself, sir," She was in the mood for a romp.

When he extracted it eventually from between her thighs she had sufficiently involved him, so that when he pegged back the brandy, he was prepared to promise to 'take her out some time, for a change' in order to hasten his own tenancy of the key's recent lodging. Mrs Ball, refined, blew out the candle.

The circuit of the evening was complete; Joe, listening to the bed-springs and Mona in familiar concert, comforted himself with the thought that T. T. would pay a great deal for the comfort of this.

Alone in bed, in the light of morning, his eyes resting on a print of a Marcus Stone, looking pale against the floral paper that was coming away from the wall in the place where the gutter leaked at Christmas, he felt misgivings.

Downstairs he heard the rattle of crockery, and Mona's hoarse morning voice apostrophising the cat, which she absurdly called 'William'. He could see her as plainly as if she was in the room—the pink cotton nightdress, the blue flannel dressing-gown, the felt slippers. She would have to do better than that if she wanted to go visiting. She was always hinting that he should bring her about with him. She wanted to see a bit of life, she said.

His reflections were interrupted by the arrival of his hostess with a breakfast tray and *The Freeman's Journal*. Averting his eyes from the salmon-pink corset, which looked hideous in day-light, and Mrs Ball's felt slippers, he read in the newspaper that preparations were on foot for King Edward's visit but protests were to be expected.

Madame Maud Gonne was rallying the patriotic element in the Dublin Corporation to re-enact the scenes that marred the last visit of her late Majesty, Queen Victoria, in 1900.

"I know what I'd do to that one," Joe remarked. "Would you mind taking your corset off that chair, Mona. I hate the sight of women's underclothing in the morning."

"Oh, we are very particular," Mona said, but she bit her lip. She liked the touch of breeding in her Captain. It kept her up to the mark; and she loved him very dearly, or else why would she continue to put up with him? It was a one-way traffic most of the time.

When he came to go he found he hadn't a penny to bless himself with and had to ask Mona for a loan. He had to admit that she was open-handed. Easy come, easy go. That was Mona.

"You're not a bad old sort," he said and kissed her.

He was the better for it. A simple kiss, but it had the warmth of feeling. Mona was elevated by it from a thing to a person.

"Be off with you," she said, delighted. She watched him with mild pride as he stepped out. A gentleman. You had to admit it. But of no use to her in any way except for the odd tip for a race. But her's were more reliable than his. She had an instinct. He had none, although he thought he had. He was one of life's losers. You could see it even now in his affected jauntiness. He was bracing himself, not walking on air. He lived on that, and knew it gave no foothold. But Mona went as near to loving him as she had ever loved anyone, more than any other man, less than her mother who had gone the same hard road, about as much as she loved William, who was now mewing to be fed.

"I'm still fit. I can still do it. I'm as good as ever I was," Joe's fear of losing his patron was more pressing but not as deep-seated as his anxiety to preserve his potency. Mona acted as a recording angel. At least, he could look any man in the eye and challenge him to a cross-country on any mounts he chose. It was all he had to offer women, after compliments; and, unfortunately, with society departmentalised as it was, he had to keep his light under a bushel in the very quarters where he needed every resource he could command.

XVI

THE PLANS THAT were formed, sitting round the fire in
Buttercup Square, were invested with the glow of the coals and the
general happiness. In the morning light they looked more remote.
Made by a loving group, all with a common interest, they had to be
carried out with the help of the uncommitted and sceptical world.
Alan, for instance, had gone to bed feeling like Young Lochinvar,
but as he gazed through the raindrops sliding slowly down the
window-pane he saw no comfort in the grey pavement or in the first
stragglers, holding up their collars to keep the rain out.

Admittedly the prospect would have chilled a braver heart; and
after lunching with a friend, at rather unnecessary expense, he felt
less despondent. He had arranged to meet Milly in a tea-shop at
five, and then he would go back to dine with his aunts.

Milly kept him waiting; she couldn't help it; her nose was red
from exposure to the weather; she needed comfort and was not in
the mood to come to Alan's rescue. He looked a little glum when
she arrived and this disappointed her. Even when she explained the
delay—she had almost run to minimise it—he had still a ruffled air.
He explained it by his own despondency, and she did not help
matters by saying, "You are afraid of what your aunts will think."

"I haven't given them a thought. I hope I have got to an age
when I can decide upon my own career." But he would not have
sounded so peeved if she hadn't guessed precisely what had lowered
his spirits since yesterday.

Milly, who had been frantic at the delay (she had been caught by
the parent of one of her pupils and held for questioning), feeling
bedraggled from the rain, and hot from hurrying, had expected to
be met with eyes of love, and Alan's lack of patience cast her down.

"You had better not delay. You might be late for dinner."

"I don't mind if I am late."

Milly was not impressed. She had not thought about the rain.
She had looked forward all day to getting this glimpse of him. She
had seen them warm one another in a mutual glow, and thought
that Alan might have seen her home. Now she would refuse his

escort and urge him to hurry back to Blackrock, to the aunts who hated her.

"I'm sorry if I seemed fussy," he said, ashamed. She looked suddenly woe-begone. It was all in such a sad contrast to the splendours of yesterday. Harrison's tea shop, at the best of times, was not a very convivial place. It was an appropriate setting for gloom. She looked wanly at the buttered toast; and the sponge-cakes that in happier circumstances she would have finished off quick enough—she was hungry—now looked like funeral meats on the willow pattern plate.

Alan was not good at such a moment. He was too lacking in fortitude. What had been so wonderful about Milly was her radiance. She made everything seem easy. Her uncle, too, last night had woven a magic spell. Splendour and starlight. Now rain and despondency. Love shouldn't be like that: love should give life, colour and warmth: love should, above all, be happy; and here they were in tears in a tea shop. There were tears in Milly's eyes now, and he had to blow his nose to suppress a sympathetic flow.

"I was so anxious to see you. I felt sure something had gone wrong. I didn't in the least mind waiting for you. If I had been quite sure you were coming I'd have waited for you for ever—gladly."

He found her fingers under the table, and she let him hold them while, with the other hand she used a little handkerchief to repair her eyes. They were the centre of interest to the other patrons in the restaurant, elderly persons with square toes and string bags.

"It doesn't matter if the parliament scheme falls through. In two years I will have my money and the place. We will do very well, and I should have an income from the bar if I stick to it."

Milly felt better now. She let the toast go, but she sampled a sponge-cake.

"I wish I could help you," she said. "But if Uncle Joe's friend is prepared to put up the money, why shouldn't you stand for parliament? I would like you to be famous. If I were a man nothing would stop me. I'd become Prime Minister. I would make the most splendid speeches. It must be wonderful to move a great crowd, to feel it welded into a whole by the spell of—one's voice."

"I'm pretty useful at debating, but I don't see myself as a demagogue. I think I should feel a fraud raising people's expectations without being sure I could fulfil them."

"If you don't believe in yourself, nobody will believe in you."

"If you believe in me, Milly, I will believe in myself."

The red had gone from her nose. The look of strain that had made her face pinched had gone as well. She was beginning to glow again; and Alan was under her enchantment. There was nothing in the world he would not do for her. Time was going by—half an hour ago he had been fretted by delay—now all he asked was to sit for ever, looking at her.

At six o'clock a tired waitress put a bill for one shilling and sixpence on his plate.

"The toast has gone to waste," Milly said.

"What of it?"

To Milly, living under conditions when every penny had to be counted, his dash was attractive. He had long eye-lashes which came down over his dark eyes when he looked at her. His mouth was long and, for a man, rather full. If he went home with her, he might kiss her, but he couldn't if they parted here, in Westmoreland Street, convenient for his tram. Buttercup Square was off his route. He would be late if he went home with her. She hoped he would, although she would protest and say she was quite happy to go home by herself in the tram.

But he excelled himself and hailed a passing cab. Inside it they fell into a corner, his lips on hers until the driver's discreet cry to the horse, who needed no encouragement to stop—it was dying on its feet—reminded them that they were in Buttercup Square. He told the driver to wait and saw her to the door. Someone was opening the Terrys' door with a latch key. Milly caught a glimpse of Charley's reproachful face as the door closed.

Her day had ended splendidly and she was ready to sympathise with Dolly, who had had a very unpleasant innings with Lady Kelly.

Her ladyship had found no reference to her party in *The Irish Times* and until *Irish Society* arrived, in which a full account was promised, she could not be entirely happy.

Many aspects of the afternoon pleased her, if Mr Lane's fugitive appearance held out little promise of any closer aquaintance. She wondered if after a day or two it would be politic to write and ask his advice about a portrait. If she had a portrait of herself painted, a photograph of it, suitably framed, would make an appropriate present for Dolly instead of the cruet. She probably expected money, but she was marrying a man who, presumably, could support her. To give her money might be interpreted as an earnest that she could expect more. And that was now out of the question. Dolly had behaved with singular ingratitude and a slyness that was wholly out of character in getting engaged, or even in entertaining the idea without first obtaining her approval. It was a tacit admission that the connection was undesirable. And inviting these Roches to her party was inexcusable. The girl had lost her bearings. She had been so timid, annoyingly so (Fanny Kelly liked *spirit*) and all of a sudden she takes leave of her senses, issues invitations, gets engaged, and all without so much as 'by your leave or damn your soul', as her father's coachman used to say, when she was supposed to be out of hearing.

She decided to be cool with Dolly. Her expression of thanks was received coolly, her exclamations of pleasure at the entertainment were listened to without any response. But when Dolly said the Bernard Roches particularly enjoyed themselves, Lady Kelly raised her eyebrows. "I don't think I know anyone of that name. Surely you must be mistaken. Only my particular friends were invited yesterday."

"You said I could ask them," Dolly cried, hurt by this behaviour.

"Did I? I had no recollection of it. I'm glad to hear they enjoyed it, then; although I should not myself derive much pleasure from an entertainment at which I didn't know anybody who was present."

"They enjoyed themselves very much."

"I am glad to gratify them if you are going to be connected with them. I was surprised that you should think it fitting to get engaged without informing me."

"But I didn't know until yesterday. Bernard proposed at the party, at twenty minutes to five."

Lady Kelly assumed a wintry smile and shook her head slowly in absolute scepticism.

"I'm not a damn fool, Dolly."

These occasional lapses into violence threw Dolly into panic always. They were like the eruptions of an earthquake.

But by lunchtime Lady Kelly had called off the war. She wanted to hear about Milly. Everyone had commented on Milly's appearance and her total lack of propriety in talking all afternoon to that handsome young man, Alan Harvey. Lady Kelly was anxious to hear more about him. Dolly ingenuously told her all she knew, not noting a rising resentment in her listener's demeanour. She looked like a python preparing for a meal.

"And is the young man a Catholic?"

"No."

"I thought as much. Mark my words: he will not be allowed to marry Milly. Anyone could tell you that. The girl is making a fool of herself. And I think you would be doing her a kindness if you let her know it. You can say you have it from me. I should certainly advise her not to make such a show of herself. I can't understand your mother. If I were Carrie, I would have called her to heel in a brace of shakes."

It was very difficult to make Dolly unhappy at that time, but her employer succeeded. Her cutting manner carried more conviction than Uncle Joe's fireside prophecies. It was more in keeping with Dolly's experience. She was quite satisfied with Bernard herself, but she knew that Milly would be harder to please. Alan was perfect for her. She would be happy with him. This woman was always saying how much she wanted to help them; but when it came to the most important event in their lives, she seemed to derive a pleasure in belittling their chances of happiness.

"Try and help her. You can do it. I'm sure his old aunts will do what they can to prevent his marrying Milly; but they love one another and I don't know what she will do if anything goes wrong."

"Learn to put up with it as better women have before her" was all the Prestons' patron had to say.

She was thirty and Dr (as he then was) Kelly forty-eight when she had married. His proposal after Sunday dinner, when everyone else withdrew as if at a sign, was not unexpected. He had walked home with her after Mass on three occasions, and then the parish priest called on her father, and her mother told her that everything was arranged. She had only to consent when the proposal was made. She had nourished a secret passion for the manager of her father's business for some years, but she knew it was hopeless, and Dr Kelly, from humble beginnings, had at last put up his plate in Merrion Square. She had said 'yes' and Dr Kelly made a suitable little speech; but he didn't kiss her. He told her afterwards that he would have but he thought she might take the familiarity amiss. He was the most polite of men and always begged her pardon before he caressed her, and that was not often or for long. He told her that he would have preferred to become a priest but he had doubts about his vocation. He explained to her at considerable length, before the honeymoon, the reasons that had dictated his decision to propose. He had concluded that at her age she would be willing to accept him although he realised his age and appearance would not have recommended him to a younger woman. They had no children. The title had gone far to solace her. She would have 'done it' for that she told herself in her more sober moments.

Dolly knew nothing of this or she might have forgiven a bitterness which only revealed itself in sudden bursts. She was careful to avoid any further unpleasantness. Milly would eat her if she heard that she had not only discussed her but implored this woman's help. Dolly tried to like everyone; but she could not like Lady Kelly now. She would have to get away from her. It would require more courage than she felt she had; but Carrie, perhaps, would write and say she would have to keep her at home to get the trousseau ready and be prepared for a letter in reply ordering her to leave the arrangements to Merrion Square.

If Dolly could have seen Alan's return home she might have given Lady Kelly credit for a clear-eyed view of the case. He changed from the cab into a tram at the corner of Lansdowne Road, as the pace of the poor horse, livened up occasionally by the whip into brief staggering trots, was almost as slow as walking on his own two legs.

With Milly's kisses on his lips he defied his aunts. Miserable old women, why should he bother what they said? Nobody could prevent him from getting what his father had willed. He was twenty-three years of age. He could cock a snook at the whole family. But, as always, the bleakness that descended on the house, whenever his aunts guessed he was up to no good, petrified him. He had planned to overwhelm them with the news that he was about to stand for parliament. It would wake them up to the sort of man they were treating like an infant. But, somehow, over soup, he found that he lacked the impetus to begin; and at the main course it seemed hard to explain how news of such import had not been broken at once. The apple-pie came up and went down; coffee followed; and still nothing had been said. Aunt Jane's topic was the Royal visit in the summer. Susan wondered if the Union Jack flown on the last occasion would serve. The moths had been busy. Jane thought not. Susan begged leave to differ. They wrangled.

After dinner Alan went to his study to work. He joined his aunts before bedtime and drank chocolate. By then he decided that at breakfast over the newspaper was the time to make an announcement of this nature. "What do you think of the idea of my standing for parliament?" He had to pinch himself: it seemed so unlikely. And when he came down to breakfast he had decided that it would be foolish to mention the subject until he was quite certain that Joe's plans had matured. He had promised to report within a matter of days.

The report didn't arrive as soon as Alan's uncle, the Bishop. He rang up unexpectedly to say he was coming on a visit and particularly wanted to see Alan.

A visit from their brother was the greatest thrill life had to offer the Harvey 'girls' (as he liked to call them). The house was given a spring clean, stocks sufficient to supply a regiment on the march were laid in, and nothing else was discussed. The servants were given new aprons, and the hall-door, waiting for it until the weather was more suitable, got its coat of white paint. The Bishop came up to the Synod once a year, but stayed for that occasion in the University Club, which was convenient to the Representative Church Body's building, and occupied by other bishops, giving it during the week the appearance of a rookery.

He came up to Viceregal entertainments, when his name got into the newspapers, and on other occasions unbeknownst to the ladies in Blackrock who derived greater stimulus from his society than he did from theirs.

They knew this, and the compliment was all the greater. That he should expect to meet Alan was quite natural. Alan was his god-child, and if they were his guardians the sisters never failed to consult the bishop where Alan's well-being was concerned. His worldly wisdom was beyond question; his spiritual strength went without saying.

Alan never found him easy to get on with, but when younger was grateful for his half sovereigns. His uncle was a widower, having married a lady much older than himself as a step, his critics said, on the road to preferment. She was connected with the Beresford family, who had a magnetic attraction for bishoprics.

Uncle Tom elected to come for luncheon on a Sunday. He arrived by train and walked the half mile to the Harveys' house on Merrion Avenue at a stately pace, bowing slightly whenever he encountered a glance, and he encountered many because there was an air of consequence about him. He was grace personified; after-dinner grace. His progress was not unlike the mail-boat's stately arrivals at Kingstown Pier, a sight with which the people in these parts were familiar.

Jane at a top window was the first to sight him, and her cry, 'Here he comes', was taken up by Susan, putting a final touch to the table, and relayed to the kitchen. It reached Alan in his study, copying out a verse he had composed on waking and proposed to leave in Milly's letter-box that evening. The Bishop had declined an invitation to stay. He would lunch, take tea, and depart.

Alan's verses owed a little to the influence of Swinburne; he could only attempt poetry when he was in love; and he had only been in love three times. Never, never in love as he was now with Milly.

> Never did lover love like this!
> O lend me again those luscious lips!
> I faint, I fail, such heavenly bliss
> Pierces my heart like a hunter's knife.
> Heal the hurt before life slips
> My darling, my darling, my love, my wife,
> One more embrace, the scale o'er-tips . . .

He could go on like this indefinitely. Milly, he was surprised, did not find in herself a corresponding urge. "I suppose I am a more prosaic sort of animal," she said; but she kept his poems in a special bundle, tied with a different coloured ribbon from the one that bound his letters.

Like Drake, on another occasion, Alan refused to be hurried. His uncle could make his way up the drive without encouraging waves from the steps. He was going to read over his poem. He might not get an opportunity later.

It ended, he felt, abruptly; but if he went on he would be involved in another verse. The image of a pursuit in the woods was one that came to him frequently, and he confined himself to classical mythology. It enabled him to write things down that might embarrass her, he thought, if they were given a more contemporary setting. It was the difference between Titian's nudes and Manet's nudes; one was nude without, somehow, being naked: with the other, a girl in the buff was a girl in the buff. And he didn't want to think of Milly in that way. Since he had come to know her he disliked even the conversations of his friends because of the way they referred to women.

"O world," he demanded, "be nobler for her sake!"

Not wholly satisfied, nor yet without a certain pride in his facility, he folded the page meticulously, and addressed the envelope with a care that was unnecessary as he proposed to deliver it by hand. But Milly invited perfection. Nothing but the best was worthy of her.

He put the envelope in his pocket-book and went out to meet his uncle in the hall. The meal went well. The Bishop liked an audience, and there was none more attentive than his two sisters. They rose from the table in a glow, leaving Alan with his uncle. Coming in, the bishop said he wanted to have a word with him; and Alan, behind his benignity, sensed a purpose other than civility in this visit. He examined his conscience, and insofar as there were matters known to them both, he could think of nothing that was likely to cause friction. He had done quite well in his examinations. He had not asked for money. He had been attentive to his aunts. Unless they by any chance had enlisted him on their side against Milly. That possibility only occurred to him when his uncle pushed back his chair from the table and said, "I want to ask you a straight question and I expect a straight answer; are you engaged to be married?"

"I am not," Alan said at once. Then he felt his face hot, and saw his uncle's unwavering eyes noticing it.

"I am glad to hear it; and it confirms my opinion of the fellow and the rest of his story."

Alan's mind, busy with conjecture, suggested no reply. He waited. The Bishop re-arranged himself more comfortably for narrative.

"I had a call the other day from a young man called Bernard Roche. He has taken over a solicitor's practice in Waterford, and his visit was in the nature of a courtesy, I suppose. I confess I regarded it as an impertinence. He was a most self-satisfied young man, and he was pleased to tell me he was not only a friend of yours but likely to be connected through marriage. He was engaged, he said, to a Miss Preston and you were engaged unofficially to her sister. He expressed surprise that I was unaware of the fact.

"I had hardly time to recover from this when he said that you were to stand as a candidate for the Irish party in Westmeath. I must say at that I thought the young man had taken leave of his senses. He mentioned your sponsors as a Mr Talbot Thompson and a Captain John Dunne. I was taken aback, said it was all news to me, and tried as civilly as I could to disabuse his mind of any idea that I would be able to further his professional or social career in Waterford.

"My first impulse was to write to you, but I thought I could spare you unnecessary bother if I checked up on the young man's story. My own solicitor has a knack of getting information about everyone at a moment's notice. It was only when he told me that there were such people as Mr Talbot Thompson and Captain Dunne, that they hunted in couples, and that Dunne had a widowed sister, called Preston, with no money and two daughters on her hands, that I felt in duty bound to take up the matter with you."

He paused and took a slow sip of the port he had been persuaded to take after coffee. There was something in the ceremonious way he did it that told Alan he was being given time to prepare his defence.

"You can guess," his uncle continued, brushing crumbs off his apron, "how relieved I am to hear from your own lips that there is nothing in the story because—" he raised a plump hand to check Alan, about to intervene at this moment—"because I need not tell you how calamitous such a connection would be. Thompson, I hear, has so unsavoury a reputation in London that he is blackballed whenever he tries to join a decent club. Dunne is a shopkeeper's son from Mountmellick, who was cashiered from the army. Mr Roche, your putative brother-in-law, is the grandson of the hardware merchant in my town, and for the son of a soldier and the grandson of one who was murdered by Fenians to stand for the Irish party would be an act so disloyal, so contemptible, that I would find myself obliged to cut off any communication with you if I heard you had even contemplated it."

With this he turned as if on a pivot and raked Alan's abashed countenance with a large and luminous eye. Alan struggled to say something. He felt as if he were waist-deep in quicksand, and that if he could not establish a foothold on firm ground soon he was lost. But his uncle, having rehearsed his part, was determined to play it out.

"What occurred to me," he began, and then made an unepiscopal noise which by looking enquiringly at the ceiling, he seemed to imply came from somewhere up there. "I shouldn't drink port in the middle of the day," he said, and then, frowning at his glass, "What occurred to me was that you might through good-nature and inexperience have given these people sufficient encouragement to seem to justify their presumption. I don't want to enquire into your manner of life. You are now a man; but I am your uncle and I am very fond of you, my dear boy, very fond indeed. I have neither chick nor child of my own, and it has sometimes occurred to me that we don't see as much of one another as we should. I should like to think"—here moisture blurred the eye fixed on Alan—"I should like to think that if you were in any sort of trouble—and the best and wisest of us gets into trouble sometimes—that you would turn to me. You can't confide, in the way I mean, in your excellent aunts. Men of your own age lack experience that only time—believe me—can bring. If you are in any difficulty confide in your old uncle. Let us put our heads together."

Whether he had more to say Alan never knew, a repetition of the former sound led to a concentration on the ceiling as if determined this time to find the vent.

Alan had his opportunity. His uncle obviously knew everything. Now was the moment when he could proclaim his independence and justify his pledge to Milly; but he found that the words wouldn't come. What he heard himself saying was: "I think I should explain. I am a friend of the Prestons, and even if their uncle is disreputable—and they know it, but what can they do about it?—they are very nice people. Mrs Preston is a perfect lady, and her husband had a tremendous reputation at the bar. I do know that. I met them with the Days, at the dance they gave for the girl's coming out. And they have entertained me very kindly. I know about the shop; but that was not the family's fault; the uncle ruined them by his extravagance. You can't hold them responsible. As for parliament, that was a sort of joke. Talbot Thompson, whoever he is, wants to put a member into parliament, and the uncle asked me if I'd like to be a candidate. We were ragging. It seems to me that young Roche was trying to impress you. He is rather consequential and he is engaged to the elder Preston girl, a nice girl, but not very pretty."

The Bishop's eye never left his nephew's face. It was a knowing eye with the soft stare a cow's has, as encouraging and as non-committal.

When Alan finished, there was a moment's silence. Then the Bishop said, "You fancy the pretty one."

Even this reference to Milly was enough to bring the gallant to a sense of shame. Miserable, he redeemed himself so far as to say, "Milly is very good-looking and a perfect lady."

He was aware of the apologetic tone in which the ladyhood of the Prestons was made an issue; but his uncle had distorted the picture and dragged in every damning circumstance. It was an exercise in dialectics, an attempt to show Alan his folly. Neither was in the least doubt what was in the mind of the other.

As if to partake in a communion of fellowship with erring humankind, the Bishop raised his glass and lowered the contents; then, very slowly, closing his eyes, he licked the last drop off his rather full lips. There was nothing impulsive about him; and his attitudes were calculated; but their appearance was conciliatory. He had come, not to accuse, but to help. Alan was out of his depth.

"Don't think your uncle was always proof against a pretty face, dear boy, or that he doesn't understand your situation. Believe me, we all go through it; and I am not such a benighted ass as to tell you you will look back on this some day with a smile. I can quite believe what you say about these Prestons. I'm sure they are excellent people and that the girls are well brought up. You must forgive me, who has never seen your Milly, if I seem hard-hearted when I say that they will do very well but they are not our sort of people. I met young Mr Roche who is engaged to the elder girl. That is their mark. As you say, it is not their fault they have shops in the family. There is nothing to be ashamed of in owning a shop. There is no need to explain or excuse it; but, at the same time, we don't marry shopkeepers in our family. On the whole we have done the right thing. We have lived up to the responsibilities of our position. I am sure you have not the least intention of marrying this young lady. But you should think of her. She is poor. You are going to be comparatively well-to-do. She has no position. You are a Harvey of Lingfield. Is it fair to turn her head and fill her with impossible hopes? The mother is, I am sure, all you say; but when a young man who is a catch comes along, can you blame her if she puts down some bird-lime for him? Mothers do. Even in our lot we have match-makers. I could tell you tales. Don't break hearts, Alan. It is a cad's trick. This girl will find a husband, if she is pretty, just as her sister has, from someone in her own set. But if you turn her head you will make her discontented. Your aunts tell me you invited her out here. Was that wise? Was it fair to them? I am only asking you to take thought, to consider others as well as yourself, a hard thing to do at three and twenty."

"I haven't been thinking of myself. I wish you could meet Milly, Uncle. You'd see what an exceptional person she is. I have never met a girl so intelligent as well as pretty, and she could be anyone. I hope the aunts were not unfair to her. They gave her a rotten welcome."

"Your aunts are excellent women, Alan, but you presented them with a difficult situation. Of course, they took fright. And you can't blame them if they tried to protect you in the only way they knew how."

"But protect me from what? Listening to you, Uncle, one would think Milly was a street girl instead of an angel. Her father was a barrister, a member of my own profession. I've met her family. They are charming."

The Bishop smiled, patiently.

"I take your word for it, Alan. In the ordinary course I'd have nothing to say; but where my nephew and his future is involved I feel a duty to grasp his hand when I see him on the edge of a precipice."

"A precipice! That's absurd."

"If you marry a girl like that, and put yourself outside the pale, you'll spend the rest of your life regretting it. I don't want you to look back and say nobody helped you, nobody warned you, nobody held out a hand."

Alan said nothing. A load of depression had settled on him. He did not feel strong enough to shake it off. He felt his family and everything to do with them as jailers; but he lacked the energy to declare his independence. His uncle seemed to have grown. He filled the whole room, absorbed all the air.

"It's too hot in here," he said. "Would you like to come into the study?"

"I think we ought to join the girls in the drawing-room. Don't take me up wrong, Alan. Think over what I say, and remember, if you want to talk to me or if you find your situation difficult, don't be ashamed to let your old uncle know, and don't be too proud to ask him for help. Bless you, boy."

As with many stout men he had a rubberlike resilience, and there was a certain bounce in his walk which set off his pomposity and suggested good cheer as well as self-satisfaction. His entry lifted the spirits of the two women, who were wondering what was happening in the dining-room.

Alan followed him, hating his great round bulging back, hating the old faces that lit up on his entry, hating the misery of it all. Here were only wrinkles and the prospect of boredom; less than ten miles away, was Milly. He could leave them and join her. He could stay with her for ever. What power had they to keep him here and passive, while they planned to ruin his happiness, to make his life as narrow and dreary as their own? Whatever the power was, it held him. He passed round coffee cups. He sat down. He crossed his knees. He listened.

"I have a little scheme on foot," the Bishop said at four o'clock precisely. "I meant to keep it as a surprise for Alan's birthday; but I am no good at keeping secrets. I've been talking to the Marquess, and he agrees with me that this scheme of Wyndham's is the beginning of the end for the landowners in this country. Little by little the flood gates are being opened; and if we look into the future we can only see a time when the peasants will not only have taken the land, they will take over the running of the country. Read the signs: the Local Government Act of '98 was the death blow to the landed interest in local affairs. Now we have compulsory sales to tenants. Look at the agitation to put a Roman Catholic Chapel into the grounds of Trinity College! And it's not the peasantry who are doing these things. The cracks are within. It's the politicians. They think by throwing sops they will keep the hounds at bay and forget that appetite grows by what it feeds on. You can postpone the evil day at the same time and by the same measures as you ensure its coming to pass."

Alan hardly listened. He thought of Milly in the cab, Milly's lips on his. He wished this old bumbling bee would take himself off.

"I thought you were going to tell us something cheerful," Jane said in her downright way. "Susan and I were saying just that before you came."

The Bishop smiled. Susan gave a nervous glance at Alan. He kept his eyes on the shining toes of his new boots.

"Patience. I believe in marking out the ground. What I am trying to say is simply this: Alan's future probably lies across the water. I think he should continue his bar studies in London. And now let me take the rabbit out of the hat. I've kept you waiting long enough. Alan, as we know, doesn't come into his income until he is twenty five. It so happens I've had a little windfall, a thousand pounds."

The ladies clucked and crowed.

"I don't want to blow it, and thank God I have sufficient for my simple needs. What I suggest is that Alan takes it and uses it to keep himself properly in London. Later on he can pay me back. He will have the means to do that; and I believe, once he finds his feet, he will have a much brighter future at the bar in England than in this country, judging by all the signs. May I say—in case Alan is getting ready to shout me down—that I spoke of this to the Marquess and he said that if he were in Alan's position he wouldn't hesitate. He told me that I was to say so. He takes a real interest in you, Alan. I've mentioned that before. It's very gratifying, I must say."

There was implied in this—and it escaped nobody—that the Marquess would be perturbed, to say the least, if he knew what had been recently on foot—Irish Party candidates, Milly Preston, Talbot Thompson, bankrupt uncles, shops in Mountmellick—a ghastly picture for a Marquess to contemplate. Alan threatened even his Uncle's most valued friendship by his irresponsibility.

The idea of losing their nephew made the two women desolate. They were moved to tears at the prospect and at the Bishop's kindness, for they had no doubt that the scheme and his loan were all the result of Alan's folly. They were going to have to pay for it. But he had this exciting prospect before him. He had only to shake off a little girl whom he would forget in three months. They had to give up the first object of their existence; the Bishop to put off the enjoyment of a thousand pounds. Would the boy ever realise what was being done for him? Would he ever know what love really meant? Would he ever be thankful? Probably not. He would see himself as an injured innocent, as a victim.

Such was life; but what mattered was to do the right thing, cost what it may. Well, thank God, they were brought up that way. And thank God for the Bishop. And thank God for the Marquess and all the forces operating on the right side. Cheerfully would they make their sacrifice too. Thank God they knew their duty. As for gratitude—one must not look for that.

Damp and questioning eyes rested on the object of so much bounty. How was he responding? Alan kept his eyes on the toes of his boots. When he raised them he was lost. They waited.

"It's very kind of you, Uncle," he said "but—"

A sigh broke from his aunts. All this and the boy was so far gone that he could only respond with a 'but'. The Bishop moved his head, a gesture that told them to be at peace. He could deal with 'buts'.

"Are you going to tell me it is a quarter to six already," he said later, taking out the great turnip watch the Marquess gave him. Nobody was, of course. Nobody wanted to. His presence was comforting to the girls. So long as he was there, Alan had an excuse for doing nothing. When he left, the prospect to Alan of an evening with his aunts was daunting, nor was he quite sure how he should behave towards them. If the Bishop's visit was an act of complicity, he should strike out. They tried to rule his life, these old women buried in the past; he could cope with them on their own ground, but if they started to plot against him, life would become so intolerable it would be better to go away. In this manner the idea of going to London took lodgment. Of course it meant being away from Milly, but they could write; there would be holidays. Perhaps she might even come to London. She was so independent and capable; he would look around and find her work to do.

Perhaps the Bishop's visit, which seemed so disastrous and fatal, was, after all, a blessing in disguise. Of course, he was trying to break up the understanding with Milly. But why not hoist him with his own petard? Why not accept the offer, go to London, keep faith with Milly? Leaving her out of consideration there was much in what his uncle said. The future for landlords in Ireland was dim; and he, although he liked the countryside and paternalistic dealings with peasants, did not at all relish a prospect of being ruled by peasants and country shopkeepers. There was nothing radical in Alan's nature. All his instincts were in line with his relations'. What separated them was age and love—Milly, in fact.

When the Bishop finally went, Alan pretended to remember an engagement to dine at the Inns and accompanied him into Dublin, leaving 'the girls' to talk away to their hearts' content. Earlier in the day he would have dreaded the Bishop's company; but now that he had decided to turn his uncle's plan to his own purposes he rather relished it.

No resolution is a secret; Alan's manner denoted a change of heart; the Bishop observed it at once, but he drew the wrong conclusion. He thought he had won; he did not know that he was being played with. He was satisfied. He would not seek to press home his advantage. Enough to have sown the seed.

And therefore, when they came outside, after an expression of gratification for his entertainment and regard for the girls— "wonderful characters, true as steel"—he threw off his earlier preoccupations and decided to entertain his nephew with the manner that had got him where he was and made him a favourite with the Marquess.

He had never depended on theology for preferment; and it was his capacity to make common sense his rule of life that endeared him to laymen. He was never, as the Marquess observed, 'unduly pi'. He dined out regularly, ever since his wife died, in houses where she would have objected to the arrangements. Charming women from London without their husbands were always given the benefit of the gospel lesson about the throwing of stones. Reproof was reserved for outrage. When the Bishop thundered from the altar he had his congregation one hundred per cent behind him.

When a stray cat rushed past them, he said "If I had a stone handy, I'd have pegged it at him. Reminds me of Oxford days, we were terrors to strays, dogs or cats. It was sport. We were great raggers in those days."

He exchanged a greeting with the lamplighter when they met him on his mission. "Gas was a wonderful invention. I hope it will never be displaced by electricity. My scientific friends tell me that it is now acknowledged in Germany that the bad summers we have been getting are due to the increased use of electricity. I don't believe in tampering with nature. God had His plan—and you may see it in the social as well as the scientific sphere—and man interferes with it at his peril. The pace of modern life is unnatural. The Marquess was trying to persuade me to buy myself a motor-car with that money I hope to see you using in London. I said to him: 'Tyrone'—I always call him by his christian name, knew him since he was a child 'if a chariot was good enough for Elijah, I think it should be good enough for me'. I thought he was going to choke. 'Have you heard the Bish's latest?' I hear he has been saying everywhere he goes. Bless him."

A tram hove in sight, and the Bishop quicked his pace. "This will save us a walk."

Trains, he felt as a rule, were more consonant with his dignity than tram cars, but he had a frolicsome side; and it amused him to board the humbler vehicle in the company of a youngster, and a good-looking youngster. They made a spectacular pair, he well knew. He was proud of his nephew's looks; and the wisdom of his decision to help him to remove them to London struck him forcibly as he let his shrewd but luminous eye move calmly over the faces of their fellow-passengers. It was comfortable to be sure of one's position, to stand right with God, and to be able to look with pure benevolence at faces which one would never have to look at again.

The Bishop felt himself under no constraint to lower his voice. So far as he was concerned his fellow-passengers were entitled to listen to what he had to say if it amused them. And in his tone this was apparent.

He dropped his voice when it suited him, as when he discovered that he had nothing less than half a sovereign in his purse, and wanted Alan to produce the necessary pennies for their fares. He dropped his voice to ask how long Susan had had the habit of winking; he had not realised it was involuntary, and had winked back during the luncheon. And he dropped it again when, to Alan's surprise, he invited him to come to the pantomime, now ending its long run at the Gaiety Theatre.

Nothing in the solemnity of his manner when he pleaded another engagement to excuse himself from dining at Blackrock suggested that he had a spree of this sort in mind. It would have been so pleasant, Alan thought, if he could have suggested that he would fetch Milly in a cab, and then the three of them would have had 'a really jolly evening'. But that was out of the question.

"I'll dine at the club. I may meet some other lonely old buffer," he said. He had, Alan remembered, a passion for the stage and regretted that his parents had never allowed him to follow his vocation. "If you must play-act, go into the Church," his father said. "You can enjoy yourself preaching sermons."

They parted company at the corner of Dawson Street. A hint of furtiveness in Alan's manner was due to his having to pretend to be taking a northward-bound tram, when in fact he intended to go in the other direction.

"Think over what I said; but don't keep me waiting too long. We mustn't waste time if you are to take up your studies in London; and if you leave it there I might be tempted to use the money on the installation of bathrooms in the Palace. God bless you."

The Bishop in his benevolence was not keeping a proper lookout and a cyclist, cornering at speed, missed him only by a fraction of an inch and sent his silver-topped cane flying across the street. He was at once surrounded by a sympathetic crowd of bystanders, one of whom retrieved the stick and received an absent-minded sovereign as a reward. The Bishop became on the spot a beloved object.

"Are you right, your Reverence? Or is it kilt y'are? It's them scorchers. They have no regard for man nor beast so long as they can go scorching along the roads terrifying the life out of decent pederasts, moving as God meant them to instead of tempting providence on contraptions meant only for monkeys."

Another sovereign bought the silence of the speaker, who was wrapped in a shawl.

A member of the Dublin Metropolitan Police, almost as impressive in appearance as the Bishop, now came on the scene and was overwhelmed in his turn by willing witnesses.

"I thought he was kilt," one woman said. Another was prepared to testify that not one, but a swarm of bicyclists, had been responsible for the outrage.

It took half an hour to get the Bishop to his club and to persuade the Constable that no damage had been sustained. It was an expensive experience. Alan left his uncle in the smoke room of the University Club, staring moodily at the statue of the Earl of Eglinton and Winton, across the way. Hand outstretched in the gaslight, he reminded the Bishop of his recent recklessness. Those two sovereigns rankled all evening; he forgot the offer of a thousand pounds.

Milly had a holiday on Saturday, and this one she spent alone contentedly. She had no desire to go with her mother and Dolly to a tedious entertainment. She did not expect a visit from Alan; but she rather revelled in the quietness of the house. Thinking of Alan, sure of him and siding with him in her mind against the opposition of his family, she almost took a positive pleasure in his absence, as a child will in hoarding up a cake or sweet and postponing the pleasure of devouring it.

Conscious of the duty to improve her mind, she sat down with a novel by George Eliot and a volume of Newman's Essays. Her own thoughts, she discovered, were more exciting than either and seemed to get between her eyes and the printed page.

She gave up the effort and glanced instead at the society paper which Carrie religiously bought to keep up with what was happening only to depress herself by the weekly reminder that she might as well have been living in New Zealand for all its relevance to the life she led. Now that the girls had seemed to get over their lack of opportunity, she was possibly less upset by the details of balls and weddings and at homes they were never invited to attend.

Milly had developed a satirical approach to the subject. Sometimes its artificiality revolted her; and she considered how someone so human and good at heart as her mother, and who had tasted the bitterness of its insincerities, could still hanker after the life it represented. She got, of course, her own amusement by seeing through pretensions. Some of the happenings reported were plants, occasions unworthy of notice.

What sort of person ran the paper, Milly wondered as she read that "Mr Fred Hatton, who plays the Grand Vizier at the Gaiety Pantomime, as well as being Assistant Stage Manager, was born in Belfast. Like most Irishmen he is rapidly pushing himself to the front." What kind of mind was capable of conceiving that paragraph? She studied the photograph of Mr Fred H. Hatton. His hair, brushed back, was crinkled like sand over which an incoming tide has crawled. He looked too harmless to push himself or anyone else. It was the effect these studio portraits had.

Her eye rested on the features of Mr Lewis Waller in a trilby hat. He was better-looking in his showy way than Alan, but only just, and not so young, not young enough. Carrie would take seats for the matinee. He affected her strangely. The girls laughed about it.

She read about the dance given by Sir Charles and Miss Cameron. " 'Not a ball', the hosts assured their friends in the interval since the invitations had gone out." Sir Charles had won a medal awarded for sanitary work, and his guests congratulated him on his success. "Mrs Power O'Donoghue, who, being in mourning, merely looked in, wore a black tulle dress, flecked with jet, and jet arrows stabbing her hair."

Her brief appearance must have paralysed the dancers at what was not a ball. When was a ball not a ball, Milly wondered? Was this merely an excuse to economise on refreshments?

What degree of mourning would have forbidden Mrs Power O'Donoghue to do more than 'merely to look in', and what were those arrows like?

Somebody knocked at the door. She had been told never to answer it, but she called to Mary to keep to her quarters as she crossed the hall. She always felt uneasy when she heard her tramp upstairs to do what they could do so easily for themselves.

Milly opened the door.

"Alan!"

He looked, she could not tell how, 'different'.

"Mother's out. She went with Dolly to a music party." But when he took her in his arms she added, "Mary's downstairs."

She was about to eat her supper by the fire and invited him to join her. This meant, inevitably, Mary's appearance, a succession of speeches, spectacular noises in the kitchen, Mary's reappearance, further speeches. Even when she eventually withdrew, Milly observed that she was likely to pop her head in at any moment to ask how they were getting on. So he did not sit as close to Milly as they would have liked.

There was something unsettled and unsettling in his manner. He was too demonstratively affectionate; she would have preferred him to be tender and less hectic. He asked her about herself in an unwonted and unconvincing way; as a rule they talked about his affairs, and she surmised that this marked change was due to something that had happened recently. Her misgivings returned. It was foolish to have felt so safe. When he went so far as to enquire after Dolly's doings, she decided to smoke out his secret.

"What have you been up to?"

"Up to?"

"I know you. There's something afoot that I have not been told about. What is it?"

Then he told her everything; but he told it wrong. He was not sober enough about it. He made too little of the threat of separation.

"Where? How?" she said when he suggested that she should come and work in London.

He was upset by her tone. He liked encouragement.

"Honestly, I think Uncle's right. What future is there for me in this country? Our lot has been sold up the river. The writing has been on the wall ever since that old humbug Gladstone stuck his nose into our affairs. I hear what is going on. You don't know about the seditious newspapers that are in circulation. There's a branch of anarchy as busy in Dublin as it is abroad . . . a man called Griffith, a most vindictive scoundrel. You should see some of the poison he poured out when our men were fighting in South Africa. The pro-Boer lot are carrying on their mischief. There's a man called Martin in my club who is an out-and-out rebel. Of course, he is a Catholic. Oh, I beg your pardon. But you know what I mean.

"If the Liberals get in they'll revive the Home Rule cry; and then there's all the Irish language revival. Such rot. It sounds harmless enough; but I'm told that it is being used as a cover up for real revolution. Balfour thinks he can buy them all off; but that won't work. We are in a minority here; and if the British Government is not prepared to defend us we have no future."

Milly listened, unimpressed. Why was he giving her a history lesson? Although she was a Catholic she had been brought up with the same ideas as his. Her family had been over-anxious to impress Protestants with their loyalty and had played down their religious difference. They wanted to be let in on the Protestant monopoly; they wanted to be privileged and to cut a figure socially. They were as anxious as the Viceroy himself to keep the Nationalists out of positions of influence. 'Castle Catholics' was the current term of Nationalist contempt for the Prestons' attitude; and Balfour had been heard to say that all the best men in Ireland were rebels, his supporters were lackeys.

As Alan went on Milly found his argument less and less attractive. It was, somehow, unworthy of youth. It was middle-aged, and as he spoke he crumpled up and lost his beauty. But that was not what upset her. She took no interest in politics and, being away for so long, knew nothing about them; what did disturb her was a conviction that Alan was only talking as a screen.

"Go to London. Sell Lingfield. Forget you were Irish. Shake off nationality and Catholics and riff raff of that description. Become a club man in St James's. Do everything your uncle expects of you. But don't ask me to encourage you. You will have to forget about me."

"Forget you, Milly! How? Why?"

"It's part of the plan. You know quite as well as I do that the reason for this sudden decision is not the political situation. Why not tell the truth? Your relations have determined to rescue you from an undesirable entanglement, and the only way to do it is to bribe you to go to England."

"Bribe me! Milly! I won't let you say that. It's untrue. It's damned unfair. And it's not even a gift, merely a loan. Do you think I want us to be separated? I only want to do what will bring us together. Uncle made no conditions about the money."

"He doesn't need to."

"What do you mean?"

"He knows you too well. If once you go away you will shake Dublin and everything to do with Dublin off your feet. And that includes me. Why not be honest?"

"I won't let you say that. I won't."

He had stood up to move plates about, and Milly, on a low chair, spoke into the fire. Now he knelt beside her and put his arms round her. She stiffened and turned her cheek away from his kisses. He became desperate and by exerting all his strength drew her back. When he leaned over to kiss her, she lost balance and lay in the thick black wool of the hearth rug, which made her face the whiter by contrast. He held her head and pressed his lips on hers, bruising them. Still she didn't yield to him; it had become a trial not so much of a physical strength as of will. Her surrender when it came astonished him. He knew very little about women and nothing at all about passion. It was as if she had come apart; some force in herself was too strong for her, and it called out to what wasn't there in him, although he stormed her lips, her eyes, her hair with kisses. Under her blouse he felt for the first time the small round firmness of her breast. She tried weakly to take his hand away. But she had lost all strength. He could have done with her as he pleased had the response in his loins to the sudden stiffening of the nipple under his hand overcome him.

His pursuit was over. She was his. Everything in her behaviour, since the day she joined him in the cab in Capel Street, made obvious that if this moment came they would pass the stage of drawing back. Respect, timidity, he was freed from everything that would normally have kept him in check by her surrender.

But at the very moment when everything he had dreamed of was his for the taking, he had a sudden impulse not to take it, an impulse that had in it no regard for her, there was neither tenderness nor compassion nor reverence in his resistance, no last moment effort to save her from herself, but a clear vision of his own situation. Here was all in life he wanted to possess and he could possess it; but having possessed it, he would himself be possessed. Love was to be paid for with freedom. The cave was a cage. What he thought he valued most in life should have come as a concession not as a free gift. What should have been a conquest had become a surrender. There is before the first time lovers lose themselves a moment of choice when hesitation is refusal. Alan hesitated. He was not ready for that, yet.

Her eyes were closed. He kissed them. He sank his face in her hair. The ticking of the clock on the mantelpiece was the only sound in the room. Neither of them had heard it until then; it marked the running down of passion, measured the cooling of blood. When Milly asked him to move his arm as her's had gone asleep, her voice was her own.

When Mary came in loudly to fetch the trays, she decided that there had been some 'coolness' between them. She regretted this, as she had rejoiced for them in the opportunity they had by being alone to forward a work of which she wholly approved. Then she noticed Milly's blouse and decided that the young gentleman must have forgotten himself. It would explain the coolness. They ought to get married soon if that was the way it was.

"You'd want to put a comb to your hair, Miss Milly. It looks as if the sparrows had been nestin' in it."

She would not make mischief; but she was genuinely anxious lest 'the mistress' might notice something amiss when she came in with Miss Dolly; the young man might get his marching orders. That would be a pity.

Milly jumped up and looked at herself in the overmantle, in the corner of which she saw a printed card. Lady Kelly, it said, had changed her at-home day from Friday to Thursday.

XVII

WINTER SLIPPED BY: Milly gave up coaching and started to attend the College of Art without making use of Mr Lane, whose pursuit Lady Kelly abandoned when he made it clear that she was of no interest to him unless she would buy pictures. As Lady Kelly derived little pleasure from pictures and none from the work of the artists Lane recommended, she decided that he was a charlatan, and told her circle that she had determined on no account to let him darken her doors again. She kept up with Carrie, in whom she succeeded in arousing a sense of guilt over Dolly; and in this way retained a connection with the family and at the same time let it be understood that she had suffered from the connection.

Dolly, without any prompting from her mother, sent her little propitiatory gifts—thin volumes of essays, handkerchiefs, sealing wax in a pretty box—and these were acknowledged on sheets of mourning paper, retained after seven years for use in such a case as this.

The excitement of the School of Art and confirmation at an early stage from the teachers that she had considerable talent as a draughtsman gave Milly the outlet she needed. She came and went to the classes and did not mix at all with the other students, from a shyness that was mistaken for conceit. Milly had a proud way of walking; holding her head high, and being rather tall and young, the impression she made was of arrogance. Her smile was attractive and disarming; but it was slow to come. When talked to she had an attentive way of listening that lent her an air of seriousness. There was a youthful formidableness about her which her precocious talent assisted. It frightened even Lady Kelly; it had made Alan's aunts realise at first meeting that their nephew was in grave danger.

During these months, while she had no cause of complaint about Alan's attentiveness, there was still some constraint in their relationship. Both of them were aware of it. Their love-making was by mutual tacit consent kept in strict bounds; neither wanted to look into the abyss again. Alan put down the subtle change in their manner towards each other to resentment because he made no formal proposal, and let their relationship be understood. He tried to explain to Milly that an official engagement would involve him in such a wealth of family trouble that it was only prudent to put it off until a suitable moment came. That this was not necessarily his twenty-fifth birthday he suggested, without being specific as to what other prospect he had of independence. His uncle's death? But he was not more than sixty and in robust health. A change of heart on his aunts' parts. But they never saw Milly, and Alan was careful not to let them know—whatever they may have guessed—about his engagement. Milly was never mentioned in Blackrock.

Alan said he had written to his uncle declining his offer. He had decided to complete his law studies at the King's Inns in Dublin. When he was called there was little difficulty, he understood, in being called in England if the prospects in Ireland then had deteriorated as his uncle predicted. Alan told Milly this to put her mind at rest. He was impressed by the extent of his sacrifice. And he could hardly conceal his disappointment that Milly was not more enthusiastic, more surprised, or more apparently grateful. She took his renunciation almost as a matter of course. He did not show her the letter or admit that he had used a phrase in it designed to mislead the Bishop about his motive for getting Alan to London. Milly had made it plain enough that if she were in Alan's shoes she would have told her family to go to hell. She would certainly not have tried to hoodwink them. And an instinct that the truth would not please her prevented her from enquiring too closely about the details of the correspondence.

She did not want a formal engagement. She had no desire to flaunt an engagement ring. As they could not marry until Alan was twenty-five, she was quite satisfied to wait. The interval was not going to be dull; she had discovered a new and powerful interest in life, her growing talent. She was in love with Alan, and if she saw him now without his old aura, she did not love him less. he charmed her, he attracted her. She would not want life without him; but he was incapable of her depth of feeling. He had caused her to betray herself. Deep—very deep—down, she bore him a grudge.

Some day she would have to have it 'out with him', in the meanwhile like a pea under a mattress it spoilt what should have been perfect. If Alan looked at another girl or praised one or did not enter at once into her enthusiasms, she felt resentment, and then was ashamed and annoyed by her ungenerous attitude. Pettiness warred with her idea of herself. But there were days that were as happy as the first, when love shone from a clear sky.

The skating rink was still one of Dublin's standing amusements; but it had lost—as did everything in the city eventually—its social *réclame*. Willie Wilde, in hopeful search of a rich wife, and usually engaged to at least two current prospects, used to fancy himself as a gallant figure on roller skates, but since the evening when someone came to a fancy dress party as Jesus Christ, word had gone round that the prudent should lock up their daughters and keep them away from the rink. A girl who frequented it in 1903 earned a reputation for being 'fast'. Reggie Terry, it need hardly be said, was a regular visitor, and his attendant was Kitty Hopkins, than whom there was no more fluent performer.

Some of Milly's art class were making up a party and asked her to join them. It was the first gesture any of her new companions had made towards her, and she did not want to refuse. But having done the agreeable thing, she was faced with the prospect of an argument with Carrie, who was bound to disapprove. Some busybody had begged her not to let 'her girls' be seen at Earlsfort Terrace. Milly was too busy to wish to make an issue of this, but she was an expert, having learnt to skate on ice at school, and would have enjoyed the forbidden exercise. If Alan had agreed to go with her, she would have gone surreptitiously; but he shared Carrie's views that the rink was not a suitable place for Milly to be seen. She rather liked him to be stuffy on her account. It made her feel secure, as if they were married and he had the right to rule her conduct; not that she had as yet made up her mind about the extent to which a modern woman should allow her husband to dictate to her. Dolly, when they argued about it, took the view that a girl would do whatever pleased her husband. What satisfaction was to be got from disobeying him and having rows? Milly thought that this was mere tyranny. Once a husband learnt that he couldn't order his wife's life to please himself he would learn to be civil. After all, he had something to lose if they got on bad terms.

Dolly, scenting 'Milly's awfulness' about to raise its head, closed the subject. "I can't see any prospect of disagreement when two people really love; they will only want to please each other," she concluded.

She saw marriage fixed on the barometer at SET FAIR; Milly already knew that its temperature would rise and fall. She was much cleverer than Dolly, but not so wise.

When Alan said that he had to work and would not see her for a few days, Milly felt under no constraint to tell him about the party. It would only lead to an argument; and he had shown himself rather suspicious of the Art School, having a poor opinion of artists, even the local variety.

Milly was surprised to find how much lawless pleasure she got out of the prospect of an unconventional evening. She avoided telling Carrie a lie by describing the entertainment as a birthday party at the Art School, which it was, and not adding that they were going to finish their soup, sandwiches and beer in Kildare Street and then walk along the side of the green to the skating rink opposite Alexandra College and behind the grounds of Lord Iveagh's mansion.

There were twelve in the party, a few of them were paired off, and she discovered that she had been assigned to a young man with a strong Belfast accent. He had given her furtive glances in class, and she now realised that the party was not as casually got together as she had supposed. He must have put someone up to inviting her; and they were left much together. Artists, she had been told, were licentious; but this young man, whatever was going on in his head, was morbidly shy. He had a way of shutting an eye and screwing his face up on one side whenever he said anything, which she found disconcerting. And when she tried to ask him a question, to encourage him to talk about himself, he was studiously cautious. She couldn't get him to assent to any proposition. And there were frequent silences between them, which he seemed to find natural, as he winked whenever she was about to despair, and seemed to be quite happy so long as she stood near and watched him eat.

Going to the rink the party marched up the street in three rows, linking arms. Some of the girls were smoking cigarettes, and nobody wore a hat. They were stared after—wild bohemians, the sort that went to the rink nowadays.

Milly felt happy. She anticipated no trouble from her admirer who, for all his bohemianism, lacked the self-confidence of Reggie

Terry, the first familiar face she saw when they came out on the floor. He waved at her, but Kitty Hopkins shook her head contemptuously. She was on the floor with the acknowledged champion. She would have Milly know as much.

But Milly's turn came. She had been the best skater at school; and very soon she was attracting the attention of the room. Irwin, her partner, was adequate but she in herself eclipsed all competition.

During an interval she was approached by Reggie. "Kitty's wild. Mad jealous," he told her. "I didn't know you skated. You must come with me. There would be nobody to touch us."

"Miss Preston's with *me* I'd have ye know," Irwin said in a stage whisper to Reggie. Reggie shrugged his shoulders and returned to his partner, who burst out at once into complaint. But he continued to smile. He was on top of the world. Some of the other men in the party were better performers than Irwin, and Milly would have liked to partner them; but she found that she was monopolised by Irwin. He had secured her, he explained, by paying for her admission. Nevertheless she enjoyed herself although the floor was too crowded; and as the evening wore on and the skaters increased in number it was often hard to make progress. Instead of sweeping round the whole floor, it was more rewarding to mark off a limited territory and glide round that.

For some reason the groups on the floor thinned and Milly took the opportunity to circle round the floor, leaving her usual corner. She was going very fast; Irwin was unable to keep up; and before she realised what had happened she was giving a solo performance. She had been accustomed to skating on ice, and it had taken her some time to accustom herself to the new conditions, but she had got the hang of it and now, as on the pond in Guelderland, she let herself go. All evening she had been trying to suit her mood to her company, but Irwin's dry little jokes and flirtatious depth-soundings, in the accents of Belfast, which would make even the Song of Solomon sound like a bill of sale, had heightened a longing to be with Alan. The rink orchestra was plodding cheerfully through a Strauss piece; Milly, in imagination, was holding Alan's hand; the floor was empty; they were waltzing on skates, delighting in their skill, their youth, their beauty, their love.

Soon the rink's patrons would resume—nobody could monopolise the floor—but for, perhaps, two minutes' space they rested and watched this beautiful creature showing off. 'Showing off' is what Kitty Hopkins, Queen of the Rink, described Milly's wholly unselfconscious performance. But she noticed that her remark lay where it fell, neither Reggie, fingering his moustache, nor the other men around had ears for disparagement. Their eyes were too full of uncritical admiration.

Alan, was not a dedicated student of law. He kept away from Milly with the best intentions; but he was unable to work continuously, and he had come from a chilly dinner in his club with an officer whose tale of woe had lowered his spirits. The rink at Earlsfort Terrace was hardly the equivalent of Vauxhall, but it was a way to fill an idle hour. It attracted amorous adventurers. The officer had been complaining about his wife. She was extravagant for one thing.

"What a stunner. I'm going to find out more about her if its the last thing I do," he said, his depression swept away by the sight of a girl skating as if she had left earth and was circling in the air with the first swallows of Spring.

"Dammitt, she would do for Brynhilde. I hope she is not surrounded by a ring of fire."

He was, strangely enough, a Wagner enthusiast, an enthusiasm which, when he looked at Alan, he decided was not shared.

"What's up? What's the matter, old man?"

Alan looked as if he had seen a ghost.

Milly, aware now of being the centre of attention, decided, after one more delicious circuit, to rejoin her companions. Faces were a blur, she could only make out the salient points of the hall. She arranged in her mind to skate off the floor at the entrance to the rink where the crowd was thickest and she could be lost to view, suddenly embarrassed by the fact that she had performed for the benefit of the whole assembly.

As she drew in she heard words of praise and admiration. She knew she deserved them. Skating was one of the things that she really could do better than other people. But she was already feeling the slightly sick reaction of the shy when they give way to an impulse of exhibitionism. She would have liked to disappear.

She looked round for her friends and when her eye fell on Alan, standing with a companion, she looked at him unseeing as if it was a trick of imagination. Then she looked back and met his angry disapproving eyes. For a moment she could neither move nor speak. "But you said you were going to be away," the sentence that agitation sent up first, was the most damning of all. She had no time to deliver it or to find a better. He said something to his friend, ignoring Milly, and then turned away.

"I say!"

The remark was made by Alan's friend, who had had no time to realise that he was being left alone in the field before Milly brushed past him, looking, he noticed, pale as death.

She pulled off her skates and ran out on to the street. She saw Alan's back. He was walking towards Stephens' Green.

"Alan! Alan!"

He walked on. She was sobbing when she caught up with him and placed a hand on his arm. Very firmly he took it off, keeping his gaze ahead.

"I'm with the School of Art students. It's a party. Come and join us. Oh Alan, don't be angry."

He stopped on this and turned to face her. She could only dimly discern his features in the gaslight. It made his face very pale.

"What am I to think? I go away for a few days and come back and discover you making an exhibition of yourself in public at the rink. At the rink!"

The place she had chosen rankled most of all.

"I didn't mean to. It just happened. I was skating with one of the students and he couldn't keep up. Before I knew what had happened I was on my own. As soon as I realised that everyone was looking at me I stopped. I did nothing wrong. You mustn't try to make me think I've been wicked. I haven't."

"I am glad you are happy about it. You must rejoin your friends. They will be wondering what has become of you. It's quite the thing for girls to slip off with strange men at the rink, you know."

"Well if it's such a terrible place why did you go?"

"I'm a man."

"And would you have slipped off with some girl if I hadn't been there?"

"Milly, I think you should go back to your friends."

"Not until you give up being so horribly angry."

"I'm afraid I can't change my moods to order. I wish I could. It must be convenient to be able to."

"It's not a mortal sin to go to the rink. You know it. I was at a party. Everyone wanted to go. What was I to do?"

"Oh, do as your friends do, by all means. But don't ask me to approve. That's all."

With that he turned away. She did not follow him this time. She stood petrified, watching him go, watching his figure become a shadow and the shadow merging with the gloom at the end of the street where the gas light picked him out again as he crossed over to the park and disappeared. She thought she could still hear his feet, growing fainter and fainter.

"Is that you, Milly? I was wondering where you'd got to."

Irwin had to repeat himself before she became alive to his presence. She walked back to the rink beside him.

"Who was your friend?" he asked. Milly heard "Hoojer frénd?" and the sound conveyed no meaning. But when he added "He was in a kind of a hurry," the message went home. But she made no attempt to answer. When they got to the entrance, she came to herself again.

"I'm very sorry, Irwin, but I can't go back to the rink. I don't feel well. Do you think you could get a cab? I'll collect my cloak."

Irwin, bitterly disillusioned about the way the evening which had started so well had collapsed, did as he was told. He had no spare money for cab fares, and if he was paying for one to transport a girl he expected a return. He was frugal, not riggish. Milly, so inaccessible-looking as a rule, had seemed almost in reach this evening; but the silent girl who stepped into the cab and sat like a caryatid in the corner held out no such promise. He could hardly see her in the dark. He might have noticed, when they passed a street light, that her eyes glistened. He did not suspect any cause for tears; he was not thinking about her now as a person, but as a girl in a cab for which he was paying. He did not know how to begin. His pleasantries were greeted by monosyllables. They were in Rathmines now. Time was running out. He took a hand. Surprisingly it was warm. Quite a strong hand. It lay in his like a stone. He came nearer and put an arm round her. A mailbag would have been no less responsive. But she made no effort to disengage herself. Now the shadow of the Church of the Three Patrons was looming up against the sky on the left. He dived and landed with his lips on hers. He was kissing a stone and the taste was of sea salt. But still she made no response. He tried to open her lips with his and made no progress.

"Go on, Milly. Give us a kiss," he said. If only she kissed him once it would be something. They had passed the Church of the Three Patrons and turned left.

"What's the matter with you?"

For a moment he thought she might be dead.

"Is it near here?" the cabby asked, turning round as he shouted.

Milly, suddenly rousing herself, tapped on the glass. The cab came to a halt. An overwhelming feeling of having been cheated filled Irwin's simple soul. Milly, not knowing or caring how his mind worked, arrived independently at the conclusion that she should pay for the cab. She did not want to be under any obligation to Irwin. His attentions had affected her as much as if she had been caught in a hail shower. Quckly fumbling in her bag she found a half-crown, and as she got out of the cab, too quickly for Irwin to hinder or help, she handed it up to the driver.

"Good-night, Irwin. Thank you very much," she said and walked rapidly in the direction of Buttercup Square.

The driver, having examined the coin, gave vent to his pleasure. "There's a lady for you! A real lady!" he said. "Where to now?" he asked.

"I'll get off here," Irwin said. His digs were miles away, but he was not going to let Milly's unexpected assistance go to waste. She was a decent girl, he decided, but cold; shy, perhaps. He must be more persuasive and less masterful in his approach in future. It was a lesson to him not to be so concerned with getting value for money. It tended to a short-sighted view and a rushing of fences. Irwin, in his way, was something of a philosopher.

XVIII

"I WAS WONDERING where you had got to!"

Alan, sunk in a chair in the cavernous hall of his club, winced at the cheerful sound of his friend's voice.

"I say. What's happened? Are you feeling all right?"

"I shall be all right, Carslake. Something has upset me."

"Too bad! Nothing inside? I mean—you don't feel ill or anything? What about a little drink? I could do with one myself."

Alan was loath to admit, even to himself, that his woes were susceptible to such mundane consolation: but he felt like a drink.

"Could you split a bottle of port?" Carslake said hopefully.

"To tell you the truth, old man, I could do with it. I've been going through hell lately. If you ever marry, Harvey, take my tip: begin as you intend to leave off. I hadn't a bean when I married Tessa, but we lived as if we had money to burn; and now the silly kid doesn't know how to pull her horns in. There's nothing for it but to write to her father. He has the stuff, but it's the devil to extract it from him. I suppose that's why he has it."

Captain Carslake then rang the bell and ordered a bottle of '64.

"Might as well be hanged for a sheep as a lamb, old man. Here's to you, Harvey. Tell me what happened. But first let me tell you: when you left, that stunning girl came right over to me. You could have knocked me down with a feather. But before I could even bid her the time of day, she rushed past me. For a moment I thought she was in pursuit of you! If she were, you wouldn't be in the dumps now. These things don't happen. Only in dreams. But I suppose they must happen to some chaps. I mean—if she was running after someone, he was one of the lucky ones. She didn't look particularly cheered about it, come to think of it. She looked as if she had seen a ghost. I wonder who she was."

Alan sipped his port and said nothing, whereupon his friend returned to the recital of his own anxieties. Of these Alan had had enough during dinner. It was time to make this fellow listen to him for a change. They spoke the same language. You could talk to a chap like this and know it wouldn't go any further. The port was a seal of confidence.

"Carslake, old man, can you keep a secret?"

"I hope so, Harvey. Anything you told me I'd keep under my hat. That you can rely on."

Alan shifted in his chair. His friend topped up his glass. He sipped it slowly and began: "That girl at the rink—the one you have been talking about—I am in love with her."

"By Jove."

"We were as good as engaged."

"I must say, you are a dark horse. Well, what's happened?"

"It's a long story."

"Let's have it."

Carslake had it all. By the time Alan had finished, the decanter, acting as an hour glass, showed that time had run out.

"But I wouldn't break off just because she went to the rink. Damn it all, old man, she explained that she was with these art class friends of hers. Not the sort of company I'd like to see any girl I wanted to marry mixed up with, I'll allow. But still. I wouldn't wreck my life for that. You are not engaged, after all. She hasn't your label on her. Until you have you can't expect her to answer to your beck and call."

"But why did she go to the rink when my back was turned? It has shaken my faith in her, Carslake. And you have heard what I have gone through for her. My life has been hell. Damn it, man, I gave up a thousand pounds. I risked a break with my uncle. I threw up a career at the English bar. Am I not entitled to something better than this?"

"Naturally, you are put out."

"Put out! Put out! That hardly describes what I am. I'm broken, Carslake, broken."

What could his friend say? He poured the vestigial remains of the bottle into Alan's glass, hoping in vain that he would suggest a partition. But he was not observing the condition of the decanter; his anger had turned to self-pity. It was a more comfortable feeling. He was grateful to Carslake for his ministrations. Friendship was a beautiful thing.

"She's a damned good-looker," Carslake mused. He would have gladly exchanged tiresome Tessa, who had bandy legs, for a girl like that; and here was a man who had cast her off because she went skating. The ironies of life were inexplicable. He rang the bell and ordered a second bottle.

"But she might come over to your side. And, anyhow, you can take the boys. Her church has to be satisfied with the daughters. I can never understand why you Irish make such a song and dance about the religious question. Some of my friends married Catholics; it was regarded as a bore; but nobody blew up about it. That's prehistoric, I should have supposed."

"You don't understand this country, old man. You don't know how people feel about these things. It's bred in the bone. It's history. Besides it's not merely a question of religion. She has an uncle—"

"So has Tessa. Millions of them; and aunts too, by jove."

"Carslake, I know you well enough to tell you things I wouldn't mention to any other man. The whole set-up is unsuitable. There's a shop in the background. My brother-in-law to be—but don't ask me to go into details. I am only giving you the lie of the land."

"If you want her badly enough, old boy, none of that would stop you. What can your relations do about it, after all?"

"One doesn't like to feel one has let them down. My uncle—"

"To hell with him. Good God, if I had a girl like that in mind, I wouldn't give tuppence for what my uncle thought about me. Can he disinherit you? Have you expectations? Well, old man, only you can decide whether you can afford to risk that. It's a tricky position, certainly. Take my case."

But Alan, at that moment, was not prepared to take any case but his own. They were well on with the second bottle.

"Are you trying to suggest that I don't love Milly?"

"I didn't say that, old man. Now, be fair."

"Carshlake, I am asking you a straight question, and I expect a straight answer: are you suggesting that I don't love Milly?"

"Of course not, old man. You wouldn't be in the state you are in if you didn't love her. That stands to reason. Before I proposed to Tesha—"

"I don't suppose any man has ever gone through as much as I have done for Milly. I'm not going to let even my dearest friend suggest that I don't love her."

"I'm not suggesting anything, my dear fellow. I was just going to tell you—now, what was I going to tell you? Funny, that. It seemed to be absolutely vital to what we were talking about. And

189

now I can't remember what it was. Let me give you a little more of this port. Best thing in the club, if you ask my opinion. What was I saying? Oh, yes. I've got it. Before I proposed to Tesha—"

"Carshlake, you are avoiding my question. I am asking you if you think I don't love Milly?"

"I was trying to tell you—"

"I don't care a damn what you were trying to tell me."

"No need to get abusive, old man. After all, what in Heaven's name does it matter to me? I was only trying to help. What I was trying to tell you—you're not drinking up. I say, Harvey, old man, that girl at the rink was a stunner. I don't know what all this talk is about. I wish I was in your shoes. Not that I don't love Tesha. Before I proposed—I was dithering about it, I must admit. You see, I knew she would accept me and that always sets a man back in his tracks. Scots blood, I suppose. Anyhow, I was talking to my colonel. A wonderful old boy. He didn't want me to get married. Thought I was too young. So I was. Dammit."

"That's part of my trouble. You see—"

"We were having a drink in the mess, and he said to me 'Carshlake—I'd give you this advice if you were my own son—if you want to know whether you love a girl or not, you bloody go and sleep with another woman: you'll damn well know then.'"

"But I don't want to know whether I love Milly. I wouldn't be in the state I am if I didn't love her. Would I? Answer me that?"

"I know. Still, you are thinking twice before you propose to her. You're like I was with Tesha."

"There's no comparison. You're married to her for one thing."

"That's because I did what the colonel told me. You must pull yourself together. You can't throw your hand in, Harvey. There was a woman where we were stationed, very pretty she was, too. I knew her form. Every officer in the regiment pretty well knew her form. Red hair, if I remember right. Well, I went and spent the night with her, and do you know what happened?"

"I don't want any of that sort of talk, Carshlake."

"I'm telling you for your own good. I went straight to the post-office and sent Tesha a telegram, pre-paid. 'Will you marry me?' She accepted by return. And, my God, I sometimes wonder."

"But I know I love Milly. I don't need to prove it, man."

"Then, why don't you go and ask her to marry you?"

"Must we go over all that again?"

"Can you get her without offering to marry her?"

"Carshlake, if anyone else but you had said that, I'd have hit him in the face."

"You're a difficult man to help, Harvey."

"And who would I go to anyhow? Not one of the tarts in this town. You don't suggest that."

"As a matter of fact—I happen to know this by rather an extraordinary coinsh—coinshidence. Tesha—"

"Oh, Tesha."

"Tesha has been selling clothes to some woman who lives in Ballsbridge. She bought a brooch from her, and robbed her in my opinion. I had a job to get at the truth. When I did eventually, I went and tackled the bird in her nest. Ball is the name. I wasn't looking for anything, you understand. But I got the impression that if I were, it wouldn't have been difficult to persuade her. I have her address; and if you were to call you could say I sent you to tell her that I'm quite happy about the brooch. I paid too much for it in the first insh—insh—inshtance. If you like I could drop you over there now. It's the only way to settle your problem. Let's finish the drop in the decanter and be on our way."

"Carshlake, I'm not happy about this. After going for Milly about the rink, it seems incon—inconshish—incon—I'd be letting Milly down."

"You're a man, Harvey. Remember that. And Milly looks like a girl who will want a man not a mouse, if I'm any judge. I shall never forgot her, skating there, alone, this evening. She looked like—who was it I said she looked like, Harvey?"

"I can't remember, old man. Where did you say this friend of yours lived?"

"Per—Per—Pershy Place."

"Pershy Place. I know Pershy Place. I could do with some air. But I'm feeling better, Carshlake. I'll be all right when I get some fresh air."

The two friends, walking a little unsteadily, as when the blind lead the blind, made their way down Leinster Street and Clare Street to Merrion Square, and then along Lower Mount Street. Of the two Alan was in better shape. Carslake had been drinking steadily since the afternoon.

By the time they arrived on Mount Street Bridge, Alan was

quite clear about his own intentions. He wanted to go home. For one thing, he had never been with a woman in his life but once, and that was after a football match when he was so drunk that he had only a vague recollection of eyes gleaming in the dark and after-taste of having been cheated. He had never repeated the experiment; and that vague evening was one of the incidents in his life which he had deliberately buried so deep in his consciousness that it had come to belong with his recollections of dreams. He never confided his experience to anyone; and his friends were never bloods with stage-door conquests or hearties who knew the town. It was understood by Alan's set that you were respectful towards the girls of your own class. If you wanted to maul a girl, there were always girls in shops, and waitresses it was easy to pick up. Tarts were something else. That was dangerous.

The nighttown with which many a medical student was familiar was a closed book to Alan. He hardly knew of its existence. Nor did he pursue 'common' girls for the sake of sport. He went to as many parties as he wanted to. Girls liked him. Plain ones were easy to kiss if one wanted to; but Alan kissed pretty ones, too. The prettier they were, the more flattering it was. Like men who are natural athletes he set little store by what others struggled for and took pride in. He was used to all the girls he had grown up with. Milly's fascination was not only in her looks but owing to her being altogether different from the girls he knew. They talked of the same things and the same people in the same way. They were so predictable. He was never certain what Milly would think or say on any topic.

Love and desire were to him two wholly different concepts. Since he had fallen in love with Milly he resented smut. He would have maintained that love in some way transcended sexual feeling had it not been for the incident after the bishop's visit, when he was alone with Milly in her mother's house. That had taught him a great deal, but it had lowered Milly's intrinsic value in his eyes. It had made him cautious. Carslake's idea had appealed to him, in spite of himself, for several reasons. If a woman he had never met could satisfy his desires, then it was clear that he was making a romantic fool of himself about Milly. Pride made that hard to believe. He would have liked to have explained the state of his mind to Carslake. That was why he sought his company. He wanted to tell him about the girl who called to him from the dark.

And the disappointment. He wanted to consult Carslake's experience. Was it different where love was? And if so, how could a visit to Mrs Ball tell him that?

He didn't want to admit to Carslake that he had practically no experience. Unless he did, Carslake couldn't help him. But to do so was to admit to a pose of sophistication ever since they met and took a liking to one another. Carslake was not very bright; but he was kind. He would understand; but how to begin? It would look as if he were losing his nerve. Besides, Carslake was not easy to explain anything to. He was rather drunk.

They reached a familiar spot. It was where he parted company with Milly's uncle when they came away from Buttercup Square together. Another dagger in his conscience. But he was doing this for Milly. He would have gladly backed out of it if it were not going to solve their problem as Carslake's colonel said. What was he going to say to this woman? Was it as easy as Carslake made out? Would she expect to be paid? To ask Carslake all this made him seem a child. Carslake held his elbow and kept pushing him forward. He seemed excited.

"This is it. In you go. And remember, old man, you may rely on me to keep it—" Carslake relaxed his elbow pressure to put a forefinger to his lips.

Then he lurched off; but stood on Huband's Bridge, in the shadow, to make sure that Alan did not run out on him. He had the singlemindedness of a drunken man, an obstinate loyalty to an idea that had taken root and provided a point of return for a mind that was revolving in circles in a world that threatened to turn over.

He watched Alan's blurred outline, watching him heard his irresolute knock, saw the window go up and heard a voice that sounded not sweet on the night air ask who was there. Of Alan's reply he could only catch one word—'Carslake'. Then the window shut, and a little later the door opened. Only then did Carslake feel free to retrace his footsteps. He contrived to move forward on a curved course, feeling benevolent and at peace with all the world.

Alan, miserably sober now, cursed Carslake keeping guard like that until he was drawn in to a hall covered in dark wall-paper and smelling evilly of cats. The only light was Mrs Ball's candle. She had on a lace night cap under which her hair escaped in golden bobs. Otherwise he could only discern large eyes of baby blue staring rather shrewdly from a network of tiny wrinkles.

She led the way into a room and lit first a gas-light hanging from the ceiling in a red silk shade, then the fire in the grate.

"Sit down there Mr—what did you say the name was?"

Alan had been careful not to say, and the question took him by surprise. Among the various terrors of an encounter of this kind, because he set such store on respectability, he listed blackmail high. But something in him resisted the idea of giving a false name, and he was too polite to refuse to answer a not unreasonable question. "Alan," he said.

"Any relation to Charley Allen, the vet? I saw he got married recently."

"Alan is my christian name."

"Mona is mine. Are you a friend of Mrs Carslake? You must be if you turn out at this time of night to transact her business."

"I come from her husband, Captain Carslake."

"He called on me himself the other day and I thought we settled everything then. Why has he sent you? I'm not going to re-open that transaction. I would not have had any dealings with Mrs Carslake if I had known she was not as good as her word. Officers and gentlemen indeed! When a woman has no man behind her, Mr Allen, she very soon discovers what that noble phrase amounts to."

"Captain Carslake was perfectly satisfied. He spoke of you most appreciatively and recommended me to come to you."

"Well, that was very kind of him, I must say."

There was a pause during which Alan felt that he was shrinking under the scrutiny of those faded pansies with beads in the centres which held him in a rather motherly regard.

"It's late to call. I very nearly refused to answer the knock, but I was half expecting a friend of mine, and I can think of nothing worse than to call on a friend and meet with a sleeping house and a locked door. Can I offer you any refreshment? I have some sherry wine a gentleman friend gave me, or, perhaps, you prefer something harder; but you shouldn't at your age—how old are you, Mr Allen?"

Still under a vague dread of blackmail Alan hesitated and then said "Twenty-four", not only that she might have wrong particulars for her file but to counteract the shrinking feeling.

"Twenty-four. That's a lovely age. I'd have put you down as younger as that. Sweet seventeen and never been kissed," she said enigmatically.

"Your eyes," Alan said, desperately, "are an attractive colour."

"They are blue, love. Like blue-bells I've been told. But if I went by what I was told I would be in a queer street. Would you like a cup of tea? I was going to make myself one when you knocked. Then you can tell me what is on your mind. I always say there's no business that isn't the better for being washed down with a sup of tea."

"Thank you very much," Alan said. He by no means wanted tea but he was anxious to gain time. What did one do on these occasions with a woman like this? Pretend to be in a sudden passion and seize her? Or make a cold-blooded proposition as if one were hiring a cab? Surely she made the running? Somehow the idea of a pot of tea was foreign to his idea of unbridled lust.

"Just you rest yourself there; and don't let that cat bother you. She is apt to leave remembrances behind her, poor thing. I haven't the heart to dispose of her. I'll be back in a jiffy."

He leaped to his feet and opened the door for her. She gave a little bow and then caught the lapel of his coat in her hand and let it slide through her fingers. Now, he thought, she is beginning to make overtures. But all she said was "That's a nice bit of stuff. You didn't get that here."

"It's English cloth."

"Made by Johnston; I have a gentleman friend who swears by Johnston."

Mrs Ball had turned back a pocket flap to acquire this information.

Alan's unease increased; she now had a line on him. When she went down to the kitchen he looked at the exposed label and saw his name written in black ink. He was no match for this woman.

From the kitchen came the strains of "The Belle of New York". He could make a bolt for it now but how would he face Carslake? She would be bound to tell about it and make him look a fool. Curse and damn Carslake! Why couldn't the drunken fool mind his own business and leave him alone?

Mrs Ball was expert at tea-making, to judge by her speed of return with a neatly laid tray of biscuits, a tea-pot under an embroidered cosy and willow-pattern china cups.

"How do you like yours?"

"As it comes, thank you."

"Tea first or milk first?"

"I beg your pardon?"

"Do you like the tea put in first? Some do, some prefer it the other way."

"Tea first, thank you."

"Sugar?"

"Thank you. I mean no sugar. I'm sorry."

"There you are. Be careful. Your hand is trembling. You haven't been on the binge, I hope. Naughty boy!"

Alan made no reply. He concentrated on tea-drinking and found it provided neither solace nor inspiration.

"Have some more?"

"No thank you."

"A biscuit."

"No, thank you."

"Sweet enough as it is."

"I beg your pardon?"

"I said you were sweet enough as it is."

"Oh."

"Am I to call you Alan? or Mr Harvey? You haven't told me yet."

"Alan, by all means."

"That's nice. And you must call me Mona. I never feel happy when I'm called Mrs Ball, It reminds me of so many things I want to forget."

"I'm sorry for calling so late. It was Carslake's idea."

"Now that you are here, what does it matter? 'Call me early, mother dear, for I'm to be the Queen of the May'. I like to put my feet up in the evening. Are you sure you won't have another cup of tea?"

"Quite sure."

"Now, tell me why you called on me. In trouble? You look worried. What can Mona do to help. Most of my business is done with ladies. Very exclusive. Very personal. Very private. If I talked—my dear!"

"Carslake suggested it."

"Well, that's sign certain he must be satisfied, isn't it?"

"I said he was when I came."

"Well, that's all I want to hear. Now you must tell me how much you want."

"What do you usually give? I mean—I shouldn't like to ask unless you expect . . ."

Mrs Ball smiled in a conciliatory fashion. "Perhaps you would like to show *me* what you've come to tempt Mona with."

Alan jumped to his feet; his hand clutching his mouth.

"You have been drinking. Mona knows. Mona knows the naughty ways of men. Sometimes she wishes she didn't. Life for a woman isn't all a bed of roses. Not by any means."

"I'm not drunk. I assure you, I'm not."

"I didn't say 'drunk', love. I would never say such a thing to any gentleman. I only intended to convey you had been drinking a little more than the little tum can take. Young tums are more easily turned than old tums. I'll give you something for it presently."

"May I kiss you?"

"Mr Harvey! You surprise me. If I had thought for a moment—"

"Your eyes are like blue-bells, Mrs Ball. Mona."

With that Alan who had risen to his feet hurled himself on top of Mrs Ball. She was sitting on one end of a sofa, and in bending down to push away the little table on which the tea-things lay, the top of her dressing-gown fell open showing a night-dress underneath.

She was small and had no chance of resisting Alan, who had plunged, as a determined early morning bather dives before reluctance urges a retreat. But she managed to slip from under him down to the floor in a confusion of flannel and lace.

He felt ridiculous, stretched on the sofa, his face in a cushion. He knelt down beside Mrs Ball who was looking at him reproachfully.

"I love you," he said.

It came to him as the only dignified move available in this game he had involved himself in.

"What would happen if anyone came in and found me here, like this?" Mrs Ball enquired.

It was a question of which at any time Alan would have required notice before attempting an answer; but now an awful nausea seized him, and he heard her voice as coming from an infinite distance and with no relevance to him.

"I'm feeling ill," he was able to say. Then he rushed out of the room: one way led to stairs going in different directions; the other presented only a door to be negotiated. Alan went for the door. He was sick outside, in the front garden, under the visiting moon, sicker than he had ever been since the day he first tried to smoke the gardener's pipe. But afterwards, although he was shivering, he felt as if he had purged himself of a nightmare. Without thinking of what lay behind the door he had left open in his haste, he followed the moon where it led him, over the bridge, along the canal, all the way to Buttercup Square.

XIX

To MILLY'S WINDOW Alan came, half hoping that she would sense his presence and appear like Juliet at her casement. He called her name, but not loudly, and finding the exercise sweet continued to whisper it aloud. He felt exalted and purified and, as people do on certain nights, independent of the law of gravity. He had only to will it and he could sail over the fence. If she came to the window he would certainly float up to it.

But the window turned a blind eye to his powers of levitation and the slow step of the Metropolitan police ringing on the pavement drove him away at last.

He had thought of scribbling her a few lines on a page of his diary and slipping it in the letter box; but it might meet profane eyes so he decided instead to go to the rooms he was sleeping in and write from there; then he could return and leave an envelope in before Milly got up. All the way from the Square to Leinster Street—where another law student put him up on his nights in town—he composed his letter. Much of it was a précis of Romeo's address to Juliet on the balcony; very little had to do with the incident earlier in the evening, when Milly ran after him and begged his pardon, and he had spurned her. He had come through a cleansing fire and the encounter in Percy Place was like the Circe episode in Odyssey. Carslake, with his colonel's nostrums, was Polyphemus vainly hurling rocks from the abandoned shore. Such a fellow was to be pitied for never having known love in all its strength, a great white light, too brilliant for mortals, known only to the great lovers of history, to which company in modern times had only been admitted Milly Preston and Alan Harvey.

He did not bother to undress, and was unsure when he was asleep, when awake; the bell of St Andrew's Church, Westland Row, clanging at six o'clock, was his signal to rise.

The letter was very long but, in the morning light, presented a difficulty which had not been apparent under the moon. However ecstatic, he had somewhere to say he was sorry; and he felt in no mood for abjectness. Last night he had rediscovered love, and he wanted to share his excitement. He wanted to describe the miracle. It came about after the degradation of Percy Place (was the old colonel right after all?'. But he had been saved (by heroic virtue?) from wallowing in the mire provided on the premises; he had stepped back from the edge of the abyss; he was free from stain (blot out those minutes of pantomime with the woman with the painted face). What mattered were not the sordid preliminaries but the ecstasy. It was the glad tidings of that he wanted to bring to Milly before breakfast. And yet ... The trouble was that he did not feel guilty or repentant or despondent. He felt simply glorious. And yet ...

He must say 'I am sorry'. Had he taken a perverse pleasure in his strength when he saw Milly looking woe-begone because he was angry? Carslake had called her a stunner, and envied the man whom she pursued. Carslake could not imagine what it was like to have that radiant creature suing for forgiveness. She had been forgiven. The scene at the rink, the port at the club, the interior of Percy Place, the agony in the garden, all these had been submerged in the splendour of the *Liebestod* at the end. He had sung Milly's part for her. They had soared into the empyrean together. He merely wanted to inform her of this; to break the news.

Perhaps, what was pulling at the end of his pen was the reality of Milly's personality. That was a substantial fact which would not take on the stuff of dreams at his whim.

The excitement with which his letter began petered out as he drew towards the close, as if the spiritual champagne upon which it had been composed had lost its initial effervescence.

"If I was beastly to you at the rink, I am truly sorry; but when a fellow loves anyone so much as I love you he must not be held responsible for what he says on the spur of the moment when he discovers her at such a place with people unfit to breathe the same air, much less skate with her in public. Meet me at Harrison's at four-clock; and I promise not to refer to it then or ever again. Your devoted Alan."

The letter entered the letter-box at number seven Buttercup Square at five minutes to eight o'clock. With a nice clean feeling, as if after bathing, Alan walked away to spend a day during which he would give very little of his mind to the principles of Equity or the law of Marine Insurance.

He arrived at the tea shop five minutes late, having been caught at the door of the Kings Inns by a long-winded old counsel with a penchant for casual reminiscence, to find Milly not there. He waited for half an hour. She did not come. He decided that she must have arrived early—as he intended to—and been hurt when he was not even up to time. Of all days to fall victim to a bore! One of the difficulties of a lover is that he has to live in an oblivious world.

What was to be done now? If he could see Milly alone he would go straight to the Square; but he did not want to face Carrie and Dolly (whose half-critical expression was beginning to get on his nerves). Eventually he wrote a note explaining his delay, and decided to call with this after dinner. He might meet Milly; if not, the note said to come at the same time to-morrow.

There was light in the window of the drawing-room behind the closed curtains, he was longing to knock, and yet hesitated. He did not want to meet Milly with other people. He dropped the letter in, and went out to Blackrock, really to see if Milly might have written to him there. She had not.

Next day he arrived at Harrison's a quarter of an hour before time and waited with increasing excitement until five o'clock, at which moment he expected her to appear, like the sun rising, in the doorway. But the door remained shut, and when it opened a few minutes later it disclosed a thin man in clerical dress with a drop on the end of his nose.

Alan waited half an hour. It was his measure. Could Milly be ill? If she were, surely she would ask her mother to tell him. It was only as he walked down the street with no plan at all in his mind that the awful possibility he had lost Milly occurred to him for the first time.

His wandering brought him to the end of Kildare Street; he could call at his rooms where his friend, Stephens, would certainly be in, at work, or walk past the College of Art, a direction in which Milly might be discovered. He walked in the direction of the College.

A large man with a beard was standing outside Leinster House, a big, shaggy man in a loose coat. His appearance was familiar. His bulk and the amplitude of his gestures concealed his listener; Alan, looking back, saw a girl in the embrasure of the gateway. She was listening intently. He knew that look better than any in the world. To recognise it was to feel jealous at once that anybody else should be privileged to see it, even an elderly gentleman in an old-fashioned greatcoat.

Alan stopped and waited for Milly to see him. Whatever the bearded one was saying he had all her attention. She did eventually catch Alan's eye, caught it, and as deliberately dropped it again, turning slightly so as to give her full face to her bearded friend, leaving Alan to look at a bundle of gold hair under a large straw hat and a back carved, it seemed, in marble.

He waited; she continued to ignore his presence: as if he had been slapped in the face, he reddened and walked on.

His mind had been full of Romeo and Juliet because he had been saved from degrading their love. Milly knew nothing about that. His letter must have seemed wildly irrelevant to their last encounter when she pleaded for pity. Alan was not inclined to resort to literature in perplexity, but a few passages lingered since school, and he remembered now a more appropriate portion of Shakespeare about

> . . . one whose hand
> Like the base indian, threw a pearl away,
> Richer than all his tribe—

Could there be a more perfect epitaph for his tomb than that? His former English master, to whom he paid no attention, said that Shakespeare had an answer for every question life could put. Wise, prophetic man! Milly was probably spending all her time with art students now, throwing herself, abandoned, at some lecherous bohemian, some elderly Silenus. And if she were, who was to blame? Who cast her off? Who trampled on her in the mud? How divine she looked—as Carslake said—at the rink. A young queen. An angel.

Two hours later, he arrived, sweating, at number seven, having left a cab which refused to quicken its pace and ran the last quarter of a mile.

Mary, looking joyful, let him in, and announced his arrival to Carrie, alone in the drawing-room.

"How is Milly?" he asked.

His tone would have been appropriate to a fatal accident; and Carrie, who had been upset by Milly's silence and sadness for the last few days, assured him that her daughter was well, and decided in her own mind that his appearance was likely to remedy her recent loss of spirits.

"She is upstairs with Dolly, helping her with her trousseau. I'll tell her you are here."

In the ordinary course Mary would have been summoned from the kitchen—she was in fact eavesdropping on the landing—to tell Milly of her lover's arrival; but tact suggested that Carrie should take the opportunity to leave the scene.

Alan, feeling suddenly too large for the little room, waited as outside an operating theatre for Milly to appear on a stretcher.

She, too, looked taller when she came in, and her lips scarcely moved at all when she greeted him. She sat down on a straight-backed chair without suggesting that he should settle himself, and sat with her hands together waiting for him to begin. He had pictured their reunion as a rushing together, a whirlwind in which words would be blown away by kisses. Never had his euphoria or his dread pictured this scene before a silent accuser.

"I missed you yesterday. I waited again today. Then I thought you might be ill. I rushed over to find out."

Milly made no gesture to suggest that she was touched by this solicitude. Over and around them hung a silence. Alan felt no power in him to dispel it.

Since she had met Alan she had danced to his tune; Milly had decided she would dance no more. She had been at fault. She should not have gone to the rink without telling him, and left herself in a position to have to explain and ask for pardon; but she had humiliated herself. She had grovelled; and he had spurned her.

When she was at her lowest ebb on the previous afternoon she had been told that Mr Hone, the professor of landscape painting, had been looking for her. She had missed his class, unable to stir herself to go. She met him next day coming out, and apologised. He was notoriously reserved and greatly venerated because his own pictures, some people said, were thought very highly of in France, where he had studied with the Barbizon group. His appointment was a sort of recognition of his genius. He was not a run-of-the-mill teacher.

It took him a little time to work out what the pretty girl was apologising to him for. He was aware of no offence. Then he remembered. He had almost by chance laid eyes on a brilliant sketch, quite original and out of the common run, and asked who had painted it. So this was the girl. It is never very difficult, even when a man is shy, to talk about one's trade to a pretty woman who wants to listen. It is always delightful to a generous soul to recognise talent and to encourage it.

Hone asked Milly all about herself and invited her to come out to St Doulough's where he lived and paint the cows in his meadows. He painted them himself every day, and if the butcher called it was possible sometimes to point out a beast for sale on a canvas instead of going for a tramp in the fields.

Did Hone think she would ever be a good painter, a really good painter? She would, he said, if she believed in herself, if she lived for her art. He did not himself have to live by his painting. He painted to please himself; not everyone could do that; what was fatal was to paint to please anyone else. But it was a great, a rare, a wonderful pleasure to find—as he did very occasionally—that someone else derived pleasure from and understood—that above all—what he had attempted. It was lonely not to be understood; but so long as you were true to yourself you could be content. She must go abroad; she must find kindred spirits. At almost any time an artist could find someone else working on the same lines as himself; he did when he was young, at Barbizon.

Listening to the old gentleman, who was courteous and diffident about himself, and unlike some of the more conceited students who patronised her, Milly felt as if a hand was being held out to her from Heaven. She had received encouragement before, but this was different in kind. It was—so modest was this man—like recognition by a fellow-artist.

She could not find any way to express the vividness of her gratitude. When he had gone, she would leap at the sky. At that moment she looked up and saw Alan. He had seen her and was waiting for her to leave her old hero and join him. He was quite confident. The man who had tried to crush her was waiting for her to leave the man who was showing her the way to Heaven. She was no novice in cooling presumption. She had the knack of killing with a look. She decided to kill Alan.

Ever since that encounter she had lived as if in some unnatural element—under the sea—devoid of feeling. She would have said that her flesh was impervious to pain if she had not hurt herself a moment since with Dolly's needle.

Having killed Alan, there was something of anti-climax in having to meet him in the drawing room; and she would have refused to come down if it had not seemed the lesser of two evils. The alternative set up a course of explanations and anxious watchings and soundings for which she did not feel inclined. And she was determined not to spoil Dolly's excitement or push her off the centre of her little stage. Moreover, she felt that Hone had given her a new strength. She could deal with Alan, dead or alive.

When she found herself alone with him, it was not as she expected. The room seemed to her to be full of ghosts. Alan had only played the role of conqueror in the past; now he had lost it and acquired no other. He was neither tragic nor hateful nor pitiful nor sinister. Where he had been was a blank, and she had no words to fill it.

They were alone together looking at their love in ruins. What did one say on these occasions? What could one say?

Alan made a gesture of despair, in a room that left no space for such luxuries, and in doing so knocked over the standard lamp with its shade like a petticoat. On the floor it brought to mind a woman; and there was something in the thought of Mrs Ball prostrate on the carpet that filled Alan with a sense of Nemesis. What he had been taught in the nursery was true. One was punished for one's sins. Men who visited the Mrs Balls of the world had to lose the Millys to the virtuous. Something in Milly's pose made Alan certain that she knew all about Mrs Ball. She knew about everything. She saw into his very soul. He bent down to pick up the lamp and in doing so bumped into Milly. Their heads cracked together.

"I'm sorry. I'm so sorry. Damnably clumsy I am."

"It doesn't matter in the least."

But it did. There was a red spot on her forehead. There would be a bruise. Somehow that small defined area of outrage seemed to crystallise the larger vaguer miseries and murders of the last few days. Its scale was a comfort. It could be dealt with.

"Milly. Milly. I wouldn't hurt you for all the world. Can you forgive me? Milly. Let me see. Is it bad? Let me kiss it."

She let him see; and it was not bad, and she let him kiss it. When he had done so the formidable silence, having been broken, had gone. With it the ghosts had gone; and love that had been a sacked city was now a skyline of golden domes and dreaming spires.

XX

My dear T. T.

I have returned from your country estate and am celebrating the feast of the national apostle with my sister and her children. They all ask to be remembered very kindly to you, and are, may I say? enormously looking forward to the Easter holiday. While I am on the subject I must complain that you have been so reticent about the sort of gathering you have in mind. I invited the Roches. I think you liked them. The young man is marrying my niece, Dolly, and I felt that they would not want to be separated at the holiday. I was also considering young Harvey, whom you met, as a suitable addition. He comes from one of the best families in Carlow and, apart from the fact that he has found favour with my other niece, is the right sort of person for you to produce in the county. That will be enough of the young idea, I'm thinking! You may remember Lady Kelly—we went to a party in her house in Merrion Square—I met her the other day and she was enquiring so kindly after you that I wondered whether you would consider her a useful addition to the little party. She is rather formidable, as you may remember, but I see clear signs that underneath the armour there is a soft spot for you. Let me know. If I can round up a few of my county friends I'll do so. I want you to come into Westmeath with flags flying and trumpets sounding.

The work in the house is almost complete. I made a useful contact in the village who helped me to secure staff; but you will need a housekeeper and a Scottish steward. Tell me if you want me to get busy about these, or can you make your own plans? I hope you approve of what I've accomplished up to date, and I'd be grateful for a line about the other matters. In comparison with T. T., I always say, the sphinx is a chatter box.

Yours ever to command,

Joe.

To his St Patrick's day's letter Joe had a reply by return of post.

Charing Cross Hotel
March 18th, 1903

Dear Dunne,

I don't mind your inviting all your family, and I remember Lady Kelly. Don't ask more than the place will hold. I'll see about the other matters when I come over. Remember that I said that I wouldn't spend a penny over a thousand on the repairs. I was robbed for the furniture.

Yours truly,
Albert Talbot Thompson.

T. T's letters were always brief; and they were never without an undertone of sourness. Joe usually took a morning to recover from them; but by lunchtime he had regained his usual spirits. The foreman at Derravaragh had estimated that £1,500 would see the repair work through; and Joe didn't doubt that T. T. knew in his own mind that he would have to come up a bit. He liked to crack the whip; and he could never be gracious on paper. Better forget about him and concentrate on the favourable omens.

He had never known Carrie in such good spirits as she had been recently. She saw very little life, God love her. And the girls, no doubt, were looking forward to being in the country with their lovers. The prospect warmed his own heart; he wanted to perform some prodigy. He longed for universal approval and triumph. If the Viceroy had appeared at that moment, Joe would have invited him. Nothing, he felt, as he strolled down Grafton Street, was outside his range. Carrie whom he met and invited into Mitchell's for a cup of morning coffee, confided in him that Milly had been upset but had magically recovered.

"I wish she were settled, Joe."

"Give me time, Carrie. Give me time. I have great hopes of T. T. I shouldn't be surprised if he left me in charge of his Irish interests. He has other fish to fry. In that case I shall move down to Derravaragh. You can come and entertain for me. It will make all the difference to Milly. She can snap her fingers at the whole synod of bishops then. The young man will come to heel when he finds himself facing competition. Remember, there's a garrison in Mullingar."

Joe had fished a cigar out of one of his many pockets; when he was making plans for the future he liked to watch the smoke of a good cigar. It seemed, somehow, appropriate to his thought and its upward floating motion, lighter than air upon which it rested for a space, *en route* for the ceiling; its transparency, its circling motion; its copiousness, engendered by an imperceptible effort; not to mention the opulence of the aroma all induced content and a faery glow that is outside a sceptic's experience.

He told his sister about his recent additions to the party and expressed a hope of other notable prospects.

"Pity he chose Westmeath. It's one of the few places that I'm not in at all." Perhaps the wisest course was to go down to the country and move about, he reflected. He might make friends with the neighbours. So far he had only got on to terms of comparative intimacy with one of the many local publicans, through whom he was engaging the household staff. And he was on nodding terms with the police.

"What is Mr Talbot Thompson going to say to all this, Joe? Are you quite sure he doesn't want to be consulted about Easter plans?"

Carrie recognised the expression in Joe's face. It came when anyone else would register frustration or despair: it was inevitably the harbinger of disaster.

"T. T. gave me *carte blanche*. He likes you all; but I think he expects me to rustle up some of the County. When I first met him—this is in the privacy of these four walls—he had recently sold up a place in Warwickshire. He had gone down there intending to do things in a big way, but he wasn't let in. Nobody to beat the English at signalling KEEP OFF THE GRASS. Without saying anything they let him know pretty plainly he wasn't wanted. He got an opportunity to sell out at a profit—trust T. T.—and he took it. He never told me about this, T. T. never talks. But I gathered it from a fellow who had been pretty close to him for a while—well, as close as anyone can get to T. T. An oyster is garrulous in comparison. But I read between the lines; and I must say I encouraged the move to Ireland. I thought it might be helpful for us all. What worries me now is the thought that T. T. may run into the same trouble in Westmeath that he met in

Warwickshire. He may consider that I painted a wrong picture of the local scene and exaggerated the enthusiasm of the County for newcomers. He doesn't hunt. But I suppose if he contributes to the hunt they will be glad to have him. What do you say? You've met T. T. How do you see him going down in Westmeath?"

"It all depends. From what you say he sounds like an outsider; and I don't see people troubling themselves to make his acquaintance. You know how sticky people are. Does he know anybody? Has he any introductions?"

"That's the trouble. He expects me to supply these. Now, if he had only gone to Cork or to my own county or almost anywhere else, I would have been able to pave the way. But the simple truth of the matter is, as I realised when I found myself installed, I don't know a soul in the place."

"You've never said how you met T. T. first of all. Is it a secret?"

"It's a long story. Someone I know recommended me to somebody who recommended me to him as a person who might be useful in putting a certain matter—confidential, you understand—through. T. T. doesn't like to get involved. He acts through agents to cover his steps. He's very deep. I carried through this negotiation, for which I understood I was getting a handsome return; in the end that came to nothing, but it brought me in touch with T. T. and I put the suggestion of his coming to Ireland to him. He came over to see for himself."

"You know nothing about him really."

"I've picked up information here and there. He has a finger in many pies. He was in South Africa for a time. You can't avoid making money in South Africa. It sticks to your boots."

"Anyhow, it's very kind of him to let us come down. I am looking forward to a week-end in a country house; but I beg of you, Joe, to make quite sure that he knows what you have let him in for."

Joe nodded in a way Carrie knew of old. It meant that he wanted to move away from a subject. He gestured for silence. Carrie listened. All she could hear was a barrel-organ in the street playing 'O Sole Mio'.

"It's a pity you didn't keep up your music, Joe," Carrie said.

"I thought of being a pianist once; but, as the priest who taught me at Stonyhurst said, it was hardly a career for anyone who aspired to be a gentleman."

Carrie recognised that the time had come to go.

"This has been pleasant; but I must be about my business."

He waived the point with his cigar. She was free to go; but he did not want to break the spell. She hesitated; second nature by now, after a life's experience: Joe always performed the host's office as regards invitation, but he did not always have the where-withal to complete the operation. He put two fingers into a waist-coat pocket and withdrew them, put them into another and came out this time with a half sovereign between them. She nodded and so did he. There was nothing to waste words on. Soon she would be anxiously consulting her shopping-list; but Joe would sit on while the ashes collected in the saucer of his coffee cup and made a diaphanous pattern of grey on his canary-coloured waist-coat. He would sit on oblivious to covetous eyes in search of a vacant table, oblivious to the chatter around him, oblivious to the forth-coming inevitable confrontation with T. T. and the growing list of items to be dignified with the title 'miscellaneous' in the earnest hope that such comprehensiveness would paralyse enquiry at the threshold. For his reverie was concerned with a young army officer galloping on a black pony over the sun-scorched grass of a polo field, of a young rider squaring his mount up to the final fence in the military steeplechase, of a young subaltern, charmed by the sound of his own voice as it beguiled the small ear of his colonel's wife, on a balcony under a full moon, with cicadas chirruping in the garden and bougainvillaea spreading its concealing leaves over the balcony rail. A soldier's life. From there as gradually as the blue smoke that was now wreathed around him, the scene changed. Now, a lean master of hounds roared at a presumptive novice, a veteran at a crowded table descanted on the virtues of the port, a wise magistrate distributed even justice from the bench, a grizzled head bent over the blue-veined hand of a countess come to stay.

Now the cigar was a stub; and from the table everything had been cleared away except the plate on which the bill lay folded. He took it up sadly, put three pence where it had been, and presented his half sovereign at the desk beside the door. He liked the feeling of change in his pocket. He ran his fingers through it as if it was grain that he was going to spill out for hungry hens. He itched to spend.

Across the road he saw Lady Kelly emerging from a visit to the Carmelites in Clarendon Street. How long was it since he had been to confession? He couldn't remember.

She was a fine-looking woman, reminiscent of a sailing ship, with all her canvas spread, running before the wind. It would be interesting to discover how she would list if he was on deck. But the pleasing fancy was dispersed by the recollection of T. T's cryptic letter. Did it not imply that he had merely arranged to entertain his own family for Easter at T. T's expense? Lady Kelly was something. At least she had a handle—of a sort—to her name. He stepped across the road. She greeted him archly. He was encouraged. He said that he had heard from Mr Talbot Thompson who was anxious to know if she would like to come with the Prestons and other friends to his place in Westmeath for Easter. If so, a formal invitation would follow.

Mention of the Prestons sent an almost imperceptible shadow over Lady Kelly's unwrinkled countenance. Then she said she had delayed making Easter plans because of the King's visit in July; but the idea of a trip to the country pleased her. 'A change,' as Sir Patrick used to say, 'was as good as a rest.'

Captain Dunne—he was always 'Captain' to Lady Kelly—expressed delight. He would tell T. T. at once of his good fortune. He took off his hat. She bowed, and then put off, under full sail.

He stepped out briskly along Nassau Street. At the corner of Kildare Street, as always, he stopped to enquire of the porter in the club whether Major Saunderson was in. To this question the invariable reply was another question: 'Is Major Saunderson expecting you, sir?' And when he admitted that this was not precisely the case he would be told that Major Saunderson was not on the premises. It had become a habit, a ceremony of innocence. It could have been performed by gestures, each was so familiar with his part.

Coming down the steps, a large figure, coming in, tweed-clad, with heather in his button hole, stopped and smiled.

"I think we got more than we bargained for on Wednesday," it said.

"I thought so too," Joe replied. The tweedy shape laughed very cheerfully at the recollection and passed on into the club. Joe, on his way now to the Shelbourne Hotel, wondered what it was that he was supposed to have agreed about. The mistake about his identity had greatly encouraged his morale. Without the least idea of what he was doing he pressed forward in a glow of confidence. At the entrance to Leinster House he decided to go in and glance at the papers. He was not a member of the Royal Dublin Society; but he had used the premises for years, and the porter confused him with a former Vice-president and always made him feel especially welcome.

Joe looked round the reading room to see if he could recognise anyone. In a corner, behind the *National Geographical Magazine*, he thought he saw Lord Swords. For six months, some years ago now, when his fortunes were at their lowest, Joe had been employed to follow Lord Swords, and when he presented cheques to passers-by to explain to them that it was an amiable weakness and seek to recover them. Joe lost the job; and he heard afterwards that his patient had developed other delusions and was no longer in circulation. But he was here; and what was more, he remembered Joe and seemed to be delighted to see him, rushing across the room, expressing his pleasure so vigorously that there were indications of disapproval among the other occupants. Somebody pointed to a sign which said SILENCE.

Lord Swords followed Joe into the hall. But once they were alone he had nothing to say. All his energy seemed to have been concentrated on the greeting. Joe was also at a loss for words. A routine enquiry after the health of an old acquaintance has embarrassing implications when you believe he has been in an asylum.

"It's years since we've met," Joe said.

"I'm perfectly all right now, you know.'

"You are looking very fit."

"It's very kind of you to say so. Of course, I have to take it easy. I used to do too much. I enjoy it here. There's so much to read and they have concerts in the winter. All for two guineas a year. I didn't know you were a member. If I had seen your name in the list I'd have certainly got in touch with you. I am frequently at a loose end."

As if angry with himself for his carelessness, Lord Swords picked up a members' list off the table. Joe panicked.

"You are not by any chance free at Easter. I've taken a place for an English friend of mine—well known in the City—I'd like you to meet him."

Lord Swords gave encouraging nods.

"I was going to say if you did happen to be at a loose end you might like to come and join us. Only a small party, my sister and her girls, Lady Kelly and I hope we shall have young Harvey, whom you probably know, one of the Carlow Harveys."

Lord Swords dropped the members' list and brought out a diary.

"That's uncommonly kind of you, Mr Dunne. I'm not quite sure whether I'll be free to travel at Easter; but I'll certainly take a note of it and let you know. What's the address?"

Joe slipped the members' book into his pocket while Lord Swords was writing in his diary.

Out in the street again he began to question the wisdom of what he had done. His old patient certainly appeared to be quite sane again; but if T. T. was in a bad temper and inclined to be captious he might refuse to give Joe credit for his bag up to date. It would look better on paper than in reality, a condition to which T. T. was too well used in business ventures to relish when he found it in his guest lists.

But as always with Joe, he had reassured himself by the time he reached the Shelbourne Hotel and met Alan coming out.

Joe was inclined by an excess of bonhomie to conceal a certain unease Alan aroused in him. It rubbed old sores. One side of him—the underside—was complacent that his niece might marry into a circle from which he had always been excluded; the other wanted to avenge the past. When the upper-side was in the ascendant Joe hoped that Milly would spit in Alan's eye.

Today Joe was *up*, but his purposes were all constructive, and he regarded Alan's appearance at that moment as further evidence of the divine plan. After greeting, Joe leaped in at once before he allowed himself to be discouraged by a look in Alan's eyes that signalled escape.

"Made your Easter plans yet?"

"I shall be staying with my uncle, I expect."

"In Waterford."

Alan nodded.

"The Prestons are coming down to Derravaragh, Talbot Thompson's place in Westmeath. I wondered if you would like to come along."

"I don't know Mr Talbot Thompson, unfortunately."

"You've met him. He's a first-rate fellow when you get to know him. But that's not easy. He's close is T. T. I want to bring him out and the best way is to give a blow-out when he comes at Easter. He gave me a free hand to ask whoever I liked; and the grub will be good. I am in charge of the commissariat. I will guarantee the grub."

"It is very kind of you, but I don't like to let my uncle down."

"That's the bishop, I take it. Why not bring him along? There's room for everyone."

"I'm afraid my uncle's Easter duties will hardly allow him to leave Waterford."

"Quite right. I forgot that. But I'm sure when he hears you will be with young people he won't want to involve you in his Easter Duties. I can't see you reading the lessons somehow. I'm sure Milly will be disappointed; I'll have to see what I can do with the Garrison in Mullingar. Fortunately there's no shortage of men in that quarter."

"I don't think there's any need to look for company for the Prestons. I should imagine they are looking forward to country quiet."

"What's that, young fellow-my-lad! When did a girl think the country was spoilt by a uniform or two on the landscape? Not in my time. If you leave a girl like Milly to her own devices you can't expect her to stay in purdah, you know. Unless both of you become anchorites over Easter. Are there no young people in Waterford? There used to be."

"Uncle goes to the Castle at Easter. And we shall meet our friends there. It's an annual event."

"There you are! What's sauce for the gander is sauce for the goose. While you are disporting yourself at the Castle, Milly must be allowed to throw a loose leg."

"I dislike that expression."

"If it comes to plain speaking, I dislike to see a girl like my niece being led on a string. And so far as I am concerned, if I can find amusement for her in Westmeath I shall encourage her to take it."

Alan was now in a rage. He was accustomed to think of Joe as unworthy of serious consideration, liked to think that he could always count on quelling him with a glance if the necessity to do so ever arose. Now he was looking at eyes in which there was a sort of sly defiance. It was sheer impudence.

He was not going to be led into discussing Milly with this mountebank uncle of hers. Did she know this invitation was in the wind? Why had she not mentioned it? After what had happened yesterday he didn't want this fellow to go back to Buttercup Square and give his version of this conversation. What had possessed him to mention the party at the Castle? He had left Milly under the impression that he was solely governed by concern for his uncle's widowed hearth. She would think him treacherous. He hadn't meant to deceive her about Easter, but had grown so accustomed to the wall between his two lives that he forgot it was a partition erected by himself, solely for his own convenience.

His righteous indignation hardly convinced himself; it did not convince Joe. This was familiar country to him. He had travelled it many times, knew every turn and twist of the road. The gaze of the two men met; and Alan, for the first time, read criticism of himself in those smiling eyes, and knowledge and latent antagonism. He read also that Milly was a point of principle for Joe, if Joe had a point of principle. She was the only ground upon which he would ever fight a moral battle. His deeply cynical gaze was a challenge, and he had now, when he exerted energy to use it, the overwhelming advantage of age when it has right on its side.

Alan capitulated. He forgot his moral indignation. He took out his pocket-diary. He seemed to be making calculations of ways and means. Finally, he said he would try to come. He would put it emphatically: he was sure he could come; but he would have to make excuses to his uncle. He didn't like to do that.

Joe, his point won, became sympathetic at once. "If he has ever seen Milly, he won't require a long explanation," he said. "Even a bishop is not immune to a skirt."

"Oh, I'll arrange it with my uncle," Alan said, loftily now, resenting the familiarity of the other.

"If you have any friends who would like to come down, I could get a mount for them, you know."

"Thank you. I wouldn't dream of it."

Alan bowed, and left Joe to pick up the bails he had scattered with his last ball.

XXI

LADY KELLY RECEIVED the invitation to Derravaragh
with unconcealed delight. It was made out by Joe in T. T's name,
and sent from Derravaragh. For all her formidable presence,
nobody had ever asked her to stay in a great house before. Derravaragh, compared with the mansions at which the nobility entertained at week-ends in England, was a modest abode. But in Lady
Kelly's mind it assumed the proportions of Blenheim, and in her
imagination she could see the distinguished guests arrive, the comfort of it all, the splendour of the appointments, the brilliance of
the table talk, and a sudden extension of her social horizon
embracing not only the county families of Westmeath but of the
neighbouring counties as well.

Henceforth a great deal of her time would be spent in the
country she decided; and she wished Dolly were at hand, as in the
old days, to accompany her when she went out to equip herself for
a round of visits to the first families in the land.

She had been impressed by Mr Talbot Thompson from the
moment she laid eyes on him. She liked the sort of man who filled
his clothes, and of whose presence, because he took up so much
space, one could not but be aware. Sir Patrick had been meanly
built. He had looked inadequate beside her, even in his court suit,
which revealed the poverty of his legs. Not until he became a
corpse did her spouse look really dignified. A shroud became him.

In a way she would prefer if the house guests were not *too*
grand for her first visit. It would be pleasant to bring home to her
host how well-equipped she was for these occasions. Lady Fingall
acted as hostess for Sir Horace Plunkett, a bachelor. Why should
she not play a similar part at Derravaragh? He could hardly find
anyone available better equipped to grace his table. Poor Carrie.
She lacked presence. Was she setting her cap at her brother's
wealthy friend? The Prestons had revealed such an unbecoming
streak of slyness that she wouldn't put it past her. But by inviting
her, Mr Talbot Thompson showed pretty clearly that he knew
what was what. Carrie would not do at all in a county setting. She

was just a pretty little portionless widow, such as one may see listening to the band for nothing any day you care to take a stroll on the pier.

She might, she told herself, looking into the glass on her dressing table—she might have to drop Mr Talbot Thompson a hint that the Prestons were not quite all their uncle was probably cracking them up to be. She owed it to him if she accepted his hospitality. But he would probably ask her advice in any case. She knew she had made an impression when they met. This confirmed it.

Joe Dunne should not have landed his relations on the man. It was a typically Irish thing to do, and probably made a very bad impression. What had Carrie to contribute? Dolly was off the market. Milly could benefit very much from an opportunity of this kind. She would see for herself how the best people behaved. She could have seen it long ago if she had had the sense to come to Merrion Square when invited. As it was she was a perfect hobble-dehoy, flirting openly with a young man at her Academy party; it must have made a very bad impression. Milly, if it wasn't too late, could certainly learn something from a week-end in good society.

On second thoughts she was glad Dolly was out of the way. She could not make her own preparations and ignore the Prestons. She did not want to be lumped with them. They would go down to Derravaragh practically as dependents. It was an act of charity inviting them. Her coming was on another level. It set the tone of the party. She dispatched her reply, reluctantly, to her host at his country house. Had she known his London address, she would have sent her reply to him there. As it was, she was too eager to get it back, to wait while she fished out his address in England.

She enclosed a formal acceptance with a note offering to assist in any way while her host was abroad. His staff might be unused to local customs; he had only to command her and she would be at her service. She made a reference to the Royal visit in July, and said that for anyone else but Mr Talbot Thompson her preparation for that occasion would have constrained her to refuse to leave home for a moment.

In order to be with Milly at Easter, Alan was forced to lie. His uncle, he knew, would be in communication with the ladies in Blackrock, and no excuse of work or illness would be accepted;

neither would mystery about his movements. That would bring matters to a head. That they would come to a head eventually and might as well be settled now was a course that did not recommend itself to him. Meanwhile, a miracle was awaited; the death of all Alan's relations was the only one that would get him over his difficulties. He would imperil any expectation he had from his uncle and aunts in any event, and the longer he left them in suspense the less likely it was that they would reconcile themselves to the idea of the match. Carslake said as much in his incoherent way; but Alan's reply to him was a reminder that he didn't know Alan's relations or how unpleasant they could make life for him. "Life is damned unpleasant sometimes, old boy. You learn that as you go on. Tessa's—"

But Alan had heard enough about his friend's troubles with his wife's extravagance; it seemed a small burden to bear in comparison with his own.

This ought to be the happiest time of his life, but it was spoiled by the need for secrecy. He let his uncle think he was coming to stay for Easter and decided to invent a call to England as a last minute excuse. Carslake agreed to send the telegram to Blackrock and even to play the part of the stricken deer. There was no end to his good-nature; but even when he rehearsed his role he could not avoid saying, "I think, you know, it would be better for everyone in the long run if you plucked up courage and had it out with the bodyguard. It's not as if you had any reason to be ashamed of Milly. I wouldn't mind a walk down the aisle with that on my arm."

The lie hung over Alan and depressed him. Milly had been the cause of it. By his devotion he was involving himself in unworthy behaviour. He looked in from outside, taking his uncle's point of view, discouraged by what he saw.

But the telegram worked so well, and his aunts—Susan in particular—were so proud of his determination to put off a delightful week-end with a gay house-party in order to sit with a sick friend, that he was put on good terms with himself. That is how he would behave if the circumstances arose, he was sure. The aunts rang up their brother to break the news; and Alan was relieved to hear them repeat the name Carslake several times and to mention his connection with the peerage of Scotland.

He left in a cab for Kingstown; but once outside the gate,

directed the driver to Broadstone Station, where he was meeting the Prestons. He and they were going down by train. Lady Kelly was being driven by the Roches in Bernard's new Talbot. The Roches were pleased to oblige her, and to accept her inevitable snubs as one does the smells in the lion house. The rest of the party were delighted with this arrangement. Their host's decision to invite the tyrant from Merrion Square had depressed them; but they were independent now; Dolly was no longer to be sat upon, and it was decided not to let her spoil what promised to be a happy holiday. Joe had escaped censure by saying that T. T. had insisted on Lady Kelly's presence. He had done his very best, but even from his headquarters in Westmeath he had been unable to establish any contact with the local families. He consulted Carrie about the wisdom of inviting officers met casually in Mullingar to join them; but she advised him to take care. It was not as if a ball were in view. Mr Talbot Thompson might object that the garrison would not further his interests in the county. That left Lord Swords as the only card in Joe's hand. If he, as appeared to be the case, was *compos mentis* again, it would look well in *Irish Society* to read that he was among the guests. In England T. T. had never slept under the same roof as a peer, even one so eccentric as Lord Swords, Joe was reasonably certain.

"Your uncle is trying to do his best for everyone. All we can do is to show we appreciate it and enjoy ourselves. I hope, for his sake, Mr Talbot Thompson will realise how much trouble he has given and show his gratitude to Joe in some practical way." That was what Carrie told her daughters when they complained about Lady Kelly's threatened presence. Joe had, after all, arranged for them to spend the week-end in the country with their lovers.

"It's like *A Midsummer Night's Dream*," Dolly said.

"With Uncle Joe playing Bottom." Milly knew the play better than Dolly did.

"Milly, dear!" Carrie found Milly distressingly outspoken.

They were laughing among themselves, and looking charming, Alan thought, when his cab delivered him at the station in good time. Even Dolly, whom he had begun to resent because she glanced at him critically, looked attractive with her youth and slenderness. A train journey with them, and Milly facing him in the carriage, was a perfect prelude to a holiday. Everyone was happy today. Alan, for once, was gay. When his face lighted up with laughter, Carrie understood Milly's enslavement. Arthur had not been as classically handsome as Alan; but he, when she first met him, had something of the same fascination. Both of them were men that nature intended as lovers rather than husbands; but those are the men that women want to marry. When Alan was in good humour he had a caressing manner. It was unfortunate that he should ever have to grow old. In the comedy of life such men are cast for romantic leads; when they become too old for them they ought to leave the stage. Alan, she decided, would not age well, but he might become a good, conventional husband. There was nothing mysterious about him, none of Arthur's depths to plumb. He was all on the surface.

As she looked at Milly's unconcealed pleasure in his company the thought occurred to her for the first time—'even if the marriage comes about, will Milly be content?' She would develop; Alan would only age. Perhaps it might be better for Milly in the long run if this romance blew over. God, no doubt, if He saw this, had arranged it all. Better leave it in His hands. He had looked after Dolly. It remained to be discovered, when all is known, what His purpose had been in killing Arthur off so soon. That it would all be made plain, Carrie never doubted, or never doubted for long. Faith kept her going. And today, as the April fields raced past the carriage windows, smiling on the three young people she saw God's blessing on them all, and was thankful.

God's blessing, plainly was not on Uncle Joe when the train drew up at Multyfarnham and he was espied at the entrance in a motoring coat, too large to be his own. Harassment was written on his every feature; and that appearance of being poised for flight was more in evidence than it had been latterly. Carrie read Joe's face, even from the end of the platform, like a map.

"I wonder what has gone wrong," she murmured to Dolly. Alan had gone to fetch the porter, who was already occupied with other passengers. Joe gallantly attempted a wave and a smile; but as they walked over to the Benz he confided his troubles to Carrie. "T. T. hasn't arrived; and has sent no word. I sent him three telegrams. I didn't know how I was going to explain this to Swords, but he is not coming. His solicitors wrote to say there is some trouble in that quarter. Pity. I'm having hell with staff, I'll tell you all about it. Where is Lady Kelly?"

"The Roches are driving down with her. They expect to arrive in time for afternoon-tea."

The women had brought veils for the journey; but a recent shower had put down the dust and they were not necessary. All three sat inside. Joe took the wheel, and asked Alan to swing the starting—handle.

"Keep your thumb behind the handle or you may break it if the starter kicks," he warned.

Alan made several attempts, and was very red in the face before the engine started. Then he took his place beside Joe, rather resenting the manner in which the latter ordered him about.

Joe, the man of many accomplishments, was still new to motor-car driving. "I want T. T. to put a car in for the Gordon Bennett. It would be a tremendous start in the country if he pulled that off. Though I say it as shouldn't, I think I could take on any competition at this game. It only requires nerve. Don't look back."

The last observation related to a hen that had scurried across the road.

"Every time I've gone out in the Benz it's cost me five shillings in restitution money. I don't mind chickens, but I hate it when I run over dogs."

Joe, at the wheel, was temporarily transformed. Worries had blown away. There was an atavistic gleam in his changeful eyes. He missed a pillar of the entrance gate by a hair's breadth, and with the throttle full out raced up the drive, and drew up in a shower of gravel at the steps of Derravaragh. It took his passengers a moment to recover before they could look around. The house was a Victorian castellated mansion such as brewers had built elsewhere in Ireland; neo-Gothic, grey. It looked across a lawn of grass, waist-high, towards the lake.

"It will look very different when we get it ship-shape," Joe said to Alan, noticing that his eyes had rested momentarily on the gravel, through which a crop of early grass was making a coy appearance.

"Leave your bags where they are. I'll get someone to bring them in," Joe said.

Dolly rhapsodized over the lake. "What a perfect setting," she said.

"Setting," Alan agreed, rather grimly.

Joe took Carrie's arm and ushered her up the steps. "I was let down. The villain who promised to get me staff has landed us with every unemployable stray in the parish. The kitchen-maid had an epileptic fit this morning. I believe most of them have never been in a house before, and the chef, it seems, was sacked from the Greville Arms for drinking. I've been trying to sober him up, and I have put all the drink under lock and key; but you will have to give everything a look-over. It's just as well T. T. is late; but I wish I knew when he intends to arrive. Imagine the Marchioness of Merrion Square if she drives up and finds only ourselves in residence. She will not be amused."

Carrie had indulged in a modest fantasy of the coming weekend. It included no responsibility for house-keeping, pleasant food, well-warmed rooms, sufficient servants, ease. She expected no greater entertainment. Her dream vanished. She found herself in a strange house, with raw servants, superintending bedrooms, arranging meals.

Joe took the young people for a tour of the gounds: they returned to find luncheon laid out. Joe had taken the precaution of laying in large stocks. Mr Talbot Thompson's credit had been launched on a princely scale in the town, whatever might be the fate of his social career in the county. Cold meats were laid out on the sideboard, and the guests helped themselves. A part of the afternoon was going to be devoted by Carrie to a crash course in the mechanics of waiting to the likeliest of three sisters, none of whom had undergone the experience previously.

After lunch, Dolly stayed behind to help her mother. Joe, in desperation, went out with a gun in search of rabbits. Alan and Milly went down to the lake. His spirits had slumped when he arrived at the door of Derravaragh; and the chaotic conditions within, the absence of their host, the farce of the whole proceeding, made him regret that he hadn't 'done the right thing' and gone to Waterford. A friend from Oxford, Rose Power (the first girl he ever kissed), and other attractive young people would be there now in high spirits, waited upon, surrounded by hosts of friends; everything as it should be. Here it was like an Irish comic novel; and when the awful Kelly woman and the consequential Bernard with his obsequious parents arrived, he wouldn't even be able to be alone with Milly.

She was determined to enjoy the afternoon with Alan. They had never been together in the country before. As to the chaos of her uncle's contriving, she was upset only on her mother's account. The brunt of it fell on her. Whether or not their host was there didn't seem to her to matter. She had come away to be with Alan, and he had come to be with her. They should not allow any circumstances to spoil that. It was foolish, she now realised, to have encouraged Joe in his fantasy. But as they had, and it had suffered the fate of all his others, it was better to try and see the funny side of it. He would himself eventually. That was the most endearing of his traits and the explanation of his survival.

The sun had come out in full splendour, having sulked behind clouds since their arrival. Milly smiled into it, closing her eyes, then turned to Alan as if to ask him to follow the sun's example and come out from behind his clouds. He was always reluctant to leave a sulk; but Milly was determined not to let him spoil the day by clinging to the present one. She knew him too well now. He would come tomorrow, when the day had been wasted, and ask her to forgive yesterday's bad temper.

They were walking side by side. He had not taken her hand. Suddenly she stopped—the house was out of sight—and took his face in her hands. "Alan. You are not to spoil the day. I forbid you to."

"I'm sorry," he said, not prepared to capitulate at once, "but quite honestly I think it was an outrage to bring you down here. I wonder if your uncle is quite right in the head."

"Don't be cross on our account, dear. We are all as happy as larks. I am only sorry Mama has been landed with the housekeeping; but all will be well, you will see; and, anyhow, what does it matter. You didn't come all this way to see Mr Talbot Thompson, did you?"

"Certainly not. But I think he shouldn't be allowed to get away with this behaviour. I think your uncle is greatly to blame for exposing you to such a cad as the man must be. I blame myself. He looked a very fishy customer, I thought."

Milly did not reply at once. She gave Alan a glance which he did not recognise, a quick glance. Then she took her hands away from his face and looked down.

"What's wrong?"

"I'm worried."

"Don't let it worry you. You are not responsible."

"I am thinking of something else."

"Of what?"

"Of you."

"What have I to do with it?"

"Nothing. It has nothing to do with you. It's so frightfully unimportant. In a few days it will be over. In the meanwhile we shall have spent a week-end together in the country. And yet you complain like an old colonel returned from India with a bad liver. You may criticise Uncle Joe as much as you please, but at least he isn't a prig."

"Are you suggesting that I am a prig?"

"You have been behaving like one."

"I know I have a great many faults, but I never thought anyone would ever call me a prig. Ask Carslake. He knows me. Ask him if I am a prig."

"I don't want to call anyone into consultation. I wanted to be happy. I wanted to laugh. I did not want or expect to have to listen to a lecture."

They had come now to the edge of the lake. At this point it formed the base of a triangle of water at the tip of which a headland hid from view the upper end of the lake. There were trees everywhere. To the left the lake lay under the side of a high hill. A rook flew out of a copse where the upper met the lower lake, and wheeled across the water, flying low; then it changed course and made for the trees on the hill, with strong strokes of its black wings. Within a few feet of where they stood a fish rose; and little circles, growing larger, spread across the surface of the lake.

Alan took Milly's hand. She let it lie in his; but it was her turn now to slow the pace of reconciliation. Why should he always be the one to sulk and grumble? Why should she have to live on the margin of his disapproval? Why should her relations be subject to his critical scrutiny while behaviour of his had to be accepted as the vagary of divine right? He took it for granted that she would love him and wait on his convenience; all the concession was on her side. It was intolerable. So she did not return the pressure of his hand and took hers away when she saw primroses under a bank. She stopped to pick them with a conscientiousness which gave him the impression of rejection although, to an onlooker, it might have seemed that there was an indication of distraction in her unnecessary thoroughness. He began at first to help her, but she was picking faster than he, having apparently more dedication.

All he achieved was to get in her way, for which he several times apologised.

There was a limit to the number of primroses. She stood up with a large posy in her hands and looked around. He followed her gaze and was relieved to see no more flowers in the immediate vicinity. "There might," she said, as if they had come out to make a collection, "be some over there where the wood comes down to the water."

"The path is very wet."

"This is very dull for you. I'm sure Uncle Joe will lend you a gun if you'd like to murder rabbits."

"I don't find it dull."

"Picking primroses? I don't think that is an occupation for a man. And you are not very good at it."

"It seems that I am good for nothing."

"I think I see some over there, near that shed."

He feigned an interest by looking where she pointed, towards a battered-looking building on the path, just before the land rose up steeply.

"Is that a boat-house, do you think? Let's go and see."

This time she took his hand, and he allowed her to lead him like a child.

The house, when they arrived at it, turned out to be a crazy structure of planks over a small rowing-boat.

Milly looked into it. "I can't see any oars."

"Here they are, hidden in the grass."

"Let's go for a row."

"Do you think the boat belongs to the house?"

"Let's assume it does, and if someone disputes our right apologise graciously. That's half the battle; most people are so reluctant to apologise, or apologise too abjectly. I'm an expert at apologising."

"I suggest that you do the apologising for both of us if the occasion arises."

"Agreed; and you steal the boat. That's a fair division of labour."

Milly sat in the stern, Alan rowed. It was one of his accomplishments; and he was pleased to show himself off in a favourable light. He took off his coat and rolled up his shirt sleeves, hoping Milly noticed the fine development of muscle.

She put her hands to the coil in which her hair was held and shook it free. It fell around her like a cloak. She tossed it back from her face. The sun sparkled on her hair, on the water, on Alan's white shirt. No sound competed with the straining of the oars against the rowlocks and the plash of the water as the oars pushed it away. Sometimes it slopped gently against the side over which Milly hung an idle hand. Their eyes met and they smiled, rejoicing in each other. This is how it should be, this is how it would be, forever now.

When they came to the intersection of the two sheets of water, Alan rested on his oars and let the boat ride. Sometimes it was still, sometimes movement in the lake sent the water slapping against the side, and the boat rocked gently.

"I think this is the lake on which the children of Lir spent three hundred years of their lives," Milly said.

"I wish we were the children of Lir."

"They had to spend it in the form of swans."

"I don't think I'd like that. Who were the children of Lir?"

"It's an Irish fairy tale."

"Oh."

A shadow passed across Alan's face, a barely perceptible cloud.

"I wish we could row to the end of the earth," he said.

She sensed behind the softness of his expression a yearning, not so much to travel with her, as to escape from Ireland and his problems.

"We can go to the ends of the earth if we really want to."

"Now, I mean, in this boat."

"It would be easy then."

"I should have to row."

"You row very well."

His smile altered; he was pleased she had noticed. He feared she might not have. But she didn't attach great importance to his prowess or she would have remarked on it before. Had the conversation not taken this turn she might not have mentioned it at all. She was not easy to impress.

"I nearly got my blue."

"Your blue?"

"At Oxford, for rowing. Had I stayed up another year I was certain of it."

"Let me tell you something. This is the first time I have ever been in a boat. There was a lake near our school in Holland, where we skated in the winter, but we were never allowed to boat on it."

Another cloud passed over Alan's face. She was sorry she mentioned the skating. It was the one incident in her relation with Alan for which she reproved herself. She had not been perfectly true to him. At the recollection, her colour changed almost imperceptibly. She looked at him shyly to see if forgiveness was complete, and noticed that he had reddened and looked down. In the water he saw a puffy face, with small lines round the eyes, very close to his. He felt warm breath and through it a faint far scent of brandy, then a stronger smell of sweat and powder.

"He hasn't really forgiven me," Milly thought; but she felt no resentment now. She leaned forward and as she did so her hair cascaded over her face in a penitential rush of gold. Alan shipped an oar, and bent forward to seize the hand that she held out as if asking for forgiveness now. He pressed his face against her hand, keeping his head down, grateful and ashamed, bitterly ashamed. If only he could erase that evening from his memory. Damn Carslake! What possessed him to confide in such a commonplace fellow? It was profane. There were tears in his eyes when he looked at Milly. Of these he was at once ashamed. It was unmanly to cry.

But Milly blessed them. He was really moved, she knew, by the recollection of the threat to their happiness because she had been silly and he unforgiving. There was no condecension in tears. His washed away even the priggishness she had charged him with. Now between them all was perfect as on the first evening when they kissed in the hall. They had been allowed to return to Eden, and they must never do anything that might cause them to be expelled a second time.

Alan let her hand go; and so as not to have to meet her too candid eyes, busied himself with the oars. The boat had begun to drift towards the further shore.

A flock of wild geese rushed overhead, with a warning cry, leaving their sadness on the air. A sharp wind came across the lake, staining the surface with streaks of grey; ragged clouds followed in its wake, coming over the hill; the trees seemed to close in on themselves, withdrawing their shelter from the lake.

Alan said nothing but began to row. He looked determined now.

Milly liked the thought that her safety was in his hands. So long as they were together she had no thought of danger.

Rain fell in cold deliberate drops, a space between each; then in a shower of thin needles; then as a flapping sheet through which could be faintly seen the gloom of the wood.

"We'll make it," Alan said. He had been alarmed, because he had had experience of the treachery of lakes; but now they were under the shelter of the shore, and he knew he could get them safely to the slip.

After he tied up the boat, they held hands and ran along the path. She stumbled and he grabbed her arm, pulling her towards him. Rain ran from her hair in little streams down her cheeks. Her eyes glowed. They stood together in the storm; it wrapped them round.

"I like the taste of rain," she said.

It had not occurred to him, but he decided on reflection that he did; off her mouth, off her skin, off her eyes and ears, off the sea-weed that was her hair. Then they ran hand in hand towards the house.

XXII

THE APPEARANCE OF Milly and Alan, apparently half-drowned, coincided with the debouchment of the Roche party from the Talbot, and dampened the effect of Lady Kelly's entrance. They had to be hustled off to their rooms and hot water fetched from the kitchen, Carrie standing over the housemaids to superintend their efforts. They declined, however, on principle to go further than bed-room doors, on which they thumped and shouted: "Yer water."

A man-servant had arrived during the afternoon from the Greville Arms, having heard from the chef that he was in clover.

"I don't mind now," Joe told Carrie. "There is someone to wait at table. T. T. will have to admit we are keeping up appearances. I'll tell the fellow to stay in the hall and remain on view, that's the main thing."

He was there to fuss over the luggage in the Talbot, and to carry in Lady Kelly's excessive baggage.

Joe's spirits rose again. What of it if T. T. never arrived? For a whole week-end he could act the part of host in a country mansion. It was a dream come true, if only a fleeting one. Instead of going anxiously to the door and peering down the drive, he gave himself entirely to his guests, and whenever he thought of T. T. sent up a prayer that his ship had sunk in the crossing with all hands. His fantasy grew once he gave it rein. Carrie's assistance was exactly what he would have wished for in his own mansion; they were in constant consultation about ever-recurring crises; and when the guests were assembled in the drawing-room and about to go into dinner, Carrie had to take Joe aside to advise him that the butler, she had just been informed by the chef, was the boots in the Greville Arms and had never waited at table in that establishment. Joe made his familiar gesture, a gentle brushing aside of hostile forces, an expression of faith; but the intelligence possibly accounted for a certain stiffening of the back as he led Lady Kelly into dinner. To her he had confided his belief that T. T. had met with an accident, and he begged her to honour his confidence so as not to alarm the others. But there was no indication during dinner that anyone was giving a thought to the fate of their mysterious host. Joe saw to it that his cellars yielded an ever-flowing supply of the choicest wines, sent down from Dublin.

The ex-boots, if unorthodox in his methods, was an effective waiter. He was inclined to join in conversation, having an answer ready for any query put to the table; and he was not satisfied merely to offer dishes; he recommended them, and urged the taking of larger helpings.

"Have another of the spuds. It will do you good. There's plenty more where those came from."

With a sure instinct he recognised in Lady Kelly's demeanour a likelihood of discouragement. He was satisfied to push the dishes at her, and sometimes from the wrong side. But Joe intervened on those occasions and sent him round to come again.

Lady Kelly, for all her decorum, had a pronounced weakness for men. Had Joe neglected her she would have taken a hostile view of the entertainment and seen the absence of her host, even if due to drowning, as a personal affront; but Joe overwhelmed her with his rickety charm, insisting that he recognised at last the person whom she reminded him of—the Jersey Lily, Edward's loveliest mistress, whom he had often seen in the 'eighties.

It was a perfect comparison, the risqué and the Royal in the happiest conjunction. Lady Kelly's bosom was seen to swell; and the former boots, who thought he heard her being compared to a Jersey cow, was fortunately able to conceal his mirth until he reached the kitchen, from where the roar reached the dining-room. The staff had already taken a dislike to her Ladyship.

Whenever Joe addressed Mrs Roche, sitting on his other side, Lady Kelly turned graciously to her left and snubbed Mr Roche. He took it with a good grace. He was enjoying his dinner, and Carrie, on his left, was pleasant and sensible. They were discussing wedding arrangements. Joe had put the lovers together, and it was just as well. Bernard pontificated about Joseph Chamberlain's visit to South Africa, and got on Alan's nerves; but Milly's foot played on his as if it were a piano pedal. The sweetness of the afternoon hung around them both, cutting them off, as if they were on an enchanted isle. Bernard was anxious to impress Alan and more than once brought up the subject of his uncle; when this happened

Dolly asked him to fetch her shawl, or dropped her napkin, and succeeded by her wise manoeuvres in heading him off.

Champagne was served with the sweet course, and Joe rose to his feet to toast the engaged couple. Milly kept her eyes on her plate in anticipatory embarrassment. It would be very like Joe to refer to Alan and herself. The dangerous moment passed, and all was well. Only then did she meet Alan's eyes. There was perfect sympathy between them. He, too, had had his anxious moment.

After dinner the men sat on for a very short port session. Bernard showed signs of wanting to continue his political lectures and Alan made an attempt to hide his impatience. "What a bore the fellow is," he told himself; and, not for the first time, he winced at the prospect of having such a connection in the same town as his uncle. If only Milly were less devoted to that sister of hers. There was a time when everyone connected with Milly had a glamour for Alan; but lately he had begun to pick on their disadvantages. It was as if he held them responsible for the difficulties in his path. Listening to Bernard, he thought again that he must take up his uncle's offer to go to London. It was the only way in which marriage could be saved from continual humiliation. He would wait until they got back to Dublin to discuss it with Milly. She must not think that it meant a weakening of his resolve; and when Dolly married, why should not Milly and her mother settle in London? Milly could study art much better there than in Dublin.

Joe, ever watchful himself bored by Bernard, suggested that they should join the ladies.

Among the furnishings that he had added to the house was a grand piano—for which with other items T. T. would be confronted in due course. Joe had ordered it with this party in mind. He was never one to wreck his ship for want of a ha'porth of tar. Of all proverbs it was the one to which he most often had recourse.

As soon as they joined the ladies he proposed at once that they should have a concert. He insisted on choruses, and aroused in Lady Kelly an unexpected urge to sing some of the numbers with which she had entertained her parents' circle in happier days. Her voice, surprisingly, was soprano. Joe and she sang a duet. Mr Roche sang a patriotic ballad. Bernard recited Longfellow. Alan did not attempt to shine; but he stood beside Milly when she played.

Carrie, too, took no part in the entertainment. From time to time mysterious knocks on the door summoned her to consultation in the hall. For safety's sake she made a tour of the bedrooms. Lady Kelly's in particular was inspected to see that the bed was warm, the fire alight, and the necessary furniture in decent order for when the night came.

It was she who gave the signal for bed. The evening had excited her. She looked with tenderness on Joe. In a wild rush of bonhomie she offered Carrie the use of Merrion Square for Dolly's wedding. Bernard made a speech of thanks which everyone could have done without. It might have gone on indefinitely if Joe had not cried "Hear! Hear!" and clapped him on the back at the end of a sentence. "We must have a night-cap after that," he said. Punch was in preparation. The former boots brought in the bowl. By now he was in no condition to wait on anyone, having too obviously waited on himself. Mr Roche, the soberest of the party, led him out of the room.

Joe filled the punch glasses and then raised his own. His eye, too bright for caution now, met Milly's. She was only able to beseech him by her expression not to spoil the evening when a loud knocking on the hall door made everyone put down their glasses.

They waited to discover if they had imagined it; then an even louder knock was accompanied by a rattle as if someone was trying to push the door in.

Joe led the way, followed by the others. The hall was lit by bedroom candles which Carrie had prepared just before and placed on a table. Once again the knocker pounded on the door. "Its like Macbeth," Dolly said. "Its T. T." Joe corrected her. There was in the sound, in any event, the threat of doom. The door was fastened by a bolt and chain and it creaked on opening. Against the night sky, lit by a full moon, the large figure was unmistakable. It took somewhat longer to recognise in its shadow another.

In any circumstances a man arriving at his own party in his own house provides a certain incongruity. The welcome is going the wrong way. And when staged in semi-darkness—the candles made the merest flicker—the effect was massively discouraging.

"We must install gas here," is what Mr Talbot Thompson said; and in the circumstances everybody felt the appropriateness of the observation.

Bernard was responsible for fetching the lamp. His curiosity was creative in its intensity. He lit the scene. Mr Talbot Thompson was wearing a motoring coat and a trilby hat which he now took off. He bowed to each of the ladies, repeating their names until he came to Mrs Roche, when memory deserted him, so he bowed twice instead. To the men he raised an hierarchic hand as if in benediction.

Standing in front of his companion, who was discocooning herself of a motoring veil, as if he were putting her up for auction, he said, "Let me introduce you to Mrs Ball."

Mrs Ball, freed at last, peered shyly round, then she ran in a kittenish way up to Joe, grasped his hand and stared wistfully into his face.

"I know Mr Dunne," she said. Then she looked around and saw Alan, who had stepped back into the drawing-room, making himself more conspicuous as the room was well lighted.

"And here is another friend. How are the Carslakes? Don't tell me they are staying here too. I'm surrounded by friends. This must be Milly. Joe is never tired of talking about you."

She took Dolly's hands in hers. Nobody corrected her. Nobody spoke a word.

"Mrs Ball is hungry," Mr Talbot Thompson said. "We could do with supper. What have you got for us, Joe?"

"I'm afraid the servants have gone to bed," Carrie said, "but I am sure we can find something."

"Don't tell me. Let me guess. You must be Carrie," Mrs Ball said to her.

"If you would bring them into the dining-room, Joe. I'll see what I can find. Dolly, will you look after Mrs — "

"Ball," said Mrs Ball.

"There's a fire in the dining-room," Carrie said, so that Mrs Ball might relieve herself of her fur coat. She stood holding it, like a retriever with a bird, waiting to be relieved of it, but nobody volunteered, so she handed the coat to Mr Talbot Thompson, who put it on a chair on top of his own.

Joe led the way to the dining-room. The new arrivals followed him. They passed Alan, who had wedged himself into the space between the door of the drawing-room and the stairs. Mr Talbot Thompson bowed gravely as he passed; Mrs Ball paused and offered to settle his tie.

"There. That's better," she said, adding, "That's a nice piece of cloth," as she patted his waistcoat. Then she went back to where Milly stood alone and, lifting up a candle, inspected her features.

"No. You're Milly. Joe said you were like your father, and he's right. You are the spit and image of Arthur. I'd know those eyes anywhere."

She pressed Milly's arm reassuringly, then called out, "Wait for me," and hurried after the retreating men.

There was a pause as after a distant and disturbing noise before Lady Kelly said, "I am going to bed."

She took a candle-stick and led the way upstairs in a silence that spoke of outrage not to be entrusted to the inadequate resources of common speech. Dolly followed. Mrs Roche came behind. Her spouse was on her heels. Bernard brought up the rear. When Lady Kelly was berthed, he would visit his parents. He had much to say. Milly stayed behind. She was alone with Alan. It was imperative that she should talk to him before they went to bed. He had not left his corner until the coast was clear; now he came out and took up one of the remaining candles.

"Good-night, Milly," he said, and went upstairs, leaving her alone in the hall.

She was sleeping in the dressing-room off the room shared by Carrie and Dolly, an arrangement suggested by Carrie who was never quite happy alone.

Carrie said very little to Dolly beyond agreeing with her that it was unusual for a lady to come into the country with any man other than her husband, and to put forward as an instant impression that the lady was most emphatically not a lady, did not look like one, or behave like one; and was a most unsuitable person to introduce to a country-house party. The less said about the matter the better; but the week-end would now take on a very different complexion; and it was becoming a pleasant family party, with even Fanny Kelly joining in the fun.

Dolly was longing to ask her mother how Mrs Ball had become acquainted with their menfolk, but found she could not form the question. She was perturbed at the impression this aspect of the matter must have made on the Roches, and she was by no means looking forward to listening to Bernard on the morrow. Carrie did not introduce the topic; and as Dolly brushed her mother's hair they enjoyed that sort of communion which is born when two people are keeping silent on the same topic at the same time.

Milly went into her room with a quick 'good-night' and closed the door. Dolly decided that she was angry at having Alan singled out by this mysterious Mrs Ball. It put him at a disadvantage with Bernard whom he had been quietly snubbing ever since he arrived. Bernard had nothing to explain. He never had; he never would have.

Before she went to bed Carrie went into Milly's room, shutting the door behind her. Dolly looked with dismay at the closed door; why was her mother discussing with Milly what she had not been prepared to discuss with her?

Milly had thrown herself on the bed without undressing. Carrie sat beside her and put an arm round her shoulders. Neither moved, neither spoke; when Milly sobbed, Carrie brushed her hair gently back from her forehead as she had done when the children complained of head-aches in nursery days.

"I know, darling, I know," she said, and when Milly gave a sudden movement as if throwing off some unseen pressure, added, "It's better not to ask. We are not supposed to know. I blame myself for this. Poor Joe! Disaster is his element. That awful man! Don't let it spoil things with Alan. I know it is very hard; but I would try to forget this evening as if it was an evil dream. I'll speak to Joe. He must talk to that man. I'd have given my right arm for this not to have happened. Your Papa—" But then she stopped. And after a while she felt Milly's arm round her. They lay beside one another, not speaking, feeling the beat of each other's heart; not mother and daughter, not woman and child; women together, weeping as women.

"I must go. Dolly will be wondering. Dolly's all right," Carrie whispered. Then she put the covers over Milly and went back to her room, where Dolly was pretending to be asleep.

Milly did not sleep. She re-enacted the scene in the hall over and over, recalling every face, every word. What was more inexplicable was the feeling of having seen it all before, of knowing it all. She recalled a day when she was about ten years old, in her father's library. There he worked and on no account was to be disturbed; there, important, mysterious, and sometimes fascinating strangers came to see him; and through the door, in the hall, she could hear the muffled sound of voices and imagined strange secrets. The children had their own books, but she had read them all, and she was alone; Carrie had taken Dolly to the dentist; the old nurse had a day out; the fire in the schoolroom had gone down. Milly went on a prowl. She went from one room to another, wondering at the four-poster in which her parents slept. Even now she came in on Sunday mornings and got in between them. Dolly didn't any more. Then she went into her father's dressing-room. Over the chest of drawers hung a picture of a most beautiful young man, dressed only in a leopard-skin, holding in his arms a young woman with a stately figure. Her long hair hung down over what looked like a night-gown. They were standing on a marble terrace among high pillars. "Wedded," was printed underneath, "after the painting by Lord Leighton."

It fascinated and puzzled her.

From the contemplation of that she went downstairs and looked into the dining-room to see how many places were laid. If there were a party, she would have to stay in the nursery. She hoped not. When her parents dined alone, Dolly and she were allowed to come down at coffee and were given what remained of the pudding.

The study was forbidden territory; but Milly looked in and saw an enormous fire blazing in the grate. It looked inviting after the miserable flicker in the school room; and the leather arm-chair had a compelling attraction.

First she had to find something to read. Two walls were given up to law but a third was packed to the ceiling with other books, sets of novels and plays, history books and, Milly saw on the lower shelf, books in paper covers. These were mostly in French, but some were in English. She picked a novel at random. Soon she was immersed in it.

The heroine had a very sad life until she made a successful appearance in the theatre; but this, according to the writer, led to trouble with her lover, a young man to whose origin some mystery attached. Admirers called on the heroine in her dressing-room; one, an aristocrat, hideously old, took her out to supper and made her drink wine. There were other scenes when he and other men visited her in her bedroom. She seemed to live in a bedroom. There was much that Milly could not understand.

She felt a shadow, but couldn't take her eyes off the book. It was like a blow from Heaven when a hand reached out and took it away from her.

"That isn't suitable for you. You must not rummage among my books."

"Have you many unsuitable books?"

"You will always find some in any library."

"Why do you keep them if they are unsuitable?"

"Unsuitable for little girls of your age. Grown-ups and children are different. But you have to grow up to realise that."

"And grown-ups can read unsuitable books. Do you read them?"

"Unsuitable for children, I said."

"But why?"

"Because there are things that children don't understand, that they will only know about when they grow up."

"But why can't they be taught them now? Why do they have to wait?"

"I don't play Hunt the Slipper. You don't believe in Father Christmas any more. Each age has what is appropriate to it."

"But you could play Hunt the Slipper if you wanted to."

"Children have to be looked after. When you grow up, it will be time enough to look after yourself. You trust your Papa, don't you?"

Milly loved her father, but, at that moment, he neither looked nor sounded trustworthy. He liked her to read and was proud that she began to very young. It was he, not she, who had been found out.

"But I was enjoying the book even if I couldn't understand it all. There's a very rude woman in it who takes off her clothes when there's a gentleman in the room. I don't believe that, do you? Nobody could be so rude."

"Exactly. That's why you shouldn't read about it."

"I wanted to find out why she did it."

"Milly. You must listen to me. We don't lock doors in this house. But I absolutely forbid you to take books of mine without first asking me for my permission. Do you understand?"

"But——"

"I don't want any buts. You are welcome to come in whenever you want to, provided you keep quiet. There are hundreds of splendid books to read. You don't have to delve into this sort of thing. You must not take any book without showing it to me."

"May I show it to Mama?"

"Don't worry your Mama."

All that she ever remembered of her clandestine reading was men sitting in evening clothes, with their hats on, while the heroine undressed. It warred incessantly with the picture in the dressing-room, the marmoreal figure in the leopard-skin. Lovers naked did not shock her; and she had been enchanted by a picture of Rodin's 'Kiss', which a girl had smuggled into school, as the last word in exciting depravity. What was horrible was the idea of a woman being treated as if she were a horse under inspection over a stable door. Although she had recently learned that Lord Leighton's pictures were emotionally false, the picture in her father's dressing-room, like her first idea of God as a bearded old man, persisted in her idea of what love with Alan would be like. It was impossible to reconcile with that other picture, of men in evening clothes, sitting with their hats on, watching a girl undress. But the people in those scenes had no exact definition. They had the vagueness of imagined faces. Now the faces were supplied. Why had the woman said she was the 'spit and image of Arthur'?

She fell asleep before the clock in the yard hammered out three. In a dream she saw a crowd round a figure on the road; she pressed forward, pushed her way past staring men in heavy frieze coats. A man was lying on the ground, his head in a pool of blood. Her father. She knelt and took his hand in her lap; but when she looked down she saw, not her father, but Alan, staring at her through glazed eyes.

The clock striking five woke her up. She got out of bed and dressed herself. Then she sat down at the table which Joe, so careful of everything dispensable in life, had furnished with headed writing-paper.

Dear Mama,

I am going back to Dublin to get my things; then I am going away to study. I shall write when I know my plans. Don't worry, I have money. I can't stay here now. Tell Dolly I will write to her.

With fondest love,

Milly.

She left the envelope on her pillow, and opened the door into the bedroom. Little snores were coming from Carrie's bed. The door was beside her own, and she did not have to cross the room to open and close it, without shutting it for fear the click of the bolt might give her away.

The hall door was too ponderous; she got out of the french window in the drawing-room and set off down the drive. There was certain to be an early train; and she counted on walking to the station in little more than an hour.

XXIII

BERNARD, HAVING LEFT his parents' bedroom, knocked on Alan's door. He had found them surprisingly obtuse about the situation; they were enjoying their week-end, argued that they should let Lady Kelly give the lead if any form of protest was to be made. Meanwhile the Christian course was to assume that the lady was a relation of Mr Talbot Thompson's, a sister-in-law, perhaps.

But Bernard was essentially a busy person; and in relation to the Prestons he saw himself as a protector. Once married to Dolly they would feel the full weight of his concern. But now he decided to consult Alan; they should both take the same line. If Dolly was in peril, so was Milly—more so, in fact, Alan not having yet assumed the responsibility he should have. At the back of Bernard's brain was an idea of making this the occasion to hint to Harvey that his conduct was in question. His dilemma would be delicious; he must either show concern for Milly and thereby declare his interest, or remain indifferent and forfeit her regard. Bernard, who noticed—without often understanding—everything, had seen that Milly was much more upset than Dolly by the events of the evening. It surprised him as he had regarded her as modern and inclined to be fast in comparison with Dolly. He intended to advise her in due course about her general demeanour if she came to stay in Waterford.

Bernard knocked twice; but there was no reply. He said who he was. There was silence within. Baffled, he withdrew. He wanted to talk to somebody, and even thought of looking for Joe; but Joe was a person with whom he had failed to get to grips. Joe seemed to laugh at him; and you can't lecture anyone who laughs. Reluctantly, he went to his own room, and lay down to think about the morning and his plan of campaign.

Alan lay in bed staring at the ceiling and not thinking. When the worst you can imagine happens there is nothing to do: the condemned criminal has had his mind made up for him; everything that worries men who wait on death in due course has been made irrelevant; the impossible has taken place; all the uncertainty of life has been resolved; death has been provided; the hour arranged; there is only to wait.

After perhaps an hour, this paralysis wore off; a still small voice summoned Alan back to reason. The confrontation of Milly and Mrs Ball was the worst that could happen to him. It had happened. Was there not a measure of relief in this? Ever since he had taken the stupid Carslake's advice he had felt at a moral disadvantage. He could never tell Milly about that sordid plan. Whatever of the past, once he had met her and they had love to share, it was as much his trust as hers. He had been outraged to see her at the rink; and yet, within three hours, was prepared to test his affection to the music of Mrs Ball's mattress. He had not looked at Milly: and he had assumed everything; but what, after all, had he to account for? He had been preserved. Mrs Ball knew her uncle; she had gone up to Milly in an impudent way and referred to 'Arthur's eyes'. Arthur? Milly's father!

He must find out more about the woman. Would Carslake know? Damn Carslake. Carslake was the cause of all the trouble. But, hold on! Was he being quite fair? Carslake had only offered in his blundering way to help. The source of the trouble was his infatuation for Milly. Had he not fallen for her attractions, he would be now in Waterford and possibly engaged to Rose Power. That was what his uncle wanted. Rose had made no secret of her feelings at Christmas. It was flattering; every man in the county was on Rose's track. She had everything to recommend her. But he had set his face against his own interests; he had sacrificed his prospects, his social position, his relations, his friends—for Milly.

Here he was in a gloomy house, bought furnished, by some rag and bone merchant, hob-nobbing with a hopeless outsider of dubious honesty, Waterford town folk, and a ludicrous knight's lady. It was a sorry mess; and could Talbot Thompson's appearance with the Ball woman not be seen as an act of Providence? An awful warning? Was he not compelled to decide at once whether to go on—and soon he would have no choice; busybody Bernard was probably preparing a writ for breach of promise in his mind even now—to go on and face the inevitable decline in all his standards that a union with such a family involved or break at once. In the long run it was probably in Milly's interests too. If she were not intent on marrying him she would go very far as an artist—and was it right for her to bury that talent in marriage with a man whom she (through no fault of her own, poor dear!) would have contrived to reduce to a hopeless mediocrity?

His duty was clear. That chap, Bernard, would come snooping again before breakfast. Get away before that. There was a train at breakfast time. He would get up as soon as there was a sound in the yard and get someone to drive him to the station. Excitement prevented him from sleeping. He rose in the dark and wrote Milly a short note. He was going to Waterford and would write to her from there. He could not accept the further hospitality of their present host. (Further than that he did not go in the final draft. Before it there were others. In one he ran over the history of their love and begged her to forgive him, but he knew that a parting was now best for them both. Another was full of outrage. The final version left everything to her imagination.)

He had it ready at six o'clock. Then having shaved in cold water, he packed and went quietly downstairs; there he hesitated, uncertain what to do with Milly's letter, when the baize door leading to the kitchen premises opened and Joe appeared in riding-clothes.

Alan must have looked like a thief surprised; and he saw Joe's eyes move from the envelope to the small suit-case.

The two men looked at one another; and Alan got no comfort from the intelligence behind the eyes which held his under their scrutiny. It was ironic indeed to have been the subject of divine intervention in the evening and under a moral disadvantage with Joe before breakfast.

"Where are you off to?"

The question fired Alan. He was not going to listen to that tone here, and from him.

"I'm going up to Dublin. I wonder if you would be good enough to give this letter to Milly."

"And what takes you to Dublin?"

"I've explained in my letter."

"So far as I am concerned you can to to Hell if you want to, but I think it's rude to Milly, apart from the obligations you have as a guest."

"Those, I discount."

"I see. Am I to give Mrs Ball any message? She will wonder why you have gone so suddenly."

"I should be grateful if you would just give Milly that letter. Is there anyone up yet who would drive me to the station?"

"I'm sure one of the men in the yard will bring you in the trap. I am going for a ride myself, and there is no one else here who can drive the motor-cars."

With that Joe bowed. Alan had a strong desire to knock the smirk off his face; he had expected him to order a car, and did not at all relish having himself to recruit a driver in the yard.

"Good-bye, sir," he said and went through the door, uneasily aware of Joe's eyes on his back. In the yard he met a boy carrying a bucket and found him more than ready to drop the task for which he was employed to harness the dog-cart he had never been allowed to drive.

"So long as Mr Dunne says it's all right, I'm your man, sir."

Joe had come in to look for a pair of riding gloves. He exercised every morning a hack that he had bought on his own initiative, for Mr Talbot Thompson's health and amusement. It gave him an appetite for breakfast.

He paused now, wondering whether he should tell Carrie about Alan's departure. Last night's arrival had affected him in several ways, disappointing his hope of playing host, ensuring a not-to-be-looked-forward-to confrontation with his principal, and landing him an unpredictable liability in the shape of Mona Ball. T. T. should not have done it. He knew who was coming down; and this was a gesture of contempt. Mona had rather queered his pitch by greeting him as an old friend. It was a surprise to see that she knew Harvey. Rather old for him; and, besides, what did a fellow who saw himself as Milly's suitor want to have anything to do with Mona for? Worst of all was the reference to Arthur. He must flay her alive for that when he got her alone.

Depressing to think that the past and the future had roots in Percy Place. Damn Harvey! Milly would be better with a decent man with fewer pretensions. Mona had hinted often enough that she wanted to spread her wings a bit; but she must have known what he would think of her coming on this expedition. Had she hopes of T. T.? Was there something going on there? One never knew with T. T.

He went back to the yard. Someone was tapping at the window. He looked up. Carrie in her dressing-gown was signalling to him. He waved at her, and went back into the house to meet her at the top of the stairs.

"Milly's gone. She left a note on her pillow. You must find her. What's going on, Joe? I'm terribly anxious."

Joe stood speechless; before he could summon words the wheels of the dog-cart sounded outside on the gravel.

"That's Harvey, Carrie. He has gone off to Dublin in a huff. He will pick up Milly on the road. Can't we leave matters to take their course? We couldn't have planned anything better. It's fate. They will be engaged before the car gets to Mullingar. Take the word of an old-stager."

Joe never failed to re-light candles of hope in Carrie. She went to the window and saw the dog-cart spanking down the drive, beside the lake on which the sun rising over the hill laid a path of gold.

"Please God," she murmured. "Please God."

Joe put his hand on her shoulder. "If he's any good at all, this will clinch it," he said.

They stood together watching until the cart disappeared from sight behind the trees. Carrie, in a sleepless night, had many questions prepared for her dangerous brother; she forgot them now.

"We must stick to the ship," he said.

"It sank long ago."

"You have the girls."

"They will be gone soon."

"I'd help if I could, Carrie, but you see how it is."

"Who is Mrs Ball?"

"Oh, one of the Balls."

"Where does she come from?"

"Ballsbridge."

"Joe. There's nothing funny about anything to do with this."

"I was quite serious. It is just a coincidence. She does live in Ballsbridge."

"I don't care where she lives. Who is she? What does she do? Why is she here? Where did you meet her? Alan knew her too. You had better not tell me."

"I am her trustee, as a matter of fact."

"Joe; you once told me that whenever anyone said 'as a matter of fact' he was lying."

"Did I? Well, I'm a sort of honorary trustee."

"Of what, may I ask?"

"Oh, you know. Her husband was in the Merchant Service."

"I don't see what that has to do with it."

"I knew him. George Ball. A very decent man."

"Did you introduce her to our friend?"

"Did I? Oh, I see what you mean. I suppose I did. I wouldn't jump to conclusions if I were you, Carrie. It's not fair to Mona. I expect T.T. told her to hop into his yoke, and drove her down. After all, he knew there was a party here. It's not as if he had planned a rendezvous. It was open and above-board. Mona is not quite up to snuff, I know. But she has a heart of pure gold. And that's more than can be said for——Oh, good-morning."

The door behind the window in the corridor at which Joe and Carrie were standing had opened; framed in it Lady Kelly looked not unlike the Statue of Liberty; but her raised hand had no light in it; she was beckoning to Carrie.

"A word with you, my dear." She drew her in and closed the door; an eye had fallen on Joe, and glanced off as quickly, as though he were the wall of a racquet court.

"What are you going to do, Carrie? For myself I have decided. I shall not be here when that man comes down to breakfast."

"Joe says we are jumping to conclusions. After all, it's not a crime to travel seventy miles in a motor-car with a man."

"Don't be a fool, woman."

"Fanny, you have no right to speak to me like that."

"Have you thought of your daughters' reputations? What are the Roches going to think? What will Mr Harvey say? I saw that he knew who she was. Perhaps you should talk to him."

"He's gone."

"There!"

"And Milly."

"Not. . . Oh my dear . . . Not . . ."

"Milly went on foot, first thing. Alan has only just left."

"We shall go too, you and Dolly and I. The Roches can follow in their own car. I think Captain Dunne, as a gentleman, will see how we are all compromised if we stay any longer. My dear, you are quite, quite sure?"

245

"About what, Fanny?"

"Milly and Alan."

"What do you mean?"

"That they haven't . . ."

"You can put your mind at rest."

"That is a relief. I am sure you feel like going down on your knees and thanking God for that."

"I never had any doubts about Milly."

"No. Of course not. I only thought . . ."

"I shall go and get dressed and tell Dolly you want to go. We can breakfast in the train."

"My dear, I am past considering breakfast."

Carrie went to her room, and found Joe talking to Dolly.

"The Astronomer Royal is a Ball," he was saying.

"Joe, leave us to get ready. Lady Kelly insists on us going. We can't very well let her go on her own; and I agree that it will be better for everyone if we can avoid the awkwardness of an encounter this morning."

"You are all running away. Carrie, this is ridiculous."

"Go and get the motor-car, Joe. I am not going to have that woman going up to Dublin to spread scandal; and I want to pick Milly up. You distracted me from my plain duty."

Joe, muttering to himself, did as he was told. It was all very well for people who had nothing to do with T. T. to take up this attitude; but what about himself? Was he to be left to face the music? Bringing Mrs Ball down was not a mere disregard of convention; it was a challenge. It was meant to convey that T. T. wanted to show who owned Derravaragh; it was a thrust at Joe.

He pondered these matters, and then went into his own room and packed quickly, not omitting smaller items purchased with the object of furnishing the dressing-table and wash-stand, items included under 'miscellaneous' in the estate account.

The Benz started up without difficulty and was at the door before the ladies appeared. The former boots from the Greville Arms had not forgotten the practice of a lifetime. He appeared as if by magic to bring down the cases. Carrie gave him half a crown, Lady Kelly a shilling.

He stood on the steps as the Benz drew away, the engine running very sweetly, and waved unnoticed. Dolly, looking back, might have seen him if her attention had not been distracted by the sudden opening of a window over the porch. A head was thrust out and a voice shouted. But whose it was and what it said was a matter of guesswork. Dolly guessed, as it happened, correctly, but Lady Kelly, who saw it all, nodded at her with familiar ferocity to keep her guesses to herself.

The women in their different fashions were upset; to walk out of anybody's house as a gesture of disapproval is traumatic; in any sensitive soul it must produce the same reaction as a blow; it is slapping one's host in the face and in the presence of his servants. Lady Kelly assumed the role of Nemesis in person. Her bearing and theirs made plain she had assigned the parts of servitors to the others.

"Does Mrs Roche *know*?"

Dolly wriggled, uncertain whether an action taken on her own initiative might incur sovereign disapproval. "I knocked on Bernard's door and told him. It would have worried them, don't you think, to come down and find us gone and no explanation."

Lady Kelly never signified immediate approval; it might lead to a relaxation of effort: she considered, and then nodded gravely. "You will find that Mrs Roche is glad to have been given a lead. She knows what to do now. I daresay they will set out after breakfast; but they may be involved in discussions. I was determined to avoid any risk of that."

Dolly sat up close to her mother for comfort, and to comfort her. She knew that she was unhappy and not only because the holiday had proved such an undignified fiasco. When she thought that life might be taking a turn for the better, Mr Talbot Thompson had demonstrated that it was still its horrid self.

Carrie pressed her hand. Dolly, following the direction of her mother's eyes looked at Joe.

In the driver's seat he was back to his Munchausen self. Only a few minutes ago he had drawn close to Carrie, had seemed in his own way to feel with her and for her, bound together as they were to the gaunt ruin of the past. But now he was Sarsfield swooping on the siege train at Ballyneaty, Hannibal crossing the Alps, Fred Archer, on the favourite, coming round Tattenham corner, Joe, the crack driver, on the last stretch of the Gordon Bennett race. In his ears sang the cheers of the crowd; on every side handkerchiefs, scarves, shawls, coats, flags, were waving. He knew the taste of triumph.

The bell in the Franciscan chapel at Multyfarnham stopped ringing; the people of the village, attentive to their Easter duties, were turning out of their cottages to be in time for Holy Communion and eight o'clock Mass.

"There they are," Joe shouted exultantly; the women craned forward to see. A dog-cart was standing on the side of the road and Milly was talking to the driver. As if the performance was arranged for their benefit, she stepped up at the moment Joe called out, the boy on the box getting down and taking his place behind. The Mass-goers made way to let the car pass on and closed ranks in its wake. Joe hooted his horn for leave of passage, waved gaily at the early morning worshippers, and in a final burst of high spirits—hope sprang eternal in Joe's breast—gave a valedictory blast on the horn as the Benz passed through the crowd.

The horse, they were now on his tail, leaped forward at the sound of the horn. What happened then, watched by the three women and Joe (through a spectral haze), took the pattern of a ritual dance. The horse stood still as if to consider from what direction danger threatened; Alan shook up the reins; the horse backed; Alan pulled and struck once with the long whip; the horse stood; Joe blew a merry toot on the horn.

"Joe!" But Carrie's cry was lost in the general murmur as the cart backed sidewards into the crowd and, with a loud whinny, the horse plunged forward. The left wheel of the cart had mounted the doorstep of a house, and when the horse ran away the passengers were thrown towards the right, overbalancing the cart. It righted itself at the same moment (the horse was now in a gallop). Alan lost hold of the reins, and the boy leaned forward to grasp them. Had he stayed in his place, Joe explained afterwards to Carrie, the horse would have come to a halt at the level crossing; but in the event he upset the precarious balance and the cart veered to the left, where the road sloped down to a wall. Alan was thrown over the cottage wall into the midden; Milly was less fortunate. She fell on stones. The boy tumbled over on his face, on the driver's seat, and managed to get a grip on the reins and bring the horse to a standstill.

Nobody in Multyfarnham has ever been quite certain who sent for the priest. He gave the last rites to both the young people;

Milly first, her head wounds were bleeding; and then to Alan, the nature of whose injuries were harder to distinguish. Afterwards, on learning his mistake, he apologised very handsomely to Bishop Harvey. There was no way, he explained, of telling that one of the young people was a Protestant; and Alan, he reminded his Grace, was covered in manure.

XXIV

My dear Milly,

I received Mrs Preston's letter by this morning's post; will you please thank her for me and tell her I shall write from London where I am going tomorrow. I am truly heartbroken to hear what a time you have had. I would have come to see you before leaving if it were possible; but I am not really quite fit again, and I shall travel by Rosslare/Fishguard and not come up to Dublin.

My accident has made a great change in my outlook. I suppose it does to everyone who, but for the grace of God, might have been killed, and yet escapes with no more than a broken leg. I see that I have been drifting along, hoping for the best in a vague future, in a manner that was as unfair to you as it was to me. I am thinking now of *you*.

My uncle, who has been an angel to me ever since I came down to recuperate, took the drawing you did of me up to Dublin and showed it to Dr Mahaffy. He is on the Board of Governors of the National Gallery. Mahaffy says it is so good that he cannot believe it is by a woman. He thinks that you should go abroad like Miss Purser did and study. If you do, he says, you will make a great name for yourself. But after what Mr Hone told you I don't suppose you require other opinions.

When my uncle was in Dublin, he met an old College friend, back on leave. His job has to do with placing young lawyers in judicial positions in Burma. He says that if I went out there after I was called I would start to make at once what I might wait ten years for in London or Dublin. Anyhow I had already decided to sell out the family interest in Carlow. It was a hard decision; but I think a right one.

If I am going to Burma, my uncle's friend advises, it would be highly foolish even to think of marriage for at least ten years, for many reasons.

From what I told you in the past I greatly fear that you may think I am writing this under Uncle's influence. Believe me, he does not even know that I am writing; and he has been faultless in refusing to press me in any way. The decision is my own and I accept full responsibility for it. I have grown up, I feel, in the last few weeks.

If you do not agree with me about this, and if you choose to consider that I am in honour bound to get engaged to you, tell me, and I will. I know that I will never meet anyone I shall love so much. I wish things were different and that we could have found our happiness in one another.

Before I close I have to tell you that your uncle called at the hospital. Aunt Jane spoke to him very plainly; and I must say I think the man must be mad. It is the only charitable explanation of his conduct. I believe that if you took proceedings against him for negligence you might recover substantial damages. An Irish jury would take a pleasure in compensating you lavishly out of the defendant's pocket.

As he is your uncle I suppose you won't do this; but it seems quite wrong that he should escape scot-free. But such is life.

I must go now if I am to catch the post. I hope you will soon be fully recovered and able to forget your heart-broken

Alan.

XXV

I DON'T THINK I'd go near her today, Joe, if I were you. She's being wonderful, but you know it is still very soon, and I am anxious not to upset her."

"She wrote me such a wonderful letter. I never thought she could bear to look at me again."

"She has gone through too much to bear grudges, Joe. The worst moment for me was when she insisted on looking at herself in the glass; but, you know, she didn't seem to care."

"Can the doctors do nothing? I told you I will give everything I have. Not that I have anything. I will sell newspapers at the Pillar for the rest of my days gladly—if I can make Milly well."

"There will always be a dreadful scar on the forehead; but she says her hair will hide that. She has infected us all with her goodness. You know I came to hate you, Joe. I never thought I could bring myself even to look at you, but Milly made me feel ashamed of that."

"I don't blame you, Carrie. What do you think I've said to myself? But I want to do what I can for this family. I want to leave some memory of having been other than a curse. Is Milly decided about being an artist?"

"Absolutely, I believe it has saved her life. It gives her something to live for. She talks so sensibly about it. Who knows, she may have a wonderful career. Even now, Joe, I haven't lost faith that God knows what is best for us if we leave ourselves in His hands."

"I wish He would make up His mind about me, Carrie. Time is running out. I've something to tell you. I'm finished, as you know, with T. T. The man is a common blackguard. I hold him responsible in my own mind for our present misfortunes. Forget about him. I want to make the way easy for Milly. I want you to have money to take her to Paris, or wherever she wants to go, as soon as Dolly is off your hands. The only way to get you money is to sell Merrion Square."

"Fanny Kelly has a ten year lease, Joe. What is the use of covering that ground again?"

"You could sell if she got out."

"She will do nothing of the kind; and Milly would never forgive me if I asked her to, as a favour."

"She will, Carrie. She is going to go in August."

"Who told you this?"

"She did. This morning."

"I don't believe it. Joe, this is another of your chimeras. For God's sake be careful. I can't endure much more. What did you say to her?"

"I arranged that she should take a fishing lodge on the Slaney. She is leaving Dublin. She is marrying me."

"Joe! Joe! Joe! What lunacy is this?"

"I did it for Milly, and for you. I don't want you to think that the idea of free fishing influenced me; but I will have to do something."

"And this is all agreed to. Joe, are you quite, quite sure?"

He put a hand in his breast pocket and took out a printed Conditions of Sale. On the end of it was the name Fanny Kelly. It stated that she bought the premises set out on the face of the document for two thousand pounds. Not a marriage contract; but in the circumstances an equivalent.

Carrie looked at her brother as if for the first time: she felt touched a little; she was, even in her present condition, amused. Gratitude she did not feel. She could entertain almost any sentiment for her brother; but that was beyond her capacity. He was in such arrears now that he could never pay off his liabilities. She had admired his skills; he could, at a pinch, turn his hand to anything, provided it was not to his own or his family's advantage; but she had never given him full credit for his inventiveness, his inexhaustible capacity for espying opportunity. It was a sort of genius.

"Do you think you will be able to get on with her? Is it not too great a price to pay?"

"There's nothing, I've already told you, I wouldn't do for Milly."

"But you must not marry Fanny Kelly for Milly's sake. What is past is past; and to end your days in misery will be no consolation to her. I'll rake up the money somehow. I can sell this horrid little house."

"And live where?"

"Dolly will find me a cottage. I may come in useful down there."

"I didn't tell you—you had too much on your plate as it was—but I had an unpleasant experience at the hospital. I thought it the right thing to call and enquire for that scamp, Harvey. Some old woman came up to me and said that if the law was in a fit state I'd be charged with attempted murder. Then a solicitor wrote to me. Bernard kept me right about that."

"I'm sorry."

"I wish he had broken his neck. But Milly was always too good for him. It's a curious thing, Carrie—you won't understand me—but I shall never spend a peaceful night until Milly tells me she has forgiven me. There's nothing so cruel in life as to injure those one loves. It seems to be my mission. Why? God knows I am the least vindictive man I've ever met. I have never set out to injure anyone."

Carrie did not feel able to enter on a discussion of Joe's unwilling vocation, and he had settled himself in a pose with which she was all too familiar, on the only comfortable sofa.

"I must go up to Milly now, Joe. The doctor will be coming soon. I can't ask you to take pot luck today."

"I'm going. Don't worry. I just wanted you to know. You can make plans with Milly now."

He felt discouraged. His gesture had buoyed him up all morning; and whenever the thought of the salmon stretch on the Slaney entered his mind he had erased it by sheer force of will. Now he would be driven to think about it, having naught else for comfort. Even his sacrificial gestures, it seemed, were fated to go for nothing.

Carrie had never kissed him since the accident; and even now, when she saw that he was cast down, she couldn't bring herself to. But she patted his arm.

On the street he stumbled into a young man who was turning in the next-door gate. He had forgotten the Terrys. This one remembered him.

"How is Milly?"

"On the mend, I hear."

"Tell her I was enquiring for her."

"I may not see her for some time."

"I'll call then. But I don't like to bother Mrs Preston. I don't suppose this would interest *you*."

Joe took the leaflet which was pushed forward in shy defiance and looked at it reluctantly. He was not attracted by leaflets and even less by the sort of person who distributed them.

He read:

EDWARD'S VISIT TO DUBLIN
MEETING OF PROTEST COMMITTEE

It was enough. He handed it back.

"I'm sorry. It doesn't. I wore his Majesty's uniform once, I'd have you know. Good-morning."

He was elated a little by the encounter. It put him in the mood for a meal. What could he afford?

There was only silver in his trousers, and not much of that. He had the habit of slipping half sovereigns into his jacket pocket so as to come across them by surprise in moments of crisis. But today there were none. He emptied out his pockets, and in the process discovered an envelope. It had lain there unopened for some time. It was the letter Alan gave him to give Milly when he was leaving Derravaragh. Should he read it; would it matter now?

Or should he destroy the letter? To give it to Milly now without reading it, would be cruel. And if he opened the envelope Milly would be outraged. Alan was her God; and he had separated her from her God, he, Joe who was going to marry Fanny Kelly to give her an artist's training, Joe who loved her and felt closer to her than anyone else in the world!

That last scene with Alan came back very vividly to mind. Alan had been afraid to look him in the face. Alan consorted with Mona Ball. Alan was leaving Milly in the lurch even before the accident. The evidence was there, in that letter. If Milly knew, she would see Alan in a different light. But Milly must never know. Milly must go to her grave believing that she would have married him were it not for Uncle Joe.

He had come to Leeson Street Bridge: he always stopped here and looked down the canal; the overhanging trees made the water look green; the grass edges of the canal were green; through the branches the sky took on the green of all the rest. An idyllic spot, such calm, such cool. He thought of two lines, beautifully appropriate, which he incanted always when he stood here. He had other lines for other places.

> Annihilating all that's made
> To a green thought in a green shade.

It always made him feel better, when he recited verse, like shaking hands with a celebrity. There were these furnishings in the mind to be taken out and enjoyed in private, an undiminishable treasure, unlike half-sovereigns in coat pockets. They added subtly to one's self-respect. After all, however battered, they were evidence that inside the Joe the world thought it knew was the real Joe. So much of his most hopeful endeavour had been attempted in the full light of day: there was always an audience for disaster. The best, as now when he felt the poet that was somewhere in him answer to the call of beauty—the best was a secret. He took out the envelope. It had 'Milly' written on it in an unformed writing. He held the envelope so tight that he felt the letter through the cover, the message Milly never got. She would never get it. Never. He tore the envelope into four even squares and dropped them, one by one, into the green water. They lit, without making an impression on the smooth surface, then floated slowly downstream, to the next lock. He watched them, one behind the other, until they were out of sight. They reminded him of a family of swans; but, then, everything reminded him of something else: as Fanny said that morning, quoting *his* sister this time, all his geese were swans.